Thirteenth

C. M. Rosens is an author of dark, genre-bending speculative fiction, particularly Gothic horror with tentacles and eldritch family drama, with body horror as a recurring theme. She is mainly to be found travelling between the hills of Wales and the plains of England, but loves visiting friends and family all over the world when she can. She has a PhD in a niche area of Medieval British Studies, and these days mostly applies her research skills in fiction rather than academia, which she enjoyed but doesn't miss. Her work is heavily influenced by the histories, mythologies and folklore of places she grew up in and lived as an adult.

Also by C. M. Rosens

Pagham-on-Sea

The Crows
Thirteenth

THIRTEENTH

C. M. ROSENS

CANELO

First published in the United Kingdom in 2024 by

Canelo
Unit 9, 5th Floor
Cargo Works, 1-2 Hatfields
London SE1 9PG
United Kingdom

Copyright © C. M. Rosens 2024

The moral right of C. M. Rosens to be identified as the creator of this work has been asserted in accordance with the Copyright, Designs and Patents Act, 1988.

All rights reserved. No part of this publication may be reproduced or transmitted in any form or by any means, electronic or mechanical, including photocopy, recording, or any information storage and retrieval system, without permission in writing from the publisher.

A CIP catalogue record for this book is available from the British Library.

Print ISBN 978 1 80436 745 2
Ebook ISBN 978 1 80436 750 6

This book is a work of fiction. Names, characters, businesses, organizations, places and events are either the product of the author's imagination or are used fictitiously. Any resemblance to actual persons, living or dead, events or locales is entirely coincidental.

Look for more great books at www.canelo.co

Printed and bound in Great Britain by Clays Ltd, Elcograf S.p.A.

Prologue: The End

14 May

Gran's house was the oasis of calm Katy Porter craved. She could hide in the guest room – her room – headphones on and music up, pretending everything was fine.

She couldn't hear the sibilant hiss of her mother here, complaining about the bloodstains on her father's shirts. There were no low murmurs in college corridors as another missing person's picture was plastered to the walls.

She uncrossed her long, strong legs and stretched out the cramped muscles, rubbing her calf. Midnight had been and gone.

She dreaded her looming seventeenth birthday, the days ticking down like a time bomb. Parties sucked. Mum was wound up like a spring and Dad was usually out. When he was home, he was ominously quiet. He hadn't said more than three words to her since he'd picked her up from the leisure centre two days ago. They'd stopped at the traffic lights, where she'd heard a muffled pounding from the boot of the car. He'd said nothing when she looked at him, only stared back at her in tight-lipped silence.

Katy had said nothing, either.

She'd wondered how much this one resembled her.

Katy spent as much of her time at Gran's as she could. It was the *good* kind of quiet here, and as the youngest of thirteen, Katy luxuriated in the chance to breathe.

'This'll be yours when I'm gone,' Gran had said this afternoon, and sliced Katy's arm with a fruit knife to daub her blood on all the locks. The wound still itched, distracting her from the stack of flashcards and her neat, handwritten notes.

She gave up on A-Level Chemistry revision and studied the fresh cut on her arm. Gran had seemed on edge today; she hadn't been herself all week.

Now the cut was freshly scabbing beside old, faded scars, where Katy, as a tired, miserable child, had once looked for the Beast she knew lived inside her. She'd tried to find it, to tear it out, but all the blood and flesh got in the way.

Gran had put a stop to that.

Katy swallowed, resisting the urge to trace them with her fingernail, and pulled her sleeve back down. It was just precautionary, she told herself. Gran wouldn't die or leave her. She *needed* Gran. Gran was like the cliffs, like the woods, like the ancient long barrows that slept under the cyclical sun. She *couldn't* die.

And yet…

Her stomach gave a warning lurch.

Something was wrong.

Everything was in its proper place: the armchair, draped in a pink and grey hand-crocheted blanket; the heavy wardrobe, half full of Katy's clothes and the other half of Gran's old romance paperbacks; the three framed oil paintings of the Weald with Gran's signature at the bottom. Katy's own cross-country medals glinted, draped over the vanity mirror. Gymnastics certificates and trophies filled the shelves. Gran collected all of them, since Katy's mum said they didn't have room for stuff like that at home.

Katy turned onto her back. The ceiling was smooth, crisp and magnolia, familiar and plain. No cracks crept across its surface, nothing to tease her imagination with patterns and faces leering in the lamplight.

'Are you there, Grandad?' she whispered. 'You wouldn't let anything happen to Gran, would you?'

Sometimes she heard the Voice in her head, answering back like an echo. Gran said this showed she was special. Grandad didn't talk to everyone.

Tonight, he was silent.

Katy bit her lip, nipping the skin away until she tasted blood. 'Gran's just being careful, right? It's not her time yet. She'll be around forever.'

Grandad said nothing.

Maybe he wasn't listening tonight. Maybe he wasn't there at all. Maybe she was mad, Gran was mad, they were all mad... *All the best people are.*

She turned onto her side, her headphones crunching under her head. She struggled up to switch to earbuds.

The cottage was silent. Oppressive emptiness rushed in to fill the gap left by the music.

She listened for Toffee, Gran's ginger tomcat, but there was no sound from outside her door. There should be *some* sound. Gran pottered about downstairs until gone midnight, her low chants and soft muttering always reassuring. Katy frowned, crossed to the door and cracked it open.

'Gran?'

Gran's hearing was bat-sharp, but there was no response. Katy hesitated, her hand still on the door handle. Her chest tightened.

'Gran?' It came out as a croak this time, quieter than intended. She tried to clear her throat, but her mouth was dry.

Heart pounding, Katy crept out onto the landing. Her bare feet made no sound on the carpet, padding slowly to the stairs. It was dark down there, all the lights off. She glanced down the corridor, but Gran's bedroom door was still ajar, her coverlet neatly turned down. Toffee wasn't in his usual place on the end of the bed, just visible from where she stood.

Katy frowned.

She was just doing a ritual in the cellar, that must be it. Although the alignments were all out, it wasn't a significant day, no one (to Katy's knowledge) was going through the Changes at the moment, and there wasn't any reason for her to be down there.

Grandad was still silent, the Voice absent from her head.

She half-wondered, in a moment of grossed-out fascination, if *that* was what Gran was doing, summoning the mythical family progenitor and doing the nasty with unearthly appendages in the deep dark of the cellar below.

Her imagination rebelled.

Katy crept downstairs, but there was nothing to hear but the rush of her own blood in her ears.

There was a raw, meaty smell in the air, like a butcher's shop. Katy recognised it from her dad's garage, her brother Liam's storage unit, the way it clung to Uncle David like cologne.

Nausea churned her stomach to water.

'Gr-an?' Her voice cracked.

The living room door was ajar, but the room was dark. Gran had been up late, making a costume for little Cousin Maisie's school play. Maisie had the part of a cow that said 'moo' and learned stuff about staying safe in the summer holidays.

Had she fallen asleep?

Steeling herself, Katy swallowed a hard lump of panic and pushed the door all the way open, feeling for the light switch. She flicked it, and her fingers came away sticky.

Light burst onto a bloody scene, winking off shards of shattered mirror glass.

Katy stood still, throat too tight to scream. A chill of dreamlike horror pierced her mind, irrational but from her darkest, most hidden place:

Did I do this?

It wasn't real. It couldn't be real. It was a scene exactly from Katy's recurring night terrors, in which the Beast ripped apart her family one by one, except the Beast was always her.

She *couldn't* have done this.

She hadn't Changed yet.

Someone was here while I was upstairs, she realised, horror prickling the base of her skull and flooding her with electricity. *Someone came in here and did this...*

Gore caked the furniture, soaking into the chintz covers in ragged-edged splashes, sprayed over the ceiling, was drying on the walls. Katy stared mutely at her fingers. The stickiness was grey and slightly mucus-y. It took her a second to work out it was brain.

Shattered bones and a broken ribcage lay in a puddle of fleshy mess on the floor by the armchair. Vertebrae were pulled apart and littered the carpet, and there was no sign of the head. That is, until Katy looked down.

Gran's slack mouth gaped inches from her foot, her eyes ripped out of the sockets leaving hollow holes, bloody red mats in her tangled grey hair.

Katy couldn't scream, the fist of horror clenching her throat. All that came out was a wheezing squeak. She nearly kicked it away from her instinctively, but her feet wouldn't obey.

She stumbled backwards through the door, wiping her hand on her jeans and falling over everything in the hall until she found the front door, and only then did her scream erupt from her bursting lungs as she fled into the night.

Chapter 1: Kidnapped

10 January

Be on time, be on time, please...

Katy found a well-lit spot on the station platform, the only soul waiting for the last express train to London Victoria. An aura of frosty vapour hung in the air around the lights, her breath streaming in front of her, drifting over the edge of the yellow line. Her handbag bumped against her side as she fidgeted with the strap, hard-shell suitcase glittering purple in the bright LED glare.

The orange display blinked. The train was five minutes late.

She wrapped her knitwear layers closer around her, thick jumper still not enough to keep her lean frame properly warm. From her position on the platform she could see up and down the track in both directions, the Cyclopean red glow of the stop signal in the darkness, the shadows of the car park behind her where some of the streetlights were out. A few people had left their cars there overnight, despite the signs warning them it was at their own risk.

Most things are at your own risk, Katy thought. Like crossing the road. Telling people how you feel. Running away.

Dad's really going to do it this time.

He'd been gearing up for something over the last eight months, and she wondered if the only reason she was still alive was because Uncle Marcus, the new Head of the Family, had told him not to touch her.

Or to wait.

Either way, Katy had been waiting for the axe to drop ever since Gran's... she hesitated over the word 'death'. It was such a neat word that glossed over what had happened.

No one would tell her who'd done it, though she was certain *somebody* knew.

She wanted the Beast to deal with it – she wanted to learn how to rip it out of her flesh and become it, set it on the killer and tear them apart. It might be any of the elders, or Gran could have had some enemy outside the family that Katy didn't know about. She couldn't imagine anyone being strong enough. Certainly not her dad, although he wasn't sorry Gran was gone.

Her mum was embracing being a grandmother herself these days and was babysitting all weekend for Kim and Adam, so it was just her and her dad alone in the house.

As soon as her mum left, Katy knew what he was going to do.

They'd been polite to each other. Ian Porter was good at frosty politeness. He made himself innocuous with it, made you think he wasn't interested in you, and so most people assumed he wasn't dangerous.

Katy knew better.

She knew what came next.

He said they were going to go for a long walk on the Weald together. *Bonding*, he'd called it. He'd never used that word before. He'd never wanted to take her anywhere.

Katy had locked herself in her room and called her best friend, then her oldest brother. Wes said staying with him was fine. He hadn't sounded keen, but he hadn't asked questions. He knew what Dad was like.

Besides, there was something she needed to tell Wes face to face, and she didn't know how to. Not yet.

She hadn't banked on the train being late. Had her dad noticed she was gone yet? What would he do when he did?

Come after you, you stupid cow. That's what. He'll come after you and he'll kill you.

There was movement between two parked cars.

Katy pulled her case between her and the entrance to the platform, bouncing on her toes to warm up her cold muscles. Running was what she did best.

A short man who would barely come up to her dad's chest appeared from the car park through the open barrier, hands in his pockets. She recognised the walk and the grey hoodie before she saw his face and fought to keep her breaths deep and even.

Not him, she pleaded, but at least it wasn't her dad. *Shit, how did he know?*

She darted a glance at the board. The train was now ten minutes late. Biting down on an already over-gnawed part of her cheek she nipped raw skin away and winced, dragging her case closer like a shield.

'So, you're off then?' her least favourite cousin called over to her in his gruff, deep voice, nodding at her suitcase. 'Not even going to say goodbye?'

There was something dark and sticky on his top, splashed across his chest and smeared into the grey joggers. As he moved, the light changed it from black to deep red. He'd been reading entrails again. That answered her question, but not in a reassuring way.

Katy tightened her grip on the handle, knees locking. 'It's all sorted… Wes is picking me up, I'm going to live with him…?' She bit back a 'please?' at the end, but her voice still went up and made it sound like a question.

He's only my cousin, she reminded herself. *He's not what they say he is, he's not a god, he's not* my *god, I don't have to listen to him…*

Ricky Porter approached with an easy swagger, stopping a few feet away. As he lifted his chin, his grin sliced through her. 'Sure about that, are we? You never asked *me* if you could leave.'

The train was now showing as delayed.

Katy gripped the handle of her case, knee bumping against the hard shell. She feigned cockiness, trying to match his attitude with her own, drawing herself up to look down on him from her few extra inches of height. He looked up at her with faint amusement, and she ground her teeth.

'You're not Head of the Family, and I didn't ask him, either. I can make my own decisions.' It still came out higher than she wanted.

Ricky found this funny. 'Uncle Marcus? He bowed the knee to me and tore his own eye out because I told him to. Head of the Family don't mean shit. *I'm* the One and Only. I'm the one you need to check with, aside from the fact it's polite.' He paused. 'Why d'you think you're still alive?'

'I'm not a kid, I can go see Wes when I want to…' Her mouth dried up as she registered what he'd said. She wasn't sure she believed it, but Ricky wasn't known to lie.

Would her dad take Ricky on? Did he really hate her that much?

'You're still a minor,' Ricky reminded her.

'I'm seventeen.'

'Like I said.' He looked her up and down, cocking an eyebrow at her knitted layers. 'Did your mother not tell you to put a bloody coat on?'

Katy hugged herself and flushed despite the cold, tips of her ears burning. 'Piss off, you pervert.'

She regretted it as soon as it dropped out of her mouth like a stone, plunging to the ground in frost-pale mist.

Ricky's grin sharpened, revealing a set of filed teeth. He let the insult slide off him, eyes bright with amusement.

'Did you even bother to tell her? She still owes my mum fifty quid, by the way.'

The bile in his voice nettled her for reasons she couldn't explain. 'She does not!'

His eyes gleamed. 'Ooh, that was defensive. They've done a right number on you, haven't they? That's all right. Fam'ly's complicated.'

The last thing she wanted was to get into this with the man who had poisoned his own parents over a teddy bear. That was the story she'd heard, anyway, and she nearly threw it back at him, but it was a waste of breath.

Katy flashed a look down the track, stretching into darkness, and back to the board. There was no sign of the train. It was still showing as delayed. The gate was open, barriers unmanned, the cafe on the other side closed up. She was still the only passenger waiting on the platform.

Cameras. Where were the cameras? There must be some.

Katy swallowed, dragging her case a little further down the platform and into the pool of light, where the CCTV hung below the lamp.

Her cousin let her retreat the few yards, shaking his head. 'They don't work, you know. Haven't for weeks.'

Katy glanced across the platform to see if the train to Hastings was on time.

'Don't do it,' he warned lightly.

She'd have to leave the case with all her stuff, her chargers, her hair straighteners, laptop, clothes, favourite pillow... Her fingers twitched involuntarily on the handle. She tried to move the handbag strap over her head to secure it if she had to jump down onto the tracks and drag herself up the other side. But then what? He'd follow. Could she do it as the train was coming, would she make it in time? Would it be going slow enough? Could she jump on before he got there?

'You won't make it,' he said, with enough casual certainty to spike her gut with doubt.

The train wasn't due that side for another five minutes. Her ticket wasn't valid in the other direction.

What was beyond the station? The TravelInn hotel, some rooms lit up on the upper floors despite it being the off-season, and beyond that, the high wall of the Jubilee Estate. Her mate Rocket lived there; he'd help her. She dipped her hand into her pocket for her phone.

Something whipped out and wrapped itself around her arms, pinning them to her sides. It pinched and pricked at her through the woollen layers, and she knew exactly what it was before she looked down and saw the sucking, needle-toothed mouths in the muscular coil around her waist. Her cousin hadn't come any closer. He didn't need to. There were more of the things sprouting out of the back of his head, the hood down now, the lengths twisting in the chill air.

Silvery mucus coated her jumper, sticking to the threads like the tracks of snails, numbing her skin in patches where it soaked – or ate – all the way through.

Katy couldn't help it. She took a panicked gasp of breath, and the coil tightened against her diaphragm. She quickly gasped another, and it tightened further as she panted out, so the third gasp was too shallow, and there was not enough air on the platform, not enough oxygen in the air, the darkness of the night pressing down, smothering, muffling, and she couldn't scream or cry or breathe.

Shit, she thought, dots bursting in front of her eyes, *I can't breathe…*

He let her gasp and loosened the coil. A great, cold gulp dried up her throat and filled her bursting lungs.

Two breaths, and the coil tightened again as soon as she tried moving her hand inside her handbag. Prickles of panic spread over her face, her eyes bulging with the effort of fighting for air.

'I ain't stupid,' Ricky said conversationally, without rancour. 'You think you know best. I thought the same when I was your age. No one could tell me a bloody thing.'

She struggled, but the numbness was spreading. He'd bitten her – his coils had bitten her. The injected saliva was creeping through her veins, cold as a needle in her blood. She couldn't feel her fingers, couldn't feel anything in her bag.

What if it reaches my heart, what has he done, what is it what if—

He was still talking. 'I thought, no point in askin' 'er, she'll only take my advice the wrong way. Better do it direct. Your brother's a useless twat, no offence, and the omens don't look so good for you travelling right at the moment. 'Sides, you need to learn a few things afore you achieve your destiny, an' you'll learn best from me.' He squeezed, a few more coils whipping around to support her, mouths biting through her jeans, taking out her legs. 'You're welcome, love.'

Her knees weakened, joints like jelly. She leaned on the suitcase handle, but her weight pushed it down and she sank with it, legs useless and limp beneath her. They twitched like they didn't belong to her, heels kicking over the yellow line, and there was no one around and the cameras didn't work and there was no train. Her bladder was water-weak, stomach dissolving in the churning fear.

She tried desperately to breathe with quick, shallow breaths, fighting to pull herself up again, but the case was a mountain and so far out of reach, and she had no control over her body anymore.

Ricky laughed, and a hot flare of hatred burst in a thousand coloured dots in front of her eyes.

'Relax,' he said, crouching over her as her vision failed. His face was all angles, eyes glowing like stop signals. Something was thumping arrhythmically near her right ear. She twisted to see what it was – her hand was bouncing limply against the suitcase of its own accord, like a puppet that didn't belong to her at all.

He set her head straight again so she was looking straight up, eyelids twitching but unable to close, barely able to feel his dirty fingertips against her cheeks. A cloud of his breath hit her with a puff of raw meat, fresh like a butcher's shop, but warmer, wetter. She knew that smell.

Her lips tingled, throat constricting, vision growing darker. She was too numb to be afraid. Her vision doubled, trebled, unfocused.

Cousin Ricky loomed over her, three-faced and blurred, like a bad drawing of a storybook troll. 'You ain't going anywhere, Katherine.'

Everything faded to muzzy grey, lights blurred and blinding, before the night swallowed it all and the swirling smudges above her winked out into icy black.

—

Wes Porter stood with his hands in his pockets at Victoria Station, lost in the crowd. Well, as lost in the crowd as he could be with oversized epaulettes on a jacket Freddie Mercury would have killed to own.

He'd already had a coffee, it was too late for another, and a beer would be better but a pornstar martini twice as good. His nerves were on a knife-edge, jangling a warning.

No one could ever remember his face, but in London that was true for everybody. He wandered over to the nearest shop on the concourse, bought a packet of cigarettes and watched the vague expression of the server, unchanging as they looked away and he tapped the card machine. They hadn't even looked at him in the first place; the fact his face melted from memory the moment it was out of view, erased by something as swift as a blink, didn't matter.

He'd always loved London.

Katy's train was delayed, but it wasn't cancelled. He missed the announcement giving some generic apology and wondered if he had time to go outside and smoke.

Neither of his partners were home this weekend, which gave him a chance to think about what he was going to do with his sister longer term, before they came back. She'd called and asked to stay the weekend, but he'd guessed from her tone that she was planning on staying longer.

Wes idled the time away by texting Hugo something flirty and encouraging but didn't get much back. He was probably being boyish and deferential with his father's clients, panicking every time the talk got technical.

He texted Charlie, too, but she was prepping for her photography exhibition and not in the mood for sexts. Wes itched to hit up a few of his casuals to while away the time, but he was waiting for Katy. One saucy invite and his nerve would crack. He couldn't do that.

He checked the Arrivals board again and shuddered.

Thinking about his baby sister, their thirteenth-child-of-a-thirteenth-child, had become an exercise in creeping himself out. Now there was only one year left until her eighteenth birthday – no, far less than a year, wasn't she a Gemini? – and then those dreams of hers would become reality, the Beast would be released from where it lurked under her skin, and it was every family member for themselves, survival of the fittest.

Unless something happened to her first.

He tapped his foot out of nervous habit.

Where the fuck is this train? Why am I doing this?

He toyed again with the idea of going out to smoke, but he knew if he walked out of the station now, he would keep going, leaving her lost and alone. He couldn't do that. He'd promised.

His phone rang.

Katy.

Rolling his eyes, he answered and straightened up. 'Hey, how long are you going to be?'

'She's not coming.'

The voice sent a chill down his back. He tensed with a deep breath, grip tightening on the handset.

She's dead.

The instinctive thought punched him in the gut, not with grief, but relief. The guilt bubbled swiftly after it, and he leaned back against the wall to steady himself.

'Evening, Richard. What an unpleasant surprise.'

Cousin Ricky *hated* being called Richard. This time, though, the gruff voice retained its aggravating calm.

'That's int'restin',' Ricky said after a pause. 'Not, "what the hell are you doin' with my sister's phone", not, "where is she, what've you done with her…"' He chuckled. 'Do you actually give a shit?'

Wes let out a slow breath. He found himself squeezing the cigarette packet in his pocket and scraped the plastic with his thumbnail. 'Course I do.' The world was swimming, narrowing into a dark point. He blinked, shaking his head, and sank his lanky frame down onto the floor, back pressed against the wall. 'Where is she? What have you… What *have* you done with her?'

There was another silent pause, pregnant with an unspoken accusation. 'You askin' what I done with her body?'

Wes shook his head, fighting to get his thoughts straight. 'You – you haven't. You haven't hurt her. You'd have let Uncle Marcus do it months ago if you wanted her dead. Why would you do that? She's no threat to *you*, is she?'

Ricky gave a low, humourless chuckle. 'Bet you wish I had, though. Bet a little part of you jumped for joy just then.'

Wes's cheeks burned. 'Fuck you.'

'Scares the living shit out of you, don't she?'

There was no background noise wherever Ricky was. Wes held his phone away from his ear, wanting the bustle of the station to fill the gap, to wrap the cocky bastard's voice in something more palatable than the awful, accusing silence. He focused on the crowds of people in the station, the bustle and the conversation, the snatches of music from the shop behind him, the burble of a mangy, hobbling pigeon, after whatever filth it could peck off the ground.

'You still there? You gone awful quiet.'

Wes's voice cracked. 'You can't control her, you know that, right? What are you up to? Why d'you want her?'

'I don't want to control her. That's what Gran wanted. That's what *you* want. She don't need to be controlled, she just needs... a bit of direction. I offered to help before, if you remember, but Gran wouldn't let me. Wanted our Katy to be *her* little protégée. Things is diff'rent now.' Ricky chuckled, and it sounded ugly. '*Much* diff'rent. Remind me, when they called the vote after Gran died, you know, to see whether they'd let our Katy reach her eighteenth or no, which way did *you* vote? I misremember.'

'*Where is she?*' Wes raked a hand through his hair. He wasn't going to be riled, not by Ricky bloody Porter trying to be clever.

'She's fine. Don't fret.' Ricky yawned. *Yawned.*

What a bastard.

'I'm off home, thought I'd give you a ring, let you know she ain't coming.'

Wes forced himself up on shaking legs. 'Cheers,' he said bitterly.

'Evenin's your own now, but omens ain't looking good. I'd take care, if I was you. Maybe don't go home for a bit.'

'Am I s'posed to say thank you?' Wes pushed off from the wall and strode towards the nearest exit. People jostled and milled around him, a reassuring hum of life drawing him out into the night.

Ricky snorted. 'You didn't seriously want her living with you, did you? I can't protect her up there, not from all the possible little accidents Uncle David and his lads could dream up, and you can't do as good a job as me. Anyway, won't she cramp your style? What would you *do* with her?'

Wes shook his head, trying to ignore the fact he'd been asking himself the same questions since he'd agreed to let her stay.

'What are *you* going to do with her?' he returned, but Ricky was evidently enjoying being inscrutable.

'Not your business, I told you.' Another pause, this time the sound of Ricky working his way up to small talk. 'You all right, are you, otherwise? What are you going to do now?'

Wes inwardly cringed and attempted to flag down a black cab but failed. He kept walking, catching the traffic lights at a good moment and propelling himself across the road. 'That's none of *your* business.'

'Aw, come on, don't be like that. Just asking.'

'Why? We're not friends.' Wes halted in a doorway and clamped his phone to his ear with one shoulder so he could open the cigarette packet. 'Don't… don't hurt her. And don't...' He hesitated, searching for a word that would really sting. '...Don't *infect* her, neither.'

'Infect her?'

'There an echo your end? You know what I mean.' He got one out and stuck it in his mouth, fumbling for his lighter. 'Telling her all that future stuff, getting her hooked on fate and prophecy and all that crap.'

There was a long pause, which gave him time to light it and take a decent drag. Standing apart from the rivers of wintry people, bundled up in the glare of the headlights and dull roar of the city, Wes felt inexplicably adrift, alone. The ugly, urgent desire to hit his cousin where it hurt rose up in him like pus from an old scar.

Ricky sounded indignant. 'I'm tryin' to help.'

'You're a disease,' Wes told him, savouring the nicotine hit. 'What you do, it's like an addiction. I think Uncle Marcus is right, I don't think we need a soothsayer. Maybe we should be getting rid of *you*, instead.'

There was nothing but the sound of Ricky's barely controlled breathing.

'You got rich because of me,' Ricky reminded him, and Wes was gratified to hear the tightness in his voice. 'You got *everything* you have because of *me*...'

'Yeah, thanks for that. After what you did, you fucking owe me.' Wes blew a smoke ring into the bustling street. 'Worked out great. And you're the one who's going to die alone, but don't go dragging my little sister down that path of fate and destiny and all that bollocks, that's not fair. She'll figure you out. And when she does, she'll add you to her little List, and you'll be brown bread like the rest of us.'

'Fuck you.'

Wes grinned, smoke wreathing between his teeth and scrawling his vice across the dark, cold street. He took another vicious, glowing drag. 'Still want to know what I'm doing this evening? Cos it still ain't you.'

Ricky hung up.

Wes relished the moment, but it didn't last.

'Fuck you too,' he muttered, bounding out of the doorway to finally flag down a taxi.

He dismissed his cousin's warning as a bluff, but as the taxi got closer to his Kensington address, he started to doubt. Ricky didn't bluff well. He was pathologically honest, which always tripped Wes up after a whirl of parties and crowds and people who thrived on drama and double-speak.

Wes watched the city crawl by, guilt and relief doing an unpleasant tango in his chest.

He climbed out of his taxi outside a Georgian building on a bare, swept street of grasping twigs and frosty streetlights. Wes was currently living rent-free in the penthouse provided by Hugo's dear old dad, who would cut Hugo off without a second thought if the poor boy displayed any sign of independent thought, or, indeed, if Hugo senior ever found out about Wes.

Someone was waiting for him. A stocky man in a nondescript suit, with the weathered look of a seasoned enforcer.

Wes's stomach dropped.

Maybe don't go home for a bit.

Ricky hadn't been bluffing.

Too late now.

He cleared his throat and adjusted his silk scarf. 'All right, Mister Bill?'

Mister Bill – not his real name, but a moniker given to him because he always turned up when people missed-a-bill – blocked the door, taking a deceptively relaxed stance. 'Your uncle Barry wants a word.'

Wes shook his head. 'No, I done my bit for this month, he can't go adding days when he feels like it, that wasn't the…'

'You're coming with us, son. Don't make it difficult.'

Wes spotted a car parked in a residents-only spot and blew out a slow breath.

Thank Grandad that Katy hadn't actually shown up, hey? Ricky Porter, you sly old sod. You could have bloody warned me properly.

He rubbed the back of his neck. 'Look, the last batch made me lose time. I don't… I got places to be, you know, I…'

'You should have thought of your busy schedule before you stole from him, shouldn't you?' The man's monotone was matter-of-fact, but Wes detected a hint of judgement.

'It was just a bit of ket for fuck's sake, I only took it for a bit of fun, it wa'n't the Crown Jewels.' Wes rubbed his face, noticing the bigger man never looked directly at him. He knew better than to stare at Wes's face for too long. 'All right, all right. I'm coming.'

Charlie was going to video call him soon, and he had to answer. He'd promised.

'Can I call my girlfriend?'

'After.'

Wes clicked his tongue. 'Come on, mate.'

'No phones.' The man took a step towards him, and Wes retreated into the arms of two other muscular blokes whose footsteps he hadn't heard.

One grabbed his arms and the other searched his pockets. It was all done in a few seconds – a swift pat-down, wallet, keys and phone confiscated. Wes cursed inwardly.

They walked him to the waiting car.

'This had better not fuck me up,' Wes muttered.

One of the men smirked, only briefly, and Wes groaned. They put him in the back, one either side of him, and for the second time that night Wes found himself going somewhere he didn't want to go.

—

Uncle Barry's set-up in London was beneath an animal shelter. Mister Bill led Wes down to a maze of cellars where his phone wouldn't work even if they hadn't taken it off him and into the clinical testing lab where Wes had had some of the worst and best trips of his life.

Barry Wend-McVey, a stout, balding, middle-aged man with no visible eldritch additions to his physique, lumbered around a dentist's chair, one meaty hand on the leather back.

'Wesley!'

'Uncle.'

'You got a face like a slapped arse, son. Thought I'd say it so's I can remember it.' Uncle Barry chortled. 'Ah, balls, what did I just say? Never mind. You're the gift that keeps on giving, ain'tcha? Hours of fun for all the family. Park your backside there and strap in.'

'Kinky.' Wes knew the room intimately by now, its stainless-steel accoutrements, the squeaking cages of test subjects, of whom he was one.

He knew from months of experience there was no way out of the room except through the door, which was ridiculous on his uncle's part. There should always be *two* exits, preferably one that didn't involve going through Mister Bill, in case the meat-mountain ever got a better offer from someone even more unpleasant. Wes didn't trust anyone when money was involved. He'd mentioned it to Uncle Barry a few times, but Uncle Barry only laughed and said Bill was loyal. That wasn't comforting.

'These are the perfected lot,' Barry said from behind him. 'I want you to flog 'em for me. Parties. The kind you lot go to. Fifty quid a pill.'

Wes rolled his eyes and fiddled half-heartedly with the cuffs on the chair. 'Each? What do they do, suck you off and call you a cab?'

'Dirty little bugger.'

His uncle handed him a small pill, white and round, about the size of a tic-tac. Wes hoped it was posh molly, but Uncle Barry tended to go in for more dramatic effects than mild synthetic euphoria.

'Let's see what happens. Unlock your true potential, all that jazz.'

'Oh, it's not these again?' Wes had tried a version of this before and spent two days unsure of whether his thoughts were manifesting in the real world (unlikely) or if he had finally had some kind of psychotic break (far more probable). It had been awful, and the best he could describe it was like lucid dreaming, without it being either lucid or a dream. Charlie said he'd talked a lot of crap, and forbade him from doing it again. He hadn't told her it wasn't exactly a choice: better she think he was just an arsehole than worry about him being actively in danger.

He took the pill, and a twitchy little lab-rat in a white coat, on a break from cooking meth by the smell of him, handed him a glass of water.

Wes took the pill dry, pushing it back into his throat and swallowing.

It didn't take long to kick in.

Thoughts swirled before his eyes, manifesting in clouds that he could walk around, touch, manipulate. He danced with them, tripping over things that didn't belong there, parties and sex thrown together with strange dark landscapes he'd never seen, family arguments chasing him down corridors where a red, sticky cocoon pulsed, blocking his path.

He knew there was something he needed to do, something he ought to remember, but his head filled up with silvery threads and sparkling dust, and he gave in and lost himself in the visions and chased the thoughts he wanted to last.

He soon forgot about his sister.

Chapter 2: Lord of the Flies

11 January

Fairwood House was silent under the moonlight, but it was not dreaming. It was thinking.

Its Georgian façade covered an internal mess of add-ons and various architectural misadventures, the thirteenth-century stone crypt the only remnant of the monastery it had been built on top of, some Tudor timber still in residence, but the rest had rotted away and been restored fully just under a year ago. The locals nicknamed it The Crows, and it didn't mind that, but *he* liked its original name.

Him.

Fairwood contemplated its lodger. Richard Edwin 'Ricky' Porter, autodidact, taxidermist, car thief, had got rid of its resident spectre, a violent whirlwind of arson and destruction, but now he haunted its halls and passages instead, filling it with the scent of soil and sweat and crusting blood. He kept things neat, at least, and didn't spit on the bare floorboards. But yesterday he'd come home with something wrapped in old newspaper and muttered some incantations, and it felt… different.

He was given to muttering to himself in gruff, self-taught Old English, but the house wasn't old enough to understand that, its thirteenth-century stone roots more attuned to Medieval Latin, with the vaguest recollections of Anglo-Norman and a lost dialect of Middle English. The only owner it had had who'd studied Old English at university was nowhere near fluent and had forgotten much of it before she'd come to the house. Carrie's memories were not useful for deciphering his rhythmic verses, and it didn't know if he was reciting some saga or riddle to himself, or if he was composing something new.

That aside, someone's heart was up its kitchen chimney. It could feel it there like a fleabite, the fresh organ nestled against the brick and starting to rot.

It waited for him to come home and explain himself.

It was waiting a while.

He came through the gates just after midnight, a girl over his shoulder in a fireman's lift, towing her suitcase in his other hand.

She was a skinny, athletic-looking thing, and though the house had never seen her before, her aura was familiar.

It braced to reject her and keep them both outside. He had gone too far. He knew the rules.

Ricky grinned in his cocky, crooked way, like a naughty schoolboy who knew he was about to get away with something appalling.

'Evenin' love.'

The heart in the chimney gave a small, feeble thump, and the house found it couldn't resist. Its gates creaked open without a fuss.

...Ricky, what have you done?

'This is my cousin,' Ricky announced, shifting her comatose dead weight on his shoulder. He made it look easy, but Fairwood's windows could see him sweating. 'Her name's Katherine. She's gonna be stayin' for a bit, hope you don't mind.'

...Ricky...

'It's not for long. Promise. All for a good cause, I'll explain inside.' He trudged up the gravel drive towards the porch.

...You'd better.

'You'll really like her, but don't get attached.' Ricky struggled up the steps and the front door opened to admit them. 'Cor, she's heavy after a while.'

...When you said we might be having guests, this wasn't what I had in mind.

Ricky's angular face tilted in the light of the entrance hall, hood slipping back and revealing the puckered skin at the back of his shaved head. Those lips were currently shut, set in a curved line of scar tissue.

'The fam'ly's not happy. It's getting a bit complicated.'

The house released a deep draught, joists groaning all through its attics and upper floors.

...We will talk about this. At length.

'Yeah, of course.' He gave his burden a pat on the back of her legs. 'Not now, hey, she's sleeping.'

Fairwood contemplated pushing the consciousness of its rooms and passageways into a single point, condensing all facets of its personalities from across its floorplan into one multidimensional avatar.

Ricky usually listened to the avatar – it looked like the late owner, Carrie Rickard. Carrie had died eight months ago of an aneurism, but thanks to her dying wish, her form and mind lived on in the walls. The avatar was so good it could fool her still-living parents on the phone or by video chat, and even once in person, but with Ricky it didn't have to try as hard.

Carrie was the part of the house who made coherent decisions when the various rooms could not agree, and

Ricky tried to get around her the same way as when she'd been alive, as if, apart from her melting out of the walls and floor occasionally and not needing to eat or drink or breathe, he hadn't really noticed the difference. Or at least, he pretended he didn't to avoid feeling guilty about it, and pretended so successfully that he had, at last, convinced himself.

Ricky didn't know what to do with guilt, Fairwood realised.

The house decided against manifesting for the time being and let him struggle with his cousin up the stairs.

'She weighs a bloody tonne,' he complained, halfway up. 'I carried her from the station already, how about a hand?'

...*She's your guest.*

'Very funny.'

He dropped her off on a camp bed in one of the six guest rooms, none of which had been properly furnished yet, and retreated to the room that had been Carrie's. All her things were still there, her clothes, her bedspread, the room exactly as it had been. It welcomed him wearily, one of the more genial upper rooms.

The one Katherine Porter was sleeping in was less impressed, its boards still bearing the chalk marks of an ill-judged séance. The room didn't recognise her, but Carrie did.

Carrie had seen the girl once before, when she'd had tea with the girl's grandmother. The girl was a few months older now, and her makeup made her look older still, but she couldn't be more than sixteen or seventeen. Even in sleep, she had the sulky cast to her long face that Ricky sometimes had, a Porter family trait. She had been introduced to Carrie as Katy.

Fairwood absorbed this information and siphoned through Katy's dreams to get to know her better until it touched something dark and oily in her head that resisted with a slavering snarl. The house recoiled.

...What have you brought here?

Ricky shook his head, stretching out his muscles on Carrie's bedroom floor, and didn't reply immediately.

Fairwood's rooms whispered in concert, debating what to do. Ricky, irritatingly, had become adept at tuning them out.

'She could kill me, you know,' he said, as if this would win him points. He kicked off his shoes and lay on the bed fully clothed, protecting his back lips with his arms, staring at the ceiling.

Only now did Fairwood focus itself into a point, Carrie's face forming a pattern in the cracks and lines above his head.

'I could well believe that,' she said. Her voice was almost the same as when she'd been alive, just a little deeper and more resonant.

Ricky fixed his eyes on her with an unguarded expression of relief that she'd appeared, and the house feasted on his silent adoration.

He looked oddly delicate in this form now, short and lean, all bones and angles, tired skin and heavy eyes. He'd been proud of his body, Fairwood knew. He'd honed it, trained it, and it was entirely his. Now his Changes were complete and his beauty, his glory, had been set free... his body betrayed him, couldn't keep up with the demands he made of it, and it was slipping out of his control. Carrie-Fairwood could see that, and she knew he knew it too.

When Ricky felt out of control in one area, he always tried to take it back somewhere else, usually by killing someone, or poisoning them, or, in this case, taking charge of who the house allowed through its gates and abducting his cousin. It probably made logical sense to him, but that didn't make it better.

'God, you look awful. I told you, you're not looking after yourself. Why didn't you eat your dinner? You've already got a calorie deficit to make up from the last time you Changed.'

He blinked up at her. 'Oh, I... didn't feel like it. Got put off my dinner, like.' His cheeks tinged. 'Seeing what Uncle Marcus sees is a right pain in the arse, wish I'd never eaten his sodding eye.'

'What did you see?' Carrie-Fairwood asked, although she didn't really want to know.

'Aunty Ida. Far too much of her. At their time of life, too, bloody hell.' He shook his head, looking ill. 'All the politics and clandestine bullshit I can stomach, that was the *point*, but all the rest of it, shit me. I wish that'd occurred to me sooner.' He made a face, and Carrie couldn't help but laugh. He managed a weak smirk and changed the subject. 'All right. In all genuine seriousness, on a scale of one to fucked, where d'you think I am when her in there Changes?'

The house creaked, breathing around him.

'...Into whatever the hell is in her head?' Carrie could feel the snarl reverberate through her, enough to reduce her to splinters. She winced. 'I'd say you're fairly up there, mate.'

He nodded, swallowing. 'Yeah, that's what I thought.'

She switched to voiceless communication, in case Katy's hearing was sharper than the average seventeen-year-old coma patient.

...Does she know you killed her Gran?

'Not yet.' His grin was weak. 'Still can't see my own future prop'ly. Maybe I get out of it, hey? The family cull, I mean. What d'you think? She might not mind so much, not if I'm useful to her.'

The avatar pushed itself into her humanoid form, sucking the life out of the room around him, and climbed down the wall.

He made room for her to lie beside him, propping himself up slightly so his tendrils had space to emerge. She heard them thrum against his oesophagus on the way out. She probed his mind, and his thoughts mingled with hers.

He didn't want to look at her.

'It's all right,' he said. 'In the long run, it'll work out. And you won't have to worry about me bringing body parts into the house anymore, I know you don't really like that.'

'About that heart up my chimney…'

'Yeah – I… Can we talk about that in the morning, love? It's… it's nothing, honest. It's for your benefit, that's all.'

'I highly doubt that.'

He sighed. 'Best of intentions, I promise.'

She didn't say anything. Ricky's best intentions led to some fairly gnarly situations, so that didn't fill her with confidence. She watched his face as his eyes slid into sad, vacant staring at the ceiling. His lips tightened, and he looked far older than twenty-nine.

'What'll happen to you when I'm not here? I've tried and tried, but I can't see that, either. You're technically dead, see, and I can't quite manage seeing the fate of the dead. Yet.'

He was thinking about dying, she realised, and the room chilled around them.

      ...Don't be defeatist. This isn't like you.

'Nah, it's fatalistic, not defeatist. There's a diff'rence.' He shrugged, swallowing. His eyes were moist. 'I didn't think I'd get this far,' he admitted. 'I got everything I ever wanted. That was a proper surprise. Started to think the entrails were lyin', but here we are.'

She pulled herself into his side and rested her head on his chest. Ricky had almost grown used to it, used to feeling safe, used to the weight and texture of her against him. She had grown used to him, too.

'I wish you hadn't done it,' she whispered.

'What? Which bit?'

The house wasn't sure. It wasn't really his fault. Carrie had always been doomed to die as Ricky foresaw, and not even his interventions could have saved her. They had just made things a whole lot more complicated.

'Yeah, that's the problem, isn't it? All of it, I guess. I wish you hadn't... looked in the first place. I don't know. I can't unpick it. I don't know where it started.'

'You wish I was something else.'

'Not exactly.'

He breathed in her smell, loamy, warm, an old library in summer, the one she knew he liked. It relaxed him a little.

'You want me to be like our Wes? All made-up principles and vegetarian?'

'I wish you'd see people as more than spare parts for you to use.'

He grinned. 'You want a lot.'

'I wish you'd see *yourself* as more than spare parts for other people to use, that would be a start.'

'Oi! Haven't you heard? I'm a bloody god.'

She got comfortable, pulling his arm over her. 'You're still an arsehole.'

'Charming.'

She looked up at him, windowpane eyes seeing through his. 'You don't want to die, do you?'

He shuddered behind his fixed smile. 'You're right, I'm being... Nah, ignore me, I'm... I'm not thinking clear tonight, that's all. I ain't gonna die.'

'You're not sure.' Carrie-Fairwood didn't like it when he wasn't sure. He may be a colossal prick, but she was sentimental about him, like a broken gargoyle that had taken on its own charm and had become a feature just as it was. 'Why not just kill her now?'

'This a test?' He glanced down at her, but she was serious. 'Nah, she survives to Change. I seen it.'

'Does she *only* survive because you refuse to kill her because you think she survives?' Carrie sat up, narrowing her eyes. 'Is this one of those self-fulfilling things? What if I did it?'

He made a low sound. 'You'd go in there and smother her with a pillow, would you? Crush her windpipe? Drown her in the bath? Little household accident?'

'I've lured people in before and hurt them.'

'Yeah, when you were rotting, this is different.'

'How?'

He stroked her hair, teasing the strands between his fingers. 'Love. You won't succeed. I've *seen* it. It's a waste of energy, she'll survive. An' I don't want to see you damaged. Let her be. If it's my time, it's my time.'

She shook her head. 'You're an agent of fate, not its slave. An agent ought to have some agency of their own, don't you think?'

He shrugged, eyeing the enamel contours of her bare shoulder. He traced them with smooth fingertips then ran his hand down her arm, letting it glide along the polished surface like the waxed veneer of the bannister rail. His touch connected them with a mutual sense of belonging.

'You're getting better at this. It's nearly right. I c'n still tell, though.' His smile was crooked and shallow. It slipped away as she pulled herself closer, watching him. 'You're the first place I ever properly stayed in, apart from at home. Never spent a few nights away before until you let me in.'

She paused, his memories slipping through her mortar. 'That's not true. What about when you were a kid, and—'

'Doesn't count.'

'And that time you slept rough for a bit...'

'You're the first place I *wanted to be*, there, happy?' He rolled his eyes. '*That's* what *counts*. It was my choice to be here. That's what I mean. My first place away from home. My parents' place. You know what I mean.' He looked away. 'You really cross?'

She studied him, wondering what difference that would make. 'Yeah, a bit.'

He only nodded, a short jerk of his chin. 'You sorry to see me come home tonight?'

'No.' She tried levity, because he really looked like he was going to cry. His cheeks were drawn, eyes pink and moist. His jaw fluttered as he clenched it. Carrie tapped his breastbone lightly. 'You only have to look at my grate and it catches fire.'

He snorted and it turned into a choking cough.

'Be-behave.'

That was better. Her mind turned back to the current problem, comatose on the camp bed in her guest room.

'How many people have *you* killed?'

Ricky pondered this, not ever having kept score. 'Not as many as you think. Only a few a year.'

'Since when?'

He yawned. 'Fuck knows. Don't matter much now, does it? I only done for a couple since I moved in here.'

'Give the man a medal.'

'I done everything else you asked.'

She stroked his face and he leaned into her hand. His eyes moistened, but he was getting better at holding it in. Something twisted inside her chest where her heart had been.

'Turn the light off, love.'

She didn't need to reach for it. The lamp went out, and the house drifted into gentle, quiet slumber, letting his thoughts merge with its dreams.

Ricky's Memory: Soothsaying in October

Ricky sat alone in the coal cellar at Fairwood House, deep in contemplation. Around him, dead birds were arranged in a rough pattern in various stages of death and decay, their entrails spilling onto the candlelit floor. One was still twitching, clinging grimly to life with every ounce of fight it had, but as he watched, the light winked out of its bright, agonised eye, and it twitched once more and lay still.

(Interesting…)

He allowed himself a slow yawn and a stretch, unsure of the time. Maggots danced inside a magpie to his left. He nodded at it, poring over the putrefaction. His jaw fluttered.

Merlin Silvestris could prophesise accurately *without* reading the dead, he had read about it before. He ached to be that powerful.

He'd thought that with his beauty now fully revealed, his glory fully manifested, the secrets of the cosmos would fall into place before his eyes regardless of which form he was in.

Yet here he was, a few months on, and he was still rooting about in corpses and couldn't see his own future. The forbidden desire hadn't gone away, either. He tried not to think about it, but poking at the ruined bodies only made it starker, mocking him. He could see any number of things in his beautiful form, feed upon the energies of lesser things, open his third eye and bask in the wonders of what was yet to come... but he still couldn't *change* it.

The dance of the birds in the sky on previous evenings had told him he wasn't going to be the sole master of Fairwood House for long. All right, lodger, she didn't like it when he used the 'm' word... He'd killed a few to make sure, finding satisfaction in their decay, but the entrails told him the same thing. She'd find others to fill her rooms, a house like this couldn't be content with only one inhabitant. It wasn't what she was built for.

He couldn't blame her for that.

He picked up the freshly dead sparrow, still at last, its final shudders only underlining what everything else had revealed. It wasn't often he lost his temper, but its beak was gaping in a mocking laugh and he couldn't stand it. He clenched his fist, squeezing until the sinews stood out on his forearms, until he felt the small bag of flesh and bones burst and crack and ooze between his fingers.

The coal cellar watched, that vengeful part of her she kept under lock and key, and he fuelled her thirst.

...Why are you angry?

He grinned in the flickering dark. 'Shouldn't I be? You said I'd be your lodger, your only one. That's not what these say. We're going to have guests.'

...When did I promise you that?

'We don't *need* anyone else. *I'm* all you need. I can repair you, I can take care of you, I can...' He felt the smouldering bitterness of Fairwood's bad memories pushing at him from the walls as the bird blood drained into her foundations. She sucked it up like milk.

(Good old girl, I'll help you feel better, none-else can give you revenge like me.)

...I don't need revenge now, Fairwood whispered.

He stroked the floor, smiling crookedly at the flagstones.

Out loud, he said, 'You should've seen all their faces when I Changed in front of 'em. The fam'ly, I mean. They think I'm a god.'

...What are the eyeballs for?

The voice tickled the back of his brain, whispering gently.

He glanced around at the mason jars on shelves above his taxidermy kit. 'Insurance. I'm learning what to do with them.'

...And you really think I'd bring guests in here?

He sensed this was meant to be a joke, but he was on the defensive. 'It's tidy, ain't it?'

The whole cellar seemed to sigh.

...There's no need to be so upset. You of all people should know the future isn't a straight line.

He blocked her out of his head. He'd rather burn her to the ground himself than be just another lodger, a guest, lost in the crowd. Bird remains squidged around his flexing fingers. The little broken body flopped wetly onto the floor.

(I ain't jealous, jealousy's beneath me.)

That was almost his grandmother's voice, the mantra deeply ingrained. He sniffed at his hand, inhaling the stink of blood and contents of the burst digestive system, and wiped it off in a ragged hand towel. He blew the candles out and kicked the maggot-filled birds out of his way as he headed to the steps.

11 January

The ceiling was unfamiliar, the wrong shade of beige, and minus the cracks. The lightshade was stained glass, casting soft colours across the plaster, not wicker bars casting their caged shadows over the room.

Katy sat up.

The bed wasn't hers, either. Too small. Too hard. A camp bed. She jerked fully alert, instinctively hunting for her phone. Her handbag was nowhere she could see – the only furniture in the room was the bed she was lying on, covered in cheap white sheets and an itchy wool blanket. She threw them off. Her purple suitcase was nowhere to be seen either.

Katy swung her legs out of bed although she could barely feel them, bare feet hitting the floorboards too hard with a numbed thump. Standing took three tries. She slapped her arms and thighs, trying to get the feeling back into them. At least she was still fully clothed.

She was in an empty bedroom, floorboards waxed and clean, heavy brown curtains framing the window. There was nothing under the bed, nothing on the shelves, no cupboards to check, no wardrobe, nada. Chalk lines were palely visible on the bare boards, as if someone had let a child scribble on the floor and not cleaned up properly.

Where the hell am I?

Katy stumbled to the window, knees buckling but getting stronger, and leaned on the windowsill. She was on the second or maybe third floor of a building that faced a wide, long lawn, ringed around by a high stone wall, wrought-iron gates at the end of a gravel driveway leading to a familiar country lane. Fields stretched beyond, a melancholy wintry slash of colour below the cold grey sky. The planted woodland they called The Chase lay off to the left. She tried to swallow and realised how dry her mouth had become, how thirsty she was.

This could only be one place, and that was impossible.

Katy closed her eyes, blinking slowly, trying to figure it out.

Had Ricky brought her there?

Sixty years or more ago, a witch had cursed Fairwood House, the old manor local people also called The Crows, effectively banning all of Katy's blood-kin from setting foot there. Family legend had it that the house itself had to decide to let you in, that it lured people like a mythical, wood-and-stone siren. That sounded made up to Katy, because buildings were just buildings, but she wasn't one hundred per cent sure.

Gran had told her the blood-magic spell had been cast out of spite, because there was something powerful in the house that the family needed, and they had had to make do with lesser shrines ever since.

The curse still held for everyone except Ricky.

None of the others could set foot on the grounds or so much as touch the gates. She'd heard from her mother that some of them had tried. They said it was because he'd ascended, that he was a god now. Katy didn't really know what they meant by that. She hadn't been going to the family gatherings since Gran died, and he hadn't seemed any different than usual at the train station.

Katy tried to open the window, but it wouldn't budge and there was nothing to smash it with. Besides, it looked like she was pretty high up. Her head swam, fuzzy with dehydration and the after-effects of Ricky's bites. She didn't want to lift her top, examine her skin. She didn't want to roll up her sleeves and see the shape of his suckers. She wanted to jump into a scalding shower and scrub her skin off.

Katy stumbled to the door, blinking. She expected it to be locked, but it opened almost as soon as she touched the handle – she flexed her hand to get some feeling back and stepped into a long, carpeted corridor. At least this wasn't Ricky's shitty little cottage in the woods, where his creepy parents lurked behind the dusty windows like something out of a horror film. Her mother's sister freaked her out with her heavy black dresses and sibilant voice, and that weird little giggle, like a deranged child.

'How do I get out of here?' she whispered to herself.

A breath of air blew through the corridor that almost sounded like a word. It thrilled her muscles into action, and she stumbled down the carpet towards the stairs. Her cousin's voice from a room on her left brought her up short.

'C'mon, love, don't be like that.'

Katy jumped away from his voice, but the door to the room was closed. She stared the keyhole down, poised to run, but then she heard 'No, I never said *that*' from the other side, and relaxed. He wasn't talking to *her*, wasn't all-seeing, all-knowing.

She dropped into a crouch, creeping up to the keyhole – one for a large, old-fashioned type of key – and squinted through it. She glimpsed a bedroom, comfortably kitted out with a double bed and peacock wallpaper. Her eyes watered, trying to focus. She thought she could almost hear someone speaking to him, but she couldn't make it out.

Ricky was topless, in different trousers to the night before, and pacing. She couldn't see his face. His abdominals and obliques were like an anatomy diagram, and it looked like he'd never missed an arm day, but Katy had seen lads at the gym like that and not one of them did cardio. Cole Morgan, in her class for biology, could crack nuts with his biceps and got out of breath jogging up the stairs. If Ricky wasn't anticipating it, she just had to outrun him.

He paced out of sight, giving her a clear view of the double bed with its sunny yellow counterpane. On the bed, opposite the door, she saw a handbag strap. Her handbag strap.

Shit. He had her phone.

Ricky lowered his voice, and Katy strained to hear what he was saying. His accent had broadened, something Gran's had done whenever she got animated. In his case, he sounded more embarrassed, as if he were being told off. She wished she could hear the other side of the conversation.

'Yeah, well, I didn't though, did I? An' I said it'd be for a liddle while, but I never said…'

Katy thought she could hear a whisper, but both his arms were by his sides. Speaker? Headphones? What about the house's owner – where was she?

She gave up squinting and pressed her ear to the keyhole instead.

Who else knew he'd taken her from the station? If it was going to be a long argument, she could chance it, make a run for it now, see if the front door was unlocked or if not, find a key. But she wanted her handbag – mainly, her cash, her debit card, her train ticket (the outward one was still valid for today, she'd got an open return to avoid suspicion) and her phone – and that was on the bed in the room with her kidnapper.

'I never 'urt her, did I? She's all right.' A pause. 'Ah, come on. I wouldn't do that, I promised.' Something breathy, out of range. Almost her imagination, perhaps nothing, a draught. 'Nah, it – why'd you say that?'

Katy tried peeping through the hole again, covering one eye to help her focus.

Something blocked her vision and she pulled back, poised to run as the handle turned.

'Why didn't you say so?'

The door opened, and Katy took off.

'Bloody hellfire...'

He wasn't as fast as her.

She bounded down the unfamiliar stairs, skidding across the tiled grand entrance hall and slammed into the front doors, tugging at them to no avail. A small table with a landline and a telephone directory sat nearby, and she pounced on the wooden arts-and-crafts bowl, looking for keys.

Ricky sauntered down and took a seat on the stairs, watching her. 'She won't let you out, even *with* the keys.'

Katy found a keyring and tried one in the lock. It wouldn't turn. She tried forcing it, rattling the handle as she fought to deepen her panting breaths, chest on fire.

'Easy! Don't snap it, she'll...'

Katy fumbled the keys and dropped them. In desperation she struck the door, kicking and pounding the oak.

Ricky bounded up and launched himself at her at a frightening turn of speed, grabbing her around the middle and throwing her backwards. Katy righted herself before she fell over and sped through the nearest door. She put a two-seater sofa between them as her cousin followed her in, blocking her escape back into the hall.

'Don't do that,' he warned. 'Don't kick the door. That's rude. Doant you *ever* do that again.'

Katy tensed, looking for something that could do real damage, and spotted the poker by the fireplace. She grabbed it, knocking over the paraphernalia around the grate.

'I'll smash the window, I swear to Grandad. Come near me and I'll smash your fucking face in.'

Ricky stopped, staring. 'Let's not smash anything, all right? My face, fine, but...' he sighed. 'Look, I didn't *hurt* you. Let's calm down and start again, all right?'

'*What?* No! You *kidnapped* me.' She took a two-handed grip on the poker.

Ricky rubbed his forehead. He looked at her, frowning, and in the grey daylight she saw the shadows of heavy bruised bags under his eyes, how his cheeks sank in, how haggard and tired he looked.

Had he always looked that way?

She couldn't remember the last time she'd seen him, or properly looked at his face under the hood he always wore. He was still topless, and it wasn't only muscles standing out under his skin. There were ribs, too, the stark lines of his collarbones, and livid red stretchmarks around his hips and over his belly that looked painfully fresh. Veins stood out on his sinewy arms, but it was what came out of the back of his head that she was more concerned about.

Tendrils were snaking out of whatever the hell he had back there, and they writhed around his head in anxious knots. Her grip tightened on the brass along with a flutter of hope.

He was ill, or something.

Good.

'Can we just...' He huffed a sigh, raising his hands, and fixed his stare on a point a little to the right of her shoulder. 'It's all right, I ain't going to do nothing. Maybe you were right, you happy now?'

'Right about what?' Katy asked, shifting her weight.

'Wasn't talking to you.' Ricky gave a slight shake of his head, but Katy resisted the urge to look behind her. The hairs pricked up on the back of her neck.

'If you don't let me go, I *will* break the window, but I'm leaving.' Katy licked her lips.

He was nuts.

She couldn't swear she'd heard another voice in the bedroom with him – maybe he talked to himself. What was the curse supposed to do, again? It was meant to repel them, keep them out. What if it scrambled your brain like a magnet on a laptop? If she stayed here, would it get her, too?

'And... I want my stuff back.'

'Yeah. I got your suitcase.' He jerked his head. 'In the kitchen.'

Katy realised she'd have to pass him to find it. She shook her head. 'You get it. And my handbag. Bring them in here.'

'What for? You ain't actually going anywhere. I can't have you ringing anyone. Not yet. You do know they're watching you? You wouldn't last five minutes in London. I told 'em to leave you alone, but I wouldn't trust Uncle Marcus further'n I can throw the town hall.'

Katy swallowed. 'Wes is going to be worried. He'll report me missing. And he'll protect me, he promised.'

Ricky scoffed. 'Wes won't do shit.'

'I bet he's called the police already.'

Ricky raised his eyebrows. 'I bet he hasn't even called *you*.'

His lack of faith in her big brother stung. She tried to swing the poker at the space between them, but it didn't budge. Her shoulder wrenched, the brass twisting under her palms, but it wouldn't move. Something was keeping it in place, something over her right shoulder. The wall shimmered in her peripheral vision. She snapped her head around to look, but it was a trick of the light – the wall was firm and flat.

Katy dropped the poker. She turned slowly back to face Cousin Ricky, and her heart lurched. He was much closer than before, and he was grinning. She hadn't heard him move.

Fear webbed across her throat in a tight, hot, nauseous corset. Katy broke eye contact and darted a frantic look around the floor, but the poker wasn't where she'd dropped it. It had rolled closer to the fireplace, muffled by the rug. She made a grab for it, but Ricky pounced.

She yelped as his weight cannoned into her, pinning her arms to her sides. The tussle was brief: Katy didn't have a hope in Hell of getting him off, and he threw her onto the sofa with almost enough force to tip it backwards. Half buried in the cushions, rubbing at the studs of pain where his fingers had dug in, she glared at him.

'What the *fuck*?'

Ricky glared at her. 'Yeah, I could ask you the same thing. I *told* you this is for your own good, calm the fuck down.'

'How did you do that?' Katy demanded. 'The, the poker thing, how did you do that? Why wouldn't it move?'

Ricky seemed to find this funny. 'Told you,' he said, not looking at her but rather at a spot somewhere to the left of her head. 'She almost asks as many questions as you.'

Katy spun around, but he was literally talking to the wall.

'Who's the ghost?' she demanded, taking a leap into the obvious. It came out as a croak, and the flush of fear and frustration burned as far as her ears. 'Where's the owner? Doesn't some woman own this place?' She had a vague recollection of that: Gran had invited the woman over for tea once, and Rachel had worked with her in SupaPrice on weekends, but after about a month the woman had stopped turning up to work. Everyone assumed she'd quit.

Ricky giggled. 'She's around.' He levered himself down into a cross-legged position on the rug, pressing his knees down to the floor in a stretch. 'Bloody hell, I'm getting too old for this crap.'

Katy folded her arms, the sofa cushions a welcome comfort, although she was loathe to admit it. Tight-lipped, she channelled all her frustration into a glare.

'Around? What d'you mean, 'around'? She's dead, isn't she?'

'She ain't a ghost. And I di'n't kill her, if that's what you're thinking.' Ricky arched his back, and Katy winced as his spine cracked. The tendrils had retreated, sucked back somewhere into the depths of his body, although where they went was another matter. There wasn't enough room in there for those things *and* his organs, surely?

Katy pictured the coils slithering around inside his ribs, wriggling between the folds of his intestines. She forced a dry swallow and nearly choked on it.

'Look,' he said, without rancour. 'I don't *mind* you running away. I ain't cross with you. I'm not your enemy, Katherine. I'm tryin' to help, matter of fact. I could've told you the omens say you leaving is all bad.' He raised an eyebrow, tilting his neck to one side, then the other. 'That vote, that wasn't my idea.'

Not the Vote.

She'd been deliberately not thinking about that. She hugged herself, pushing her fingers through the holes in her ruined jumper. Her cheek was sore but she chewed it anyway, nipping skin away and tasting blood.

'It was close,' he said, as if that was a good thing. 'I can tell you who was on your side, if you want to know.'

Katy shook her head, queasiness catching her off-guard. She pressed her arms into her stomach, digging her nails through a hole in her sleeve and deep into her own skin.

'Sure?' He seemed surprised. 'Some of 'em were pretty pissed off the vote even got called. They don't *all* want you dead. They're quite keen on the idea of you killing off a few they don't like, settle some scores for them.'

Katy found her voice. 'Can we – can we *not* talk about this? Can you just – just *shut up*, please?'

Ricky blinked. 'Oh. All right. I'm not trying to be... anyway. I sorted it out. But Uncle Marcus ain't happy. And you're putting Wes in danger, too, he's sailed pretty close to the wind these last couple of years. Don't give them the opportunity to kill two birds with one stone.' He snorted. 'Literally, as the case may be.'

Tears clogged her gullet like concrete. 'Is this a *joke* to you?'

'Course not!' He dropped his gaze to the floor. 'Nah, I'm not... I di'n't mean it like that. I'm tryin' to help, believe it or not, and you won't listen, so...' He shrugged, glancing up, and she'd never seen him – or anyone – look so haggard and helpless. 'I offered you help before, remember, and you turned me down, so...'

She cleared her throat. 'What, so you thought you'd kidnap me?'

'Abduct.' His lips twitched. 'Kidnap's for profit. This is abduction.'

Katy wasn't in the mood for pedantry. 'Whatever.'

'I need you to stay around for a bit. That's all. It's... for your own good. I know you turned down my offer last time, I know Gran told you to, but I don't think you understood me proper – it was naun else but mentoring I was offerin'. Think of this as your second chance. All right?'

She rolled her eyes. 'I knew what you were offering. I didn't want it.' She hadn't fancied being his disciple at fifteen, and she sure as hell didn't want to be his disciple now, either. 'Do I get a choice?'

'Not really, no.' He gave her a tired glance up and down, and she hugged the cushion tighter. 'But there's two ways this can go, yeah? One, you see sense, we do it my way, and you get the run of the house, the grounds, whatever you want, go see your friends, do whatever, but don't go to London. Stay here, where I can keep an eye on you.' He shifted his weight. 'I can teach you how to, you know, Change. Prop'ly, ascend, you know. Teach you how to control it. Then you can bugger off, do what you want, go to university like you want to, it's your life. I may have... one thing I'd like you to do for me, after, if you were feeling like you owed me, if your life's worth something to you.' He shrugged, as if his generosity was no big deal, and she narrowed her eyes.

There it was. He wanted something.

'Not a big thing,' he said, as if to reassure her. 'I, um. I'll tell you about it later, if you want to unpack and get yourself sorted...'

'What's the other way?' Katy interrupted him.

Ricky stopped, train of thought broken. 'What?'

'You said there's two ways we can do this, what's the other way?'

He stared at her. 'You're... Come on. You're seventeen anyway, you're still a bloody minor, an' Wesley should know bloody better than to agree to this bullshit.'

He levered himself off the rug, nostrils flared. The ceiling creaked, and he shifted on the spot as if the sound had reined him in.

He continued, softer, but cockier. Katy itched to punch him.

'I spoke to Wes last night. Told him you weren't going to show up.' Ricky shrugged, jerking his head at the door. 'Go on, your handbag's upstairs. Check your phone, if you like. See how often he tried to call you. How many texts d'you reckon you got?'

He wouldn't ask if the answer was more than 'none'.

Katy pushed back against the cushions and wished she could slide between them and be lost forever in a dark, warm world and cease to exist. She dug her nails deeper into her arm, leaving bruised half-moon indentations and clamped her teeth together so hard they ached.

I'll kill him. I'll rip his heart out through his throat and shove it up his arse.

That was Uncle David's favourite threat, but it was satisfying. She wasn't sure if she was thinking of Ricky or Wes, not that it mattered. She should have known it would all go wrong.

She chanced a glance at her captor, simmering with hate. It deadened everything else until all there was to feel was the hot squirming in her chest and a spreading numbness in the pit of her stomach.

'Okay.'

Ricky scowled. 'Okay, okay what?'

'Okay, I'll unpack.' It came out as a whisper.

Weak. Spineless. Stupid.

Her cousin nodded, satisfied. 'Good girl.'

Katy dug her nails into the old scratches on her forearm so deep they drew blood. Pain shocked her, gave her a release, enough to twitch her lips into a cold mask of obedience. 'I'll take my stuff upstairs.'

'Yeah. Let me show you.' He led the way, a spring in his step as he headed for the door, and Katy hated him in that moment more than she had ever hated anyone before.

'Don't you worry,' he said over his shoulder, as she grudgingly pulled herself up to follow. 'You won't be here for long.'

Chapter 3: Dangerous Liaisons

12 January

Wes hung around in the clean white sweep of the gallery's corridor, lurking with a glass of champagne to clear his head.

His thoughts were thankfully back on the inside of his skull, although for some time he had been able to observe them externally, walk around them, view them from various angles like holograms – *well done, Uncle Barry* – and his mood, more or less, had evened out. There were some memory blanks, but he wasn't sure if they were important. He could flog these little darlings for twice the price to those who appreciated their educational application.

The exhibition was not his style. Manipulated photographs of carved-up faces, set alongside the doctored images of vintage Soviet propaganda and bleak fragmented landscapes that played tricks with perspective and told stories in negative space; that wasn't for him.

He had elected to wear his flashiest dress shirt, bold crimson silk with diamond buttons, a pocket square of wasp-yellow, black skinny jeans that left nothing to the imagination and had probably cost more than the catering for this event. He knew he was being unkind there, but tiny things on sticks weren't his idea of a good time.

He took three vol-au-vents from a passing plate with a Vegan label, eyeing up the chorizo things on another circulating tray. He caught the eye of the server, a lithe androgynous youth in crisp black and white whose complexion would have made Raphael throw down his brushes and weep, and winked.

Charlie was busy, deep-red curls piled in a messy bun at the back of her head, tumbling out around the wide silver headband set with pearls and crystals. She was her competent professional self this afternoon, braving the January elements in a fake-fur-trimmed Grecian gown of silver and gold, cheeks highlighted with bronzer and glitter. She shot him little glances now and again, but she was trapped by a semi-circle of sparkling socialites. Her eyelids were caked in gold, so much so that it was a wonder she could keep them open, the glittering powder bleeding into thick charcoal black smears that hollowed her eye sockets out and streaked across to her temples.

This was her Fragile Icarus persona, of course, the woman scorched by a flight of fancy few had dared take.

Of all the guests at this grand opening of her exhibition, Wes was – predictably – the only one who had turned up in colour. He loitered, conspicuous and loud, defying the 'Snowflake Aesthetic' theme as a matter of principle.

'Are you with anyone?'

The scratchy voice at his elbow made him start, nearly spilling the champagne. He popped a vol-au-vent into his mouth, chewing to cover his surprise, and cast a glance at his accoster.

'Shit me, Huey.' Wes sagged, backing up to the wall.

Hugo straightened up, chiselled jaw and clean-cut grin earning him instant forgiveness. He dropped the false voice, returning to his soft, neutral-with-a-hint-of-culture drawl.

'Language.'

Wes grinned back and looked Hugo up and down. His suit and tie were rumpled as if he'd only just got off the train. There was something about him, some unspoken absence, that made him blend in with Charlie's fractured landscape behind him. His broad shoulders were drawn up but slightly stooped, like a broken crag, uncombed hair tousled and unruly, disarranged by the wind. His smile wanted to be warm, the warmth was there, fighting, but it quivered into a cold, quiet death and slid into a worried frown. He had yet to divest himself of his old college scarf, but someone had taken his coat and furnished him with a champagne flute as well. Wes noted the pinched paleness of his cheeks, a pinkish tinge to the whites of his eyes.

'What're you doing here?'

Hugo frowned, a deep crease wrinkling his broad forehead. 'Supporting Charlie, of course.'

'You're not meant to be back for a few days.'

'Counting, are you?'

Wes offered him a vol-au-vent and ate the other one. 'Always.'

Hugo sniggered like a naughty schoolboy over the soft ambient music, earning them both a stern glance from another guest.

'They like you to be quiet,' Wes murmured as Hugo's shoulders shook. 'Pure as the driven snow in here.'

His partner recovered himself. 'Quite the crowd.'

'She's doing really well.' Wes nodded in Charlie's direction and gave Hugo a sidelong glance. 'How are *you* doing?'

There it was – the guilty tic, a slight twitch of his lips that jerked a single dimple in and out of existence.

'Oh, you know. Could be worse.'

'Huey...'

Hugo drained his flute and took another one. 'Champagne's good, at least.'

'It's not a cash flow problem, is it?'

Hugo winced at the indelicacy.

Wes cocked his eyebrow. 'If that's all, you only have to say.'

'I hate to ask, but – the rent's due and – I was, I was wondering...' He faded away, leaving the question unformed and hanging between them.

Hugo's father paid the rent for him every month, like well-oiled, well-heeled, greasy-palmed clockwork. The senior Mr Chalmondley – pronounced 'Chumley', of course, in the way that Featherstonehaugh was pronounced 'Fanshaw' – had never failed in this respect, although as far as Wes could tell he'd failed in almost every other.

Wes, on the other hand, happily lived in the penthouse and never paid for anything as a point of principle, but he'd intended the principle to be a fuck-you-very-much-Mr-Chalmondley-Senior, and not something that made Hugo this embarrassed. It was another reminder that Wes hadn't grown up in an environment where talking about money was crass, and as far as he could make out, crassness of any kind in Hugo's world was a failing akin to a televised national scandal.

'Give me a few days and I'll have the whole lot in used notes,' Wes murmured back, and was rewarded with a bark of relieved laughter. Hugo seemed to shrink into himself as he regained control, tense and trembling.

'I wouldn't ask, you *know* I wouldn't ask, but I'm in a bit of a bind… I think I might… need to move anyway… I'll – I'll talk to you about it later.'

Wes went cold, stomach turning to lead. For a moment he considered gripping him by the collar and kissing him hard, making him stare into his forgettable face and willing him to addiction, but that came and went with a fierce wave of fear and subsided. He couldn't do that to Hugo. What he'd done to Charlie was bad enough.

Hugo cast off his gloom as Charlie approached, gliding on flat-soled golden sandals, and swept him into a fond embrace.

'Darling! You came!' They broke apart, and Charlie caressed Hugo's cheek. 'You look dreadful.'

'Oh, very nice.'

'I mean it, you look cold and bored. No wonder, lurking around him.' She shot Wes a mischievous smile and took Hugo by the arm. 'You remember Justin, don't you? And Phillip? I'm sure you do…' She pulled him off into a knot of well-dressed people, adding his splash of business-like navy to their flurry of knitted grey and ice-blue satin.

Wes shifted from leg to leg, wondering where the chorizo-server had gone, but Charlie returned and passed him, brushing his hand as she swept down the corridor to the back offices. He followed at a languid pace, waiting for her to key in the code and let them through.

As soon as he let the door click behind them, she turned, eyes glinting with their own savage shimmer beneath all the makeup, and pushed herself against his chest. The ferocity of it took him aback – she had seemed so contained in the gallery, so professional, that he had missed the signs. He wondered, suddenly uneasy, how well she could hide them.

Her voice came out in a greedy rasp.

'I need to see your face…'

Wes swallowed. She was so slight these days, her dress billowing its long pleats around a frame that wasn't there, that he could push her off with a sharp breath. He stroked her cheek and tilted his chin so she could see.

Charlie's mouth, certainly among her more talented parts, gaped in relief. He held her up as she stared at him, unblinking, barely allowing herself to breathe. Her eyes had been brighter once. He remembered them, a vivid forest green, brimming with life and adventure but always viewing it from behind the safety of a lens. He'd only wanted to show her wonders, a life of adventure and pleasure. They were muted now. Vacant. The utility-knife scars across her eyelids and browbone were faint but still there, covered with makeup except for one thin line etched into her left eyebrow, dissecting it neatly in half.

She blinked out of dry-eyed necessity. Her eyes lit up again, sparked into life by furious disappointment as his image was erased from her mind. For a moment, she looked like the old Charlie.

He kissed her, hard and long and deep and full of regret. She kissed him back, mouth as greedy as her eyes. He broke the kiss after counting slowly to five in his head and turned half away from her, pushing her gently backwards.

'That's enough,' he said, biting at the skin around his thumbnail and staring at the wall. 'Have you had a good day today?'

'Of course.' Her voice was as dull as her eyes, heavy as her joints.

'Sorry, baby,' he said.

Charlie didn't need to ask him what for. She shrugged. 'They won't miss me yet.'

Wes nodded, already unzipping his fly as she hitched her dress up and kneeled down. He turned, knowing someone else might need the office for something, knowing they could be seen through the strip of glass in the sturdy pine door. Normally that would have made it better, but he had a bizarre thought, rising out of nowhere, that Katy might show up after all and see them, and then she'd think that's what he was doing instead of coming to get her. Charlie started warming him up, but now his baby sister was in his head, staring at them through the glass.

She can bloody well fuck off, he thought, but Ricky Porter and his cocky, casual phone call rang through his head again.

She's not coming...

Charlie's mouth was warm and teasing, but he made the mistake of closing his eyes. The thought burst violently into the moment: Katy, watching, furious, opening her mouth in a silent scream and baring millions of bloody, pointed teeth...

He flinched, pushing Charlie off.

'Don't. It's all right.' He shook his head, covering his face with one hand, and zipped himself up with the other. 'You don't have to. I shouldn't – not right now. Go and enjoy your party.'

'I was *trying* to enjoy my party,' Charlie snapped, recovering. She got to her feet, and he saw her glare through his fingers. 'Where's your mask, anyway? Don't say you forgot it.'

He had. He shook his head. 'It slipped my mind, that's all, anyway we're not here very long and Hugo knows better than to look for long...'

'Oh, yeah. Of course he does. He's living with a cautionary tale.' Charlie brushed past him, yanking the door open. 'What's the *matter* with you?'

'What? Nothing, it's not *you*...'

'Oh good.' She turned a cold smile on him, poison-sweet. 'I'm so glad it's not me.'

'Are you all right?' The terrible feeling he had missed something important was stalking him, looming out of the shadows. He rubbed the back of his neck, checking his fly.

Charlie's forced smile fluttered. 'Where were you last night?'

'What?' Caught out, he shook his head. 'Nowhere.'

'We were supposed to video chat, you know I need you to be there.'

Shit. 'I didn't have signal...'

'You went out.'

'No! Not for long...'

'You know I need you, Wes. You promised me, *you* were the one who set the time, you said you'd always answer, I'd never go longer than forty-eight hours without seeing you, you *promised*...'

Wes faltered, belly awash with cold. 'Shit. Baby, I'm so sorry, I didn't think it had been that long, I didn't mean to go out last night, it wasn't *planned* or anything...'

She looked at him with disgust. 'D'you know, I wasn't going to say anything, I wasn't going to bring it up here, now, but you... You're full of shit, Wesley.'

'It's *not you*, I'm not... I'm not going anywhere, is that what...'

Charlie shook her head, silencing him. The sad vacancy stole back over her face.

Bloody Uncle Barry... She *knew* he wasn't leaving, surely? That she was a fixture in his life was something he'd resigned himself to years ago, something intertwined with his own identity that would follow him through his life, like his National Insurance number.

He pulled her into a hug and stroked the fur draped down her back in a plunging V.

'Baby. I'm a prick. I'm sorry. I'd *never* not turn up, I honestly, honestly forgot about last night, there was something that came up and it – it upset me and I didn't want it to bother you, and I should've been there to take your call, or be somewhere with signal, and I wasn't, and I'm an arsehole, and... I've never done it before, have I? And I'll never do it again.'

'You haven't been yourself for months. We'll talk about it later.'

She pulled away, stealing glances at his face as he shifted his palm across it, trying to block her view. He should have brought his mask, it wasn't fair. How could he have forgotten?

'Okay.'

She turned her back on him. 'Why don't you go home.' It wasn't a suggestion. 'You don't like these things anyway.'

Wes raked a hand through his hair, sick at the thought of an impending Conversation. Hugo's loud, boyish laugh burst over the gentle music and highbrow chatter, and that settled it. He strode off to find his coat and slip the chorizo-server his number for the hell of it, and left Charlie to deal with her public and whatever mess Hugo was about to get himself into on too much champagne and too little food.

Something Ricky had said once, a long time ago, chased him out into the street.

You're a bloody coward.

He couldn't remember the context, didn't need to. It would have been one of the many rows they'd had growing up until eventually Ricky's attitude had smouldered into resigned resentment and his own into cold, disinterested disdain.

Yeah, well. You're a fucking sociopath.

Wes thrust his hands into his pockets and ducked his head down against a gust of smoky wind, finding the cigarettes from the night before. He'd have to get rid of those before he got home. Quitting was another thing he'd promised Charlie he'd do, along with renouncing meat and not screwing his relatives.

His phone buzzed in his pocket, but he ignored it.

He was aware of cars crawling along and people jostling him as he stalked towards his own Italian sports car, impractical in the ice and snow but unforgettable either at speed or at a standstill. He was vaguely aware of a car with tinted windows creeping along the kerb, but there were plenty of those. He didn't think anything of it until his phone buzzed again, insistent.

Wes paused to dig it out of his pocket and the car paused too. It was his sister Lucy, she of the impeccable timing.

'Wes! Get in the car.' His sister's voice was artificially cultured, bubbly and bright, with a slight Essex twang she'd picked up since her relocation to glamorous Romford.

Wes groaned. 'What?'

'We said we'd pick you up, have you forgotten all about us?'

He couldn't remember even speaking to his sister in the last month, except for sending dirty memes on the sibling group chat. 'What – it's Charlie's thing today, I'm just going home, I'm not up for it right now.' *Whatever 'it' is.*

Lucy's voice went up a fraction, scraping over his brain. 'You *promised* you'd hang out with us. We *never* see you. We got tickets and everything. Uncle David doesn't just hand those out, you know. Sasha's shows are so good.'

Wes needed more than a glass of champagne and three vegan vol-au-vents for this. 'Sasha – Cousin Sasha? She's in the, um...' He stumbled over the phrase 'snuff film industry', mindful that he was in the middle of the street. '...I really don't think...'

'You *promised*.' Lucy was dangerously close to a breakdown. Wes ducked down a side street and tucked himself in a doorway.

'Yeah, maybe, hanging out sure, but not – not for watching Sasha off someone on camera I bloody didn't. When did I...?'

'*Unbelievable*. What's your problem?'

Wes cursed his family from branch to rotten root, guilt roiling up as he thought of Charlie and Hugo. He fumbled for his cigarettes. '*Snuff films aren't fucking vegan, Lucy*, that's my... *that's* my fucking problem, all right?' He nearly dropped the packet and struggled to get one out.

'Stop bitching and get in the car.' Lucy hung up.

Wes gave up for a second and thrust the packet back in his pocket. He ducked out of the doorway determined to stride off in the opposite direction, but Uncle David's boys had caught up with him. It wasn't Mister Bill this time. Wes didn't bother to register the details, apart from the fact they were built like rugby prop forwards and would make about three of him, each.

'Fucking hell.'

They escorted him to the waiting car and bundled him into the back seat before blindfolding him.

'Playing this game, are we?' he asked, not expecting a response, but got a pair of soft giggles he knew well. His heart sank.

'Girls, for fuck's sake...'

'Now you know the rules: no social media, no tracking on your phone, they'll take them anyway.'

Wes struggled against the seat belt, but that earned him the cold, metallic click of cuffs around his wrists. 'Oh, come *on*.'

'Once you're in, you're in.' Lucy sounded entirely unconcerned. 'I can't believe you'd rather be with your little people-pets than hang out with us, that's a bit hurtful.'

Wes ground his molars. 'I'm not avoiding you, Luce, I – I'd rather do something like a barbecue or a, a fucking, boat ride, not – now, nothing against it, nothing against Sasha, obviously, and I'm sure the gents in here are fine upstanding blokes doing their day job, right, I mean I kneecapped people back in the day, who hasn't...' He stopped himself and pulled it back. 'All I'm saying is, I'd prefer it if you *listened* and respected...'

'Oh, *do* shut up, Wesley.' That was Kirsty, Lucy's inseparable, identical triplet. Not physically inseparable, unless they wanted to be. The nature of their Changes meant they were largely human-passing even with all their clothes off, except for a matching pink, lightly puckered line running down one side. Dave, the absent triplet, had one on the right, although his Changes had also accelerated his second puberty and corrected what he termed his minor birth fuck-up, while Kirsty's was on the left. Lucy, the middle triplet, had two, one on each side. Both of hers opened up with greedy little teeth and clamped onto the other triplets' identical gashes with a sucking bite that made three into one.

Wes didn't want to picture the two of them if they were stuck together at the moment.

'Where's Dave?'

'Being boring.' Kirsty sounded jealous. Wes guessed this meant Dave was spending the day with Cousin Alice.

'I said I'd be back early,' he said, wriggling in his seat. 'I'm meant to be being boring too, these days.'

'It's not *long*. This was meant to be a lovely day out and nearly everyone's let me down, and now even *you're* backing out and the whole *point* of this was to spend a bit of quality time with our big brother.'

Lucy could turn the waterworks on and off like a tap, and it was awful when she pouted. He couldn't see her through the folds of material, but her voice was enough. The triplets had been the spoiled youngest batch by default, since Katy, by popular consensus, was an accident of birth, a homicidal family fail-safe, and therefore didn't count as an *actual* sibling. It was easier to think of her that way than to get attached to someone who was probably going to kill you and half the people you cared about.

Wes groaned inwardly. 'Luce…'

He felt her flutter closer, all fake feathers and wafts of her trademark perfume tickling his cheek and nose, Cousin Layla's brand, and put her head on his shoulder.

'Please, Wes, don't spoil it. I'm trying to do something nice.'

Something nice. Something forced. Something ugly.

All the same isn't it, as long as one of us is having fun.

Wes nodded, glum, taking stock of the situation. He was blindfolded and cuffed in the back of an unknown car, being driven fuck-knows-where to watch a live snuff film by some dodgy blokes who'd do far worse to you off-camera than Sasha would do to you in any of her flicks if they were being paid enough.

'Go in my top pocket,' he said to Lucy.

Small cold fingers slipped down his chest against the silk, as Lucy found the packet left over from the previous night. 'Uncle Barry's latest magic pills,' he said by way of explanation. 'Don't have a street name yet, but I call 'em Silver Lining. Pretty, ain't they?'

He heard the packet crackle as Lucy inspected them. 'They're *so* pretty...'

Kirsty must have leaned in. He heard the seat creak. '*Ooh.* Cute.'

'Dipped 'em in edible glitter.' He raised his voice, hoping to pique the interest of the burly men, not sure how many of them there were. 'They'll get you high enough to see the arsehole of God.'

Lucy gave a scandalised squeal. 'You're so dirty.' She elbowed him as the car turned a corner. 'All right, let's see. Open wide.'

'No, you have them.'

'You go first.' The packet crackled. 'Open.'

Wes could almost see his cosy future crumbling, slipping through his fingers and out of reach forever.

The small round pill was being pressed against his lips. He let her put it in his mouth, sugar-coated like a painkiller. He contemplated only pretending to swallow but made the mistake of hesitating. The car went over a speed bump and he swallowed before he choked.

Well, shit.
Arsehole of God it was, then.

—

Ricky was as good as his word. Katy got everything back, her case, untampered with, her handbag, with nothing taken from it. All her money was there, her cards, her phone.

Katy pulled her memory foam pillow out of the case first, her handbag contents scattered over the bed. She cuddled the pillow and breathed in the lavender spray on its lilac cover, texting Rachel with one hand. He'd been right about Wes — no calls, no texts. Had he deleted them to make Wes look bad?

Rachel, on the other hand, had been trying to get hold of her since ten o'clock the previous night, and had left voicemail after voicemail. Rocket had called three times, her stomach flipping as she saw his number repeated. Alex hadn't called at all, not that he would now he had a girlfriend, not that she cared. He hadn't messaged her at all since the last time he'd asked for nudes, and she hadn't replied.

She didn't want to call Rachel back, thinking Ricky might be listening.

The room had no radiator or storage heater, but it was a mild day and not freezing. She bundled herself up in the wool blanket, pressing her back against the wall. To her surprise, the wall was warm, like pressing up against a lukewarm pipe. Lucky for her the bed was positioned here, she thought, and she leaned her head against the paint. It felt strangely soft, as if the plaster were coated in a thin patina of velvet skin.

Katy tried to send her reply to Rachel, but it wouldn't go through. She tried three times, but each time it failed. The signal was full.

'Shit.' Katy tried calling, and the phone beeped at her. '*Shit!*'

Her battery drained, from sixty per cent to three in a second.

'No, no, fuck!'

The phone died and refused to turn back on. There was nowhere to plug in her charger.

Katy jumped off the bed and searched the whole room, but there were no power outlets. How was that even possible? She moved the bed out to make sure and found one hidden behind a metal grate. Someone had gone to a lot of trouble to hide it, to make the room fit some antique aesthetic she couldn't figure out. What was this meant to be, Victorian nostalgia? She needed a small screwdriver to work it free. Rocket always carried a tiny one for his reading glasses; he was always prepared for everything. Katy thumped the grate in frustration. She'd never laugh at Rocket again.

She moved the bed back and settled back against the wall, but it had gone cold. Katy put her pillow behind her and cuddled into the blanket, wondering what to do.

As if in answer, the floorboard near the door creaked, and her door opened a crack. Katy grabbed her charger and her phone and slid off the bed.

'Hello?'

It felt stupid, saying *hello* to what was clearly an empty room, an empty corridor, but the hairs pricked up on her arms. The house was quiet.

She sidled over to the window, away from the open door, just in case.

Her cousin was outside, investigating the grounds as if looking for something. She watched him, a faceless grey figure intent on poking around near the wall and glanced back at the door. If he was out the front, maybe she could get out through the back.

She dashed to the bed and shoved her things into her handbag, the important stuff she couldn't leave, and tore out of the room. The corridor was quiet, carpet muffling her thudding feet. She got to the grand staircase, bounding down the steps two at a time into the spacious, tiled entrance hall, but didn't bother with the front doors.

Turning left, she ran past the living room and down a corridor of smoke-damaged oak panels, turning right at the end where a handsome, modern long-case clock stood, ticking out the seconds before Ricky came back in, and jogged down the steps into the kitchen.

The back door was locked and wouldn't open, even when she shot back the bolts.

The key must be around here somewhere, in a drawer. It wasn't that she had a death wish. It was the principle of it, of being held under duress, of being bullied into agreeing to something she didn't want to do. She could go and stay with Rachel instead, if Ricky would protect her while she was in town. She would stay almost anywhere as long as it wasn't at her parents' place, or this creepy old house with her mad, overbearing cousin.

She heard the front door slam.

Katy cursed inwardly and tried another door, the one connecting the kitchen to the old servants' corridor at the back of the house, which Ricky had pointed out to her when he'd given her suitcase back. He had given her a brief tour, and his possessive pride in the place had struck a wrong note with her and made her uncomfortable. Maybe it was the way he'd made it sound like he was talking about a person.

The servants' corridor was now partitioned into a utility room where she could do her laundry, but beyond this were the back stairs and an entrance to the cellar complex under the house, via a trapdoor to the old coal cellar.

Katy assumed that Ricky had told her that too, and she'd absorbed it without really listening. When, though? She couldn't shake the shivery feeling he *hadn't* told her what was down there, but rather, something else had whispered it in the eddy of cold air sliding by the nape of her prickling neck.

…There's a tunnel…

Katy's legs stiffened, arms tense and vibrating with fear and cold. How did she know that? Was that her own thought, or did it come from somewhere else?

'Mistress?'

She heard her cousin's mocking voice and tugged the trapdoor open. He could only be calling for her, but he'd never called her that before, and she didn't like it. A light came on below her, revealing brick steps and a cavernous space. She headed down, hoping he wouldn't come after her yet, hoping she'd find some way out.

The coal cellar led, via a low archway on one end, to a small honeycomb of chambers beneath Fairwood House, including one that had once been a thirteenth-century crypt belonging to the monastery on that site before the Reformation. Her gran had worked at the house once, she'd told her that. She must have done.

Yes: she must be remembering stories Gran had told her, from before Gran and her sisters had upset someone and they'd all been banished from the house. Gran had a shrine in the cellar of her own cottage, of course, but she'd never taught Katy how to use it, and it wasn't as powerful as the Pendle Stone was reputed to be. She wasn't even sure where the Pendle Stone was, or what it looked like.

The cellar, lit by a naked bulb, was sparsely furnished with trestle tables against one wall and a pile of blankets in one corner. It looked like a workshop – there were knives laid out by a whetstone, a leather pouch spread open with leather-working tools and needles inside, and the cause of the stains on the floor were better left unimagined.

The jars arrested her attention.

Ricky (she presumed, who else would have done it?) had erected the kind of free-standing metal shelves her dad had in the garage and filled them with mason jars of preservative fluid and human organs. Of course he had. She wasn't sure what else she'd expected to find. The books were more of a surprise.

Cousin Ricky had never been to school, as far as she knew. He'd grown up wild, doing whatever he wanted. She'd assumed that at *some* point someone had taught him to read, or that he'd figured it out by looking at road signs and bus timetables, but it hadn't occurred to her that he actually read *books*. They couldn't all be his.

The eclectic mix reminded her of the trophies her dad kept in the garage, rings and friendship bracelets and gummy bands all thrown together in boxes, all belonging to girls who looked like her. Cousin Seth collected teeth. Wes had liked kneecaps before he'd started screwing around outside the family and grown inconveniently attached to regular people.

There were kids' books among copies of Hemingway and Kafka, and some modern stuff that looked like contemporary chick lit from the covers. Some, she assumed, must have belonged to his victims – she knew he was into human sacrifice and all that shit, everyone said so.

She pulled out a fragile copy of *Alice's Adventures in Wonderland* and flipped it open, only to find 'For Margaret, love Aunty Rose' on the inside page. She snorted and stuffed it back.

There were some old books – really old, pages yellow and crumbling at the edges – but a cursory glance revealed cuttings of newspapers from the 1940s and spidery handwriting she didn't recognise.

The name on the inside of the front leather cover was faded, but she could make out 'Nathan Porter'.

These must have belonged to Grampa Nathan, the human occultist too horrified by his own spawn to hold his kids, even when they were human-passing. Katy had never met him: he and Grandma Deirdre had died in the last cull, at the hands (or jaws) of Deirdre's little brother, Hector Wend. The first Thirteenth.

Nathan Porter's notes were mainly in shorthand, with doodles of strange symbols and odd landscapes and moon phases in the margins. She flicked through one, wondering if there was something interesting in it, but was interrupted.

'Looking for something, are we?'

She spun around, sending a jar flying and a book thumping to the floor.

A thick tendril flew out and caught the jar before it hit anything and withdrew. Ricky was standing with his hands in his pockets, watching her as if he'd been there the whole time. He retrieved the jar as his tendril wound back inside his head, the jar's contents sloshing about unpleasantly.

'Bored, are you?'

Katy fumbled for a book. 'Just, um. Looking around.'

'You c'n have that if you want.'

There was a disconcerting slurping sound as the other tendrils disappeared into the back of his head, and the smack of large, puckered lips.

Katy wrinkled her nose. 'Cheers.'

'It's crap.'

Katy turned it over and read the title. 'You think Dickens is crap?'

'Don't you?' Ricky gave an easy shrug and strolled over to the shelf, replacing the jar.

'Is that a heart?' Katy asked, watching.

'Course it is. Got ventricles an' everything.'

She rolled her eyes. 'Is that, like, a *human* heart?'

'Yeah.'

Katy stepped closer to examine one of the jars, determined to show him she wasn't scared. A chill in the air made her shiver at the wrong moment, and she caught his distorted grin reflected in the curved glass side. The eyeball in the jar was suspended in fluid, its optic nerve trailing like a drunken jellyfish. The shade of brown looked horribly familiar.

'Is this...' She frowned, glancing back at him over her shoulder. '...Is this... a *Porter* eye?'

He giggled, a childish, high-pitched sound that didn't suit his usual low, gruff register.

'They're all singin' a diff'rent tune now, ain't they? Lining up to give me what I don't even need. She plucked it out herself. Give it t'me in a box. Nice of her.' He grinned and stroked the wall of the cellar as if fondling a pet.

Katy found herself drawn to the bricks, staring at them as if something were going to happen. She clutched the

Dickens novel, recalling with a sickening flash the new bandage sported by her father's favourite sister. '*Why* do you... What's all this *for*?'

Ricky dug his shoulder into the arch, rubbing his head against it and smiled. 'Want to try one?'

'What?'

'Easier to show you than it is to tell you.'

Katy blinked. 'What am I supposed to do with it?'

'Eat it.'

'Fuck off.'

'It's fine, it's like jelly.'

'*No!*'

He snorted. 'You're going to be crunching our kin to pulp soon, anyway, no point in being squeamish about it.'

Katy tapped the side of the jar before she could stop herself, drawn to it in a morbid tug of curiosity. 'That doesn't mean I want a taste of them beforehand.'

'I can show you how to get stuff out of them,' Ricky said, cocking his head. 'How to make connections between you and them, you know? Eyes is powerful. You can see what they've seen, what they are seeing... in my case, of course, what they *will* see, but that's not for you.' His full lips twitched. 'Two out of three ain't bad.'

Katy chewed the inside of her cheek, frowning. Something tugged at the back of her mind, but the accompanying cinch of her chest made her shy away from it. A lot of things since Gran died were a blur, including the night Katy found her. Dilated pupils and floating diamonds of glittering disco lights whirled through her mind, doing lines at the Roar Shack with her friends, eyes reflecting and multiplying in mirror facets all around her. Gran's eyeless skull, brains gone, mouth gaping at her feet.

No, he didn't, he couldn't have, she was too much for him on his own, she must have been, surely...

He didn't look strong enough to kill Gran. A chill spread over her back as she realised she didn't really know what he could do.

She turned her back on the jars, grasping for something that would make her feel more in control.

'How is that going to help me?'

'If you want to control the List, you need to know *why* they're on it, don't you?'

Katy bit the inside of her cheek so hard she drew blood and sucked at it until it filled her mouth with its coppery tang. She dropped her eyes to the book she was still holding, focusing on the restful purple of the cover, a river at dusk, a rowing boat off-centre.

Ricky eyed her with some dark shade of satisfaction. 'D'you want to learn what they say about you when you're not there? How much power they think you got? What they're planning on doing to protect themselves if or when the time comes?'

Katy hadn't considered that last part. In her dreams, resistance was futile. They were ground beneath her claws, chewed to pulp, and she woke fighting through their ribbons of flesh.

'They can't stop me.' Her voice was dull and flat in the cellar, bricks deadening the sound.

He shrugged. 'Look, it's up to you, but I mean it. I'll teach you how...' He eyed her. 'I ain't wasting anyone decent on you yet. Show me you can stomach it first. Down in one, it's easy.'

Katy's belly flipped, imagining the jelly bursting in her mouth, the stringy thread of flesh scratching its way down her throat like undercooked spaghetti. 'God, no. I can't.'

'Fair enough. I might have a go at Uncle Danny up there.' Ricky nodded at a shelf he was too short to reach. Katy glanced up.

'I'll leave you to it.'

'Yeah, you do that. Don't mind if you want to watch, but you suit yourself.'

Katy retreated back up the cellar steps, shaking her head. 'I've got this to read.' She waved the novel at him. 'Thanks, though.'

Sarcasm was lost on him. He turned his back on her, treating her to a full view of the puckered skin at the back of his shaven head, the flat tapeworm lips which parted with a wet suck and opened to reveal nothing except writhing, questing knots of carnivorous coils. Katy's stomach churned up a queasy bubble of vomit into her mouth, and she retched but held it in.

She ought to be used to things like that, but worm-like things still got to her. She couldn't stomach her brother Liam's Changes, either, the way those anemone-like fronds, pale and slick like the eyestalks of a snail, peeked out from his armpits and occasionally protruded from his short-sleeved shirts.

She wondered if she'd be able to handle her own, when the time came. She knew it was what her body was somehow designed to do, like getting pregnant or having periods, but the whole process was painful or so her sister Kim claimed, and you never knew what would happen. Kim's quad, Nicole, had delighted in telling the triplets they would get something awful, but they'd got off fairly lightly and Dave had gotten exactly what he wanted. They spent most of their time joined at the hip by choice anyway.

Katy didn't need to be told hers would be awful.

She made it back into the warmth of the kitchen, a space that felt far more welcoming than the rest of the house, and made herself comfortable in the cushioned chair at the end of the table. She could charge her phone later. Right now, she wanted to lose herself in fiction, some story about how awful people were, but how it all came right for most of the good ones in the end. Or so she hoped. Frustration spoiled her concentration, though.

Why hadn't Wes called to check on her? Where the fuck was he, the useless twat?

Oh, fuck him.

Katy opened the book and dug in to spite-read.

—

Ideas sparked, half-formed, outside his brain. Wes didn't *think* them, only watched them pop into existence like planets, a whirl of words and images, shifting patterns of colours and sounds. Some were about his family, and they were spiky, dark, complicated. He couldn't get too near them. He took a stroll through the bursting nebulae and danced in the rain of sparks.

Numbers flashed in front of him as he wandered through a set, covered in blood and raining screams. He raised his arms to the ceiling and danced in it, time standing still and the clock showing three different times all at once.

15:28.

22:53.

18:12.

There were welcoming thoughts popping up to protect him as he wandered through the night sky, pornographic, sensuous, amorphous, abstract, bubbly molecules bouncing around flashing tits and arse, begging to be chased.

Cute Little Bastards.

The words formed in front of his eyes with firefly-neon flashes. He waved his hand through the letters, blurring them into constellations that arced over him in alien skies.

Wes saw nothing but black outcrops of rock, the reek of dead fish and salt on the air, and somewhere up ahead of him pulsed a red, sticky cocoon…

He knew it was wearing off when they started to happen *inside* his head again. Everything started to collapse, his universe telescoping around him and sucking back into the confines of his skull, the world rushing through his eyes as if his pupils were tunnels and his skull was hollow and sucking everything in like a black hole.

The blindfold came off at the start of the come down, brilliant light stabbing into his eyes and yanking him into a different dimension, one with depth and height making him dizzy with their defined points of reference.

It took a while for them – who were they? – to calm him down, before he realised he was in some sort of warehouse, factory, something disused by the look of the rusty pipes, somewhere old and forgotten.

Fuck you, Uncle Barry.

There was a period of blankness, memory loss, he supposed, but only in retrospect when he was sat with a drink in his hand laughing at a joke.

There was an empty bottle of champagne he vaguely recognised. Fragments of memory slotted back into the broken jigsaw. A word of welcome in an American accent he couldn't place, a bucket of ice, people in masks bound together by deliciously illicit anonymity and a top-notch security team.

He felt good though. Really good. Top-of-the-world good.

Was that the Silver Lining or the champers?

Silver Lining, surely. Champagne didn't feel like this. He could feel every individual gorgeous sparkling bubble in his brain, bouncing off his synapses.

Fuck me, Uncle Barry, you absolute legend.

The chair was comfortable. Leather. He could lounge in it, pretend he was a perfectly respectable pervert like the rest of them, definitely wasn't rat-arsed with a head full of firecrackers.

Sitting at a polished black table with silver service and a vegan platter in front of him, sipping the last of his champagne, Wes relaxed in front of the two-way mirror watching his burlesque-costumed cousin amputate a man's leg with a chainsaw.

She'd started and he hadn't even noticed.

He glanced at the digital clock display; online viewers had bets on how long it would take the guy to bleed to death.

'Did I place a bet?' he asked, too loudly, and got shushed by some American couple dressed for the fucking opera. 'Ah, piss off.' He found a betting slip in his pocket, looking for his cigarettes.

He looked at it: he'd bet fifteen minutes and twenty-eight seconds; that seemed awfully precise. Then he looked at how much he'd put on it.

Five hundred grand? Shit.

Not exactly pocket money.

His sisters Lucy and Kirsty, identical down to their clothes, Venetian masks and makeup except for their oppositional colour palette, chittered to each other about the performance and Kirsty's work gossip and finished each other's sentences.

One of them had asked him about Katy.

He couldn't remember what he'd said.

The Americans were applauding for some reason, their offensive enthusiasm grating through his throbbing frontal lobe. Why couldn't they let him watch a guy get offed in peace? Or at least masturbate to it in dignified throaty abandon like a normal fucking person, like that guy over there. Cut-glass features, swooping hair, killer eyeliner and a bad attitude.

Wes definitely would.

He turned his attention back to his cousin. The chainsaw got swapped for a dentist's drill. This was more his thing, not that he'd admit he missed it. He sat a little straighter as Sasha teased her audience, not to mention the man tied to the operating table, with the drill bit.

Oh, shit, go for the knees, sexy girl... He hoped she knew he was watching, that she'd remember, do something just for him. Why would she? He hadn't spoken to Sasha in years, why did it matter now?

What the hell is wrong with me?

'You're having fun, see, I told you he would.' Kirsty, in glamorous red and yellow to Lucy's sumptuous blue and green, mercifully still physically separate from her middle triplet, fluttered false eyelashes across the table. 'Uncle Barry's silver things are shit, by the way.'

Wes blinked. 'What?'

Lucy sniffed. 'Oh, yeah, they make you weirdly tingly and giggly, but they don't last long.'

'You didn't see your own thoughts?'

Sasha distracted them by driving the drill straight into her victim's patella and Wes grunted with sudden, surprised pleasure as the man on the next table came.

Lucy and Kirsty, to Wes's infinite disgust, joined the Americans in applause.

More champagne arrived along with a bottle of still mineral water, imported from the Alps, probably, or some such bullshit. He'd stick to the champers, thanks.

The clock was ticking.

'So, the drugs don't work?' he quipped. He was about to lose five hundred grand.

Lucy gave him a pitying look. 'What were they supposed to do? Are you *actually* enjoying this?'

Wes sighed. It was a trap, not a question. 'Yeah, yeah, that bit, the knee bit, that was excellent, and, we don't hang out enough, and, um. I'm pretty drunk.' He poured himself another glass because that was looking like the best idea at the moment and wondered if he fell in the door at five o'clock how much his partners would really mind on a scale of one to livid. '...And that's good. So. Yeah, of course.'

Lucy was only partly convinced.

'Are you *sure* you don't know where Katy is?' Kirsty asked. 'Mum's going spare. She's always looked up to you, didn't she call or anything?'

Lucy leaned across the table. 'If you know where she is you *have* to tell us. She's going to Change soon, you know. Has something already happened to her?'

He forced himself to focus, concentration sluggish. 'Already? What d'you mean by that?'

'We voted on it, remember?' Lucy's lips gleamed below her mask. 'Uncle Marcus wants her gone, never mind what the soothsayer says.'

'Didn't think he had the balls to go against his god,' Wes muttered.

Kirsty squealed, distracted by the show. 'Ooh, she's changed drill bits.'

That took the heat off him for a while.

At fifteen minutes and exactly twenty-eight seconds, the heart monitor beeped in warning and the man's vitals no longer registered.

Wes crowed, did a complimentary line off the table, started on the water, and ordered a coffee.

His sisters fawned over him, the sulky Yank with eyeliner stumbled up to flirt but stopped when he realised Wes was Sasha's cousin, another bottle of champagne popped near his ear, and Wes exulted in sheer relief and adrenaline.

All the same, the number nagged at the back of his mind. He drowned it with the rest of his champagne and returned to the water like a good boy.

He didn't place the next bet, but he wrote down a time on a napkin, the first numbers that came to mind, numbers he remembered from his trip.

22:53.

Sasha, resplendent in a fishnet body stocking and blood-spattered platform shoes, performed a flirty burlesque dance with the tools of her trade while the next victim was wheeled in, conscious and screaming.

Fucking hell, Sash. We used to dress up and play in Wonderland together, remember? Those were the days.

Wes concentrated on sobering up, watching the clock. There was no way he'd be right a second time.

The girl was declared dead twenty-two minutes and fifty-three seconds in. Bang on.

Fuuuuck.

Wes asked for chamomile tea. He tapped his foot against the table leg until Lucy kicked him, patience expired.

The third victim was wheeled in, the last one for this set.

Wes wrote down a random number that came to him, glittering at the edges. He knew it, because he remembered it. Like déjà vu, except in reverse.

Wait. Did that make sense? Perfect sense. What good was a memory that only worked backwards?

18:12.

Like the overture. Yeah, he was cultured, he knew Beethoven, just because he hadn't grown up with it didn't mean it wasn't for him.

Wes scowled into his lap.

He didn't place a bet.

After some erotic shenanigans with a pair of bolt cutters, the reappearance of the dental drill and a final flourish – a jigsaw – the unwilling 'volunteer' was sawn in half. Blood spatter coated the two-way mirror, obscuring the view.

Wes checked the clock. 18:12.

Three for three.

Well, shit.

If he could unlock his own ability to see this kind of run-of-the-mill stuff, he wouldn't need the soothsayer. Ricky would be utterly redundant. Oh, sure, yeah, the little sod could see the secrets of the cosmos, all that crap. So what? No one wanted to know that bollocks, did they? He'd made a couple of million sitting on his arse just now, for writing down four numbers in the right bleeding order.

Who needed Ricky Porter?

'That was great,' he said, faking enthusiasm like a champ. 'Let's do dinner next weekend, I'll come to you if you want.'

Lucy wrinkled her nose. 'I'm a bit busy.'

'Me too.'

Wes sighed as the others around them started leaving, ushered out by security. 'Yeah, thought so. We'll do something you fancy doing later then, is it?'

The bitterness was missed, along with the sarcasm.

'Do we need to drop you home?' Lucy asked, checking her handbag. 'Or is it okay to drop you near where we picked you up?'

'Don't go out your way.'

This, too, was taken at face value.

He only realised he was not sober enough yet when he stood up and the room spun. He sat down heavily and waited for his sisters to sort themselves out, lip glosses and purses and whatever else they'd been comparing strewn all over the table around their plates and glasses.

'Come on,' Kirsty shot over her shoulder, halfway to the door.

Wes blinked. How had they got over there so bloody quickly?

Shit, shit, shit, he thought, *I'm fucked. Nah, I'm all right. Charlie's going to kill me.* But he could take the water with him, he had a while yet, what was the time? Probably plenty of time.

He levered himself more carefully upright, testing his balance. *Yeah. Piece of piss. Sober as a judge.*

What was that revelation he'd had just now? Something to do with the soothsayer? He was sure it had been a bloody good idea.

No – gone. Never mind. It would come back to him.

Chapter 4: The Call of the Wild

13 January

After his less-than-successful attempt the previous day to induct his little cousin into what he was loosely terming 'discipleship', Ricky inhaled the edge of winter, thumb caressing the warm surface of the ceramic tile in his pocket. He thought about going to Barrow Field and breaking into the long barrow to collect his thoughts, but instinct tugged him in the opposite direction.

Perhaps 'disciple' was the wrong term for Katherine. A mentee, a pupil. Adherent. Acolyte.

He grinned.

(Zealot.)

The lanes were quiet. He wanted the walk, circumventing the town, approaching Sea View Road from the fields.

'It's a nice day,' he ventured, feeling her resistance, a prickling across the skin of his thumb. 'You sulking?'

Silence.

'She trying to leave again?'

Silence.

Normally, he liked that. Every winter he walked for miles, savouring it. Nothing but the voices and memories in his head (walk fast enough, far enough, shuts them right up), farsight waxing strong, catching glimpses of the near future in every cloud formation and bird in flight.

Today, the silence was an absence. He trudged on, moody and abandoned.

Katherine had spoiled everything. He never should have brought her in. Should have tied her up and left her in the long barrows out in Barrow Field or dumped her in the smugglers' tunnel below the woods. Now she was colonising his rooms with teenage debris, poking around in his private spaces, reading his bloody books. Couldn't even stomach an eyeball.

He sniffed, coils shifting under his skin.

(*I'm* the master, I'm their *god*, *I'm* the One and Only…)

'Look, I didn't do anything *bad*. I didn't break my promise or nothing, it's not like that, is it?' He took a light run up and vaulted a stile one-handed. The tile bumped against his thigh on the landing. He flicked his hood back up as it slipped down. 'I only tweaked things a bit. I'm not *controllin'* you.'

The tile bumped against his leg again, and he took this as a sign she wanted to be taken out. He paused, putting it down on the grass.

The mistress climbed out of the ground, swelling from the small, square point of origin, pushing her way into a human-shaped avatar where the house's consciousness could reside.

It looked exactly like the last owner, but he was still one of the very few people who knew the last owner was dead.

'*Not controlling me?*' The voice was deeper than hers had been in life, but still recognisable. 'I can't let her *out*. I can't open my doors. *Not* my choice, Ricky, and you said…'

'Yeah, yeah, I know, it's not me, though, is it, it's the old hedge witch, Miss Pritchard's curse, that's all...' He stepped back, raising his hands as she extracted one new-formed leg from the ceramic base and stepped towards him.

(Not fair, I swear she wasn't that tall when she was alive...)

'You *messed* with the curse,' Carrie said, voice ringing in the crisp air. 'I should have *known* this was going to get messy...'

'It takes the pressure off f you, tha's all,' Ricky said, frowning. 'You can't watch her for me while you're like this,' he gestured, 'An' it was only a *little* tweak to make sure she can't leave once you let her in...'

'Just a little tweak?'

'Well.'

'I'm only going to ask this one more time, *whose heart is up my chimney?*'

He shrugged. 'Some woman I found in a car park.'

Carrie towered over him. 'You *utter cunt.*'

'Oi!' He took a few more steps back, knowing unless he Changed there was nothing he could do in this form, not against a seven-foot ceramic-and-brick woman with the condensed force of a seven-bedroom house. 'What d'you call me that for?'

'What the hell is *wrong* with you? You're *deranged.*'

He sighed, huffing a stream of frozen breath into the gap between them. 'Come on, love, omens looked good for takin' her, or I'd have left her and taken another one. It's *fate*, it's not *pers'nal*. And it worked. You still keep out my blood-kin, just, you know, if you wanted, exceptions can be made by me instead of you, and that's better, ain't it? You don't know us. *I* know us.'

'Stop it.' Carrie shook her head, glass-clear eyes glinting, glossy yellow-and-silver ponytail rippling like curtain fabric. 'Stop trying to be devious, I can see through you like a bloody conservatory.'

Ricky scratched his nose. 'Not tryin' t'be devious,' he mumbled. 'Makes more sense for it to be *me* who makes the decisions about my own kin, since I'm livin' there, I'm the master...'

'You're the *what*?'

He backtracked. '...Lodger...'

Carrie's plaster face was smouldering hot-iron red, wood-burner smoke purling from her nostrils.

He'd made the mistake of telling her to calm down once before, and that had been a near-eviction crime. He swallowed down the advice.

'*Lodger*, but I'm...' He cleared his throat. 'Look, you said it was all right if she could stay, I asked first.'

'I didn't realise I had no choice about letting her back *out* again.' Carrie was going from incendiary to sullen. He recognised the draining energy in the slump of her shoulders, the slow puffs of smoke turning from ash-dark to lighter steam. She decreased in height by an inch or two, compressing back into herself. 'I don't know why I try, sometimes.'

He licked his lips, trying to find a solution. 'D'you want me to get rid of the heart?'

'And do what, shove it back in?' Carrie shook her head. 'I mean, yeah, obviously, but what a *waste*.'

'I can always use it for...'

'Of *life*, Ricky.'

He paused. 'Oh. Right. Yeah, well, she'll still be dead, whoever she was.'

She pinched the bridge of her nose, now more or less an exact double of Carrie Rickard, a life-like statue. 'Mate, can you… can you shut up, you're doing my head in.'

She hadn't mentioned eviction yet. He hovered, waiting for her to get back to her usual height. 'D'you want to go for a walk? Now you're out, I mean, might as well.'

She gave him a wearied glare.

'All right, I'll shut up, not another bloody word. Honest.'

He was rewarded with a tired shrug. Taking this as a good sign, he nodded, sidled by her to pick up the tile lying in the cold grass, and carried on walking.

Carrie followed.

The tension was worse than family meals at his grandmother's, which was apt, since that was where they were going.

She kept an unusual distance between them, not looking at him. He wondered if she wanted more attention, more sanding, maybe, if he could buy another winning lottery ticket in her name and spend it on a surprise, like a landscape garden. He'd been meaning to sort that out for months.

He got lost in this, imagining the space and the restoration of the 1920s greenhouse, estimating the amount of work it would take, the timescale, whether it would all be done in time to plant the things he wanted to grow. By the time they got to Wundorwick, his grandmother's cottage, he was whistling.

Carrie shot him a look. 'Ricky?'

'Hm?'

'You've forgotten, haven't you?'

(What? An event? It wasn't her birthday.)

She shook her head. 'You don't give a shit, do you? Rip out someone's heart, kidnap your own cousin…'

(Oh, that.) 'Abduct…'

'…You really *don't* get why I'm pissed off. It's like talking to a wall.'

'Now you know how I feel.'

Her face was stone. 'Was that supposed to be funny?'

He sensed it was time to change the subject. 'Want to see the old shrine? It's been abandoned since Gran died. Uncle Marcus is using the Foreman shrine again now Gran can't stop him.'

'Not much.' Carrie folded her arms. 'I want you to stop poncing about with body parts and get your cousin out of me, to be honest.'

Did that mean she wanted to be just his again? She wasn't hoping for Katherine to stay, she didn't want things to change either? He couldn't help the lurch of happiness manifesting itself in a broad grin.

'Yeah? You want her gone, too?'

Carrie sighed. 'Yeah, yeah, there's nothing I love better than it being just us. What's this shrine thing you want me to see?'

He paused, leaning against the drystone wall, chest squirming. 'Why d'you say it like that?'

'What?'

'Like it's *not* the thing you love best, like I'm not enough for you.' He was losing ground. Maybe he could make her laugh, and that would help.

Carrie blinked. 'Oh my God.'

'Yes, my child?'

She froze for a second, fighting it, then, as he'd hoped, burst out laughing.

'Prick.' She swallowed her amusement and cocked her head. 'Some god you are. I seem to remember having to rescue you last time your parents had you chained to a kitchen chair.'

Ricky shifted, insides lurching. 'I wa'n't expecting that. Dad got me unawares, that's all.'

'Has he still got the... weird ointment, whatever it was he used on you?'

'Prob'ly. I, er. I've been avoiding them, tell you the truth.' He was mumbling, for a brief, irrational moment afraid Gran would overhear. He remembered she was dead, he'd finally had it in him to kill her, but he didn't raise his voice. 'I don't think they told no one else about it. Dad's got it tucked away for their use only, I bet. Otherwise the others wouldn't be half as scared o' me.'

'I don't like your dad very much.' Carrie studied him, making him strangely uncomfortable.

They stood facing each other, Ricky too shy to look up now, in case he chose the wrong moment and spoiled it again, like he spoiled everyth— (shut *up*, not now, she laughed didn't she, *shut up*...)

He jerked his head. 'Shall we?'

Carrie rolled her eyes. 'Yeah, go on. You realise though, if I'm manifested here, I can't really tell what's going on at home. I've no idea what she's doing now, for example. You sure you want me here? What if she breaks a window?'

Ricky shrugged. 'She won't do much damage. I think she likes you. And I got her curious. I think she'll want to stick around.'

They went in through the garden gate, the bare earth of Gran's neat garden giving him more ideas for developing Fairwood's back lawns.

'She left the cottage to Katherine,' he said, putting his shoulder to the back door. It didn't budge. 'Hm. Love?'

Carrie took over and wrenched it open.

'Ta.'

He went in first. The kitchen had been stripped bare by relations, eager to get what they felt was owed them. Everything of value had gone. The pots and pans hanging above the sturdy table, spice rack and all its contents, the best china and the silver set, the bric-a-brac and the pot plants. He'd never felt welcome here anyway, but the emptiness served to push him further out.

He cleared his throat.

'Right,' he said. 'Let's have a look. I reckon our Katherine's been playing with this, it feels odd to me. An' did you see her with the jars? "Is that a human heart" she asks, she knows damn well what they're for, she's seen 'em used. She was looking for something, an' I bet you it wasn't a novel.'

'I remember your Gran and her sisters back in the day,' Carrie mused, looking around the kitchen. 'You know, I have… the house's memories. They used to clean me – it – every day. Your great-aunt, Eileen, was it, she lived-in for a long time. I can't remember her very well. She barely left any imprint of herself in me at all…' She shrugged, sweeping her fingers along the kitchen table. 'I have memories from the seventeenth century that are clearer than that. Isn't that strange?' She bit her lip and grinned. 'Thought she was a cut above, didn't she, Eileen Pendle? What was the "married" name she chose? Foreman.'

'All the Foremans think like that,' Ricky said, taking another good look around. 'They all think they're better than us. Never married out of the bloodline, see.'

His mother had been promised something of Gran's – some of the china, one of the tea sets. He'd have to throw his weight around if it turned out she hadn't had it. He gestured to the stairs.

'Coming down?'

Carrie smirked. 'You know how to show a girl a good time.'

He flushed, scratching at the back of his neck. His hood slipped down, but that didn't matter here. Not with her. 'You can get to know my cousin a bit better, if she has been here messing about.'

'You mean, *you* want to get to know her better.' Carrie approached the stairs to the cellar and peered down. 'Radical idea, literally only just occurred to me, out of the blue, you know, but... you could just try *talking* to her.'

He snorted to mask his discomfort. 'Where's the fun in that?'

'Fine. Do your thing.' She waved him on, but he let her go first; it wasn't like he hadn't learned his manners.

They descended into the dark, neither needing to turn a light on. Carrie was quiet again, which wasn't like her. He wondered if she was still angry with him, even though he'd made her laugh. Maybe she'd get over it with enough distraction.

When they reached the bottom and found the old Welsh dresser against one wall, and Carrie spotted the enlarged, mummified heart pinned to a shelf with several hatpins, he remembered again why she was cross.

'Here we are,' he said, hoping she wouldn't notice.

Carrie gave him a weary glance. 'Why is it always organs with you lot?'

Ricky shrugged. 'I don't make the rules.'

Her lips twitched.

'Look, I'll sort the heart out when we get back, I'll reverse it, I'll give you back your... responsibility. I thought I was making life easier, that's all. Really. No disrespect meant, love.' He shifted on the spot, chest tightening in nameless emotion, swirling too fast to grasp at it. He focused on the task at hand, pushing the feeling away, breathing through the physical symptoms.

Carrie was watching him with a softened edge of concern, as if she could see inside his skin. His tendrils were snaking out, betraying him. They retreated with some conscious effort.

She came close enough that he could breathe her in and rubbed his bicep and the back of his shoulder. He allowed himself a shy smile, tilting his head so she couldn't see it. If he showed her how much he liked it, a little treacherous voice whispered from deep inside himself, she might stop doing it for free.

'What are we doing?' Carrie asked, curiosity bubbling over at last, like he'd hoped it would. 'What's all this for? I thought there was a shrine down here...'

'This is it.'

She tilted her head. 'That? That's a... that's a dresser, isn't it? There's *plates* on it.'

'Yeah, comm-whatsit, commem'rative.'

'Are they *actually* hatpins?'

'Great-Aunty Eileen had a thing about hats, don't you remember? One's Gran's, one's Great-Aunty Olive's, and one's hers.'

Carrie arched an eyebrow. 'Oh, God, is that Charles and Diana? The royal family are important for opening portals to the other side, are they?'

Ricky sniggered. 'Don't be daft. They're just plates.'

'And family photos? Is that what all these are?' Carrie poked around on the shelves at the frames, the images obscured by dust. 'Oh, God. What's *that*?'

'Uncle David.'

Carrie snorted and moved on. 'Shit me.'

He grinned. He was rubbing off on her. 'Shall we see why our Katherine's been messing about down here? I can feel 'er. If I know what she was after, I'll know better what to offer.'

'I'm not sure I like this.' Carrie tossed her ponytail, teasing the fabric of her hair into individual strands with her stiff, cold fingers. 'You're getting a bit power-drunk.'

He stiffened, chest lurching, like the time Gran had caught him climbing up her shelves to get at the gingerbread jar.

'No, I ain't.'

Carrie paused. 'Is this you trying to bond with a member of your family you don't actually hate?'

He shrugged, looking away. The cellar was swept clean, and apart from the dresser there was nothing else there. A quick sweep of the walls showed him something had climbed up them recently, within the last few months, tracking small, smudged prints across the ceiling.

'You abducted her because you wanted a chance to chat, didn't you?'

'That don't sound like me.'

'The chatting? No. But then again, you poisoned your own parents for trying to take your toy away, so the methodology checks out.'

'I brought you along for a reason, you know, not so's you can give me grief.' He nodded at the shrine. 'Go do your mem'ry thing. You know. Extract the energy from the building, an' share it wi' me.'

Carrie pursed her lips. 'Shan't.'

'Please.'

'Slightly better. Still no. Try again.'

He took a deep breath and let it out in a slow, controlled stream of simmering embarrassment. '…If you please, Miss'us Rickard, I'd be obliged if you saw your way clear to giving me a hand.' He shook his head and added, so low he hoped she wouldn't hear, 'Some people think I'm a god, you know.'

'*Some people* need a good culling. Which is why I'll help you. The fewer of your relatives there are in the world, the better for everyone, quite frankly.' Carrie paused. 'And if I do this, when we get home, that heart up my chimney is *gone*. Right?'

'Cross mine.'

She snorted. 'Okay. Please don't do it again.'

'Promise.'

Carrie crossed to the wall beside the dresser and pushed herself into the corner it made, taking on the wood and brick aspects of the cottage and folding her frame into a sharp right angle. She pressed in, melting into the woodgrain on one side and the brick on the other.

He waited while she communed with the cottage for a while, building to building, extracting the memories in its bricks and mortar. He couldn't tell where the avatar ended and the cottage began.

He fidgeted. Ripping memories right out of the brick, imagine that. She was sucking them out the way he drank auras and energies down in his beautiful form, the way he swallowed eyeballs in this one. It was more efficient, more elegant, the way she did it. He wasn't sure how that made him feel, but he didn't like it.

Finally, she pulled back.

'*Shit*, that was *insane*.' She moulded herself back into a more human, less geometric, form.

Ricky wasn't sure which he liked best: the angles reminded him strongly of Fairwood when the dusk fell and part of her was engulfed in shadow.

'Right.' Carrie held out her hand, and he took it immediately, eager for the touch of polished wood and silky paint against his own palms. Her cold fingers locked around his wrist, and he moistened his lips, adjusting his stance.

'That good, is it?'

'Pretty good. I got most of the cottage's memories, it can see quite a way up and down the road. I'm guessing you only want the ones Katy's in.'

The vibrations through his arm were hot, like wafts from an oven. With the heat came pictures, moving, stuttering, layered, dancing in front of his eyes. His head pounded, sinuses pranging painfully with the build-up of pressure.

He siphoned through the pictures she channelled to him, and when he came to the one he wanted, he smiled through gritted teeth and let it unravel like a ribbon.

Wundorwick's Memory: Katy's Visit

The evening fell over Pagham-on-Sea, long summer sun sinking at last on air-conditioning unit shortages, extortionate electricity bills, hot, sweaty queues for all kinds of fans, and the local SupaPrice branch running out of bottled water.

Katy sat on the garden wall of Wundorwick, her grandmother's cottage, waiting for her friends. The only people she trusted were Rachel and Rocket, since both of them had some experience with what Katy termed the different-than-mainstream-natural.

The garden wall absorbed her worries, her sense of self, her maelstrom layers of overlapping thoughts, memories, ideas, doubts and emotions. She left her energy impression in the stone, and Wundorwick recognised her as its Owner-To-Be.

She'd showered and cleaned up her bramble scratches from a countryside run, covering them up with loose paisley trousers. Since Rocket was coming, she'd opted for a short-sleeved crop top she could wear with a padded bra, although she'd rather have her fingernails ripped out than admit he'd influenced her choice of outfit.

Rachel had been swimming. She turned up on foot with her gym bag over one shoulder, a lean, sporty figure walking beside a much heavier-set Rocket on his LED-pimped bicycle. Rocket lived on the Jubilee Estate, where darkness was the enemy. His reflective jacket and neon-green light-up trainers made him ridiculously conspicuous for a break-in.

'What the hell is that?' Katy jumped off the wall and dusted off her creased linen. 'I told you we need to be subtle.'

Rocket shot her a rakish grin, chubby cheeks ruddy from the exercise and summer heat. Ignoring her, he jumped off the bike and wheeled it to the garden gate. 'What are we doing here? This your gran's place?'

Katy folded her arms. 'Was. Yeah. She was killed here.'

There was no police tape left – DI Parsons had closed the case for the sake of her sanity; at least, that's what Wes had said.

Rocket grinned wider. 'Cool.'

'No, sad.' Rachel rolled her eyes and gave Katy a hug. 'You sure you want to do this?'

Katy wasn't sure, but she nodded. 'I just want to see if... if her books are still there. And, I... I want to see if I can get down to the shrine.'

'So, is this a séance? Should we have brought candles or something?' Rocket pushed the gate open and winced at its unoiled scream.

Katy shook her head. 'Don't need them, do we, if you're kitted out like a fucking Christmas tree.'

Rachel sniggered.

Rocket leaned his bike against the garden wall, where it was obscured by bushes. 'You think there'll be something here you can use to stop the Changes?'

Katy shrugged. 'Gran wouldn't say if the shrine was that powerful. I don't know. No one's ever tried.'

He hesitated, looking at the drawn curtains and lowered blinds of the smart cottage, a deep straight crease in his brow. 'Worth a shot, though. You got a key?'

Katy shook her head. 'Never needed one. We're going in the back.'

'Let's get on with it, yeah? It'll be dark soon.' No one in the Jubilee Estate liked returning after dark, and reflective gear was less a fashion statement and more a survival uniform. Another kid had been found dead between two blocks of flats not long ago, the life sucked out of his tiny body by something no one could see, without leaving a mark. That couldn't so easily be explained away by collective hysteria, or mould, or a leaking gas main.

'You can both stay over,' Rachel said, 'Dad's away again. Only one spare bed though.'

Katy nearly punched her, but Rocket was checking his phone and not listening.

'Oi! We boring you?' Katy shot Rachel a dirty look, but her best friend only grinned at her.

'My brother's messaged me, hang on.' Rocket carried on typing a reply. When he was done, he brought up a screenshot and turned the screen so they could see. 'Look at this joker. "My djinn can help you find health, wealth and happiness."' He shook his head. 'Been some weird shit going on in Brighton, this guy's probably why. He doesn't know what he's doing.'

'Great. Can we focus on this now?' Rachel headed around the side of Wundorwick towards the vegetable garden at the back.

'Hey! I'm the one with the experience, why is she going first?'

'Gran *loved* her.' Katy gave Rocket a smirk. 'You're the cavalry, not the A-team.'

'You talk like an old lady,' Rocket said. 'Don't touch anything, just in case...'

They heard Rachel trying the kitchen door with a vigorous thud.

He rolled his eyes.

'It won't open for me,' Rachel called.

Katy sighed and jogged after her. 'Coming.'

The back door was closed, locked for the first time in Katy's memory. She felt the magnetic draw of the shrine even so, which gave her hope.

'Did you bring it?' she asked.

Rocket dug in his jacket pocket and handed over a hunting knife. Katy took it without hesitation, her stomach doing backflips. 'Cheers.'

'You need us to help or...'

'Nope, you're good.' She put the blade to the back of her scarred, tanned forearm where there were fewer nerve endings than the palm, something movies always got wrong, and where there'd be less inconvenience as it healed. 'I just need a scratch.'

Rocket nodded, watching her.

Rachel fidgeted from one foot to the other. 'It's chilly. It shouldn't be chilly, we're in the middle of a heatwave. So that means something nasty, right?'

Katy swallowed, and nicked herself with a straight, shallow cut. 'This is going to be mine. It'll open for me.' But she wasn't sure.

Wundorwick, on the other hand, was already primed for the exchanging of contracts.

Katy smeared her blood on the keyhole, the stinging and stickiness making her irritable. The door felt the contract terms being sealed and completed, and creaked open.

'Okay, we're in. The first aid box is in the cupboard, that one over there.'

'I got it,' Rocket said, beating Rachel to the cupboard.

The lights were off, Gran's electricity disconnected now she was dead. Someone had cleared out the kitchen of all the best pots and pans, and her coffee machine and microwave were both gone. The pentangle wind chime above the back door was still there, one of Gran's anchors for her home protection.

Rocket unpacked the bandage roll.

'Arm out.'

He started cleaning her cut with antiseptic wipes.

'Don't, it's only a cut.'

'You can't be too careful with cuts. Mehmet cut himself like this once, said exactly the same thing, and it got infected.' Rocket's hands were deft and firm.

'You going with them to Brighton?' Katy asked, hazarding a proper look at his handiwork. He tied off the bandage ends and grinned, a bold sparkle in his eyes.

'Course.'

Rachel smirked. 'Bring us back a lamp.'

'Ha, ha, ha.' Rocket held Katy's hand longer than he needed to, checking the bandage.

Katy's heart hammered so loudly she was certain he would hear it. His fingers lingered on her wrist, and his grin was knowing.

She pulled her hand away, nodding at the door to the cellar in the far corner of the kitchen. 'I'll go down, see if I can get some answers from the shrine. Or see if Gran's old books or diaries or something might help. She keeps – she kept everything down there.'

'Won't they have moved it?' Rachel asked, staring around the bare kitchen.

Katy shook her head. 'Nah, I don't think so. We need the books near the shrine, Gran always read from them there... doesn't make much sense to take them, does it?'

'Unless it's a way of limiting access,' Rachel pointed out.

Katy had thought of that but was hoping this wasn't the case.

'Let's see.'

'Who'd have the books, if they've moved them?' Rachel was checking the empty cupboards. 'Wow, they've cleaned out everything, haven't they?'

'Don't.' Katy couldn't start crying now. Her voice snagged on the lump in her throat. She shook it off and focused. 'I won't be long.'

She headed for the cellar door, conscious that she had never been down there without Gran before. The pull of the shrine was stronger as the door opened onto dark steps leading downwards. It drew her onwards with a sharp pinch in her chest, like the summons of a family member, but sang more deeply into her soul.

Katy ran her hand along the brick as she made her careful descent into the familiar darkness, her phone providing a dim puddle of light for her feet. Its pale blue glow illuminated the chalk images scribbled on the walls by countless grandchildren – drawings of too many limbs, too many eyes, gaping mouths and worshipping figures.

Katy found hers about halfway down, above the tread of the eighth step. A badly drawn hound with a muzzle split like the petals of a snowdrop, covered in spiky triangles. She wasn't sure if she'd drawn it because it was what she *wanted* to be, or what she knew she was becoming. As she neared the bottom of the stairs, someone had drawn their own version of 'Scream' by Edvard Munch, a large chalk face distended in grief and dread with hollow, white eyes.

Standing finally on the flagstone floor, Katy's phone light picked out the shrine against one wall.

It was an antique Welsh dresser.

Pendle portraits in silver frames were arranged on the uppermost shelves: her grandmother's parents, Thomas Pendle and Ann Youngblood; Thomas Pendle's brother, John; and John's son, Richard, a rare only-child and as such gifted with the second-sight, after whom Cousin Ricky was named. Gran had hated Dicky Pendle. No wonder. He'd chopped up his wife and buried her under the floor.

There were framed pictures of her grandmother, too, along with Gran's two sisters, Olive and Eileen, and commemorative plates from a royal wedding.

These pictures cluttered the whole top shelf below the dresser's scalloped pine canopy, and on the second shelf, around Katy's head height, the light picked out glass vials, jars and strange things in shallow dishes that might be bone or teeth, or something else entirely.

On the third shelf, above the main board, there were only three objects: a mummified heart pinned to the wood with several hatpins, and two twisted candles, one either side.

Below this, scattered on the main board of the shrine, was the prism and metal rods that Gran used to open a dimensional portal, the wicker basket for offerings, a number of strange minerals that changed shape when you looked at them from different angles and seemed to glow with an eerie metallic light, and a list in Gran's handwriting.

Katy picked it up, heart beating harder, and the nearest metallic object gave off a cold glow as her fingers brushed its side.

It read:

> *Liver*
> *Onions*
> *Tinned pears*
> *Tinned peaches*
> *Ice cream*
> *Toilet roll*
> *Cat food*

Katy crumpled inside. Tears rushed up to choke her. Gran's handwriting made it feel like she was still there, like she'd just written it and popped out. She almost expected to hear Gran's footsteps overhead, see her come down the stairs and help.

She even stood stock-still, waiting, but Gran didn't come.

Gran was dead.

Katy dashed her tears away and threw the note somewhere into the gloom where she couldn't look at it and delved into the over-stuffed drawers of the dresser, but there was only some ravenous slime-fungus in one (Katy slammed that drawer shut pretty quickly) and the robes Gran wore for special ceremonial occasions, her masks and amulets, all largely for show. Uncle Marcus had his own, of course. The smell of lily-of-the-valley rose up from the robes drawer, kicking her in the chest with more memories, more wishful thinking.

'I can't do this,' she said out loud. 'I can't do this.'

Try, a voice, not her own, said in her head. It sounded like it was hers, but there was an odd echoing quality to it.

The Voice brought her up short. It had been months since she'd heard Grandad in her head, a voice that sounded like her own but wasn't. She looked around, swallowing her grief, but everything was still.

'I don't... I don't know how to...'

Try.

Katy sighed and picked up the prism. 'I could just break this, and then they'd be fucked,' she muttered. 'If they want me gone, I could fuck them over too.'

Her doubts drowned out the Voice. *That isn't going to work.*

The prism was hot in her hands.

'Fine. I can open it, I just need the right instructions...' There was a knack to it, like a Rubik's cube. She couldn't remember where the rods went, or what you did with the weird metallic stones that looked like tools from some angles but from others were just bits of meteorite.

'Okay, I brought an offering anyway.' Katy took a bracelet out of her pocket, a thin silver chain with tiny charms. She laid it in the offering basket, and the dresser rattled against the wall. Katy swallowed.

'Speak to me? Tell me what to do?'

Kill them, the Voice asserted in her head, *Prune the tree.*

Katy winced, in case Rocket could hear it too. 'Yeah… Okay… But, like… what if I don't… want to?'

The dresser shook violently, slime bubbling over the edge of its drawer.

'Oh, God, there's even… Can we skip this bit, it's not scary. Maybe when I was like, twelve. But, come on. Slime? Really?'

The heart started to beat.

Only the hatpins kept it from jumping off the shelf.

Its cracked, ash-grey muscular walls pulsated in a slow, dusty rhythm.

'Here we go,' Katy murmured aloud, tensing. The prism began to glow, the rods and metallic rocks vibrating with an eerie, otherworldly tone, but they flickered and vibrated alarmingly, out of sequence. 'Shit, Gran did something… What did she *do*?'

She tried to poke the stones into some sort of semi-circular configuration, but they were too hot to touch.

'Shit.'

The heart was beating faster, a metronome keeping time to a speeding countdown.

Katy's own heart hammered in time.

'*Shit!* How do I turn it off?'

She tried the prism, catching glimpses through the sides of a green mist, a room with living walls, impossible shapes twisting through multiple dimensions at once. She couldn't tell which way up the world was. The prism projected a kaleidoscope of possibilities, ever-shifting in the dimensions of its facets, too many eyes blinking back at her as she stared into its twisted heart.

The walls closed in and spun. Katy tried to stay upright but she didn't know where the floor was – it seemed to be forty-five degrees to where she'd expected, her feet uncertain of what was beneath them.

'Katy!'

She heard Rocket from the top of the stairs, but it wasn't Rocket – too many limbs sprouting from his body, too many eyes (all Rocket's eyes, replicated a thousand times) blinking at her as they opened in his skin, illuminated by a green haze.

The floor met her shoulder with a thud, falling on top of her and rolling her sideways through empty space. Constellations burst in her vision, joined up with threads of cold starlight to make the same patterns Cousin Ricky once had tattooed on his arms. They *were* tattoos, emblazoned on an alien night sky, and when she threw out her hands to find something solid, they ripped themselves out of the night and burned themselves onto her own forearms in a flash of white ink.

Katy screamed, flesh searing.

She pitched forwards through nothing, the ceiling bumping against her forehead, knocking her back onto what should have been the floor but was another ceiling to another room somewhere else.

'Katy!'

Someone grabbed her, and she spun through a ninety-degree angle, consciousness flickering through space–time in a blur of edges.

Something wrapped itself around her leg, sliming up her calf.

'Katy!'

She blinked, saw the shrine was upside down, and her limbs collapsed under her. The world turned the right way up, but her elbows grazed the tiles and her quads ached. She must have been in a bridge position, but there was no slime on her leg, no tattoos of star-fire on her arms. Rocket and Rachel were standing over her, with the usual number of limbs and eyes.

Make the List.

The Voice in her head was too much. Katy gagged on her own tongue, retched, and threw up.

It was only water and bile, but her throat stung, and her brain felt like a ball of yarn that had been unravelled and wound up again too many times.

She got onto her knees, pressing her forearms into the ground, trying to figure out if the floor was really the floor.

'Allah Allah,' Rocket exclaimed. 'What the *fuck* was that?'

Katy blinked in the harsh light from his torch app and tried to stand. Vertigo hit her in a wave, and she staggered sideways before catching herself. Rocket grabbed her, warm clammy T-shirt pressing into her side, and she figured out physical coordination.

'It was like that time Eden brought that doll into school,' Rachel said, rubbing Katy's shoulder to ground her. 'You remember that? God, I can't wait to get out of this shithole of a town.'

With a last look at the shrine, its heart now still and immobile, the prism lying harmlessly on its side, Katy let her friends help her back up the steps.

Rocket still looked shaken up, but Rachel had been around Katy's family long enough to have seen that – and worse – before, albeit accidentally during one of their childhood 'Spy' games. Sneaking around at the top of the stairs could get you into a lot of trouble when the family were enacting rites down below, especially since Rachel was only human.

'Did you at least learn something?' Rachel closed the cellar door carefully behind them, leaving the shrine to Katy's grandsire enclosed in the darkness once more.

The sun had set, and Rocket was getting shifty.

Katy shrugged. 'Gran's shopping list. That's it. Nothing else.'

'Maybe it's a code?' Rachel suggested.

'An acrostic? No. What's the word, like a… acronym? No. Memory thing, you know what I mean.'

Rocket fidgeted, glancing out of the kitchen window at the purple-shadowed dusk. 'I really have to go.'

'I said you can stay over,' Rachel reminded him. 'Why don't you both come back to mine? We can chill out and order a pizza.'

'Nah, I got to go.' Rocket gave Katy the apologetic smile, not Rachel. 'Sorry. Mehmet's picking me up early tomorrow in the van.'

'See you on Saturday? The Roar Shack?' Rachel gave Katy a little push forwards. 'Katy's not sure if she's coming.'

Katy couldn't focus on clubbing. She was still getting used to moving through three dimensions again.

Rocket was paler, too, still studying Katy's face. 'Um. I mean, yeah, if you're going, I can go…'

'Great. Gav says he can get us some pills, but he wants the money up front.' Rachel tugged Katy's sleeve. 'Let's get out of here, come on.'

He was still focused on her. 'Not for me. Katy? You okay?'

She shook herself and blinked hard. 'Yeah, all right. Let's... let's go.'

Rachel led the way out, holding the door open. Katy rubbed her breastbone, the pinch returning as she walked away, pulling her back. Rocket guided her through the door ahead of him, and when he closed it, the pinch released. She could breathe again. The world was fresh, clean, but still strangely flat.

'Thanks for coming with me, guys.' Katy needed to get out of the garden, where Gran wasn't pottering around the herb beds, where her hum wasn't floating on the air, some old tune she claimed the plants preferred. She clung to Rachel's arm.

Rocket headed over to the front wall to retrieve his bicycle.

'Message us,' Rachel said, and Rocket nodded and cycled off down the road at speed, LEDs spinning in bright Catherine wheels of multicoloured light.

'I'll stay over,' Katy said, and Rachel gave her a one-armed hug as they navigated the creaky gate. 'I don't want to be at home on my own.'

'Your parents out again?' Rachel's expression told her exactly what she thought of that.

Katy focused on the road, and the wobbly business of putting one foot in front of the other. 'Dad's working. Mum's at Kim's with the spawn. They're all she talks about.'

'We'll figure all this out,' Rachel promised, an arm around her waist. 'We will.'

She said it with so much certainty that, just for a moment, Katy believed her.

Ricky withdrew from the memory and let go of Carrie's hand. 'That was int'resting.'

Carrie frowned. 'Poor kid.'

'Yeah, well, we all got our millstones to bear.'

'Crosses.'

'Nah, I don't think so.' Ricky pulled away, turning the pictures and their import over in his mind. He'd been right about his cousin – she was alone, like him. The rare flutter of hope, beetle-light, buffeted his innards.

Carrie rubbed his back unexpectedly, her touch sending sparks down his spine. He stiffened.

'You really want an *ally*, don't you?' she asked, hitting on the term he'd settled on and hidden away, in case it didn't work out. Hearing it from her, unprompted, jolted through him with an unpleasant bump.

'That's it, isn't it? You're fed up of being on your own.'

He covered for his unease. 'Got you, ain't I? That's all I need.'

She wrapped one arm around him, enclosing him in a cupboard-tight grip, giving him a space to shelter.

'Mate, I appreciate that, but you need more than just me. It's not a *betrayal. I* have living friends. My family still don't realise I'm dead, largely thanks to you. And, I know you don't like it, but you need to get over this "friends are for other people" thing.' She gave his ribs a squeeze and let him go.

He had nothing to say to her, but the thought of her going out with other people filled him with the same kind of burning he'd felt when the dead birds told him he'd have to share her with another lodger.

(I'm not jealous. Jealousy's beneath me.)

He inhaled the long-suffering breath of a martyr. 'When we get in, I'll take the heart away,' he said, suddenly remembering. (Ought to get points for that, right?)

She shook her head, but her face was pinched with resignation rather than rage.

'Damn right you will.'

She was harder to work out than he'd anticipated, even eight months on, but he was getting the hang of it now. He filed this incident away as something else she didn't like, and jogged up the cellar steps ahead of her, wanting to be out of Gran's cottage as quickly as possible.

She's nice.

That wasn't his thought.

It brought him up short, halfway across the kitchen. He glanced behind him at the cellar steps.

'D'you hear that?'

Carrie, following him, shook her head. 'Hear what?'

'Oh, it's...' He winced, tapping his temple. 'Ne'mind.'

You broke into her *space. Can you enter another?*

He flinched. The Voice hadn't spoken to him for months, not since he'd disavowed it, not since it had promised him he'd get what he wanted but left him with a house in flames and someone who didn't breathe. Although, he had to admit, it had worked out since then.

(What's it Gran said, 'ellynge', that's the right word, lonely, ellynge, eerie. That's us, ain't it, my love?)

So why now, then, why the creeping call tugging at the back of his mind, that insidious old sod working His way back into his brain?

'Let's go.' He took her arm, savouring the smooth warmth of it, not quite alive, but close enough.

She pulled a little, resistant.

He let go.

'You still pissed off?'

'What's freaked you out?'

His cheek twitched. She always did that when you asked her something she didn't like, threw a question back at you that you didn't want to answer either.

'I said I'd make amends, I meant it.'

'Ricky.' She raised her eyebrows, lips bowing. 'What's wrong?'

'I want to get out of here, that's all.'

(What d'you think I am? A key for a lock?)

The Voice was there, clear as a bell, deep in his brain as if it had never been away.

You're the One and Only. Unique in your generation.

'Fuck this.' He marched to the door and strode out into the crisp air, taking it in with deep breaths. 'I know who I bloody well am.'

She touched his shoulder and he flinched, not realising she was so close behind.

'You're hearing it again, aren't you? That voice in your head?'

'It's... I'm not int'rested. You can't trust Him.' He squirmed as she took his arm this time, her touch making his skin crawl. Thinking about his grandsire had that effect, made him think about the day she died. He swallowed, eyes pricking, blurring. 'You go on home.'

She nodded, knowing when to give up, and crumbled away into plaster flakes and brick dust, leaving him fighting back tears alone.

Chapter 5: Persuasion

13 January

Wes flopped back against his pillows ruffling his hair, building up the energy to roll out of bed. It was too late for breakfast: brunch was pushing it. Late lunch?

Hugo usually made him get up at a reasonable hour, averting his eyes before Wes put his fabric mask on, but Charlie had taken him out to get to the bottom of whatever was going on. She'd texted three times to make sure he was awake. Each time he'd lied and gone back to sleep. When she'd challenged him on what the weather was like outside, he'd gotten Siri to answer her and sent back the reply without lifting the blinds.

The apartment was nearly silent. It wouldn't be if Katy was staying with them. That thought came out of nowhere, and he rubbed his face to erase it. She was fine.

Probably.

For a moment, staring at the familiar ceiling, he felt strangely detached, as if he'd never been in that bedroom before. The bed, still comfortable, was an island of familiarity in an alien capsule. He was *almost* convinced there was nothing outside the blinds at all, nothing beyond the door, that he would get out of bed and fall into a blinding white void that would swallow him whole...

He sat up as his phone rang.

'Yeah?'

'Wesley!' A wet voice, a slick voice, grinding his name like a wave over shingle.

He pulled the phone away from his ear and checked the display. Nothing. He hated it when the elders did that.

'Uncle Marcus?'

'Didn't wake you, did I?'

Wes flushed and threw the covers off. His feet hit the rug – not the abyss – and he curled his toes into the thick fibres, grounding himself. 'I done as you asked, stayed out of the way, been helpful to Uncle Barry. What d'you want?' He rubbed the back of his neck, taking a few heavy steps to the door. Even though he *knew* it would open into the vestry and the large lounge, when it did, he was relieved. An unsettling feeling clung to him with shadowy fingers.

'Where's your sister?'

Wes fought the sudden urge to be sick, gorge rising on an empty stomach. He swallowed a few times, shaking his head. 'I... I don't know.'

'Bollocks. Where is she?'

He didn't mean to blurt it out, but Uncle Marcus wasn't the kind of man you played silly buggers with. 'Ricky's got her.' He winced as it came out.

'What's he done that for?'

Wes stumbled to the bathroom, the white porcelain his enemy, inviting the nausea to return. He stumbled out again, disorientated. 'I don't know. She... she wanted to stay here with me for a bit, she's upset with Mum and Dad, and I think... Ricky doesn't want her leaving. So. She's staying with him for a bit. He said she's fine.'

'Well, that's a problem.' There was a sticky, watery suck, Uncle Marcus smacking his tusked lips. 'He don't like us, your Richard.'

Your Richard.

Wes made it to the sofa and flopped down, not prepared to take that on. 'He's not...'

'Oh, naun to do wi' you, is he? Only made you rich, naun else. We never needed a soothsayer in my day, made our own fortunes, worked hard.'

This was a boring speech, one that Wes and his generation had sat through from time immemorial, and always given by hypocrites who would consult Ricky themselves in a heartbeat if the circumstances were right.

Uncle Marcus wasn't one of those, though. He was an upright man of his word, straightforward and plainspeaking, exactly what they wanted in a Head of the Family. And a Foreman, of course – a true pedigree, inbred from the very first spawning of Eileen Foreman née Pendle. Uncle Marcus was certainly the foremost man of his inward-looking, inward-loving branch.

Wes eyed the gleaming surface of the breakfast bar and willed someone to appear, but the apartment was echoingly empty, and the only company was on the end of the phone.

'He'll be filling her head wi' all sorts of nonsense,' Uncle Marcus complained. 'You sure he's got her?'

'Positive.' Wes wondered what Ricky had done to hide her away so well. 'I can't do anything about it, you know we don't get on.'

'Bollocks, you can talk the hind leg off a donkey. You got enough sweet talk in you to get around the likes of her, and him, if you got the mind.'

Wes didn't like where this was going. His stomach churned, as watery as Uncle Marcus's voice. 'Why are you calling me?'

There was a pause. 'As much as it pains me, I think we're goin' to need you.'

'No, you really don't.' The weird feeling was fading, disintegrating around him like the last tendrils of a dream. The sofa was solid, Charlie's framed art brightening his minimalist world.

'I could get your little pets any time I like an' wring their necks like a couple of chickens,' Uncle Marcus snapped, walrus-boom ringing in Wes's ear. 'Your Uncle David's boys can grab 'em off the streets like a pro, you know what he's like. Enough meat on your boy for a good family roast, I'd say, an' the girl's not up to much but I doubt she ever was...'

'Leave them alone,' Wes snapped, flinging his lanky frame off the cushions and onto his feet. 'Don't you bleedin' dare.'

'Ah, there we are. I could've opened with that, but I was trying to be nice.' Uncle Marcus's tone was level, not mocking, with an underlying fist-clenching note of pity. Wes didn't even realise he'd balled up his free hand until he became aware his arm was shaking, locked impotently by his side.

'This ain't a negotiation, Wesley, I'm tryin' to be nice to you on account of your dear ole dad, who's always been a good friend of the Foremans.' Uncle Marcus chuckled, and hate coursed through Wes, slick and hot and adhering to every part of him.

Ian Porter was a slippery bastard. He'd turn on his own kids if it benefitted him. Wes remembered him at the Vote, not looking his way but facing forwards, eyes straight ahead, raising his hand to be counted as the family decided on Katy's fate…

That afternoon had left a bitter taste in his mouth.

Uncle Marcus was still talking, bullish old bugger, still in that same, level, reasonable tone. 'You're closest to the girl, so it has to be you. I was hoping you'd say she was there with you, then we could have picked her up no bother, the boys would be in and out in a few minutes. If we're not allowed to kill her we could at least keep her somewhere out of the way, try and put the Changes off for a few years. It's painful, but if she'd agree to that, Richard can hardly complain.'

Wes swallowed, tensing. 'You want me to… go get her out of Ricky's place? Where's he even living these days? If it's in that old house, I can't set foot there…'

'No, but you know the girl who bought it.' Uncle Marcus sounded like he was moving around in his kitchen. There was a faint seagull ruckus in the background, a radio, the sound of Aunty Ida monologuing in a shrill vein of complaint at a distance and something that sounded like *'What d'you want for dinner?'*

'But…'

'Go and get your sister away from that little prick before he gets control of her List, if that's even possible. Or it's curtains for your little playmates. Off you go, there's a good boy.'

You're scared of him, Wes realised, wondering how he could use that, and if Ricky appreciated the power he wielded over the elders.

'I'll drive down this week. I'm not promising anything. Leave Charlie and Hugo alone.'

'Oh, and Wesley. Maybe you ought to tell your Katherine exactly how her esteemed grandmother bit the dust.'

Wes blinked. 'She – what? How did… I mean, I don't know what you want me to tell her…'

The family had agreed not to tell Katy that their newfound deity-incarnate had killed Beverley Wend. She might put him on the List, and then they'd be down a soothsayer and money-maker. *Some* factions wanted her to know in order to force a battle royal which, they hoped, would end in Katy's defeat. Uncle Marcus was evidently hoping for the opposite, or that they'd destroy each other.

'Well, I wouldn't want her to hear it from *me*, o' course, people might think I'm biased. Head of the Family, an' all that. Everyone knows what I think about our soothsayer. Especially since he cost me an eye. God knows what he does wi' them.'

'Oh, right, so you want *me* to break it to her? Thanks.'

If Katy put the soothsayer on the List and killed off the family cash-cow, Wes's remaining sympathetic relations would turn against him faster than people forgot his face.

'Can she even kill him? Doesn't he think he's some sort of god now? What if he finds out I told her? I couldn't take him *before*.' Wes paced, chest tight. 'I'm far from his biggest fan, but I'd rather fuck him than fight him, if you know what I mean.'

'You made your bed, you bloody well lie in it.' Uncle Marcus's voice dropped and resonated like a rutting sea lion. 'I expect you back by this time tomorrow, I'm not unreasonable. Send Katherine a message, tell her to meet you, and drive the wedge in deep. You understand?'

'I understand.' Wes itched to hang up on him, but Uncle Marcus cut over his terse 'goodbye' and started talking to Aunty Ida about whether the carrots were past their best and hung up on him mid-discussion.

Wes was left dismissed and forgotten, alone in the penthouse, desperately wishing Hugo and Charlie had woken him up and taken him out with them. But he'd have been useless to them, too, and Hugo was going to dump him and move away somewhere.

There'd be a day when Charlie would get sick of him, lock him up in a cupboard like a first aid box, cut his head off and keep it in the fridge where she could stare at his face for as long as she needed...

He found himself sniggering at that image, although it wasn't funny. He flopped back on the sofa, chuckling to himself, and punched his temples with hard, bony knuckles. He punched his own face over and over, gritting his teeth with every impact and rocking against the plush grey cushions, daring himself to punch harder. He chipped a tooth and his cheekbones throbbed. He spat the chip out and punched himself again. It wasn't like anyone would remember the bruises anyway. He could beat himself black and blue and bloody, but he couldn't make himself forget.

Wes's Memory: The Vote

Uncle Marcus and Aunty Ida lived on the edge of Pevensey, in a fisherman's cottage facing the sea.

Wes hated the melancholic bleakness of the shingle and the haunting laughter of the gulls; it was a nowhere-place to him, a place you came to be forgotten.

There was no one around when Cousin Layla parked the car – for once, they were one of the first to arrive. Layla's terse messages had made it sound like she didn't want to pick him up from the station, which had surprised him. He wondered what he'd done this time.

Layla Wend-McVey had dressed more sombrely than usual on this occasion. She gave Wes a withering glance, cornflower-blue eyes from the McVey side so unlike the family brown, and he wondered if she felt out of place there.

'Ready?' he asked her.

Layla hadn't said a word to him the whole drive, and she only shrugged now.

Wes was running out of topics on which to monologue.

Layla got out of the car and wrapped her cardigan around her against the salty breeze, even though it was set to be another scorcher of a day.

Wes followed suit. 'Lay! Wait!'

She locked the car behind him without stopping, marching over the shingle in sturdy cork wedges, shaking her head.

'I can't *help* being her brother!'

'It's not about *that*,' Layla finally shot at him, coming to an abrupt stop. Her pretty face was distorted in a snarl. She had a vague resemblance to their grandmother in this light, the same cast to the jaw when she set it firmly in anger, but the McVeys had bright blue eyes and a strawberry tint to their hair, distanced from the other branches by a few generations of out-breeding until they were more human than human-passing. Some Wend-McVeys barely Changed at all, but Layla had been one of the lucky ones. Her glory, as some of them called it, had broken through just before her twenty-first birthday, making her the pride of that branch's generation.

'I saw the soothsayer the other day. After what he fucking said to me – is that true? It had *better not* be true.'

A cold hand clutched Wes's chest. 'What did he say to you?'

The apples of her cheeks burned. She stopped, her whole frame quivering. Her prehensile tongue darted out from under her top, thrashing at the air before whipping back into her navel.

Wes took a guess, hoping to mitigate the damage. 'Look, that was *years* ago. And it was only the once, and we were kids, you know, I wasn't with you just to make him jealous if that's what...'

She stared at him, her increasingly slack-jawed incredulity indicating he was not only barking up the wrong tree but had pissed in the wrong garden. He swallowed, scratching at the back of his neck.

'Shit.'

Layla's eye twitched twice, her only movement. In her shimmering skirt and uncharacteristically high neckline, she was a frozen statue of beige and mint green, like a gorgon or a plump-breasted demi-goddess.

'Are you actually staring at my tits? I'm up here, arsehole.'

He dragged his eyes up to her face, which was a far less pleasant view. She was furious.

'Who broke into Uncle Barry's practice and nicked a load of ketamine last month, Wesley?'

Oh – that.

'Hasn't he got CCTV?' Wes didn't show up well on video.

She punched him, right in the arm. Pain spasmed up his bicep and pins and needles broke out in a prickling web.

'Jesus!'

'You fucking thief! You rotten junkie bastard!' She flew at him, prehensile tongue of many talents going for his throat. He tried to fend it off, the teeth slashing at his skin, attempting to wrap around his neck and puncture the jugular.

'You *don't – steal –* from – your own fucking *family* you *arsehole*, what the fuck – is – wrong with you?'

He couldn't fight off the tongue *and* her fists, delivering a hard rain of blows. Wes had very little padding on his lanky body, and every hit glanced painfully off a bone. He doubled over under her assault, the lashing tongue slashing and cutting at his arms and scratching his plastic mask to pieces.

'Whoa! Whoa! Lay, come on! I never, I never honest, he's chatting shit!'

'He's a fucking *soothsayer*, he tells the fucking *truth*, that's his fucking *job*!' She kicked him hard, aiming for his groin, but he managed to twist away and she caught him right on the knee. Wes fell back onto the stones, losing his balance as the kick took his leg out from under him.

Uncle Marcus was running out of the house with heavy, pounding strides, a juggernaut under full steam.

'Layla! Leave him be!'

Layla kicked him again, this time in the kidneys, and stopped panting.

Wes curled up, aching all over and laughing with relief.

The laugh was a mistake – before Uncle Marcus could grab hold of her, Layla kicked him again, square in the back of his thigh. Pain shot through his leg.

Wes howled in agony and laughed and swore into the shingle.

Uncle Marcus yanked her back so roughly that she nearly fell herself, and Wes was heaved to his feet, legs buckling under him.

'Get a grip on yourself, boy,' the Head of the Family snarled in his ear. 'You're a representative of your generation, Foreman help us. What's this about?'

'*He's* the one who stole from Uncle Barry,' Layla said, pointing at him in livid accusation. 'I wasn't going to say anything, I wasn't, not today, but he's a – He deserves everything he gets. Who steals from their own *family*?'

'You stick whatever you want up your nose or in your arm or in any orifice of your choice,' Uncle Marcus said, one massive hand around the back of Wes's neck giving him a teeth-rattling shake. 'But don't let me hear about you stealing from family again, or there won't be leniency. Layla, get in the house and help your aunts.'

He threw Wes forwards, pitching him back down onto the shingle. Wes threw his hands out to stop himself sprawling flat on his face and fell afoul of something sharp. He righted himself, palms bleeding and embedded with dirty sand.

'If I ever hear you've had your grubby fingers in the family pot again, or anywhere else they don't belong, I'll have to tear you apart myself, even if it is from a Wend-McVey,' his uncle growled, tentacle-beard wriggling with displeasure. 'Married-ins they might be, but I can't be seen to be biased. Do you understand?'

Wes nodded, straightening his mask. 'Yes, sir, Uncle Marcus, sir.'

'Cheeky little shit,' Uncle Marcus muttered, waiting until he was sure Layla was out of earshot. He clapped Wes on the back. 'Thought you said you wouldn't get caught.'

'Soothsayer dropped me in it,' Wes said.

Uncle Marcus rolled his eyes. 'Well, it was a fine theory. George was supposed to deal with him, but a little bird told me that didn't happen either.'

They watched Layla slam the front door of the cottage behind her as a few other cars started pulling up as close to the house as they could.

'No. I heard the same.' Wes rubbed his knee and thigh, wincing. 'Cor, our Layla's got a good punch. She still kick-boxing, is she?' He caught his uncle's unimpressed expression and shrugged. 'Look, I gave you a good cut of the profit, didn't I? I won't do it again, not unless you ask. I wouldn't do it just for me, you know that. I'm a family man.'

'You're a selfish piece of shit,' his uncle said matter-of-factly.

Wes scowled. 'Yeah. Well. Cash is cash. I got two partners to look after.'

This earned him a seal-like bark of amusement from his enormous relative. 'You've got yourself a cushy little nest with two human posh kids who'll pay for everything,' Uncle Marcus corrected, deep brown eyes twinkling. 'You're a lazy, good-for-nothing little tosser, that's what you are, Wesley Edward Porter. You've got no ambition, no drive. No work ethic. You're a funny sod, I'd be genuinely sorry to see you go, but if you're not on that List of hers I'll eat my waders.' He looked him up and down. 'Look, if the Wend-McVeys push this, I'll have to give 'em what they want. You know that. Mebbe you c'n sweet talk your Uncle Barry.'

At the mention of the List, Wes was abruptly reminded why he was there. It eclipsed even the threat of Uncle Barry's inevitable wrath. He moistened his lips.

'How d'you think the vote will go?' It came out croakier than he'd intended.

Uncle Marcus shrugged. 'Do I look like our soothsayer?'

Wes took in his barrel-chested uncle, resplendent in thick-soled boots, old brown trousers patched at the knees, sturdy braces and an off-white vest.

'Nah, too well-dressed.'

Uncle Marcus let out a belly-laugh and clapped Wes on the shoulder, causing his aching legs to buckle again. 'Right. In we go. Let's get this over with.'

They joined the others trooping up to the cottage gate, Wes limping over the loose stones. He was determined to do the right thing by his sister, even if he was on the List. He couldn't say as much to Uncle Marcus, but that was his genuine intention. He'd told himself so, over and over, every day that week. He was going to vote not to kill her.

His phone buzzed in his top pocket.

He had an unread message from Hugo – the usual *I love you, have a good day* – and a longer one from Charlie. He paused, nodding at his relations as they processed past him, levering himself onto the wall to answer them and turn his phone off.

'You coming?' Uncle Wayne rasped, string vest of living flesh pulsating over a skeletal torso.

Wes jerked up. 'What? Yeah. Yeah, I'll – I'll be right there.'

'Hurry up.'

Shit. Shit. Shit.

He was the last, now, the only one still outside.

The door opened. Aunty Ida. 'Wesley? I think everyone's here now, are you coming in?'

He heard someone behind her say, 'Maybe he wants to abstain,' and he pocketed the phone, numb.

'No, I'm coming.'

Charlie needed him, needed to stare into his face or she couldn't function. Had he really forgotten that, when he was rehearsing his good intentions in the mirror, telling himself he would choose his sister's life over his partner's sanity? Or perhaps when he was dead and gone to the Other Place, the Outside, wherever it was that his kind go... it would be as if his whole existence was erased, forgotten in a blink. Charlie would be cured, live her life without him, without a single memory of his imprint on her life.

That, for some reason, made him feel worse. Hollow. A shadow of a thing.

'Yeah, coming, hold the door.' He switched on aeroplane mode and limped up the path as fast as he could and slipped in, adjusting his mask.

The living room was packed, even with some of the elders manipulating space to make it seem bigger. The family were their true selves, appendages and unearthly flesh on display, gaping maws and coils dripping with excretions, a mass of humanoid and otherworldly flesh.

Wes removed his mask and faded forgettably into position, the only one among them who could drive people to madness by his *absence* in their memory. Given the choice, he'd have taken the coils.

They'd be better off without me. I'm an aberration. Never should have existed.

Uncle Marcus was droning on about how it was a serious matter, how the gathering was unprecedented, how important all this was. The soothsayer wasn't present:

then again, he was meant to be neutral. The Head of the Family got the casting vote in the event of a tie.

Someone piped up about tradition, Bill Shaw, of course, unimaginative to the last and believing he was strong enough to be untouchable. This was quickly countered. Tess Porter reasonably pointed out that, since Katy was only the clan's *second* Thirteenth, 'tradition' was a loose term in this case.

Besides, Uncle Marcus added, this wasn't a vote for foiling fate, as no one could outrun their wyrd. Think of it as a temporary reprieve. There would be other batches of Thirteen in time.

Wes stood in silence throughout the debates.

If it went Katy's way, if they let her live, she'd start to Change perhaps as early as next year, and then she'd come for him. The Thirteenth pruned the family tree, cut off the weak branches. He wasn't anything close to the clan's definition of 'strong'. No. The more he thought about it, the more he was sure he'd be on the bloody List, and the weight of it began to suffocate him with the fug of warm, inhuman flesh pressed close together.

Would Charlie remember him? Would Hugo? Would he be a gaping hole in their memories forever?

He couldn't bear it. The room was oppressive, thick with mucus and ooze. His back ached. His legs hurt. Uncle Marcus droned on and on.

I need a break, I need a breather, I need to get out of here... I just need it all to go away...

'Those in favour of giving us a reprieve, and just killing the girl?'

Wes reacted without thinking. He didn't even know he'd raised his hand until Uncle Marcus looked him in the eye, nodded, and counted him in. '...Fourteen...'

Wes dropped his arm, wide-eyed, a prickling horror washing down his back. He'd voted against his sister.

No one caught his eye.

No one was looking at anyone else.

Wes stared around the room and saw his own father on the far side as Uncle Wayne leaned back slightly. Their dear old dad had his hand up, staring straight ahead. Hate blazed in his belly, burning his lungs, pulsing a flush of rage over his neck.

How could he stand there, calm as you like, that lean, mean face a mask of straightforward let's-get-this-over-with-then, and vote for the death of his own daughter? It was, Wes knew, entirely in character.

Look at yourself, Wesley Porter. You turned out just as bad.

Wes couldn't take it anymore. He pushed relatives out of the way, and they let him through.

The fresh air hit him with a bolt of sunlight, promising clarity. He made it to the garden wall, stumbling into the gatepost, and collapsed there with his head in his hands, knowing the ayes had it.

The sun beat down on the back of his neck.

A gull screamed at him in the distance.

It was gone midday. He retrieved his cigarettes and lighter from his back pocket, lighting up and taking a steadying drag.

If he had to die, let it be dramatic, let him be a hero, let him be *something*. He'd fight for Charlie too, for Hugo, for whatever they wanted to build, if they would only let him stay and be a part of it.

Is that selfish? He didn't know.

In the agony of indecision, Wes stumbled away down the beach, getting lost in the bleak sweep of the coastline, his head a mess, wiped of logic by the abrasive salt air.

Chapter 6: Strange Meeting

13–14 January

Wes plastered on his pretend smile, dabbing away the last drops of his twenty-five pounds' worth of nosebleed. People hung around with louche hands trailing over his waistcoat, buying him drinks, all the drugs he wanted. Strands of conversation wove around the thumping bass.

Who's that guy?... Why didn't I recognise him?

How does his face disappear like that?... What are you talking about?

Get him back over here... I don't know why, just ask him. Brown hair. Black hair? I don't know. Does it matter? That guy.

His phone rang, and he ducked into the opulent men's room to answer it although the signal was dodgy. 'Uncle Barry! To what do I owe the pleasure?'

'You better not be high off my fucking pills,' his uncle growled in his ear. 'I want the money tomorrow.'

'I'll... yeah, you can have it. I've got it. It's fine.' Wes steadied himself on the porcelain sink, checking out a guy with a half-a-million-pound watch as he missed the urinal. Unsurprising with a cock like that. Equally nice watch. Bet he wouldn't miss it.

'What d'you say about my cock?' His uncle asked, amused.

'Nothing.' *Shit.*

'Your thoughts better be on the inside of your skull. They're for selling, Wesley.'

Wes tried to focus on his royal-blue nail polish. 'Yeah, I got that, yes. Selling them.'

So far, external thoughts happened in just over half the cases, which Wes had been noting on his phone. No one he'd challenged to a bet afterwards had won, either. Everyone else just seemed to have a good time, nothing to write home about. Wes was starting to think the Silver Lining was wasted on the proles, even ones with half-a-million-pound watches. It wasn't as if he couldn't just give Uncle Barry his own cash, for fuck's sake. Keep them. Then the old bastard could flog them to whoever else he wanted, but Wes would have a little stash of his own.

'Good lad. Don't let me down.' Uncle Barry hung up.

Wes shook his head and eyed Watch Guy's arse as he left.

What was he *doing* here? Wes knew he didn't belong here. He missed the grimy clubs of Pagham-on-Sea where he'd grown up, where they didn't look twice at your fake ID, sweat condensed and dripped down the back of your neck from the low ceilings, and your shoes stuck to the floor. He missed the thrills and the untouchable shine of being a Porter in a place where everyone knew his grandmother and wouldn't say a damn thing.

Then again – he liked not working, he loved his partners, he enjoyed all this.

Didn't he?

He wished Charlie was here too. He missed her all of a sudden, as if something had just burst in his chest.

Charlie had a date, which was fine. She'd told him to relax and not to be an arsehole, and that Hugo would tell him what was going on in his own time. Hugo, so far, had kept nearly telling him, then bottling it.

Wes couldn't bear it. He dragged himself back to where he'd left Hugo and let the world spin around him, myriad shards of light and colour whirling and buffeting at his scattered attention, utterly lost.

He had convinced himself that Hugo wanted to break up with him and just didn't know how to do it.

Good.

Wes kept imagining him being abducted off the street by Uncle David and his boys, and the best thing he could think of was that Hugo's life-changes should include getting as far away from Wes and his fucking family as possible.

He was sure he'd left Hugo at the bar for only a few minutes, but he'd lost track of time. The club beats pounded through him, his veins electrified. Somehow, despite his size, Hugo managed to blend in like a chameleon with everyone else, even though he was the only person Wes knew who wore a suit and tie to a nightclub like this.

He pulled Hugo away from his financier friends without ceremony, mid-conversation, fuck them. Hugo shouted something he couldn't hear. The lights hit him, fragmenting him like a kaleidoscope.

Wes wanted to be like him, this warm, simple man who tried to see the best in people. Falling in love with him had been like stepping out of a vacuum and into a place where he could take a deep, fresh breath. Wes ached for those earlier, simpler, better times, but had no idea how to get back there.

Hugo pulled him away from the dancefloor, firm and brooking no argument, although Wes didn't resist and would have followed him into Hell.

'God, you're so *clean*, aren't you?' Wes pushed him down onto the upholstery, purple leather gleaming like the lights on Hugo's thick sweep of hair. 'Not a stain on you.' He meant clean-cut, like a marble statue, something even he couldn't fuck up. He prayed to Grandad that was true.

Hugo showed no signs of Charlie's addiction, but people reacted to Wes in different ways. Some of his fuck buddies couldn't even remember his name, or thought he was a different person each time. Where Charlie had thrown herself into him like an offering into an abyss, Hugo was drawn like a neglected moth offering itself up to the flame of something greater, something special, but as yet showed no signs of scorching.

Deep down, Wes had always known he'd leave eventually. Something that sweet couldn't last.

Hugo's mouth twitched. He caught Wes by the wrist, pulling him closer and into the seat. 'We've got to talk,' he said, in that apologetic way of his whenever the other person was at fault.

Wes cringed inside. 'I'll pay the rent as long as you need, I don't have to be there. I can chuck out my tenants and take my flat back if you give me time.'

'What — what are you talking about?'

Wes blinked, pinching the bridge of his nose, eyes suddenly full. 'Uh.' He inhaled sharply. 'The flat, you know, my Chelsea flat…'

'No, I mean — why are you moving out, why would we move to Chelsea? I'm not… I'm not moving to Chelsea.'

Wes looked up. 'Can we not beat about the bush? Huey, if you want to end it, just tell me, yeah, give me my marching orders, don't – don't draw it out.'

His boyfriend stared at him, the image of gentle, warm-eyed bafflement. 'Why? I mean, no! That's not... Grief, Cha-Cha said you'd take this all the wrong way...'

Wes smirked in spite of himself. He couldn't imagine anyone but Hugo calling Charlie 'Cha-Cha'. He shook his head. 'Wouldn't you be better off without me, anyway?'

Hugo spluttered out a laugh, broad shoulders shaking. 'Without you? I couldn't say boo to a goose without you.'

He grew serious, taking care to look at the silk and lace of Wes's commedia dell'arte mask and not at the eyes behind it that he wouldn't remember. 'D'you think it matters to me what you look like, or don't? You opened my eyes to possibilities I – I couldn't have imagined before I met you... and... I couldn't have stood up to Father without you, Mummy's going spare and won't even speak to me, and it doesn't matter because I've – I'm the luckiest man in the world.' He smiled, but Wes saw the pain in it. His joking tone rang false over the music as he raised his voice a little. 'Cha-Cha's folks are great. I think they want to adopt me. One of us ought to have a decent family.'

Wes swallowed. 'So... what is it? Don't... don't tell me you finally stood up to your old man.'

Hugo's shy smile twitched, and Wes burned with pride. 'You serious? That's fucking brilliant! Fuck him! You fucking brilliant man.' He kissed him hard, relief pouring out of him, sagging into Hugo with the release. He broke the kiss and grinned wildly. 'I'm so fuckin' proud of you. What – oh, right.' Everything slotted into place. 'He's throwing you out of the apartment. That's it, isn't it? Oh, God, Huey, you could have told me that. I'll pay for it.'

'Yeah. And. He – he's cut me off. Out. Completely. You know. I'm – I got a place to study for my PGCE, and I need – well, I need some money.' Hugo squirmed. 'I should've had a bit put by, I know, but I'm hopeless with savings and the three accounts in my name aren't – well, I haven't been as good with them as I said I have, tell the truth, and I didn't think the old man would *actually* cut me off, I hoped he'd, you know...' He gave a hopeless shrug. 'I hoped he'd support me, I guess.'

Wes rolled his eyes, relief flowing over him in waves. Poor Hugo. Wes had only met Chalmondley Senior a handful of times at corporate events. The man radiated *bully* like a flashing sign. He'd fit right into the Porters.

No wonder Hugo had fallen face first into the idea of otherworldly beings; he'd done so with the desperation of someone who wanted to be liked by *everyone*, even if 'everyone' included... well, monsters. Wes shook his head, trying to focus. 'I'll support you. Whatever you want, you know that.'

'But it's one more thing to put on you.' Hugo looked stricken now, twisting in his seat, bumping his ribs against the edge of the table. 'That's – that's the other thing. What's going on?'

'I can't...'

'What are you scared of?'

'I...' He couldn't. He couldn't. He shook his head, lost, but Hugo wasn't going anywhere, and he wasn't going to let him get away with silence. He winced, pulling himself up a little straighter, and studied his hands.

'Katy. I'm scared of Katy.' Wes remembered Uncle Marcus's threats. 'All of them, to be honest.'

Hugo knew a little about the various branches of his family, but he probed. 'What happened this summer?'

The chemicals had kicked in enough to drown out his pride. Enough was enough. Fuck it.

'They... *We* voted to, to... to kill her.' He couldn't look him in the face. 'And I – I don't know how to take it back, I don't know how to help her, and I don't want to die...'

'Good God.' Hugo breathed out, barely audible over the music. 'She's a kid, Wes.'

Wes crumpled. He nodded miserably, fighting tears. 'I don't want anything to happen to *you*, either. They're – they'll hurt you, if I cross the elders, and they think I can get Katy for them. She's... she's run away.'

'Good for her.' Hugo squared his shoulders. 'We can go somewhere until it's all over, right? Babe, don't. Don't cry.'

He rubbed Wes's back through the silk, and Wes folded back into him, clinging to his partner like the big naïve prat was a life-preserver.

'You can't get away from them like that. You didn't ask for this, I just dragged you in, didn't I? You could leave. I *want* you to. I *want* you to leave me, be safe, I want...'

Hugo kissed him.

Wes barely held back a sob.

Hugo broke the kiss and stroked his cheek. 'Okay, well... You can fix it. I know you can. You'll do the right thing.'

Wes wondered who the hell Hugo thought he'd been fucking for four years, but he desperately wanted to be that man.

'I'm not going anywhere,' Hugo promised him. 'Neither's Cha-Cha, and that's not because she, not just because she... can't.' He dropped his gaze a fraction, and Wes shifted, sick with guilt. 'I need you. Why don't you tell your cousin, what's his name, Ricky?' Hugo gave his shoulder a gentle, reassuring squeeze. 'Isn't he... powerful, as far as your lot are concerned?'

Wes snorted. Hugo had never met Ricky, or any of the clan for that matter: he had everything second-hand and sanitised. He also hadn't heard anything that counted as positive about Ricky Porter, but here he was, thinking the best of someone he'd never met and had only heard being critiqued.

'Ricky's a jealous, sociopathic little shit,' Wes reminded him. 'Why should he care about you? He barely cares about himself. He only cares about Katy because he's trying to use her for something. An' we're not exactly the best of friends.' He bit his thumbnail. 'I could do what he does, you know, I could be the One and Only or whatever he calls himself, I could...' He stopped, the silver outline of memory teasing him.

Shit. I really could.

Wes *almost* had an idea, a scheme, but it melted in the face of Hugo's chiselled jaw and puppy-eyed concern. He sighed.

'I don't know what to do. I don't know... I should talk to Katy, go back to town see what she makes of it, but if she thinks I'm weaker than she *already* thinks I am, she'll put me on the List and come for me faster, first, I don't know, that's what they say the List is *for*, pruning the weakest of us...' He shuddered. 'An' that's me, ain't it, that's allus been me...'

Hugo smiled at his broadening accent; he always said Wes shouldn't be ashamed of it, but Wes thought it made him sound common. So did all their friends. And Charlie's parents, who already hated him for obvious reasons, which was entirely fair.

Wes clamped his mouth shut.

'Go home and talk to Katy, then,' Hugo said.

Go home.

Hugo caught the frown before it vanished from his memory. 'That's not what I meant.'

Wes pulled himself together, knowing he probably wouldn't be all right to drive tomorrow, knowing he'd be driving down anyway, knowing he was a waste of air and he should wrap the Ferrari around a tree and hope he wasn't as cockroach-resilient as the rest of his clan.

And then what? Uncle Marcus might go after Charlie and Hugo anyway, out of spite. What would theatrics achieve?

His heart clenched. 'You know, if I die, I think I get permanently erased. I hope I do. Gran thought so. She's – she was usually right.' He twitched his lips into a wobbly smile that wouldn't stick. 'God, I hope so. I *hope* so. I couldn't leave you—'

Hugo kissed him. Not fiercely, a life-or-death kiss, the way only Charlie could kiss him; Hugo kissed him like he was fragile, like his breath could fill Wes up and cure him of whatever smoke-dark thing lurked inside.

Wes melted into him, kissing Hugo back through the pounding in his head, Hugo's tongue braving the chemical desert of his parched mouth, and he never wanted to let him go.

Hugo broke it first. 'Better?'

Wes turned his head away and scanned the dancefloor, thinking about his sibling group chat and how it was most recently dominated by Liam's dirty memes and Kim's endless baby pictures and Nicole's endless bitching.

He was their older brother, too.

What if *they* were on the List? He couldn't save everyone, and he wasn't sure he could save himself. He had no idea what the 'right thing' was under these circumstances.

He forced a smile. 'Better.'

Hugo's mouth twitched at the corner in that nervous way of his, but, for the moment, Wes hoped, was content, to believe him.

14 January

Monday brought with it its own set of challenges. Katy was afraid she wouldn't be able to leave for college, but Ricky hadn't lied to her. The front door was open, the gates unlocked. She made it to the road and jogged to the bus stop, about fifteen minutes away from the house.

She didn't have to go back there.

She couldn't go home, either. Not now she knew her dad was seriously thinking about… she didn't know what. Well, she knew *what*, just not *how*. He must be pretty practised by now. She realised she had no idea what his signature was, or if he even had one. It was something she'd never thought about, a fact about him she'd deliberately overlooked. It repulsed her, like the thought of her parents having sex.

At least Fairwood House was quiet.

Apart from Ricky, it was pretty cool to have the whole place to herself. She still wasn't sure what he *wanted*. To protect her, okay, you could put that down to traditionalism or because he believed her cull was fated. Fine. But could he actually help her control who to put on the List? It was meant to be automatic. She'd been having the dreams – night terrors, really, except where the terror was *her* – since she was six. She remembered all of them, all the names, the faces, everyone doomed to be torn apart as soon as she Changed.

She had woken screaming, thinking her hands had become something she couldn't manage, couldn't control, that she had actually torn Aunty Janey apart and her taste was still on her tongue.

Rachel said she should practise, since she was squeamish. Rachel never joined in, but she liked to watch, lying in the grass on her stomach, kicking her legs in the air, plucking daisies as Katy practised wringing the necks of whatever they'd managed to catch.

Even at age seven, Rachel was good at trapping things.

Rachel had taught her how to blend in at school, how to talk to other kids, what she shouldn't ever say. Katy wanted to tell Rocket about the squirrels, or Wes, but Rachel had threatened (twice) to stop being friends with her if she did.

Katy didn't want to be the creepy girl with no friends.

She had kept quiet, got semi-used to the sounds and the squirming, at least enough to not throw up afterwards. Eventually, Rachel had tired of their animal practice sessions and Katy stopped trying to desensitise herself with a huge amount of relief, knowing she still had her best friend.

So that had worked out okay.

She zoned out on the bus ride into town, thinking about the big house and its echoing rooms, its warm skin – walls, paint, she meant, why did she think that? – its missing owner, the way Ricky spoke to it, the gentle way he stroked the woodwork and brick, the panic in his face when she picked up the poker...

The concrete brutalism of the college was a rude awakening. It was noisy, crowded with students, drawing them into its boxy rooms and cuboid corridors, soulless and cold, the painted colours falsely optimistic, like rouge on a crying clown.

Katy thought of the grand entrance hall she'd just left, the mahogany elegance of the bannisters silky under her hand. The metal rail and well-lit stairs to the first floor shocked her back to reality. No, she wouldn't be going back there. But it was as if the house she'd left knew that, as if it was calling her back, as if it *understood her*...

What a weird thing to think.

It was only an old house.

She went into Mr Anwar's psychology class to focus on the multi-store model of memory, doodling windows and wallpaper motifs in her textbook.

Rachel was waiting for her outside after their first class of the day and pounced on her immediately, wrapping her in a big, relieved hug.

'Oh my God, are you okay? You haven't answered our messages, we were going nuts. What happened? I can't believe you're still here...'

Katy hugged her back. 'I didn't get very far.'

'What happened?'

'Ricky grabbed me.'

Rachel blanched. 'Oh, shit.' Even so, there was a frisson of excitement in Rachel's voice that Katy didn't quite trust.

Rachel had seen Cousin Ricky high as fuck and taking on Katy's siblings for a laugh, had seen what he could do with his bare hands even before his Changes. She had hidden with Katy in Gran's kitchen cupboard once when a family row had gotten out of hand and Gran had ended up showing her true face to sort it out. She had watched him reading entrails, too, and Katy wondered if that was where the idea to help her get used to killing things came from.

She wondered if Rachel still liked watching shit like that, only now she did it without her.

'Yeah.' She moistened her lips, an arm around Rachel to keep herself tethered to something solid. 'He wouldn't let me leave, but... he said he'd protect me from them if I stay in town and... he can help me control my List.'

'Can he?'

They were walking towards the coffee shop on campus, where Rocket was guarding a table.

'I guess. I don't know. He's got... he's got hearts and eyes in fucking jars.'

Rachel's dark eyes sparkled. 'Seriously? That's sick.'

'Sick in the head, yeah. He's eating them to get information, I think. I don't know how that works. And he's insane, he's talking to the house like it's alive.' Katy shuddered. 'I think he's killed the owner and put her in the walls or something.'

'Is he still... human-passing? Did you see his...' Rachel paused, dropping her voice, '...*other form?*'

Katy shook her head. 'He's basically the same, yeah, he looks... like there's something wrong with him. You know. Ill. I don't know. I reckon it's what he's doing, it's draining him.'

Rocket waved them over as they entered through the heavy double doors, the sandwich-and-drinks queue already growing. He'd bagged a round table for four, one of the good ones with decent seats. His reflective jacket was draped on the chair opposite him, a flashy marker. His big grin made Katy's heart flip.

'Hey, you!'

She beamed back, pushing her hair back behind her ear. 'I tried to reply, I couldn't get signal…'

Rachel arched an eyebrow. 'Did you try and reply to *me*?'

Katy darted her an evil glare. '*Yes.*'

Rocket scraped his chair back and gave Katy a bear hug. 'Bring it in, Rach,' he said, waving Rachel over with one arm, to Katy's disappointment. She hugged Rocket's stocky chest, and Rachel joined in. 'Right.' Rocket let them both go, and Katy drew her chair a little closer than necessary until their knees were almost touching, knowing he wasn't aware of how narrow the gap was.

'Katy got abducted.' Rachel was always first with the news. Katy was grateful – she ran out of steam by the second telling of anything, and Rachel told stories better than she could.

'Shut the front door.'

Rachel relayed the context of Cousin Ricky, Rocket's face an expressive picture of disgust and fascinated horror. He sat back when she'd finished, knee bumping against Katy's.

'Sorry – wow. That's wild.'

Katy shrugged, shifting slightly, hoping it would happen again. 'What d'you think I should do?'

Rocket shook his head. The apples of his round cheeks were pink with the heating and his thick jumper, easily twice the size of her. She imagined his weight against her instead of Alex's that night after the Roar Shack and pressed her thighs together.

'Well, he let you come to college, so can he… can he be trusted? I mean, do you think he can actually help you with the List? That's what you want, right, a way of taking everyone off?'

Katy didn't look at Rachel, who knew that was not *exactly* what she wanted. 'Yeah, of course.'

'Okay.' Rocket frowned, forehead creasing. 'Do you think he wants to hurt you?'

Katy considered this. 'I mean. No. Not *me*. I don't know, I think – I think he likes me? Like, not like *that*, I think he just...' She got lost in the tangle of Cousin Ricky's possible motives. 'I don't know. He wants me to do him a favour, but we didn't get that far. I think it's probably about the List, he probably wants me to put people on it for him.'

'Right. But once you Change, that's up to you. Could you take him? Theoretically? Like, is he... he sounds like he knows how to handle himself, but if you really knew how to fight, and you had the advantage, what d'you think?'

'In my dreams I'm... pretty much invincible.' Katy cast a glance at Rachel, who was fiddling with her purse and eyeing the queue. 'Are you getting anything?'

Rachel pulled a face. 'Hot chocolate. What do you want?'

'Tea?'

Rocket shook his head and leaned back in his chair, balancing on its back legs as Rachel stood up. 'Had a sandwich, I'm good.'

'Sure?'

'Meh. Hot chocolate, go on.'

Rachel gave Katy a meaningful look that Rocket missed as he swung back and leaned on the table. Katy mirrored him, knotting her fingers together and chewing her cheek, and Rachel left them alone together.

'Is there any way of telling what he thinks?' Katy asked. 'Any...' She dropped her voice. 'Any magic, something like that? Gran never showed me a lot of that stuff. Every time I asked, she said I was too young, that I wouldn't need it, you know.'

'I don't do magic, but... there's something.' Rocket shifted closer, pressing her leg with his by accident, and she leaned in, not looking at him. 'You can have this, if you want.'

He pulled a knot of leather cords from around his neck, scooping them out of his jumper and separating one of three identical amulets, a flat blue bead with a painted eye.

'Here,' he said, working it free and handing it over. 'It wards off the evil eye, it's from my brother's girlfriend.' There was something heavy in his face that Katy didn't know what to do about. Rocket spent most of his time worrying about his brothers and pretending he didn't. 'I think... well, I don't think she's... human. So. Anyway, I don't think it's *bad*, I wouldn't give it to you if I did. I just don't want it. Dad says I'm worrying about nothing, but, I don't know.'

Katy didn't want to probe. She took it and undid her own necklace with her half of a Best Friend heart on it. She threaded the flat glass bead onto it, and Rocket helped her re-clasp it. His thick fingers were surprisingly nimble. They brushed her neck, and she squeezed her hands together.

'Keep it next to your skin,' Rocket said. 'It usually just protects you from bad luck if someone wants something of yours, compliments you too much, you know. But this one's different. If someone wishes you harm, it warms up. That's all.'

She nodded. 'Cool. Right.'

'Hey, if we can't stop you Changing, we can keep you safe, yeah?' Rocket gave her a soft stare, and Katy's heart clenched painfully.

Rocket had been her best friend since the junk sculpture experiment in primary school, when he'd added something to his spaceship that looked cool and old, which his uncle Ömer said belonged to a mischievous jinn. He'd ended up demonstrating supernatural jet propulsion the length of the playing field, coming to rest halfway up a tree. That was how he'd earned his nickname and learned there were things in the world that you should leave alone.

Katy, the serious, silent, creepy girl, had climbed up into the tree with him to keep him company while someone fetched a ladder. She'd offered him a strawberry bootlace while he clung grimly on to his branch like a plump kitten, praying, he'd told her later, harder than he'd prayed before in his life.

Today, apparently, they had graduated from sharing strawberry bootlaces to protective talismans.

She tucked it inside her own jumper, one she'd packed for London, silver and pastel pink threads gleaming under the spotlights.

This bore no traces of Ricky's rough handling, and she almost wished it did so she could show him evidence of what Ricky was, warn him with a visual aid.

'I might go back to The Crows,' Katy said.

Fairwood's windows and casements popped back into her mind as if it had caught her unease regarding its main occupant, and whispered,

...Don't mind him.

'I want to learn to control my List, and if I can trust him... maybe I can find out what his favour is, maybe I can use that as leverage if I need to. I don't know. I don't know what to do, honestly.'

'Look, I don't know what you guys... *are*... but, if you're going to turn into something, then maybe he's your shot at learning how to stop it.' Rocket studied her with a harder edge, and Katy was reminded that he'd seen things most seventeen-year-olds only had night terrors about. 'But whatever you do, you have to be *sure*. Some paths you can't walk back from.'

She traced a finger over the round bump the bead made, hidden behind the fabric. She didn't know how to tell him she was already too far along the path she was on.

'Um. Yeah. Thanks.'

'I just hope that actually works,' Rocket said.

Katy nodded. There were already loads of people who wanted to hurt her, and Changing was pretty much her only chance.

On cue, the amulet started to heat up, a warm patch of warning against her skin, and she scanned the room. It wasn't a family member – it was Alex's girlfriend.

Katy remembered shagging Alex at a house party, then later finding Jen wrapped around him snogging his face off. That was how she'd found out he wasn't as single as he'd claimed, but Jen seemed to think Katy had known all along.

The amulet burned.

'Yeah, it works great,' Katy said, glancing away.

—

Wes did *not* do the responsible thing, and drove down to Pagham-on-Sea instead of taking the train, muffled in a silk scarf and buoyed by Charlie's pep talk and Hugo's gentle, if conditional, forgiveness.

He needed to be more open: *yes*, he agreed, *I'll try*.

You can't protect everybody. *No, I know.*

You're hurting us, you're hurting yourself. Stop acting like you don't care, stop with the theatrics.

I will, Wes agreed, wrapped in Huey's arms on the sofa, Charlie overseeing in her unobtrusive way, Hugo getting emotional, Wes like stone.

I will. You come first. You always come first, even if I don't act like it… I'll do better, I promise, it's nothing, it's a crisis, it'll pass. I'll do better.

He texted his sister on the way down, steeling himself. This was it: after this, he'd cut ties with all of them. He couldn't balance the life he wanted with the life that clawed at his back, dragging him down to the seaside town where his past ought to be dead and buried.

He couldn't face Ricky, that was too complicated. No. Get Katy away from him, drive the wedge in hard, satisfy Uncle Marcus and then… leave. Go back to London. Sell the house in Pagham-on-Sea, cut ties, let the family forget him.

He put it out of his mind as far as he could, pretending to himself that it would be that easy, as if running from family was possible, as if they had contributed nothing to what was under his skin, nothing to what was in his head.

As if you could cut them out like a bruise in an apple.

As if he wasn't already turning into his silent father.

All he wanted was stability. An even keel. A bit of fucking *sanity*.

He bit his nails as he drove one-handed, speakers blaring out something angsty and aggressive.

The road to sanity was simple.

He could get rid of Cousin Ricky once and for all, somehow; it was Ricky he kept going back down to see, Ricky's farsight that had an addictive hold on him, and now he didn't need that anymore. The 'how' part was hazy, but he'd think of something.

Simple.

Providing, of course, that during the week, Katherine had figured out the damn List. The last Thirteenth hadn't managed it, had gone nuts and put *himself* on the bloody thing, and since then no one had figured out why or how it worked, not even Granny Wend.

Or maybe the old girl had after all, and just not told anyone.

That would have been her style.

So, yeah, of course it was likely that after a couple of weeks under Ricky's private tutelage, his seventeen-year-old sister would have worked it out. Not.

He bit one nail down to the quick, flinching at the stab of pain as it bled.

The M23 was a straightforward run today. It would only take him about two hours. He was already nearing Horsham. The journey was familiar, he must have done it a hundred times, but he nearly turned off by accident at a junction he'd never taken before, not even once, and he didn't know why.

Nice one Wesley, self-sabotaging fuck.

He kept driving, paying more attention to the signs.

How hard could that be, finding a bit of sanity? Making a clean break on his terms, getting a bit of respect for the invisible man?

Whose fault is it I'm like this anyway? Ricky's fucking fault, all Ricky's fucking fucked-up fault.

He gripped the wheel tighter, speeding up.

Yeah. All he had to do was get his cousin out of the picture, tell Uncle Barry he needed another batch of Silver Lining, and take drugs to tell the future. Then the clan would come to *him*, on *his* terms, and he'd have the best of both worlds. That was better. Then he wouldn't *have* to choose, and he could protect whoever he wanted.

Just like that.

'Piece of piss,' he muttered, trying to convince himself.

—

Arriving in town without mishap and by some miracle finding somewhere to park, Wes took a seat in a coffee shop near Pagham-on-Sea College.

He kept his forgettable face hidden behind his silk scarf screen, staring at the mock Forties posters and the rustic 'make-do-and-mend' chic, mainlining espresso until Katy showed up.

He greeted her with a wave of his phone as she finally came in. 'You're okay, then.'

She looked tired, but otherwise fine. So grown up. An adult, not the kid in pyjamas with the big, serious eyes he kept picturing. How had she changed this much so fast?

She might start killing them next year.

He offered her a chair, suddenly aware he was talking to someone on borrowed time. There'd be no going back for her after the Changes. She'd be something else, something new, and this person, full of her hopes and dreams and almost-human teenage doubts would be gone forever. He found himself focusing on her with renewed intensity, trying to fix this person in his mind before she blew away.

Katy didn't say anything. She hesitated before taking the chair, fiddling with something under her jumper, some necklace pendant.

All right. She was into pastels, skinny jeans, big silver earrings, sparkling hair clips. She still had cat badges on her shoulder bag, and he could see the corner of a ring-binder covered in pop punk band stickers poking out of one end. She was still his baby sister.

She took a breath, and Wes's stomach plummeted.

'Why didn't you come and get me?' she asked.

He didn't know what to say. He couldn't say, *because I don't want you*. If that was true, why was he here?

He shook his head. 'I meant to. I – I didn't know if I could. If...' He could see this wasn't working and he didn't know where he was going with it anyway. He gave up and changed tack. 'You can't trust Ricky, you know that, right? Why don't you come and stay at ours, here, Charlie will be coming down tomorrow.'

Wes watched her, her long face and wide Porter nose balanced out with those big, expressive brown eyes and framed by straightened brown hair. It was a long face, but without the hardness of Nicole and Kim, lacking Jade's bitterness and the twists of Lucy and Kirsty's sly, furtive mannerisms. He liked her best of all of them, and that made it worse.

Katy looked him in the eye. 'What are you really doing here?'

Wes frowned. 'I'm here for you.'

'Right. But you didn't come and get me when Ricky told you he'd snatched me. You weren't camping outside the gates, were you? What did he say?'

Wes rolled his eyes. 'Charlie had a thing, and I knew he wasn't going to hurt you, I came down as soon as I could.'

'*Charlie had a thing?*' Katy glared at him. 'I'm your *sister*.'

'You know I can't leave her without warning, it's not that...' He was aware he was raising his voice and took a breath. '...It's not that easy.' He adjusted his scarf over his nose, royal purple rippling as he sighed. 'I'm sorry I wasn't there for you. Ricky's a dick. I told you this before. He doesn't know how to give you anything unless it's transactional, you take what you need and you move on, don't let him in your head.'

Katy was hard to read. Her lips tightened slightly, but whether in agreement or disapproval he had no idea. He assumed the worst. Charlie would have had her laughing and relaxed by now, not accusatory and sullen.

He sat helpless, acutely aware they were on the brink of something that felt horribly like an ending.

Her glower hadn't improved. 'What d'you actually *want*, Wes?'

He shook his head. 'I don't want you getting hurt.'

But he did. A small part of him did. He imagined his scarf around her neck, his palm covering her nose and mouth. It wouldn't take long, and then it would be over.

Her hand flew to the bump of her necklace pendant under her jumper, and her eyes were wide and suddenly wet.

'You fucking liar.'

'Katy...'

'*Keep away from me.*'

'Katy...' *Shit...*

She shook her head, grabbing her bag and jumping up. Before he could follow, she was threading between tables and jogging out of the door and down the street, bumping pedestrians out of her way and picking up speed.

Shit.

He'd barely said anything to her.

Triple shit.

He couldn't even tell the truth properly. Boiling with frustration, he jabbed out an angry text – three bitter little words – and hit send.

> :Ricky killed Gran:

He looked at it blankly for a second. That was his cash-cow sent to the slaughter, then. His stomach churned. An unwelcome memory of camaraderie and something tender but short-lived bobbed to the surface, unwilling to be pushed away no matter how he tried.

Ricky was his fucking cousin. Gran had treated them all like shit, and he wasn't sorry she was gone, but Katy would be devastated and… where else did she have to go?

'Fuck!' He caught a few glares from the other cafe-goers for that, but screw them. Adjusting his collar, he made for the door and hoped he could catch her up.

Chapter 7: Brave New World

14 January

Uncle George was waiting on the corner as Katy left the cafe. Her bead burned.

She could tell it was Uncle George by the way his shape altered in her peripheral vision, from a lanky man in a dirty brown jumper to something with too many joints, twisting and extending in a state of flux.

He didn't do anything but watch, smoking a badly rolled cigarette.

Katy couldn't remember the last time Ricky's dad had been out of Bramble Cottage, let alone the last time she'd seen him in town. He flicked the smouldering dog-end away, head on one side.

Katy ducked her head and quickened her pace.

Had Wes set her up?

Fucking coward.

She still felt a twinge of guilt that she hadn't told him about... but maybe he'd guessed. She shook it off, pushing it to the back of her mind.

The hairs pricked up on the back of her neck, but she didn't turn around. A car was crawling along the road behind her, as if looking for a place to park. It sped up, and she stumbled further away from the kerb.

A glance told her it was her dad's car. She recognised the dents in the bonnet, the colour, the dirt on the front plate. The window juddered down.

'Katherine!'

She hated that bark, the way he spat out her name. It arrested her, drew her up sharply like a leash.

It took all she had to keep walking.

The car crept behind her.

'Get in the car.'

Katy swallowed, throat burning and tight, the familiar corset of nausea cinching her stomach and pulling her into herself. Her legs were shaking, but she could run. She could run if she had to.

Her muscles quivered, barely holding her weight, blancmange on sticks.

'*Katherine!*'

She sped up.

She heard the car stop, the door clunk open.

'*Kath-er-ine…*'

She bolted, lurching into a full sprint.

She got as far as the end of the street when another car pulled out around the corner and she nearly tipped into the side of it. The back door opened, and her sister Nicole slithered out, the Harvest Party Queen, short-cropped hair messy, bloodstains on her T-shirt. Katy wasn't sure what happened to the organs after Harvesting. Nicole did weirder shit than eat them.

Katy backed off. Nicole had always shown her dominance with violence, the worst of them for that, always twisting her arm – once until it snapped – until Katy did what she was told.

Nicole's lipstick was smeared across her chin, a comical smudge of purple. She looked like she hadn't slept for a week or changed her clothes. There was a stale smell from the inside of the car, a corrupt, sweet stench of decaying food and old, stale beer.

'Uncle Barry wants to unlock your potential,' her sister slurred, eyelids heavy, reaching for her.

This was a nightmare.

Wes *had* set her up, he must've done.

Katy jerked back and sprinted across the road without looking. The adrenaline rocketed through her, and she cannoned into Gordon Street, pounding up the uneven pavement.

She raced by the parked cars lining the road, and nearly ran into Uncle David, a meaty mountain in a fedora, as he stepped out of the doorway of the pet shop.

Wes turned a corner, hands in his pockets, lanky stride erased from her mind as soon as she blinked, and she nearly cannoned straight into him, forgetting he was there.

'I was looking for you—' Wes started, catching her by the arm, and Katy spat in his face to make him recoil.

'Get the fuck off me!'

She tore away from his hand, now convinced it was all his fault, and veered off between two cars into the road. She heard Wes yelling out a warning behind her, and a car braked sharply, feet away.

She vaulted the bonnet, dodged a motorbike coming in the opposite direction, made it across the road and plunged down another side street, but miscalculated. It was an alley between the houses and the chip shop, a high brick wall cutting her off from Bourne Road car park on the other side.

'*Fuck!*' She raked both hands over her head, tugging the hair bobble at the back.

'Kath-er-ine...' That was Liam, her brother, his dirty singsong punctuated by Nicole's chortle.

The bead was blistering her skin, but she didn't need it to know how much trouble she'd be in if they caught her. Backing up against the bricks, she tried to find her voice.

'Ricky says you can't touch me,' she said, and it sounded weak. They all wanted to prove how strong they were to keep themselves off the List, keep her too scared to imagine she could ever be stronger.

Well, point proven: soon the List would contain nobody, if she listened to Rocket. She'd have the moral high ground and be weak and scared and impotent forever.

And they'd just carry on.

She didn't want to think about the stains on Nicole's T-shirt. Or who their dad might have in his boot. Or what Uncle David did for a living. Or what Uncle George got up to in the woods. Or, come to that, what his god-like son collected, ate, ripped open.

'Ricky said you weren't allowed,' she repeated, as they got closer.

Kieran and Ashley were backing Liam up. Nicole was about a foot shorter than their brothers, gliding between them with loose, spaced-out movements, every so often treating Katy to a coy half-turn that revealed the millipede-movements of her spine under her clothes.

'*Ricky said...*' Nicole giggled.

'Little prick ain't havin' *my* eye,' Liam told her, blocking her way out. The Porter boys were all largely identical, but she could tell Liam from Kieran by his greater muscle mass, and Ashley was much taller. She wondered if Ashley was actually the same height as Wes but couldn't remember.

'Leave her alone!' Wes's voice sent a chill through her. He appeared, panting, but their siblings ignored him. 'What are you doing?'

'Uncle Marcus said you'd do a shit job,' Nicole said. 'We're the back-up.'

Katy backed up against the wall and tried not to throw up. She stared at Wes in horror and hatred, and he couldn't look at her.

'This is wrong,' Wes muttered, and to his credit he sounded sincere.

Liam laughed. 'Which way did you vote, again?'

Katy couldn't hear this. It was one thing to suspect, another to know. She stared at her older brother, the only one who'd made her life bearable, and felt the world dropping away.

'Wes?'

Wes was an impressionistic blur of colour, approaching slowly, filling her vision as he stepped between her and their family. 'I fucked that up.'

'But you voted.' Liam sounded hurt. 'You voted for *us*. You chose *us*. What are you doing?'

'I'm – I don't know.' Wes didn't move. 'I don't know, I think this is wrong.'

Katy's ears rang. She couldn't focus. Had he really voted against her? And then what – just changed his mind?

'Get out the way,' Nicole snapped. 'Uncle Marcus wants her to stay with Uncle Barry for a while. That's all. He thinks he can *help* you.'

For a second, Katy faltered. 'Can he?'

'You don't need that kind of help,' Wes told her, voice low. 'Trust me.'

She just wanted it to stop, for them to all go away.

'I... I don't want to go with you, leave me alone.'

'"*Leave me alone*",' Nicole mimicked, giggling. Her whole back parted into two wings of flesh rimmed with wriggling teeth then snapped back together. Nicole had always been Daddy's little angel.

Katy tensed, wondering what she could hit them with. There was nothing around she could use; in films, there were always mounds of rubbish and handy pieces of plywood, but this was Pagham-on-Sea where the council had semi-regular bin collections. Also, she wasn't a martial arts expert, or anything remotely fucking useful.

Wes was certainly none of those things, and to top it off, his Changes were as useless as he was.

A familiar gruff voice broke through her rising panic.

'Wotcher, Cuz.'

Katy flinched, breath stopped in her throat, scanning the top of the wall behind them.

Ricky was lounging on the top, dangling a track-suited leg over the side.

Katy breathed out, full of irritated relief.

'You all right? Anything I c'n help you with?' Ricky slipped to the edge of the wall and dropped, landing on his feet. He was barely as tall as Nicole. The three Porter brothers sniggered, but they were wary.

Ricky had taken them on once before, before his Changes, Katy recalled. Beaten the shit out of them.

She hoped he'd do it again.

'Uncle Barry sent an invite,' Nicole said, the sulky spokesperson. She looked their cousin up and down. 'That new?'

Ricky glanced down at his trademark grey attire. 'Yeah.'

Nicole nodded. 'Wanna see my tits? They're new too.'

'You're all right, darlin', thanks.'

Katy considered scaling the wall anyway, but now Ricky was this side of it, it seemed safer to stay where she was.

'You can suck Kieran's cock. He's a big fan.'

Kieran leered, and Katy rolled her eyes.

Nicole caught her, and her trout-pout morphed into a snarl. 'What's your problem, you little slag?'

'I want to go home,' Katy mumbled, getting as close to Ricky as she dared.

Wes hadn't moved, but it was hard to tell what he thought about the situation with that scarf obscuring what little of his features she could see.

Ricky cocked his head. 'What, with them? Sure?'

'No, I – I mean The Crows, Fairwood. I want to go back to… I want to go home with you.'

He smiled at her with almost childlike glee. It was disconcerting.

'Uncle George!' Nicole sang out, and Katy heard Ricky groan.

'No such luck it's George Shaw,' he mumbled, and Katy found herself clinging to the back of his hoodie.

'It's your dad.'

'Course it is.' For a second, Ricky looked genuinely worried. If she didn't know better, she might have interpreted the scowl as masking a pang of fear. But Ricky wasn't scared of anyone. It was there for a moment, then it was gone, and he got his swagger back.

Wes did move now – towards Ricky, as if standing between him and Uncle George was the only sensible place to be. Katy highly doubted this was the case.

She swallowed. 'Uncle David's around, and our dad…'

'So why are we talking to the monkeys, not the organ grinders?'

Wes snorted a laugh, but Katy couldn't see the funny side.

Her siblings jostled each other, but no one moved towards them.

'Let's go.' Wes kept himself positioned between the street and Ricky, who gave him a quizzical look.

'I don't know where you think *you're* going.'

'My car. I'll drive you over.'

Ricky sniffed, hawked and spat on the ground. 'If you like.'

'I don't think...' Katy started to say, doubt clenched in her gut, but Ricky shook his head and pointed at a cloud formation.

'See that?'

'What?'

'Travel omen.' He waved a hand. 'Comin' through, kids.'

'Do you just make this stuff up?' Katy asked, squinting at the sky.

Wes chortled. All of his confidence had returned, as if Ricky had invoked some powerful magic or an utterly dependable deity.

For a moment she didn't think it would work.

Big, stocky Ashley was the first to stand aside, although he was Uncle David's girth coupled with the Porter height: a fearsome combination, but one Ricky wouldn't think twice about challenging.

Ricky's smile was soft, blunt as a butter knife, and as he turned it on Katy to see if she was following it was almost warm at the edges.

Katy dropped her eyes to the ground and let him go first.

'Which one d'you want first?' he asked her, licking his lips.

She didn't answer. Didn't look at them.

'We ain't weak,' Liam sneered. 'Won't catch us on the bloody List. She wouldn't *dare*, would you, Sis?'

She almost shook her head, but Ricky caught her around the back of the neck in a tight, immobilising grip that nearly choked her. Her shoulders rose automatically, but he propelled her forwards, hot, wet breath against her ear.

'Name one of 'em, go on. That'll shit them up.' Louder he said, 'Who's on the List, then? Which one?'

'All of them,' Katy whispered, and Nicole stared at her. 'That's not *fair*!'

Ricky patted her shoulder and her skin crawled.

'I'm helping her fix it how *she* wants it,' he said. 'Not how Uncle Marcus wants it, nor the rest of the elders, it's up to *her*. *She's* our Thirteenth, an' that's how it should be.' He dropped his voice into a low, deliberate growl. 'If you lot defy me again, I'll accelerate the Changes for her, and she'll come after you tomorrow, the day after, or next bloody Tuesday if that's what you really want. Do you understand?'

They believe me, Katy realised, as her siblings backed off. *Maybe it's him they believe, but… they think I'm a threat. They're doubting themselves.*

That knowledge tingled through her, along with a sense of power she'd never felt before.

'Let her come with us, Richard,' Uncle David said in his pleasant bass, approaching with caution along the street. He was a craggy mountain of a man concealed in a trench coat, and he glided along the pavement soundlessly like a glacier. 'It's just an invitation.'

'Am I talking to my fucking self?'

Katy's stomach turned over, but she steeled herself.

Uncle David tipped his fedora, and his lumpy profile obscured by his scarf gave the impression he had more than one face. Katy had the oddest impression he was missing an eye, although the two in the usual place on his face were intact. 'C'mon Richard. You got better things to do than babysit a runaway, that's all.'

'*I* decide what I want to do. What's my old man doing here?' Ricky jerked his chin across the street. 'Out for a stroll, is he? That's not good for his health.'

Uncle David shrugged. 'He thinks he's getting better.'

'Well he can think a-fuckin'-gain,' Ricky snapped. 'What's he said to you?'

Uncle David shrugged. 'Not a big talker, your dad. He's just lookin' out for our Katy. No disrespect meant, Soothsayer.'

Katy shrank against her tense cousin despite herself, but he relaxed at Uncle David's oily politeness.

'It's up to her,' Ricky said, patting her back.

'I don't want Uncle Barry to "unlock my potential",' Katy said, deciding to voice her own opinion before anyone else chimed in. 'I'm going with Ricky.'

'There you are. Now, no offence, Uncle, cousins. But piss off.' Ricky tugged the edge of his hood in mock respect. 'I'll take her home.'

Katy took a step forwards, and Uncle David, to her immense surprise, took a step back.

That had never happened before, either.

Wes jingled his car keys in his pocket. For a moment, Katy had completely forgotten he was even there.

'If you lot push your luck, I'll suck your brains out your heads,' Ricky warned conversationally, still smiling.

'All right? I'll drain your auras, drink you up one memory at a time, and eat your husks with rice.'

'You're supposed to eat greens as well,' Katy said, keeping her face straight.

'That's the colour of Kieran's face, ain't it?' Ricky asked, and Katy snorted before she could stop herself.

'We're off.' Ricky finally let her go and patted her back. 'Let's go.'

They let them leave.

That was the craziest part, Katy thought, reflecting as they were nearly all the way across town, not talking to each other. They just... let them go.

Uncle George never even crossed the road. He stood, staring at his son from a distance, not giving Katy a second look.

Ricky had shot his father a look Katy couldn't read, and Uncle George did nothing. Uncle David, who could snap a man in half with his bare hands, did nothing. None of them did anything.

Getting to Wes's car was a blur. She and Ricky sat next to each other in the back, Ricky with his feet against the passenger seat in front, despite Wes telling him five times not to.

She glanced at Ricky, who ignored her.

It was like a mirror-image of her life, as if she'd been viewing everything in a fairground mirror up to now. She'd let them show her a distortion, kept *her* afraid of *them*, when *they* were the ones who should be scared of *her*.

Ricky was probably the only one who wanted her to see herself clearly. That was a weird thought.

'Thanks,' she said, eventually, as they turned off onto Redditch Lane, leaving the town behind in a straggle of houses.

'No worries,' Wes muttered.

Katy ignored him, looking at their cousin instead.

Ricky grunted. 'Said I'd keep an eye on you.' He sniggered, as if he'd made a private joke. 'They were pushing their luck is all.'

'You knew that was going to happen.' Katy watched the grin slice across his face and wrinkled her nose, hazarding a guess. 'Did you see it because… Uncle David was there? You got one of his eyes, didn't you?'

'Ain't you sharp.'

'What d'you think they meant? About Uncle Barry?'

'Drugs, prob'ly. Who knows? Haven't got one of *his* eyes.'

She glanced at him. 'Can you…' she hesitated, '…read your *own* future?'

He didn't reply for a moment, hands in his pockets, interested in the fields and barren hedgerow whipping by. 'Yes and no.'

'Yes and no? You can and you can't? What's that mean?'

He sighed, winding the window all the way down. A puff of cold breath misted in the blast of freezing air. 'Means, yes, I can see my own future. Under the right circumstances, astronomically speaking.'

'What, when the moon's in Virgo?'

He gave her a smirk. 'That's astr*ology*. I mean, like, eclipses, planetary alignments, not the horoscope crap.'

Katy flipped her ponytail out of the collar of her coat and huddled in the seat. 'It's not all crap. The *Gazette*'s horoscope page is *always* right.'

'Also weirdly specific,' Wes commented from the front.

Katy shivered. 'Can you... shut the window? It's *January*.'

Wes pressed a button and closed Ricky's window.

Ricky opened it again. 'Give over. I don't like cars.'

'One too many joyrides,' Wes muttered.

Katy rolled her eyes. 'Can you see your own future or not?'

'Fuck me, it's like being with the mistress. Yes, I can, six months ahead and that's it. Needs the right time, the right sacrifice, bit of a show. Then yes, I can see my own future.'

'What sort of sacrifice?'

'Someone young.'

Katy shivered. 'Like, a virgin, or...?'

'Nah. Don't matter. Just young.'

'How young?'

He reflected. 'Anything from twenty down works the same, twenty up and it gets hazier. Not sure why, honestly. Our illustrious ancestor, the last soothsayer, he tried kids and a baby once, but his notes don't make it sound worth repeatin'. Too bloody small.'

Katy hugged herself, nausea returning. She darted a look at Wes but forgot his expression immediately. She was left with the vague idea she was not alone in her disgust, although she couldn't pinpoint why. 'So... you don't know if you survive the family cull or not.'

'I bleedin' well better, Kath-er-ine,' Ricky growled, rolling every syllable of her name around his mouth on purpose, mimicking her dad, but there was a faint trace of amusement in the corner of his eye. 'I been bloody good to you.'

Katy wrapped her coat tighter around her, and wished Wes would say something, wished they could go back to when he babysat her and let her watch whatever she wanted and took her to the park, and told her it was all right to be special, and all right to not want to be.

What if she ended up like him, a pawn of the family, tossed around between them and drowning in raves and pills and friends who shagged her then never called her back? She resisted the urge to check her phone. Alex wasn't ever going to call. She was running out of time to tell Rocket she liked him.

What a time to think about that.

'What favour did you want?' she asked Ricky abruptly, remembering. 'If I go to Uni and do what I want to do... what did you want? For your... blessing.' It sounded wrong in her mouth. She bit down on the sneer.

Ricky blinked, looking down at his lap. 'Oh. Nothing, just... I wanted to read your books, that's all. When you were done wi' them.'

Katy was sure she'd misheard. She'd expected something far more dramatic. Wasn't he supposed to demand her body parts or something? At the very least?

'My... books? My textbooks?'

'That would be all right, would it?' Ricky chanced a glance at her.

'Uh. Yeah.' She was sure this was a trap. It couldn't be that basic. 'You... sure there's nothing else?'

'Not that I can think of.'

'Can I drop you here?' Wes asked, pulling into the side of the road by the gates of Fairwood House. 'I doubt I can... just drive in.'

For a moment, Katy had forgotten Wes was driving. Fairwood House was out of bounds to her kin, and while it had made an exception for her and Ricky, she wasn't sure why, or how an exception could be made.

Ricky scowled.

'Just a minute.'

He got out and opened the wrought-iron gates wide, but paused to have a conversation with them that neither Katy nor Wes could hear. It looked both one-sided and heated.

'Is he still talking to that house?' Wes asked, a hint of worry in the tone of casual amusement. 'I haven't seen him do that since the last time we got high.'

Katy frowned. 'You used to get high together?'

'Once or twice.' Wes shrugged. 'He always liked it in the woods there, and we'd...' He trailed off as Ricky returned, flushed and scowling. 'Well?'

'Drive in.' Ricky got back in the car and thumped his foot against the passenger seat.

'You're such a child.' Wes put the car in gear and pulled slowly off, checking his mirrors. 'You're cleaning my car.'

Ricky's lips twisted in a bitter sneer, but he didn't say anything. He didn't move his foot.

'She says she remembers meeting you.'

'Who?' Wes made it carefully through the gates and they drove up the gravel drive. 'Carrie?'

'Yeah.'

Katy frowned. 'When did you meet her?'

'At the pub once.' Wes parked up, staring at the façade of Fairwood. 'Where I meet everyone.'

Katy snorted in spite of herself, but Ricky was already out of the door. He didn't even shut it behind him.

'He's a prick,' she said, unbuckling her seat belt and climbing out the same side, giving the door a careful push.

Wes took his time, staring at the house. 'Yeah.' He cleared his throat. 'This is... do you feel it? That... there's something up with this place.'

Katy nodded, but only slightly, as if afraid the house would see.

That's silly, she chided herself. She didn't raise her voice though. 'Um. I know what you mean. Yeah.'

'Everything he touches gets twisted,' Wes said, and slammed his door shut. 'Though this place never liked us much to start with.'

Katy didn't know what to say to that. Had she been living with Ricky long enough to be tainted, too? Was that what he thought? She tossed her ponytail and swallowed.

'Coming in?'

Wes nodded reluctantly, as if he couldn't say no.

The windows watched them, blank and yet... somehow curious, as if it wanted to see what would happen next.

Katy hurried after Ricky into the porch where the front door stood ajar, and only then did it occur to her that if the windows were eyes, then she was entering the welcoming mouth. She closed her eyes as she entered, feeling it gulp her down, scrapbook her between its bricks and joists, rifle through her thoughts and stir up her memories.

Katy's Memory: Her Eleventh Birthday

Very few family members attended Katy's birthdays. Gran said she could invite some friends from school instead if she wanted, but no boys, not at her age. Since she couldn't invite Ruslan the Rocketman, Katy only wanted Rachel to come, and Rachel's father wouldn't let her.

Her mum had done a buffet this year.

Her siblings weren't around, not even Wes. He was in London for the weekend, couldn't get away. He'd called her though, asked about school and her presents, and taken an interest in her gymnastics competition.

She knew the others didn't like spending time with her because she was dangerous, but until recently she thought it was like chicken pox, like everyone was afraid of catching something.

This year, Gran had sat her down and explained it was the other way around: they were afraid of being caught up in her nightmares, and only the ones who came weren't afraid. The ones who showed her their strength knew that she was special.

She was the family's big bright hope, Gran's little butterfly, she would make the family strong again, prune it back like Gran pruned the bushes in the garden. It was a big task.

Katy thought Gran was trying to make her feel better. It sounded too much like stories grownups tell you to make you do things, something that wasn't real.

But if I'm their hope, why won't they talk to me? Katy asked. *Why don't I have friends?*

That's because you'll have to prune the ones who need to go even if you like them, Gran told her. *I like this little branch, look! Every blossom is so pretty, isn't it? Pretty as all the others, but it's going in the wrong direction, and it needs to go.*

Snip! The secateurs clicked together, and the branch fell to the soil. Katy observed the blades, sticky with sap, the fresh green underneath the bush's new wound.

Just like that, said Gran, and she smiled.

Does it hurt? Katy wanted to know.

Not for long, said Gran. *Here, you try. Snip! Snip!* And Katy trimmed the buddleia with some difficulty, the tougher branches resisting her, as if they didn't want to be pruned at all.

Like them, Gran said. *There's them as'll fight you, some of them, but there's no resisting it, no fighting the Thirteenth. Snip! Snip! Snip! Chop them off. That's it. That's my liddle princess.*

That had been earlier in the year, of course, when it was not as hot, on another weekend far away.

Mum found something to fill every available second, anything to avoid being in Gran's way.

Katy wanted a cuddle, but she was eleven now, another year into double figures, nearly a teenager, and would be going to the Comprehensive in September. She hugged herself instead as everyone set up the buffet and commented on her pretty pink dress, didn't she look sweet.

Unfold your arms, let's see the sparkles.

Katy thought she ought to be allowed to hug herself on her own birthday, but she did as she was told, and everyone cooed at her as if she was seven.

It was almost a relief when Cousin Ricky showed up, much to the anger of her father and the disgust of Aunty Tess.

Sober as a judge, he announced to them all, hands raised. *Swear to Grandad, look at my eyes. 'Allo Aunty Tess, smug as ever. Mum sends her love, ain't feeling well. Where's the birthday girl, then?*

Katy gave herself another reassuring hug and he leaned behind her, squeezing her into the back of the chair. He'd ruined all of her birthdays so far apart from last year, when he hadn't been allowed in the house at all. He had dropped off his parents' gift, smoked in the garden for a bit, called her dad a bad word and left.

He'd never hugged her before. He did it like he didn't want to touch her, or he wasn't sure how to do it.

He smelled stale and sour, unwashed.

It was brief – he hugged the chair more than her, but the sensation of clumsy pressure stayed with her as he let her go and dropped something on the table beside her.

Didn't have a card, Ricky said matter-of-factly. *The old woman's not so organised these days, wrapping ain't her strong suit no more. Anyway, thought you could just get what you wanted. Better'n being told what you want, right?*

It was one hundred pounds in used ten-pound notes, grubby, smelling of smoke.

Thank you!

She'd never seen that much cash in one place, wouldn't be allowed to have it. Mum needed it. It was so unexpected, so generous, it blew away all the bad memories for a moment.

Won 'em, Ricky said, squatting by her seat. *Birthday money. Don't let 'em see it, they'll say it's too much for a kid. Take it to wherever your liddle friend's taking you.*

Katy nodded. *Disneyland*, she whispered, and slipped it under the table in her fist. *Rachel's uncle is taking us* with his boyfriend *but don't tell Dad.*

Ricky cocked an eyebrow, failing to hide a sneer.

What's your dad got against Disneyland? It's that talking black rat, ain't it?

Mouse, she corrected, giggling.

He let her laugh, checked no one was listening, and whispered in her ear.

Now, listen: don't give that to anyone else. If they're hard up they can swallow their pride an' ask me, now, can't they? That's for you. D'you understand? Our secret. Happy birthday.

She giggled. Maybe it would be better this year. She scurried upstairs and hid the money in her sock drawer, their exciting little secret, her hidden treasure.

Of course, he had a beer in his hand by the time she came back, and that was that. He ignored her for the next hour, hanging around making snide comments and seeing how far the grownups could be pushed.

Something deep inside her stirred. Something inside that hollow feeling, as if her whole body was some kind of egg.

Katy sat obediently at the table answering questions about what she wanted to do when she grew up, while the adults dissected her dreams and showed her how silly they all were, and gave helpful suggestions about other, better ways to spend her lifetime.

Then her dad called Ricky something she didn't really understand, the kind of word she'd get a smack for repeating. Ricky's head opened up at the back and vomited tendrils and slug-slime, and her father snapped with his big second jaws regurgitated from the back of his throat, and Ricky called her father something bad back and hammered him.

Then her mother was screaming, her father was on the floor with Cousin Ricky laying into him, Aunty Tess was yelling, someone else was in tears, and Gran was sitting in the garden and not saying anything at all.

When Ricky finally stopped beating her dad, leaving him curled up in the hall bleeding into the carpet, he turned his head to Katy, smiled at her, and walked out.

Two days later, Mum discovered the birthday money, screamed about it for hours, and confiscated it all. Katy was told Ricky Porter was a thief and a Bad Influence, that Ricky had given her this money to taunt her parents with, throw it in their faces, make them upset.

And then she'd cried and said how much she wanted to go to Disneyland with Rachel and her Uncles Richard and Jerry, it just slipped out, and her father had gone apoplectic and said no kid of his was going anywhere with a couple of – something else she didn't quite understand until later – and that was the end of it.

Katy cried for days afterwards, left with the obscure feeling it was Cousin Ricky's fault and he really had given her that money on purpose to make her parents angry with her.

You ought to put him on the List, her mother said, after Rachel reluctantly went off to Paris without her.

It was the first time she'd mentioned the List or acknowledged that such a thing existed. Gran was the only one who talked about it, and Katy had thought Gran was the only one who knew.

Katy tried and tried to do it, just to please her mum, but it didn't work. When she dreamed of Cousin Ricky, which she did for a few months afterwards, and then again a few years later as a younger teen if truth be told, her dreams were about that awkward hug and the fight with her dad. In some of the dreams she *was* him, and in others she was mutely egging him on where no one could hear her, watching as he kicked her dad's head in right there in the hall, and turned back and grinned.

She couldn't dream about the Beast. The Beast wouldn't hunt him down.

Despite her failure, Katy became aware of something else, something that remained the same ever since that awful birthday: the sense that she was incubating something inside her, something which, over time, was growing and filling her up. Something that fused itself slowly to her skin from the inside. Something she loved and feared at the same time, that had no name, that was, always, both something Other, while also as much a part of her as her bone marrow.

It lived within, waiting to hatch.

One day, she'd become Gran's little butterfly.

And Katy was afraid.

Chapter 8: The Invisible Man

14 January

Fairwood House, who wore its nickname proudly and with fondness but still thought the formal one suited it best, swallowed its reluctant guests.

They were propelled from the foyer as the door closed on them and drawn along the corridor to the right of the grand staircase, where they settled in the kitchen. The mixed stones of the eighteenth-century kitchen extension grew hot with excitement.

Three again, three at last!

And yet, the blood magic was still strong, still determinedly reminding the rest of the house what atrocities the Pendles committed, why no Pendle-blood should set foot there.

The hearthstone throbbed beneath the range, conflicted.

One of the old Pendles, way back when the first initials and signs were carved into the hearthstone's surface, had instilled in it a love for triads. Three 'P's for Pendle, chiselled shakily in the rock. The year, 1633. And Pendle children usually came in threes, one after the other, or as triplets. There had been three sets of triplets born over six generations. Only-children were rare in that family: the last one had been born in 1879.

Ricky Porter was the most recent Pendle-blood to be an only-child, and now he had woken up his ancestral stone and the energies that coursed through it, it needed two more to join him. It could tell he didn't like that.

Fairwood as a whole wished it wasn't these particular two, but it still wanted – no, needed – to bring them inside itself.

The house felt both its new guests as they entered with its lodger, but one left no impression other than a shifting sense of loss and absence, as if he were a hollow ghost, the fleeting wisps of a dream, dying to memory over and over.

Wesley Porter.

He crossed the floors spilling seeds of something that tasted like psychosis, a bitter edge that lingered and sunk deep into the grouting like black mould. It felt like the residue Ricky had tracked in once from the long barrow out in Barrow Field, but that could be brushed up and cleaned off. This was insidious, alive.

It itched, the invisible man an irritant burying himself deep into the substance of the house. It regretted letting him in.

It condensed its various personalities into the plaster-and-mortar shape of its avatar, a humanoid embodiment of The Crows in all stages of its history, but allowed the preserved personality of Carrie Rickard, its last doomed owner, to take the lead.

Carrie-Fairwood pushed through the oak panelling in the hall, a dense, solid wood statue. She let pale plaster smooth over the grain, letting fabric clothes part from the fake skin, and ran her stiff cold fingers through a ponytail of insulation-foam yellow. She waited a moment until the reflection in the glass front of the grandfather clock showed her something more human than mannequin, although it wasn't quite right. It was close enough, though.

She tried out a welcoming smile, and breezed into the kitchen, the warm, beating heart and stomach of the house. It was strange to recall a time when her heart and stomach were in different places.

She forgot to touch the radio and turned it on as she walked in, making her guests jump. The invisible man was no better while she was in this form – he shifted too fast to capture the essence of him, and Carrie-Fairwood remembered a time when Carrie had been alive, meeting him at a pub in town. He had played tricks on her mind, and there was only a gap in her memories where he ought to have been.

He might as well have no face. It was a screaming blur of rapid movement to Carrie-Fairwood's windowpane eyes, as if he were made up of flat layers each moving at a different speed. His clothes remained still, and were the only things she could concentrate on.

The itch he left within her burned like a cigarette scorch on treated mahogany.

'Hello!' The word stuck, but the rest didn't. Timbre, pitch, tone – none of that worked, somehow, like his whole voice was a thousand tuning forks all vibrating at different levels. 'We met at the Snake, I don't know if you remember.' He laughed. She couldn't remember how it sounded, but it left an impression of a bitter edge.

'Of course I do.' Carrie-Fairwood held out her hand. That pub trip was, quite literally, a lifetime ago. 'You're Wesley Porter, right? Ricky's cousin.'

'Wes, please.' He took her hand and kissed the back of it. His fingers and lips sent electric shocks through the avatar's wiring, and the kitchen lights flickered in distress. Carrie-Fairwood pulled her hand away.

'Great to see you again.'

Katy glanced warily up at the lights, then turned her attention to the avatar. 'Uh. I'm... I'm Katy, I'm... I've kind of been staying here...' She glanced at Ricky who was getting a casserole out of the oven as if introductions were someone else's problem. 'We had some issues in town with my... with our family and I wondered if it would be okay for me to just stay a bit longer?'

'You better not have brought the wrath of that bloody lot down on me,' the avatar warned, shooting a glare at Ricky.

Her lodger looked affronted. 'They wouldn't come here.'

'If I get a broken window I swear to God I'll make you pay for it.'

Ricky's tendrils flicked out of the back of his head. 'I'll sort it,' he promised. 'Let's – let's just sit down and have dinner, yeah?'

'I should...' Wes shifted, embedding his spores into fresh tiles, and Carrie-Fairwood grated enamel teeth, needing him to sit the fuck down and touch nothing.

...Make him sit, he's doing my head in.

Ricky barely blinked, but she knew he understood.

'Sit down,' he said, shoulder-checking his cousin and pushing him into a chair.

Katy sat first, hunching her shoulders and compressing herself into the seat as if to take up as little space as possible, toying with the fraying ends of her sleeves. It was easy to get inside *her* head.

Carrie-Fairwood avoided it, though. It was a dark place for a kid. Things squirmed around in there, the usual morass of doubt and fear and self-loathing, the hatred for her family, resentment and anguish and the deep desire to belong anyway, but underneath all that... there was something else. Like Ricky, hiding his real form below the surface of his skin, there was more to Katy Porter, and it wasn't even nearly human.

The house didn't like touching that. It sensed the damage something like that could do, once it was ready.

Wes was harder. Each time the house found cracks between the shifting layers, deep enough to seep through several at a time, another layer beneath would shift its pattern and knock its seeking consciousness away like a bothersome fly. Wes seemed unaware he was doing it, but he did keep rubbing his forehead as if he knew *something* was bothering him.

On the next attempt, Carrie's consciousness took over and focused on the things she remembered about Wes when she'd been alive. This invasive push found a chink in the shifting armour, and the house was rewarded with a sense of who Wesley Porter was. Its questing sentience struck something fetid and painful, surrounded by swarms of thoughts buzzing like house flies.

The avatar withdrew its concentration.

Ricky caught her eye and flashed a wry grin, as if he'd guessed what was bothering her.

(Leave 'em to me, they ain't that easy. You forget what we're like, haven't any but me been here for sixty years or more.)

Ricky channelled his thought into her floor as he tossed cutlery at his cousins.

'Aren't you eating?' Katy asked the avatar, noticing there were only three sets, and three plates.

'No. I've eaten.' She smiled, a painted, warm smile that her friends said made her look less uncanny.

'You don't work at the supermarket anymore,' Katy said, still picking at her sleeve. 'How come?'

Carrie-Fairwood flashed her lodger a look. 'Won the lottery.'

'O-h.' Katy looked at Ricky and nodded.

Wes snorted. 'Was it worth it?'

'Was what worth it?'

He waved a hand, and it hurt her eyes in the way pebbles did when they cascaded against her glass. 'I don't want to... overstep. Just... you don't look well.' He put his head on one side. 'I'd say you look dead, but that's not it either.'

Ricky slopped casserole on his cousin's plate. 'She's fine.'

'She's not fine.' Wes picked up his fork and prodded the meal. 'And I'm vegan.'

'Yeah, there's vegetables in it.' Ricky served Katy with a little more care and took the rest of the dish to his seat.

Wes put his fork down. 'I don't want to be a bother, I can just...'

'There's nut roast in the fridge.' Carrie-Fairwood went to get it, feeling Wes's smudged vortices of eyes drilling into the back of her. The sensation was physical, twin blunt power tools rotating between her shoulder blades. They dragged themselves downwards leaving a dull ache behind, until he was staring at her arse.

She turned around, nut roast in hand, and tried not to look at him. 'The green beans have flaked almonds with them, but no butter.' She shot a look at Ricky. 'He's practically vegan except for the raw meat.'

'' 'S more paleo,' Ricky said with his mouthful. He hadn't bothered with a plate and was digging into the casserole dish with the serving spoon.

'You'll have to excuse him,' Carrie-Fairwood said dryly, 'he's still getting used to food with actual flavour.'

The angle of the knife in Wes's hand gave her pause. She focused on it instead of on him, dredging up memories of 1786 and the night Sir John found out his wife had been too friendly with Sir Archibald Truss, and of 1643 when the steward had a lover's tiff with the cellarer. Both incidents had ended badly, and both had begun with someone holding a knife exactly like that.

Then again, Ricky Porter was notoriously hard to kill. Even before his Changes, he had survived overdoses and hypothermia, had walked away from car crashes and falls, and had got up the next morning to do it all again. She doubted a blunt bit of stainless steel was going to do him much damage. But that wasn't the point.

'You can stay,' she said to Katy, taking a seat. She nodded at Wes. 'You can't. Not for long, at any rate.'

Long enough to scratch the itch of having a three around the Pendle Stone, but no more. In Carrie's memory, Wes had seemed flirty, cocky with overtones of pervert, but she'd… kind of liked him. She'd also been pretty drunk, so now was a better opportunity to observe him and make her mind up.

Wes shrugged, and the knife shifted position. 'Fine by me. Appreciate the dinner. Very kind of you, thanks.'

The three of them ate their meal, and Carrie-Fairwood guarded the table in stiff, tense silence.

Katy finished her meal as fast as she could, cleared her own plate away and tip-toed into the living room to watch TV. The living room was a blessed relief after the heavy atmosphere in the kitchen, with Ricky and Wes glowering at each other (at least, she remembered Ricky glowering, and assumed Wes had been doing the same).

The owner, Carrie, was all wrong. It was like someone had brought a shop dummy to life, and it was trying to fix the fact it wasn't quite human. She shuddered and hugged a plump cushion into her chest.

Oh my God.

The way Ricky talked to the walls.

The way the house always felt like it was watching.

Something was wrong, weirdly, creepily wrong, in ways she couldn't quite put together. What had Ricky *done?* She was sure that, somehow, it was his fault. Rachel had worked with Carrie Rickard at SupaPrice for a while, and she had definitely been a living, breathing woman then.

That thought brought Katy up short, a thrill chasing up her spine despite the reassuring adverts on the screen.

Whoever that stiff, statue person was in the kitchen, *they weren't breathing.*

Only now did she check her phone. She had to tell Rachel about this.

As the dating show started, theme music blaring, she saw Wes had called her several times after she'd left the cafe and sent her a text.

The casserole weighed heavily in her stomach.

He'd sent her three words.

She stared at them, trembling, and for a moment they didn't make sense.

:Ricky killed Gran:

Katy's breath caught.

She read it again.

No.

That couldn't be right.

Gran had been killed by something powerful enough to rip her apart, splatter her over the ceiling, rip her head off and suck out her eyes. She had convinced herself Uncle Marcus was responsible, or the elders en masse. She'd suspected Ricky a *bit*. But he was a cocky twat, he got high and punched people, he might be a god or something now but…

But…

Her eyes. I'm a fucking idiot. He's seen everything she's seen. He knows every conversation we ever had.

The room closed in on her, as if it could sense her sudden surge of emotion. The ceiling creaked.

'You okay?' The voice came from beside her, but no one had entered the room.

Katy flung herself out of the chair, adrenaline spiking.

Carrie stood there, uncannily smooth features carved in a slight frown.

'You didn't use the door,' Katy said, a chill rushing through her. She shook her head, eyes watering. 'You… you didn't use the door.'

Carrie glanced at the door and shrugged. 'It is *my* door, you know. I can use it or not, as I please.'

Katy raked her nails down her sleeves. 'What's wrong with you?' It came out as a wide-eyed whisper, and she realised with another queasy lurch that this was rude. 'I – I mean… I mean, what… what *happened* to you?'

Carrie looked down at herself and smiled. 'That would take a long time to explain.'

Katy darted a glance at the door again. Ricky was framed in it, casually resting his arms against either side of the door jamb, blocking her escape. His tendrils twisted like thick ropes around his shaven head.

'Where's my brother?'

'In the garden, having a smoke.'

Katy shook her head. 'He quit.'

'He ain't much good at sticking to something.' Ricky dropped his arms to his sides. 'Wes said he might have told you something. About me.'

Katy shook her head, but all she could see were flashes of gore, the ruins of Gran's living room, the mess of shattered bone, the sightless head lying at her feet with half the brain gone.

She nearly threw up on the carpet.

Ricky nodded. 'So he did, then.'

'Why didn't...' Katy croaked, coughed, and swallowed hard. Her throat ached and burned with the stomach acid. 'Why didn't anyone do something?'

'To me? Why didn't anyone stand up to the person who could rip our matriarch to tatters?' Ricky stared at her. 'Is – is that really what you're askin'?'

'I'm not afraid of you.' It wasn't even a lie. All Katy felt was a deep, blinding hate.

Ricky nodded as if this wasn't a surprise. 'I see that, yeah.'

'I'm going to kill you.'

Ricky grinned.

Katy balled her fists up tight, shaking. 'I'm. I'm going to put you on the List. I swear to Grandad, I'll make the Beast...'

He growled at her, cutting her off. '*Fuck's* sake, *no!* No! You were doing so well, wa'n't she?' This was directed at Carrie, who was scowling at him but motionless. '*No*, Katherine. Come on. This has gone on long enough, get your fucking act together.'

Katy stared at him, stunned. 'My what? What the fuck?'

He marched into the room, grabbed the poker from the fireplace and tossed it at her. She nearly didn't catch it, fumbling the cold brass and barely missed impaling her foot on the spiked end.

Ricky rounded on her, finger jabbing accusingly at her face. 'You never stood up to no one, not ever. They all acted like they was too strong to be on your List and you've never figured out how it works because you got all this bullshit up here.' He tapped his temple, brown eyes flaring a deep ruby red. 'Gran calling you her little butterfly, did that never get through to you? You ain't Changing into something you're *not*, Katherine, you're Changing into something *you already are*.' He flung his arms open wide. 'So come on, killer. Come on. You want to have a go, come and have a go. No Beast, no List. Just you and me.'

The poker's heft felt pretty good in her hands this time. Katy didn't even know she'd swung it over her shoulder until she realised Carrie was growing, somehow, looming between them, and Ricky was laughing. It was the ugly, mirthless laugh she'd heard as a kid, and hated. He'd laughed like that one Yule, right before he smashed her brother Kieran's face in for making some sarcastic remark.

Everything in her was on fire.

'Come on,' he said, and she closed the gap without thinking. When she realised she was in swinging distance, doubt came flooding back. She glanced at Carrie, or whatever it was that called itself Carrie, and swallowed.

Carrie's face was unreadable. Only her glassy eyes moved, flicking to Ricky and glinting grey. 'Not on the carpet,' she said.

Ricky grinned. 'Yeah, we'll take it outside. Get our Wesley involved.' He shot Katy a dirty look. 'He voted for the elders to kill you, so I dunno what he's on his high horse about.'

Katy shuddered, tightening her grip. Anger blazed through her and burst in her brain like fireworks, every fibre of her on fire. She couldn't stop shaking.

'Outside.' Ricky marched to the door. 'You, me, an' Wesley. Let's get this all over with, and then maybe you'll finally let me *help* you.'

Katy followed him through the house and out of the back door, tension building to fever pitch in her veins. She barely registered the cold air as it hit her, the poker searing into her palms. She was going to smash the bastard's face in.

Wes was enjoying an illicit cigarette. He stubbed it out on the kitchen wall and nearly choked on the smoke as soon as she appeared.

She tightened her grip, fury unquenchable.

'Don't tell Charlie,' he started to say, and Katy swung the poker and caught him right in the ribs.

'You fucking *liar*!'

Her brother crumpled with a surprised grunt, but the hit didn't feel right. It wasn't as satisfying as she'd expected. She whacked it down again and again over his back, and the meaty thud reverberated through her hands and was instantly forgotten. 'You – said – you – quit!'

'*Jee*-sus!' Wes coughed, flat on the grass, and Ricky sniggered.

Katy spun around to face him, quivering, blood surging with manic power.

Ricky leered at her brother, that smug grin making her sick. 'Reminded her about the vote. In case you were wond'rin'.'

'Prick!'

Katy turned back to Wes.

He spat into the soil, struggling to get up.

'What did you bring that up that for?'

He got to his hands and knees, and Katy caught him across the backs of his thighs, sending him sprawling and howling. '*Jee-sus fucking Christ!*'

Ricky's giggle was higher pitched than it should have been, childlike and odd. He giggled like his mum, and Aunt Lettie had always creeped Katy out. She swallowed hard. The bead was burning against her chest, but she hadn't registered that until now.

'*You set me up!*' She didn't recognise her own voice. Her shriek tore her throat and rang in the air, and it felt good. Hitting him again felt better. 'How did they know where I was? *How did they know*, Wes?'

She relished the vibrations until she forgot them, and Wes rolled away from her, wheezing and spitting blood.

'You – they – fuck, I *didn't*, I swear! They must've been… watching the college… foll-foll-owed you…'

'You were going to give me to Uncle Barry, weren't you?'

She raised the poker again, but Ricky stepped in and tugged it out of her grip.

Wes coughed and heaved denials out of his lying mouth and she hated him, hated both of them, and she didn't need to be the Beast to tear them apart.

'I swear, I s-swear,' Wes was mumbling, and Ricky jabbed her with the pointy end of the poker to get her attention. She rounded on him, trying to snatch it back.

'Give over, let him be.' Ricky cocked his head as Katy lunged at him, and stepped lightly out of her way. Katy missed, stumbling on the uneven ground, and whirled around to try again.

'Oi! That's enough. He's a prick, he deserves it, but he's had enough. Take me on now.'

Katy snatched at her weapon and he let her grab it – but not for long. With a twist and a sneer, he wrenched it out of her hand again, side-stepping around Wes still spluttering on the ground. Katy gave her brother a good solid kick as she passed, winding him again.

Ricky shoved her away with his free hand. 'Oi! I said enough.'

'He wants me dead!' Tears pricked her vision, threatening to fall. She fought them, but the words were out. All those years of being her main ally, her only friend, the dolls' tea parties he'd endured, the cartoons they'd watched, telling her she could come and live with him when she was older... All lies, all of it worthless, all of it.

'*How could you?*' She choked on the thought of him raising his hand, numbering himself among those who wanted to get rid of her before she got rid of them.

Wes shook his head, finally able to kneel up. 'How – how *could* I? How – do, do you know what it's like, knowing...' He caught his breath and tried again. 'Look, I'm s-sorry.' He coughed up another gob of blood, and Ricky rolled his eyes.

'Stop being a drama queen, she never hit you that hard.'

'Fu-fuck you.'

Ricky snorted. To Katy, he said, 'He don't want to die, that's all.'

Katy trembled, her tears winning their ongoing battle. She swallowed a sob, balling her hands into fists. How could she blame him, really? She couldn't. She *liked* Charlie. And Hugo. What would happen if Wes died, and Charlie couldn't see his face anymore?

She sniffed, wrapping her arms tightly around herself. 'He led them to me,' she insisted, but she didn't really believe it anymore. She didn't know what she believed. Everything was slipping away from her, the future an uncertain destination the other side of a fraying rope bridge, and she was swaying helplessly out in the middle of it above a hungry abyss.

Ricky's lips twisted. 'Uncle Marcus told him where to meet you. Then he told *them*, in case Wes fucked up. And Wes fucked up.' He offered her the poker, properly this time. 'An' it's technically all my fault, because if I hadn't killed the old bat, Uncle Marcus wouldn't be Head of the Fam'ly and none of this would have happened. But I did. So. Come and have a go at me. My turn.'

Katy eyed him suspiciously, dashing her tears away.

He waved the poker.

She grabbed it and he let go, stepping back.

'Don't bother,' Wes muttered, staggering upright but keeping well out of range. 'He's worse than a cockroach.'

'How do you know what Uncle Marcus said?' Katy asked, cutting across her brother.

Ricky grinned, and winked.

She groaned. 'You ate his eye too, didn't you?'

Once again, his giggle creeped her out.

'So... you could have stopped them?' The rage was returning. 'You could have just... You *knew*, and you still let them chase me?'

Ricky shrugged. 'Tell you what, you stick that thing in my skull and if I survive, I'm not on your List, and you'll accept my help. Properly. No half-measures.'

Katy hesitated. 'What's that supposed to mean?'

'Don't,' Wes warned her, but he didn't intervene.

She looked from the poker in her hands to her cousin and his open, guileless face and that godawful smirk. 'This is a trick.'

There was no way he'd stand there and let her kill him, surely? Could she even do it in cold blood?

You ought to practise, Rachel had told her once, big brown eyes lighting up. Katy remembered her best friend's serious face framed by grass and daisy chains on lazy summer days, watching with disappointment as Katy cried and tried to wring a squirrel's neck but couldn't stop sobbing. Katy pursed her lips.

Ricky's angular chin tilted. His eyes were bright, like Rachel's. 'I ain't bluffing. I really will let you.'

Katy shook her head. 'No.'

'Aw, come on. S'easy. You swear, once we're done here, that's it, and that's that. Swear it, and have a go. That way, you get to say you took revenge for Gran, no hard feelings, and, er...' he gestured vaguely, 'I open the portal and you sort the List out.'

Katy bit her cheek. 'What's... what's the trick, how does it work? I can't kill you, not really.' She glanced at the poker. 'Right?'

God, that grin. His teeth were all she could focus on. Her mouth was dry.

He killed Gran.

'Don't you want to? Through me 'ead, stone dead?' His accent went into Cockney and back again, and she heard Wes muttering under his breath but couldn't make out the words.

'I hate you,' Katy spat, and it felt good to get that out, like spraying out poison. 'I *hate* you. You think you're so fucking clever, don't you, but you ruin *everything. Everything!*' She couldn't stop now, even if she wanted to. It all flooded out, word vomit on a tide of fury. '...*All* my birthdays when I was a kid, pretty much *every* Yule you ever bothered to show up to, you're a fucking embarrassment, *and* you took Gran away from me! You... you took her away!' She couldn't see. Angry tears blurred the garden and smudged him out of existence, the way she wanted to erase him from her life. 'I *hate* you.'

Wes sniggered, but Katy was over him, too.

'*Shut up, Wes.*'

'See, this is why I had to abduct you.' Ricky was infuriatingly calm. 'Knew you'd never come if I just asked.'

She charged him, poker raised, point first.

She expected him to dodge.

He didn't.

The point went straight into his head, her whole weight behind it, and right through into his skull.

She stared at the brass shaft. His blood ran towards her hands. She let go. It took him a second to drop.

She couldn't have been that accurate, she hadn't even been aiming.

Ricky fell straight back, the poker tip biting into the lawn and his head juddering as he landed. Katy squeaked as he hit the ground, scouring her hands on her top. The poker pranged with the impact, like a comedy javelin.

Blood dribbled from the socket. Was it blood? Or... something else? Katy swallowed, forcing herself to come a step closer, but what was bubbling out of Cousin Ricky's ruined face was a nest of thick, dark maggots that writhed as they hit the cold January air and then were still. She jumped back again, hugging her stomach and wishing she hadn't looked.

Don't throw up, don't throw up, don't throw up...

She shuddered, forcing bile back down.

He didn't move. There was no blood flow, no breath. Nothing shifted under his skin.

'Take it out,' Wes called to her, now leaning on the kitchen wall by the back door. 'It'll be easier.'

The last thing she wanted to do was touch it.

It was already stuck in the earth, and the thought of yanking soil through his head, all that dirt and infection, nearly undid her resolve not to vomit.

She steeled herself and reached for it. He wasn't moving. Okay, well, good. She didn't want him to sit up with that thing through his head.

She wasn't standing close enough to give it a proper tug, her fingers barely grazing the metal.

'Get on with it!' Wes sounded – well, she didn't know exactly, but something about the instruction made her step closer and take a proper grip on the antique fireplace tool again. She closed her eyes, took a deep breath, and squealed through gritted teeth as she yanked the poker free.

Opening her eyes was a mistake. A black clot came with it, plopping onto the frosted dead grass and breaking apart into hundreds of dead worm-like things. She dropped her weapon and danced back, scuffing her trainers on the ground in case something had lodged in them.

'Ew! *Ew, ew, ew!*'

Ricky was still very, very dead. He'd been too cocky. What if she had killed him for good? What if it was different because it was her, regardless of if she'd Changed?

It was unreal, like a dream. She wasn't angry anymore, but she didn't know what she did feel. Numbness seeped through her chest, leaving her light-headed. It was a dream. She was a good person, she had friends, she wasn't a monster, she had never hurt anyone before. It was the Beast, the Beast inside her, the Beast that made her do it. Except she wasn't the Beast yet, and Ricky wasn't moving.

'I didn't do it,' she lied, reassuring herself. 'It wasn't me. I didn't do that.'

She couldn't have done that. She couldn't even kill squirrels properly.

He *was* going to get up, though, wasn't he?

That was a bloody big hole in his head.

Wes stumbled up behind her, his hand pressing her back. She leaned into it. 'He's going to get up, isn't he? That's... *supposed* to happen, right?'

'I bloody hope so.' Wes patted her back and rubbed her shoulder. 'Fuck me, what a mess. Nice one.'

'What did I do?' Katy turned frightened eyes to her big brother, almost forgetting his own betrayal. 'I thought he'd get out of the way, I thought it was...' She looked at her hands. 'I really killed him, didn't I?'

Wes put an arm around her shoulders, but she barely registered it. 'He told me to, I didn't...' She didn't know what she was saying, nothing made any sense. 'He's going to get up, isn't he?'

How *could* he get up?

How could it be a trick?

She'd never seen him do it before, his Mike Myers routine or whatever this was, and Wes seemed less sure of himself.

The poker was covered in blood and brain.

She grabbed a handful of Wes's shirt as panic overtook her. 'Oh shit, I'm in so much trouble...'

He rubbed her back and gave her arm a squeeze. 'Come on. Leave him. Let's go back inside.'

Katy fought a little as he pulled her away, but stumbled and let him push her gently back to the kitchen. 'We can't just... Someone will see if we leave him there, someone will come and I'll have to – what if they arrest me?'

'Who?' Wes waved his free hand around at the trees and the high garden wall. 'There's no one here.'

'Carrie, Carrie, that woman, that... thing...' Katy glanced up at the house and felt it judging her. 'I'm... gonna be sick.'

'Deep breaths.'

Her stomach rebelled. 'Oh God—'

She threw up in a flower bed, and Wes stroked her hair back and kept hold of her ponytail.

The rest was a blur.

They entered the house, although it was like walking through tar – the energy in the rooms pushed against her like a repelling magnet, as if it didn't want her, either.

Somehow, not long afterwards, she was tucked up in bed with a cup of tea and a hot water bottle, and Wes was sat on the end reading from his tablet.

She wasn't sure if she'd fallen asleep, or just blanked out the past – how long had it been? She checked her phone. Two hours.

Two hours?

She could have sworn it had been twenty minutes. Her tea was cold. She'd only put it down five minutes ago, hadn't she?

Two hours?

She pulled herself up against the headboard. 'Is he still out there?' she asked, and Wes frowned.

'Who?'

She searched his face for as long as it stuck in her memory, but blinked and couldn't remember if he was being serious or not. 'Are you joking?'

Wes snorted. 'If he is, he's just being dramatic.'

Katy drew her knees up to her chin. 'I *knew* it was a trick.'

'Not a trick,' Ricky said from the doorway, making her jump. 'You got me good.'

She stared at him, horror creeping up her spine.

His right eye was bloodshot, but she couldn't see any damage to his skull, except a few partially faded scar lines through the shaved hair. He dipped his head to show her and turned around slowly on the spot.

The second mouth gaped, puckered lips like scar tissue, tendrils disgorging, dripping spots of blood onto the floor. They waved listlessly out of his skull like a wriggling infestation crawling out of his brain, and Katy's stomach twinged. She was sick in her mouth. She burped and swallowed it miserably back down.

'Nice,' Wes retorted, but that was aimed at Ricky, not at her.

Ricky sucked the tendrils back inside his head, the lips dribbling silvery mucus, and turned back to face them. 'We got that out of our system now, have we?'

Katy rubbed her stomach, shivering.

'What?'

'You had a go, you did pretty well. Now we're both off the List.' It wasn't a question.

Katy shuffled back against her pillow. '*You* were never on it.'

'Don't sound so disappointed.' Ricky approached and stopped short of the bed as Wes stuck out his long legs protectively. 'Look. She c'n learn how to control it, who's on, who's off. It's about criteria, right? It's in-built. Sub-wha'sit, subconscious.'

Wes glanced at her, putting his tablet on the bed. 'Am I on it?'

She didn't answer.

Wes stood up. 'Katy?'

Ricky cocked his head. 'He *is* on the List? Since when?'

Katy hugged the blanket. She'd almost forgotten, in the midst of all the other nightmares. She'd pushed it down, not wanting to think about it. She should have told him. 'Last July.'

One night after Gran died, in the middle of the heatwave that summer, she had woken up fighting through ribbons of Wes's flesh and skin. She hadn't told him. She'd wanted to. But the family vote was called, and he'd called her and promised he was on her side, and she couldn't say anything. He'd still voted against her in the end anyway, so she figured, in a numb, dull way, that it didn't really matter.

'*July?*' Wes's shadow loomed over her and flickered in and out of her consciousness as she looked away. 'July? I thought I might still be able to... What d'you mean I've been on the List since *July*? I was going to vote for you...' He stopped himself.

Katy glared at him. 'Yeah, and you didn't.'

Ricky crowed and clapped his hands.

Wes rounded on him. 'Shut your mouth. What the fuck is this about? Why aren't you on there? You fucked up every one of her birthdays, you punched out our old man, you made a right mess of Kieran's face, you ruined Nic's first Harvest Party, you're a fucking disgrace. Why the hell aren't *you* on there? *Why* hasn't she dreamed of *you*?'

Ricky giggled and ran his hands over the fading scars criss-crossing his skull. 'That's the question, ain't it?'

'If *he's* off it, *I* ought to be off it,' Wes said, rounding on her. 'That poker bloody hurt.'

Katy tensed, squeezing her pillow. 'Don't tell me what to do!'

'He don't mean it like that,' Ricky jumped in, unexpectedly. 'He's on edge, and it don't come out right. Say sorry.'

Wes shot him an incredulous look that Katy dearly wished she could remember forever. 'You what?'

'To Katherine, say sorry to her. Don't be a prick.'

'*Me?* What about...' Wes gave a low growl, then his shoulders slumped. He turned back to Katy, shaking his head. 'No, yeah, all right. It's not that I don't... It's not that I don't care about you. You know that, right? It's just...' He couldn't quite look at her, but she remembered believing he meant it, even though she couldn't fix the expression in her mind. He trailed into silence.

She swallowed and relaxed a little. 'It – it's not *all right*, but... all right.'

Wes nodded. He scowled, turning back to Ricky. 'But seriously – *how* am I on the List, and you're not?'

Ricky grinned, but for the first time Katy noticed his eyes were sad. 'Are you jokin'? I'm the bloody invisible man to you lot. Aside from hating my guts, I don't think she's ever thought twice about me.' He held up a hand as Wes started to argue. 'Look – one way to find out. How about we send her to meet Grandad.'

Wes balked. 'You what?'

'I can do it by myself,' Ricky said, 'But two of us'd be easier. Quick ritual in the kitchen, and we'll use the Pendle Stone. I'll do all the non-vegan bits, you do the chantin', how about that.'

'By "non-vegan bits"...' Katy thought about the organs in the cellar. 'Ew. This is going to be gross.'

Wes took a deep breath, let it out in a long, controlled jet, and attempted humour. 'Bet you're wishing you just took Uncle Barry's pills now.'

'No thanks.' Katy struggled to disentangle herself from the sheets and blankets. 'At least I know where the body parts have been.'

'All organic,' Ricky said, straight-faced.

Katy sighed. 'Fine. Let's... let's get this over with.' She was numb. She ought to feel something: she'd murdered her cousin. Wasn't that supposed to make you feel something? Stronger, more alive? All she felt was hollow and empty and sick. She'd smashed his head in with a poker and got his blood and brain on her hands, and scrubbed it off like it never happened, except it *had* happened, and – here he was.

If she'd done that to anyone else, they'd still be lying out there on the grass, and she'd get arrested. No Uni, no travelling the world. And how would she cope if she Changed in prison? What then?

She belonged in prison. She'd killed someone.

She looked at her living, breathing cousin, and it was all too complicated.

'Sod it. What are we doing?'

Ricky grinned. 'Atta girl. This way. We'll get you into the Outside.'

Wes groaned but followed them.

Katy shot a worried look back at him. 'The Outside? Like – you mean where we're supposed to go when we… do the Changing ritual?'

He gave her a sly, sideways look. 'That's what you wanted with Gran's shrine, right? You wanted to open the portal, meet with our good Gaffer, find out if you can Change early or not at all?'

Katy went cold, staring at him. 'How – how d'you know that?'

Ricky's teeth glinted at her as his lips peeled back. 'I ain't daft.'

'I never said you were…'

'You think seeing the future's all Cousin Ricky c'n do?'

Katy shook her head, firmly believing someone talking about themselves in third person was a bad sign. Maybe she'd given him lasting damage. She trailed a hand along the wall of the corridor, the warmth of it reassuring, anchoring.

'Where's Carrie?' Wes asked.

Ricky cocked his head. 'The mistress? She's around.'

'Around… where?' Katy changed tack, opting for something that would provoke a reaction. Her fingers brushed the bedroom door where she'd overheard him talking to himself, and it swung open at her touch. The sunny yellow counterpane and embossed blue peacocks on the feature wall were not his style, but she caught sight of a clean grey hoodie folded on the bed. 'You guys are together or something, right? How long have you been banging her?'

Wes burst out laughing.

Ricky whipped his head around to stare at her, eyes wide and cheeks flaring. 'It ain't like that.'

'I wasn't... It's just, you're obviously shacked up with her, you share a bed, right, so...' Katy shrugged, bemused. 'She's pretty. What's the deal there?'

'*Nothing*. It's... it's none of your business.' He looked genuinely upset.

Katy frowned. 'What did I say?'

'Leave him be,' Wes said, as they headed downstairs. 'He's not into that. Never has been.'

'Into what?' Katy dropped her voice, desperate for something else to think about. 'Girls?' She couldn't picture Ricky with anyone, but it helped to try.

Wes snorted, shook his head, and mouthed, '*Sex.*'

Ricky rounded on them at the bottom of the stairs, jaw fluttering. 'D'you want t' learn something or not? That's why you're here, none-else...' He gave up and marched off to the kitchen, flushing an ugly bruised red.

Katy and Wes followed him, Wes shooting her what she felt, rather than remembered, was a warning glance.

'...Move the table back,' Ricky said, not looking at either of them.

Katy did as she was told, Wes lending a hand, filing away this information for later. If she wanted to hurt Cousin Ricky again, at least she knew where to stick the knife.

Ricky cracked his neck, side to side, and shifted on the spot. 'Gran ever explain to you what the Pendle Stone actually was?'

Katy shook her head. 'Not properly.'

Ricky nodded and sniffed, all business now, recovered from the personal embarrassment. 'This is it.' He lunged down and patted the slab of limestone in the fireplace, upon which the black range sat.

Katy was bitterly disappointed. 'That's it? It's... it's just a...' She gestured. 'It's part of the floor.'

'Built into the house, yeah. The hearthstone of the old Pendle cottage.' Ricky patted the hearthstone, finger tracing some carvings on its ancient surface. 'Gran never said but I think the old baronet did it on purpose. Sir... which one was it? They were all Peter or John, weren't they? One of 'em, anyway.' He cocked his head as if someone was whispering to him. '...Sir Peter Sauvant, the third one. Yeah.'

Wes and Katy exchanged glances, but Ricky didn't notice and carried on monologuing.

'Witchcraft were still illegal under the statute of 1542, did you know that? No?' He gave her a smug grin. 'There was all those rumours about what the Pendles could do, though it weren't truly much at the time, I think. They got better at it. But the third lord Peter wanted some of that for himself, thought it was easy enough to take away what they needed, build it into the manor, keep the Pendles working for him, keep all that power somewhere in plain sight where he could keep an eye on it...' Ricky sniggered. 'All mine, now. How about that, then?'

Katy couldn't believe it. She'd been sat inches away from the mythical Pendle Stone for days, been eating food warmed in the range directly above it, and after all the hype and the family legends it was just a dusty slab of rock.

'That's it?'
'What did you think it was?'

'I thought... I thought it was like a meteorite or a crystal or something.' Katy stared at it. 'Are you serious? That's what the fuss is about?'

'Pretty much.' Ricky started to undress, and Katy recoiled.

'What the hell are you doing?'

Wes chortled, drumming his hands on the tabletop. 'Not what you think.'

Ricky ignored him. 'Gonna Change. She don't like me doing it indoors much, but needs must, hey.'

'I'll do the words, is that it? You channel the energy?' Wes cracked his knuckles in front of him, and Ricky nodded.

'You remember 'em?'

'Seared into my brain, mate. Don't you worry.'

Ricky stripped.

Katy faced the wall, rigid, her turn to burn with embarrassment.

'What's the matter with you? Never seen a naked man before?'

'*I'm* not undressing.'

Ricky folded up his clothes. 'Why would you?' He crouched down. 'Right. I want you to stay in contact with this all the time. Oi. Oi, Katherine, pay attention. Down here.'

Katy lowered herself to the floor, not sure where to look. She put her hand on the Pendle Stone and a bolt of energy shot up her arm, exciting her heart like a shot of caffeine. 'Shit!'

'Strong. I know. It knows you.'

He was twisting awkwardly, something bulging under his skin and settling down again, large round coils expanding and leaving livid stretchmarks where they pushed through. Some began to split and bleed.

Wes was chanting words she'd heard Gran use, words Gran only taught to the oldest of each generation. He was getting into the zone, which bothered her almost as much as Ricky's bulges.

What did he *have* in there? How was there room for anything else? What was crawling around inside of him?

Wes droned, monotonous, words blending into one another. It didn't sound like a human language. She couldn't explain why, except that it tugged at something at the back of her mind, making her think of dreamscapes where the Beast prowled and snapped at winged insects the size of large dogs. She thought the landscapes of her dreams were imaginary, based on the stories the others had about their Changes. They all talked of black sand, a source of heat, a Voice in their heads…

Wes chanted, droning on and on until it was a buzz in her brain, an itch she couldn't pin down, and the tone swam in and out of her consciousness. The words *rippled* in front of her. She could *see* them. That had never happened when Gran chanted, had it? She blinked through the haze of half-formed symbols, pale and illusory like smoke, and saw the thing inside Ricky tearing through his skin.

Katy flinched, dragging her nails involuntarily across the rock. 'Shit, does that hurt?'

'Course.' Ricky sounded like he took it in stride, but he was wincing. 'You try having something the size of a fucking tyrannosaurus living in your bloody torso.'

'A… What the fuck?'

'You should come to the gatherings, it's much more impressive with a bonfire.' Ricky tried to laugh, and his throat split open.

Katy yelped in shock. She'd never seen a full-body Change before.

Oh shit, this is going to happen to me, I don't want this, what the fuck, what the actual fuck…?!

Something pulsed through her arm, gluing her hand to the stone. She tugged but couldn't get away.

Ricky's skin split open in pieces, as whatever was underneath forced its way into their reality, all eyes and mouths and thick, rubbery hide. It expanded.

Maybe it's like an iguana, she thought, mind shutting down, unable to stop staring at it, *it grows to fit the cage it's in…*

It filled her field of vision, pulsating, feeding from her, draining her of energy and thought and movement.

Something was happening to the Pendle Stone, magnified by the energy in the kitchen, the energy in the house. Everything was throbbing around her, one long musical tone ringing in her ears as if a crystal glass had been struck. Was that the sound the universe made?

It's beautiful, she thought, overawed by its majesty. *How beautiful…*

Ricky's other form was beautiful, too – terrible, glorious. It called to the form inside her, communing with it, and Katy wanted to tear her miserable skinny flesh away and be as beautiful as that.

The energies were doing something to the dimensions around them, bending space out of shape. Katy saw the kitchen table melt, wobbling like jelly, dissolving into pixelated fragments and being swept away in a whirl of black sand.

The stone under her hand glowed with symbols, peeling off like disco lights, dancing around her head. She couldn't move.

They seared into her eyes.

The world burst into flaring fragments.

She was on her own, the slab of limestone the only thing she recognised, sat in the middle of a square black desert. Walls of navy-blue sky formed the horizons, and the sand rippled away to the edges, as far as she could see, like anthracite.

Katy stood up.

She wasn't sure if she was really there, or if this was all inside her head. She dusted off her hands, looking at the Pendle Stone. The kitchen was on the other side, under her feet. She could feel the throbbing of the Thing-that-was-Ricky and still feel, rather than hear, the low sustained chime-tone below her.

She turned slowly on the spot, taking in the vast box of space and dark light. There was no sun, and yet she could see. The sky itself was a flat, bright square of grey.

In front of her was a gigantic black chair.

Katy.

Katy knew that voice – it was *the* Voice, Grandad's voice, the one that spoke to her from Gran's shrine.

Have you made the List?

Katy moistened her lips. She steeled herself, and started towards the chair. No – it was more like a throne. High-backed, arms and high legs, built for something huge. The tug in her chest pulled her forwards.

This could be yours, the Voice whispered. *You could sit here. Do you have what it takes to sit here?*

'Who...' Her voice broke. She coughed and swallowed, throat dry. 'Who sits there now?'

There was silence.

She approached, casting a nervous glance back at the Pendle Stone. Its edges were fuzzy, the air shimmering above it as if it were hot or giving off steam. Her eyes stung.

Katy ducked her head, scrunching her eyes closed and blinking a few times.

When she opened them, the throne was inches away from her and the Pendle Stone was further away, but she couldn't remember walking any further.

'How do I control the List?' she asked, not sure if anyone was listening.

Something was wrong with the throne. She couldn't decide what it was, or what it was made of. It was *roughly* throne-shaped, but now she was this close she could see all the contours, as if it was made up of tessellating, misshapen parts welded together. It took her a moment to realise what it reminded her of was anatomy.

'Oh shit.'

She took a step back as the eyes began to open.

Mouths pulled apart, taking shuddering gasps.

Katy stumbled backwards as the throne awoke.

Kaaaatyyyyyy...

It had one voice, but the mouths all moved in unison, hundreds of them. A few faces pushed out further on long, stalk-like necks.

Katy tripped over her own feet and sat down hard on the sand. One face floated over her, its neck stretching out, swaying and pulsing in time to Katy's heartbeat.

'Gran?'

Granny Wend groaned, phantom eyes rolled back.

Katy couldn't move, chest cold and tight, unable to blink or breathe. Other faces waved on their neck-stalks.

What wriggles and crawls with no legs at all? Ties knots without hands, chills bones without breath, changes minds without words, is stopped only by death?

Katy shuffled back as the faces strained to reach her. The Pendle Stone was so far away. She glanced over her shoulder and saw it flickering in the middle distance. Something breathed in her ear.

Katy made herself look.

She was face to face with someone she recognised from Gran's family album.

'Uncle Hector?'

The only other Thirteenth. The one before her, who had killed Gran's two sisters and ended up destroying himself.

Snippets of family history flashed through her head as she stared into the grey, dead face.

'Is this... is this what's going to happen to me?' she croaked. 'Uncle Hector? What is this? What happened to you?'

Have you made your List?

'I'm getting there, I've got people on it...'

Hector withdrew and floated above her on his long, pulsing neck.

What wriggles and crawls with no legs at all? Ties knots without hands...

'I don't know, I don't know...' Katy couldn't think. She shuffled further away, heels digging into the sand.

...chills bones without breath...

Katy's bones were frozen, heavy. She forced herself up, stumbling but keeping her balance. 'I don't *know*...'

...changes minds without words, is stopped only by death?

Granny Wend lunged at her, mouth open, and Katy screamed and ducked. She fled, speeding across the sand as the necks lashed out of the Throne, limbs breaking free of their positions and wrenching the Throne out of the ground.

It was a mass of her dead family, all the family who had died in brutal, unnatural ways, broken and groaning, calling her name in one Voice.

She forced a sprint, heels spraying sand.

The Pendle Stone shimmered, drawing her on, spurred by the lumbering of too many limbs behind her. She knew how to breathe, knew how to run for fuck's sake, but her lungs ached, her breaths coming hot and ragged.

Did it matter if she slowed down?

What was really behind her? Was she even really here?

Something whipped by the back of her neck, tugging at her hair.

Fear burst through her.

Katy leapt for the Pendle Stone, slamming both hands down on it and feeling the edges give, spongey to the touch, and as the Throne lumbered louder behind her the world spun upside down. It was like the time at Gran's, when she set the shrine off without knowing what she was doing.

This time, though, Wes and Ricky were on the other side, their energy anchoring her to the Other World. She tumbled into its warm, safe box, the lid closing on the Outside, rolling onto her back on the flagstones of the kitchen and staring at the bright beige of the ceiling above her.

'*Fear*,' she said, panting, the answer coming to her as it tied knots in her stomach and crawled up her spine. '*Fear*, it's fear.'

'What are you talking about?' Ricky asked, human-passing again, dripping with some sort of mucus. His skin was new, without stretchmarks or scars, pristine, new-born. Katy barely registered his nakedness.

'The riddle. It's fear.'

'What riddle?' Wes had stopped chanting.

Katy sat up, breathing more regularly, scooting back against the solidity of the table leg. She jerked away again almost immediately as her head brushed the tabletop – she thought it was a face on a stalk. It was not.

'Do you know what it is? What the Voice is?' she asked him, trembling.

'D'you see Him? Our grandsire?' Ricky crouched in front of her, dripping skin-mucus on the tiles. 'I ain't seen Him since my Change. Doant rightly remember what the old bastard looks like.'

'Nor me,' Wes said, straddling a kitchen chair and leaning on the back. He peered around Ricky at her. 'If you see him again, I want a word.'

'No.' Katy shook her head, drawing her knees up and away from him. Ricky's tendrils were sneaking out again, curling around his skull, and she recoiled. 'Stop it, get them away from me, get away…'

Ricky withdrew, frowning, holding his hands up to the back of his head. 'What's wrong?'

'Is that where we go when we die?' Katy couldn't imagine anything worse. Queasiness roiled up into her throat. 'Oh, God…'

She threw up into her cupped hands, and Ricky jumped up to give her the washing-up bowl from the sink.

'Bloody hell, you got a weak stomach,' Wes said.

She wanted to say *It's where I carry my anxiety, actually; it isn't unusual, fuck you*, but couldn't manage the words.

Ricky handed her the bowl and Katy coughed and retched into it, the stale smell of washing-up liquid and recently rinsed dishes hitting the back of her nose. She didn't think there was anything left after last time – it was just water and bile.

Ricky got as close as he could with the table in the way, wiping her hands with a tea towel and holding her hair away from her face.

'You're all right, love. I don't think you're really cut out for this, that's all.'

Katy gagged, eyes watering. She didn't know whether that was supposed to be meant in a good way, or if he was disappointed. Ricky was hard to read.

'It's fear,' she said again. 'The answer to the List...' her throat tightened and she retched again, Uncle Hector's flat, dead face inches from hers in her mind's eye.

'Fear? What, the Thirteenth *isn't* killing weak links, they kill what they're afraid of?'

Katy tried to get up, trying not to spill the bowl or get her sick-stained hands on anything. Despite the towel, her fingers were still slimy, sticky. She was sure she had some in her hair.

'Why isn't Dad on the List, then?' she croaked, swaying. 'Why aren't you?'

'Yeah, and why the fuck am *I*?' Wes sounded sore about that, and she couldn't blame him. She crept around the table to the sink and ran the hot tap.

'Ha. Let's have a think.' Ricky sounded like he was grinning. She'd given herself away: now he knew she was afraid. 'Maybe it's a specific fear. Or maybe I'm just... not what you fear most.' He sniggered. 'What's so scary to you about him, then?'

Katy swallowed and shrugged, not able to look at her brother. 'I'll clean this up, just... put the bowl somewhere...'

'Nah, no worries.' He was lurking behind her, she could feel him there, but the hot water and soap were soothing. She kept her hands under the tap as the water turned from warm to scalding. Her hands burned, turning pink. Katy kept them under, rubbing them together, watching them change colour and barely registering the pain.

Ricky leaned over and turned on the cold water.

'It don't help, you know.'

'What?'

He didn't answer her for a moment, watching her quietly. She let the cold soothe her skin, then turned the tap off.

'I got pneumonia twice,' he said, apparently apropos of nothing. 'Did you know that?'

Katy shook her head, checking her hair.

Ricky nodded. 'Yeah. Once was when Mum said I shouldn't be in the house, you know, cause of the old man. I slept outside. Fucking freezin', frost on the ground, she gi' me a coat, told me to wait, she'd come out and get me. I waited all night, but she didn't come.' He smiled bitterly at the kitchen table, running a hand along the top of the nearest chair. 'Could've died. We *can* die like that, you know. Before the Changes. I was... seven? Maybe. I don't remember. Second time, I did it on purpose. Wanted to get ill. Got more attention, see? Childish, ain't it?' He shook his head. 'I crashed a car once, too. Nicked it from a hotel car park in town, wrapped it round a tree.' He chuckled. 'Best near-death experience I ever had.'

Wes was silent, his head ducked low.

'Why?' Katy wiped her hands on her jeans. 'Why are you telling me this?'

Ricky looked at her with a shrewd, knowing stare. 'Cos I didn't want to Change, neither.'

Katy didn't know what to say.

Wes only moved now, getting up as if his joints were heavy, and pulled out the chair for her. She sidled to it and sat, as Ricky took the sick bowl and rinsed it out in the sink now she was done.

'I thought you just did drugs and got wasted.'

Ricky giggled. 'Oh, yeah. Course. Wouldn't you? Bloody hell.'

'I don't do drugs.'

'Bollocks you don't. Don't you lie to me, Katherine.'

She chewed her lip, avoiding Wes's eye. He tended to get up his own arse about things like that, which she really didn't appreciate. 'Whatever. I don't turn up at kids' birthday parties off my tits like some people.'

Wes snorted. Ricky cocked his head, chin jutting belligerently. His eyes widened. 'Oh, me? You're talking about me? Yeah, all right, I never was good at crowds. And you can ask her, I've always been a moody bastard.'

Katy assumed he meant Carrie, although she wasn't sure where Carrie was. Ricky cocked his head at Wes. 'Or him.'

'Yeah, he has.' Wes stretched out and Katy wondered when he'd changed chairs. She couldn't remember. 'Never had a good people tolerance, have you, Soothsayer?'

Ricky shrugged. 'I like... I like being on my own.'

Katy frowned. That didn't ring quite true. Ricky shifted, and she realised with a twinge of horror that she felt sorry for him.

He killed Gran and now she's a-a monster. And he kidnapped me. She gritted her teeth.

'Being lonely isn't an excuse for being an arsehole.'

Ricky shook his head. '*Me?*'

'Don't bother, we've had this conversation before,' Wes said, leaving Katy with the impression he was bored of it. 'Over and over. Since we were nine.'

'Bollocks. I saw you lot once a bleedin' year when we were kids.' Ricky joined her at the table, turning a chair around to straddle it and lean on the chair back. 'Look. Katherine. You don't like me, I know that. I think if you get control of the List you might be tempted to put me on it. I'm not stupid. You loved Gran.'

Katy nodded, steeling herself, wondering if he would tell her the truth.

'D'you know why I *didn't* love her?'

'I don't really care, to be honest.' She wasn't ready to hear it, not yet, not now. The roiling in her stomach worsened.

He shrugged. 'Allus best to be honest. But you know I'm going to tell you anyway.'

If her legs weren't so shaky she would have walked out.

'Ricky, come on.' Wes leaned forwards. 'She's had enough for today, let's—'

'She promised me the bloody moon, our Gran. Said she'd take me in, even tried it for a bit, but the problem was this.' Ricky tapped the centre of his forehead and grinned, cold and savage. 'That's how she figured it out, see. If our Richard's *happy now*, our Richard can't see the *future* for shit.' He shook his head. 'So that was that. When I got back home, there's this girl there. Mum couldn't stand not having a kid in the house, so she'd taken one. Di'n't last long. Dad lost it when she tried to run, broke her little back.' He sniggered. 'Thought Mum'd be pleased I was home, but... I wa'n't what she wanted.'

Wes groaned. 'Not this story again. Auntie Lettie's barking, I wish you'd just send her to someone. I told you, I know a…'

'Mum stays where she is,' Ricky snapped. 'She don't like going out, just leave her be.'

Katy didn't know what to say. 'She… That's…'

Ricky shifted. 'Point is, about me getting pneumonia, crashing a car… that was… that was all *before*. Before the Changes. Before I heard the Voice. Before I had a purpose. I had a gift I didn't know what to do with, and some days I didn't know whether I wanted it or not, but it was *all* I had.' He drummed his fingers on the chair back. 'Is *any* of this hitting the right notes for you, cos this is about as, what d'you call it, "interpers'nal" as I get.'

Wes sniggered. 'No, you're doing pretty well for once. I'm impressed.'

'Gran's in pain.' Katy swallowed the laughter and made herself remember the twisted face. 'You sent her to this, this wasteland. She's… they're all… all of them, they're…'

'Part of the Throne, yeah, I know.' Ricky nodded. 'Sorry you had to see that, but you'll be sat on it one day. You won't need eyeballs, then. Not like me. You'll be a bloody queen. Ass-im-i-la-tion.' He enunciated it, making the most of every syllable. 'That's what's waiting for us, if you survive your own cull.'

'I'll control that thing?' Katy heard it again, lumbering after her on twisted limbs. 'Fuck.'

'Gran's the best of 'em. The strongest. Now you got all three matriarchs in there, if you can control 'em. You're welcome.' He grinned. 'I allus seem to do the right thing in the long run.'

Katy regretted ever sharing so much as a smile with him. She couldn't hear this bullshit, not now.

She got up, legs still weak, and forced herself out of the kitchen and into the hall.

'Oi! Katherine! What's this about fear? I can help you figure it out.'

'Go fuck yourself,' Katy muttered under her breath. 'See if *that's* the right thing to do in the long run.'

Chapter 9: For Whom the Bell Tolls

14 January

Wes went for a short walk around the gardens once his sister had gone back to her room. He had to clear his head of the energy pulsing in the kitchen, free his mind of Ricky's ripped abs, and definitely not think about that time they'd been stupid teenagers with nothing better to do than each other. Ricky hadn't been into it then, either.

Striding around the back lawns and skirting the broken wall to return to the gravel drive at the front, he felt a twinge of jealousy stir in his chest as the gables loomed over him.

It wasn't often – never, in fact – that he was jealous of Ricky. He'd always known the old ruin as The Crows, a wild-sounding name that suited its decay. Its restoration was a revelation, an epiphany, a promise that even the most broken of things could be restored to some kind of life, and that life could be glorious.

He took his time, checking on his car while he was about it. He'd been to a wedding with Charlie where they'd laid on free wraps of cocaine in the tampon dispenser of the ladies' bathroom, and he'd still got one of them in the glove compartment. He wished he had a pack of Silver Lining instead.

Wait. Did he?

The hairs on the nape of his neck pricked, but when he whipped around to check he wasn't being observed, the house was the only thing staring at him. No movement or shape appeared in any of the windows, but the windows themselves felt like they were trained on him, a swarm of irregular, rectangular eyes.

Wes shivered and got in the passenger seat, shutting the door and hiding behind the tinted glass.

He felt silly, but he didn't wind the window down, and opened the compartment gingerly as if anticipating a knock on the window.

He checked the mirrors, telling himself he was being a tit. There was no one there.

No one except the manor house.

The manor was Fairwood House again now, and no mistake. Too grand, too big, too watchful for a colloquial name. He could buy it, settle Charlie and Hugo here, fill the place with parties and art, cocktails and pearls and the Chelsea set, have a swimming pool and a tennis court.

He'd be untouchable here, with the owner's permission. *As* the owner – even better. His partners deserved the world, if he could give it to them. They'd be safe here. He wasn't sure if it would make up for letting them fall for him in the first place, but it would be a start.

It was too good for the likes of Richard bloody Porter, that was for sure, the family's new god, the Great Unwashed. He snorted to himself.

Fishing around in his preferred hidden spots rewarded him with the cocaine wrap and Uncle Barry's magic pills. Fuck it, they were too good to waste on posh oiks with no imagination. Uncle Barry would be none the wiser as long as he got his cash. It wasn't *stealing*. He'd learned his lesson about that, even if it had only been for the rush.

Wes stowed the wrap back for later and contemplated a pill.

'Main lesson being Uncle Barry has no sense of humour,' he muttered to himself. He paused. 'I'm talking to myself. Fucking hell.'

It was this place. The house, brooding, accusing, not finding him funny either. At least it couldn't see him through the tinted windscreen.

'It's a fucking house,' Wes told the pill. 'I'm losing my goddamn mind.'

One more of these wouldn't make a difference, then.

He popped it in his mouth, pushed it to the back, and swallowed it dry.

He strapped himself in, just in case.

When it kicked in, he was ready.

This time, he tried to ignore the thoughts that wanted to come out and play, and faced the ones that manifested like thunder clouds.

The red cocoon pulsed in the distance on an outcrop of black rock, and he made his way towards it, although memories of orgies and swinger parties flashed their bits and begged him to come back.

'Later,' he promised them.

He had a few more pills left, and some of the parties gave him coy little glimpses of things he couldn't remember, which might mean they hadn't happened yet. Not that he trusted his memory to work backwards properly.

He saw his cousin, grey-faced and tense, as if he was some distance below Wes in the landscape of black rock. Fish bones and dried seaweed littered the place. Wes stood atop an outcrop and the cocoon was gone. Ricky slumped below him, rubbing his belly and looking sick.

He was alone.

It didn't look like anywhere Wes had seen outside of a pulp sci-fi novel cover, or the National Geographic. It felt familiar, though.

The longer he focused on this, the quicker he felt himself coming down.

He turned from the image to find another, dates and numbers swirling around him too fast to catch. Things began piling back into his head, sucked back faster than he could snatch at them.

Damn.

Either going with the flow lasted longer, or he'd started to build a tolerance. He chose to hope for the former.

He waited until he'd properly come back to this side of reality, downed a bottle of water he found unopened in the footwell, and checked his face in the rearview mirror.

Things were still crackling a little at the edges, the mirror misty and his face swimming slightly when he tried to focus. His eyes were oddly pink, but his pupils were getting there. Not quite normal.

He blinked and forgot.

He probably looked fine.

—

As if she'd been waiting, Carrie opened the front door for him before he was even halfway to the porch, blocking his path. He paused, wondering how to play it. He barely remembered their first meeting, when she'd been alive. She didn't trust him. That would have to change, or at least, he could try the good old charm offensive. He grinned at her.

She arched an eyebrow at him.

'He asked you if we could come in, didn't he? I didn't see you, but... I'm assuming he wasn't just talking to the gates.'

Carrie regarded him with a wooden expression. 'I'd appreciate it if you didn't antagonise him. Or make fun of him. He's my lodger, and I don't appreciate it.'

Wes chose the gallant path. 'Should I be apologising? I feel I ought to.'

She moved back a little. 'Have a go, see what happens.'

'I'm sorry. I was an arsehole. I am, in fact. No excuse for it, just — yeah. It's personal, it's between me and him, but I shouldn't have been that rude.' He couldn't remember what he'd said, his head fizzed with random thoughts and broken ideas when he tried to pin that recent memory down. He kept thinking there had been a pulsing cocoon in the kitchen on one of the chairs, red and slimy and oozing. Ricky had said something to him, and the table was covered in volcanic black sand...

No. He passed a hand over his eyes, sliding his palm over his mouth, attempting focus. He bit the soft skin between his thumb and index finger, and the sharp pinch of his teeth brought some clarity back.

'God, sorry, I'm not feeling great. The drive, you know, and the family... I'm not at my best, and that's not an excuse either.'

He was rewarded with a half-smile and a slight nod.

Wes relaxed. 'Is it... all right if I stay over, just for a couple of nights?'

'Just a couple.'

'Well, I think I nailed my colours to the mast back there in town,' Wes said, as she let him inside, evidently taking pity on him. The entrance hall closed in on him, pushing those errant thoughts firmly into their places inside his head and nearly choking him with the change of air.

He thought he'd propped himself up against a statue or the hatstand, but realised Carrie had taken his elbow to steady him. He hadn't realised his legs were trembling, or that he was listing to one side. There was a floating sense of disconnect between himself, his head, and his body, as if he wasn't really in control of anything other than the small speck of whatever it was currently doing the thinking.

He wasn't even sure who that was.

'Ah, thanks. I'm fine, honestly.'

He focused, trying out the full body scan his old therapist had recommended. He'd tried therapy for a few months once, but found he didn't have the balls for it. There was too much he didn't want to talk about, and the therapist had suggested he cut down on the booze and drugs, so she'd had to go.

Gradually, the floor solidified under his feet, which in turn resumed their status as appendages he was in command of. He blinked, embodied, theoretically stable.

'Thanks – just dizzy for a second there. The light, you know.'

Carrie gave no comment.

He pulled away from her casually, taking in the entrance hall properly this time, admiring the staircase, the tiles, the bannisters.

'Don't fancy my chances with the family prowling around at the moment. They can't get me in here, can they? I don't take up much room. Cor, this is lovely. Have I said that? Cos it is.' He winced at himself as his Gran's accent – not even the current local one, but the older remnant of the way people spoke when Gran was a girl – came out of his mouth. He hoped Carrie would forget, but then reflected it would probably work for him with her. Whatever she was.

'It's not for sale, rich boy,' she said, as if she'd read his mind.

Wes grinned. 'Only cash rich. Not like I went to the right schools. I'm just a normal guy, like you.'

'Oh, yeah, we're so alike.'

Instead of showing him into the living room, they turned left, and Wes found himself exploring a wide, open room that was evidently the old dining room, where dancing must have taken place. He whistled, and it echoed back to him.

'I bet we've got loads in common. If I took you for dinner, I bet you a tenner I'd even guess your order.'

She laughed, half shocked, half intrigued. He was good at this.

'No.'

'No what? No, I wouldn't guess? Or, no, you won't have dinner with me?'

'You're not actually asking me out to dinner.'

Wes shrugged. 'Why not?'

'I'm dead.'

He looked her up and down, taking his time about it. She was on the skinny side and her perky, apple-round tits weren't all that, and there was something off about them. Like the rest of her, actually. It was as if she'd been given the shape of a real woman but had been dipped in wax and sanded down like a mannequin, the contours an approximation rather than the real thing.

He'd still give it a go.

'I don't mind if you don't.'

Carrie visibly fought a grin. '*No.*'

He shrugged, thrusting his hands into his pockets. 'So, why are we in here, then? Away from prying eyes?' He flicked his tongue out suggestively, grinning as she balked.

'Cut it out.'

He reined it in, trying to look chaste. 'Sorry.'

Carrie sighed. He could have sworn her ribs creaked, like wood. 'Wes. I'm serious. I need you to *not* piss Ricky off. Okay? I need you to *not* antagonise him, I need you to *not* be a dick. Do you think you can do that?'

He frowned. 'Yeah.' He paused. 'I thought... this would be more about my sister. Or laying down the house rules, telling me which towels to use, or something.'

Carrie's stare was icy. 'Those *are* the house rules.'

Wes nodded, that unfamiliar jealous pang returning. 'So you really – you really brought me in here to talk about *him*?'

'You can have the bedroom on the end of the corridor, second floor, on the left.' Carrie stared at him, cold and stiff. 'Use the towels on the bed. This is temporary, you understand. *Very* temporary. But better you lie low here for a day or so than have that lot carve you up for parts, I guess.'

He shrugged, disappointed. 'Fine by me.'

Carrie nodded, then closed her eyes with a frown. He watched her... *melt* into the floor a little, that was the only way he could describe it, with no clear indication of where she ended and the floor began, and he rubbed his face trying to remember how long ago he'd taken the pill. He was probably fine to drive by now, surely, though he'd been wrong about that before.

Carrie opened her glass-clear eyes, reflecting a grey winter sky. Wes couldn't see himself in them.

He swallowed. 'For what it's worth, I'm sorry you died.'

'Thanks.'

She was hard to read. The dead were inscrutable, he thought, some little phrase from his grandmother dancing into his head, and instantly regretted it. That was probably vitalist, or some shit.

He thought of Ricky, and how wasted she was on him. Wes was a people-person, it was one of his main strengths. If *he* didn't get her, he failed to see how Ricky possibly could, couldn't fathom how... whatever their relationship was, could work.

'You know he's feral. You can't tame him. He'll fuck it up like he fucks up everything he touches, he can't help it.'

'Yeah, he thinks that, too. I wonder where that mantra came from?' She arched an eyebrow. 'Must be nice to have such a supportive family.'

The sarcasm cut deeper than he anticipated. Wes twitched and adjusted his scarf higher over his mouth and nose, glad she wouldn't remember.

Carrie looked at him as if she'd read it on the back of his corneas, although there was a crease of pain clouding her face like a crumpled curtain. She averted her eyes from his face, and Wes breathed a relieved sigh.

'Speaking of which... if you want to be useful, go and find him, will you? He's gone off somewhere. Make it up to him. And if he says you can stay a bit longer, then you can. If he doesn't, you're out.' Carrie folded her arms. 'Got it? Go and play nice.'

He didn't need telling twice. He had to get out of that room, it was too big, too empty, and he was too lost in it.

'Right you are. I'll go and... I'll go find him.'

He curled his fingers into a fist by his side and headed back out, with the weirdest feeling that something was picking through the contents of his head as he went.

Wes's Memory: The Change

Everyone had breathed a sigh of relief when Charlotte Porter, a single-birth and a thirteenth child, had given birth to a single son. Her older sister Letitia, pregnant with a batch, had been delighted for her. Single-births were special. Then, of course, three months later, Letitia spawned – except it wasn't a batch at all, it was a single boy, and then Charlotte had spawned again. And everything had been upended.

Everyone thought Wes, as a single-birth, would get some measure of the soothsaying powers Pendle only-children tended to get, but that honour was his solitary cousin's alone. Small comfort for Aunty Lettie and Uncle George, who had always wanted a big family.

It was decided that Wes's single-birth was an accident of nature, a disappointment, and nothing more. When it came closer to the time of Changing, he'd avoided going to the shrine to ask for special consideration, that wasn't cool; but when it was finally his turn he descended the cellar steps in full stupid regalia anyway.

At least, he'd thought it was stupid when everyone else wore it. The wool itched and the robe was too short on him, but that meant he wouldn't fall flat on his face or fuck it up with clumsiness.

Tonight, his night, he wore it with a strange, unfamiliar sense of pride. He *was* special. He was going to Change, the first of his siblings to do it, but his cousin had gone first. Ricky was there, three months Changed and three months sober, pupils the right size, not drawing attention to himself. He'd finally been read the riot act.

Wes was hemmed in by relatives and their robed forms, humming low and muttering a chant Gran claimed she had heard emanating from the Outside. He was blindfolded, Gran tying the wide woollen scarf tight behind his head, nearly catching his hair. They slipped a hood over his head for good measure, the robe supposed to cover everything else and keep it hidden until the big reveal at the end. They marched him around Gran's garden, the chanting gathering momentum as he lost track of who was who and who was where. He could tell at first by their voices, but then they all merged into one.

It was like labour pains, some said. You felt them where the Changes would happen – usually in your head, your throat, your chest. Some had it all over. Some described it like needles, others like knives. His mother said hers had been like contractions, but in her spine.

Wes had been feeling an odd numbness all over, creeping across his skin and eating into his larynx, for three weeks. Gran said it was coming, they couldn't delay anymore. But there wasn't any pain. He thought it always came with pain.

I don't think it's the Changes, he'd said, but was overruled when Gran examined him properly.

Wes wasn't ready.

He *liked* his face, his pretty-boy face, didn't give a toss that the lads said he was 'metrosexual'. He bought into it with skincare and hair gel, wasn't ready for extra appendages and gelatinous ooze.

They pushed him through the back door, into the kitchen. He worried about leaving traces of mud on Gran's kitchen floor, stomach cold and somersaulting with each shove, each step forwards. He tried to picture the room, arms raised slightly to feel his way across to the cellar, but he was hemmed in by relatives in front and behind, someone at each elbow, too many for the tight space. How were they all fitting in? Someone was manipulating reality again. Nothing was where it ought to be. The tiles crunched under his soles like sand. He breathed through the scarf, inhaling the heat of a volcanic desert.

There were steps. Someone took his hands.

Wes descended, the darkness total. Now there was a humming, the tug in his chest irresistible, physical, like a meat hook on a reeled-in string. It was starting to hurt, a strange ache all over. Could skin ache? Was it muscle-deep? Bone-deep? He didn't know: something was sucking at his face, like he'd stepped in front of a vacuum cleaner. The suction pulled him faster down the steps and he nearly tripped. When he recoiled it felt like some invisible force was ripping his face off. Wes stumbled, trying to press his hands to his hood, hold his skin on, but he was pulled and grabbed by so many hands and thrown down to the cellar floor.

Wes landed with a hard thud on his hands and knees, not on the flagstones, but on hard grit baked by a sun that wasn't theirs. He dug his long fingers deep into it, let it trickle through them, the heat on his back. His ears rang, but there was nothing to hear but the hum and the chant, far away.

He was alone.

He stood up, knowing he mustn't take his hood off, mustn't take the blindfold off, mustn't look. Sweat prickled all over, beading against the itchy wool, sliding down his back, his face, his chest.

Where was he? Where was everyone?

He was not alone.
Welcome, Wesley.

He stood still, petrified, the Voice worming into his mind.

Take off the blindfold.

Obedience was mandatory. He couldn't help it. First the hood: he fumbled for it, tugging it off, an old sack without eyeholes, scratchy under his trembling hands. Then the scarf.

I want to be me, he thought, fingers tugging helplessly at the knot. *Please let me still be me.*

The sacrifice has been made.

What sacrifice? By whom? He hadn't made one. He was beginning to regret that, now, but it was too late.

We have heard the request on your behalf, and we have something special for you.

There was a presence directly in front of him. He could feel it there, looming, blocking the dim light source that penetrated the scarf fibres. He screwed his eyes shut as he finally worked the scarf loose and pulled it down around his neck. Whatever it was, it was gigantic. He could sense it surrounding him, feel its shadow moving across his body, hear its breath (or whatever it was doing) like a throbbing song without a tune.

Please let me be me, he thought, *I want to be me.*

Open your eyes, Wesley.

And Wes would always remember *nothing* from that moment on, not even in his nightmares, for when he opened his eyes there was nothing but darkness, and the darkness looked back.

When he came to, he was on his back in the cellar, staring up at the ceiling, the family gathered around staring at him with baffled intensity.

'Is that it?' someone demanded, disappointed.

'Shit me,' Wes heard Uncle George say, emaciated from his most recent bout of illness and leaning against the wall. 'Where'd he go?'

Wes turned his head, and there was a muffled hiss of consternation. Then some sniggers.

'What did he *used* to look like?' his mother asked someone else.

His chest cinched. He jerked upright, stumbling and tearing off the woollen robe. His face felt the same, but then he took his hands away and forgot. Wait. Was it the same? What had it been like before? It ought to have a nose – yes, there was one, still there. Was it the same shape? And the eyes, yes, two – that was right, wasn't it, everyone had two eyes, most people, anyway, all right, most people who weren't Wends... Lips, yes, only one mouth. And his nose? What about that? Yes, a nose. How many eyes? Two. Ears? Nose? Chin? Eyes?

'I need a mirror,' he croaked, struggling to breathe. *Don't panic.* His voice sounded – wait, what did his voice sound like?

They remembered what he'd said, though, because his mother was delving into her ceremonial robes and pulling out her compact. Was it his normal voice? What had he sounded like before?

He looked into the mirror with a burst of relief as a normal face looked back at him. He blinked, lowering the compact, and erased it from his memory. Wait. Wait, what did he look like? *Was* he normal? He couldn't remember what he'd looked like before. Surely there were photographs he could check against those.

He stared back into the mirror, fixing everything in his mind, seeing the face in it for the very first time. It was a face he could work with. Fine.

He blinked.

Who was that in the mirror?

Shit, Jesus, it was him.

'Almost as good as the Invisible Man,' Uncle David boomed into the thick, warm closeness of the overcrowded room, and broke the tension.

Everyone started to laugh.

Someone clapped him on the back, and Wes tilted the mirror accidentally, erasing the memory of his own image again.

'Wait…'

His mother took the compact back, and Wes tried to stop her, but they were jostling him, all wanting to congratulate him on his Change, see what else he'd got.

'Wait…!'

They were grabbing at his arms, his legs, cuffing his head to see if there was a second mouth like Cousin Ricky, digging him in the ribs to see if he was like Cousin Seth, grabbing his chin and showing him off to each other with leering grins.

'Now you see him, now you don't,' Ricky said from his corner, out of the way of everyone else, lounging back with a nasty gleam in his eyes.

Wes didn't trust that grin.

'What did you do?' he demanded, as he was shoved back towards the stairs. 'You fucking did something, what did you do?'

Someone had made a sacrifice on his behalf, asked for something 'special'. Someone had robbed him of his own face. Wes's insides trickled away, squirming coldly.

'*You* did this!'

Ricky shrugged, ducking his head to keep Wes in sight as the relatives started up the customary post-ceremony drinking song.

'Agent of fate, me. I don't *do* nothin'.'

'You're a fucking liar!' Wes yelled, and his voice whirled away, drowned out. 'What did you see? What did you say? What the fuck have you done to me?'

'Have a nice life, Wesley,' Ricky yelled over the racket. He waved his hand in front of his own face. 'Enjoy the… ha, you know.'

'Fucking *cunt*!' Wes fought the tide of his family, but they had hold of him so hard it hurt, dragging him back up the stairs. 'You did something! *You did something!* You asked Him for this! You—'

Ricky's cocky grin, his awful childish fucking giggle, shut his logic down. Wes writhed and twisted, nearly knocking Aunty Linda down the stairs, but she reached up and got him by the scruff. He tripped over the step above and she saved him from a proper fall.

'I'll get you back for this, you twisted piece of shit! I'll break *your* fucking face so bad naun'll remember what *you* fucking look like!'

All he could hear was Ricky laughing at him, the drinking song booming all around them, words lost in the heat of his rage. They yanked him back into the kitchen to face Granny Wend, long grey hair loose in waves around her shoulders, hands clasped in front of her.

'Well done,' she said, and Wes's rage subsided. Her approval was rare, like a snowflake in July.

He wanted to say he hadn't done anything, but she nodded and patted his cheek.

'Useful. Clever boy.'

'Yeah, I try.' Ricky sauntered out behind the press of relatives, and Wes's nostrils flared.

'I told you to go down to the shrine and make your own offerings, dear,' Granny Wend said to Wes, her hand tightening on his face. Her nails dug into his skin. 'But no. You wouldn't take it seriously. Better things to do, I'll be bound. Well, this is useful. A man no one can remember. Davey, you'll have a use for him.'

I'm not a tool, Wes wanted to say, *I'm not a toy, I'm not...*

'Welcome to the Firm, son.' Uncle David was somewhere behind him, a bulky figure in a robe the size of an industrial tarpaulin and his customary fedora.

Ricky came forwards a few steps, less swagger now, shiftier. 'Gran, can I go down now? You promised.'

'Later. It won't hurt.'

Wes could have swung for his cousin. His bloody farsight, of course. He'd sold Wes out with a prayer and sacrifice on Wes's behalf so that he could see the fucking future a bit clearer.

Must be on the wane again, Wes realised, *and we all know how important that is to you, now you're trying to take your place among the elders, like they'll ever accept you, you little piece of shit... I can't believe I wanted to run away with you, must've been mad...*

Granny Wend jerked his chin a few times to view him from different angles, tutting as she assessed what she saw there. Her nails dug in deeper, the pain distracting him from the horror of what had happened.

You better get me out of this, he thought, not looking at his cousin. He stared down at the kitchen floor, rubbing his face and hoping this was temporary, that there'd be a loophole. *I want the lottery numbers for a fucking year, I don't even care, I want to win everything, the football pools, the Grand fucking National, you're going to get me minted and out of this hellhole, shitty little traitor.*

'Give Richard a glass,' Granny Wend ordered as Great-Aunty Olive's batch of Homemade was rolled out. Family legend had it that it was from before the war. No one knew which war. For all Wes knew, probably the fucking Crimea.

Ricky was protesting that he didn't drink anymore, he'd been good hadn't he, since his Changes he'd turned over a new leaf as promised, done everything she wanted—

Wes grinned from ear to ear. This would wreck his farsight, and serve him right.

'Stop your complaints, boy, it's along of you Wesley's made something useful of himself. You celebrate with the rest of us.'

Useful of himself.

Fuck. That.

Wes turned and fixed Ricky with a vicious sneer. 'Yeah, *Richard*. You drink to me with the rest.'

Ricky looked ill, shocked, as if he genuinely hadn't expected to be shafted.

Wes exulted. She was sick of him, then. Maybe now *he'd* get a look-in as Gran's new favourite.

Ricky was handed a glass of thick, dark brown liquid, stinking like the sludge you had to clean out of plug-holes. The strangely sweet undertone was practically pure ethanol. One glass of Homemade would easily knock what little farsight he had left clean out of him, and once it hit him, he wouldn't stop at one. When Cousin Ricky had something inside him, he always had another. Always was a greedy little bastard. He'd ruin everything, spoil everything, like he always did.

Wes gave him two hours before he was throwing up and passing out somewhere on the lonely walk home.

Serve him right.

Hope he gets fucking pneumonia. Hope he chokes on his own vomit and dies. What's he done? What's he done to me?

Wesley drank his own glass of Homemade down, syrup-thick and reeking like fermented compost. He watched his cousin's ruination begin through his newly forgettable eyes, and swore he would never, ever forgive him.

14 January

Merlin Silvestris never needed to change his shape to see the future. Ricky knew he'd never be that good.

Getting Katy to kill him was a gamble, and his head was scrambled still from the thrust of the poker and the fact he didn't know what was going to happen. It was time to enact another ritual, he'd need another body bag of entrails to rip open and then the mistress would get upset. Katherine, too, most likely. He'd have to be careful about it and get some twat out walking alone, not college-age, but even then...

Even then, what was the fucking point?

That thought, the tail-end of a bitter tirade, brought him up short. He stopped walking.

Ricky found himself facing the long barrow in Barrow Field, hands in his pockets. He'd walked the long way around, taking his time, avoiding The Chase where his father lurked somewhere in the trees.

(What was the *point*? He hadn't asked himself that since...)

(Hell's bells and buckets of blood.)

Ricky ground his teeth and picked the lock on the gate which barred entry. The long barrow's energy thrummed with his, a familiar pull that forced his beauty to the surface like rippling hernias.

(What's the *point*? What sort of question is that?)

He patted his stomach, reassuring himself that his glory was still there. *That* was the point. He'd done it. He'd won. He'd got what he wanted. Now he was going to make sure the family got what was coming to them, that none of them escaped their wyrd, that everything would be as he had foreseen.

(I'm an agent of fate, me. That's all. *That's* the point.)

It felt hollow. It had no right to feel hollow. He didn't know why.

(Brain's a mess. That's all.)

But he didn't like Wes being in his space, he didn't like how casually he fitted into the grandeur, and he didn't like how quickly Fairwood had taken to Katherine. If she went back on her word and put him on the List on purpose, how was he supposed to stop her? Why wouldn't she? She was probably as bad as the rest of them.

He squeezed through the gate and into the last resting place of the prehistoric chieftains, long crumbled to dust and buggered about with by antiquarians, archaeologists and his own nosy ancestors. The barrow was large and deep, dark and quiet. It was the only other place, aside from Fairwood House, that he felt truly at peace.

The strange symbols carved into the stones inside had long interested scholars and the Heritage busybodies who preserved it these days, but Ricky didn't give a shit what they meant. They used to be the only things he could properly feel under his acid-burned fingertips, but now his skin was renewed each time he Changed, and the acid burns were gone. The symbols stung him now as he traced them in the dark, running his hand over the stones leading into the main burial chamber.

His hand hit the loose stone.

He didn't mean to do it. Just curiosity, was all.

He dug his fingers in and dragged the stone out, letting it thud onto the dirt. The vodka was still there, and a packet he hadn't needed for years. It wasn't as if it really mattered. He didn't need to be an ascetic to see the future, not anymore. He'd ascended now, he could do what he wanted.

(What's the *point*?)

He wasn't going to drink it.

He pulled the bottle out to see if it was full or not, to see if anyone had found it. It was still sealed, still full.

(Put it back, then.)

He put it down and replaced the stone.

(Left the drugs, didn't I? That's something.)

He wasn't going to *drink* it.

It had been there since... he frowned. Since the last time he'd thought *what the fuck is the point* and almost lost his farsight on purpose. Except he hadn't done it, had he? No. He'd gone and lit a bonfire instead and cut open some girl he'd found. Read his own future in the steaming guts, and it had all been worth it.

And it *had* all come to pass, hadn't it? He'd got everything he wanted.

(*Now* what the fuck do I do?)

Not the vodka, that was for sure. He was above that.

Ricky made his way by instinct and memory through the pitch dark of the passage to the main chamber of the ancient tomb, taking the bottle with him.

Wes could get bent. Who the fuck did he think he was, swanning in and giving her the eye, measuring for curtains?

She was *his*, she was *his house*, he'd wanted her ever since he was fucking *five*. He'd spent hours of his life wishing she'd let him in. He was supposed to have her to himself, but those bloody birds had said otherwise, and now look what had happened. He'd even invited them both in himself, so it was his own bloody fault.

(The irony of that, hey? Can't complain.)

The cap came off with a good hard wrench and he lost it somewhere in the dirt and the darkness.

(Fuck 'em.)

He'd forgotten what vodka tasted like. Each swallow filled his mouth with memories and burned on the way down. The bottle lightened in his hand, contents sloshing down his throat, filling his belly. He gasped for breath and nearly choked on the burn.

'This a private party or can anyone join in?'

His cousin's voice slid through his head, fish knife-blunt. Ricky nearly choked, spilling the spirits on the floor, and wiped his mouth on his sleeve.

'What're you doin' here?'

The forgettable silhouette slipped into the gloom away from the dim daylight filtering through the gate at the end of the passage and was lost in the shadows.

'Followed you.' Wes wasn't where Ricky expected him to be. Swearing under his breath, he sent out tendrils to find the vodka cap, backing up to where he knew the stone wall was.

'What for?'

A soft breath on the side of his neck made him jump. 'Wanted to apologise. Guessed you'd come here.'

A denial was on the tip of his tongue, but so was the taint of alcohol and his lips were tingling. He swallowed it down, cheeks burning.

Wes chuckled. 'Relax, I won't tell anyone. It's not like you *need* to be an ascetic anymore, right? I was a dick earlier, anyway.'

A pause. His cousin swam vaguely in front of his eyes, in and out of his memory as he blinked, making him dizzy. Ricky shifted his weight to counteract it and tried to focus on something else.

'You know what to do next, right?' Wes asked.

He hadn't got the faintest idea. The bones were silent, the omens vague. The family were restless, and he could see through enough eyes now to be sure they weren't about to do anything surprising, but without clear guidance he had no idea what to do even if they did stage a coup. Since all the future he needed to see involved himself, it was a blur, hidden from him. He wouldn't admit to any of that in a million years.

'I c'n open the portal again, yeah.'

'If you want I can take you out,' Wes said. 'We can go to the pub or something, I'll stand you an orange juice.'

Ricky shifted back until he was sure he was more than an arm's length away from his invisible cousin, and a tendril tasted vodka on something hard and round in the dirt behind him. He retrieved the screw top and tried to replace the cap without making it obvious.

'Yeah? Why would you do that?'

'Because you *don't drink*, do you?'

(Shit me.)

Ricky sagged. 'Can't, anyway. Banned from 'em all.'

'What, still? Nah, bound to be somewhere they won't care. The Mermaid's changed hands, we could try that.'

Wes seemed closer, and Ricky tried to pinpoint him in the dark but as soon as he stopped speaking, he could be anywhere.

His lips had gone numb. His brain was shutting down slowly, sinking into a buzzing miasma. He cursed himself.

'Don't fancy it.'

Wes snorted. 'Right, you'd rather get pissed in the dark on your own.'

'What the fuck do you care?'

'I *don't*, I...' Wes sighed. 'Mate, come on. For Katy, yeah, can you just... keep it together for another few days while she sorts her head out? I'd appreciate not being hammered with a poker again, honestly. Then I'll fucking join you.'

It was the 'mate' that got to him most. Wes had always had a way of sliding under your skin, even before he Changed. Ricky fought the rising urge to down the whole bottle out of spite and smash the smug bastard's face in.

But the mistress wouldn't like it.

He dropped the bottle and scuffed it out of his way. He hadn't had *that* much, by the sounds of it. It sounded at least half full.

(See?)

'Nah, I'm all right. Doant you worry, I wouldn't show you up in public.'

Wes hung back. 'Didn't think you...' He hesitated, and Ricky's guts gave a cold twist. 'Didn't think you had any at all. I mean. I thought you were doing really well.'

(Patronising prick.)

'Disappointed?' Every muscle was tense now. He fought his breaths, concentrating on the tension in his jaw and keeping his fists balled tightly.

'No.' Wes's tone was too slippery to hang on to, but it left him mollified. 'Not at all, no, it's. I, um. I'm really sorry, I didn't...'

Ricky wasn't sure if the spirits had made him nauseous or if that was just nerves. Being alone with Wes was never a comfortable experience, for reasons he had never bothered to pin down. His thoughts ran aground.

'Piss off.'

Now both sanctuaries were desecrated, he may as well sleep in the bloody Chase and take his chances with the old man. Knock on the door and watch his mother's face fall when she opened it and saw him standing there, why the fuck not.

Wes followed him along the passage, keeping his distance. 'It wasn't meant to be a lecture. Fuck knows I can't lecture anyone.'

'*Yes*, I can keep it together,' Ricky snapped, wishing he would disappear. 'Course I can.'

'You still make that herbal stuff? To take the edge off?'

Ricky shook his head. He'd given most of it to the mistress when she'd been alive, and since moving in, he hadn't really needed any. His stores of most things were low, as it happened. He didn't ought to need them, anyway, not now he was a god.

'Want me to get you anything?'

Wes was closer, and Ricky headed back through the gate with half a mind to lock him in. Not that it would do any good – Wes was as good at picking locks as he was.

'No.' Ricky scowled, his glory stirring within him. He stopped at the entrance, barring his cousin's way back to the wintry field beyond. 'I don't need anything off of you.'

Wes shrugged, loitering in the gloom. 'Let *me* talk to Katy then.'

(Oh, because you can talk better'n me? You allus got the right words, have you?)

Wes kept talking as if to illustrate this point, and Ricky slid further into bitter rumination.

'Give her some space to calm down tonight, but let me have a good chat with her tomorrow, and we'll see if we can… you know. I think I should stick around, remind her of all the times I babysat when she was a kid, looked after her. I reckon I can bring her around to seeing your way of thinking with Gran, if you give me a chance. I shouldn't have dropped you in it there, that was cowardly, and I only did it because Uncle Marcus—'

'Is this 'cos I didn't go to school?' Ricky demanded, stuck in his own train of thought. 'You sayin' I don't know the right things to say?'

Wes gave him a look. 'No one's saying you don't have a way with words. It's just… it's not always a way people want to go.'

Ricky scoffed, but his brain caught up with his ears. 'Uncle Marcus did what?'

'He rang me and threatened—'

Ricky's memory cleared. 'Oh, yeah.' He knew what Uncle Marcus had done, the threat against Wes's… whatever they were. He'd seen that through Marcus's eye. He should really look forwards, see if the old bastard got eaten in the cull. Not that it mattered much. He'd already seen enough to know Katherine *would* Change, and plenty were going to die that way.

(You can't fight fate…)

The wind sliced across his face as they exited the tomb, grass still frosted in patches and tufts despite it being a clear, bright day. The winter sun was low in the sky for just gone noon, reminding him of last January, when he'd bought the bloody vodka in the first place with Gran's shopping money. She hadn't been pleased but she hadn't said anything.

(What was the *point*?)

He was back to that, then, the spiral ready to go again, and at the bottom of it was some kind of oblivion and fuck knew he'd missed that. He was already dizzy, and the pleasant spin dulled his senses and sharpened his simmering anger.

'Hey.' Wes caught up to him, bumping his arm. 'I mean it, I'll take you for a drink. We can have a chat, you know, I – I think we ought to. Talk things out. If I'm going to be staying, it's not just her that has house rules, is it? It's your place too. And we haven't… I appreciate I'm the last person you want to spend time with…'

'Doant flatter yourself.' Ricky's teeth chattered, though he wasn't that cold. He ground them together, locking his jaw. 'I got naun against you, it weren't ever pers'nal.'

Wes snapped the padlock back in place behind them and shook his head. 'Felt fucking personal.'

Ricky sighed, but the tension was bone-marrow deep. 'We really going to do this again?'

'My fucking face is fucking personal.'

He regretted leaving the vodka behind. 'Told you, I never *specified* anything. You got what you got. Believe what you like.'

Wes overtook him with longer strides, pivoted on his flashy leather shoes and walked backwards. Ricky tried not to look at him, that bitter smile sliding in and out of focus.

'Fine, all right, fair enough, history's history. It's *now* that matters.'

(Grandad's sake, does he ever shut up?)

Wes stopped dead, blocking Ricky's way. 'I've got things – people – I don't want to lose. I *know* you know how that feels.'

Ricky froze. He opened his mouth and his teeth chattered in the knife-edge chill, and the words got stuck somewhere behind all the pictures layering up into a solid wall in his head.

'No cocky bullshit?' Wes asked, hands thrust deep into the pockets of his coat.

I bought that coat, Ricky realised. (I bought him that. An' everything he's stood up in. That was me, he got that all off of me.)

He squared his shoulders, sticking out his chest. 'I don't want you staying long. I want things back to normal.'

'What the fuck's normal?' Wes asked dryly.

Ricky giggled in spite of himself. He was starting to feel light-headed.

Wes's smile turned sly. Or, at least, that was the fleeting impression it made, and Ricky was left wondering if he'd made it up. Suspicion pricked through him.

'How does it work for you?' Wes asked. 'Seeing the future in entrails, bones, all that?'

Ricky paused. Wes had never once taken an interest in *how* it worked before. He only cared that it did.

'Why?'

'Curious.'

Ricky frowned, in the mood to be deliberately obtuse. His tongue was clumsy, and he tried not to slur. Half a bottle in one go used to be nothing. A starter. Not even so long ago. Or maybe he was misremembering.

'I see what I see, except when I don't. But now I... see more or less what I want to all the time.'

'So it's like a vision.'

(Bloody hellfire, he's persistent.)

'No. More like... I read the signs, and I remember.'

Wes sniggered. 'Like a memory, just... forwards.'

It wasn't quite like that at all, but he just wanted to get home again. Not that it was peaceful there with Katherine the Great sulking in her room or Wes now lurking around running his grubby hands over things that didn't belong to him, but at least it was temptation-free and the mistress gave him space to clear his head.

'Something like that. What you want to know that for?'

Wes shook his head. 'Just realised I never asked. I been thinking about it, like – how I ought to have been the One and Only, how that didn't work out... Doesn't it strike you as odd, that we're the only three single-births in the whole family? And we're *Porters*, not purebreds?'

Ricky rubbed the back of his neck. Wes taking an interest in his birthright for the first time in twenty-nine years was not going to end well; that was instinct kicking in, not the vodka. He cleared his throat.

'There's naun wrong wi' being a Porter.'

'No, course not.' Wes ran his hands over his oversized collar, jewelled brooch twinkling and catching Ricky's eye. 'I'm not going to say anything, by the way, if you're worried. About...' Wes jerked his head at the long barrow. 'I wouldn't do that.'

Ricky forced a smile, trying not to think about the times Wes had dropped him in it for point-scoring with Granny Wend, but they weren't kids anymore.

(You're up to something, Wesley. I know you.)

'You don't trust me, do you?' Wes shrugged, brooch glinting in the dull sunlight, and started walking. 'That's all right. I wouldn't trust me, either.'

They walked back the shorter way to the house in silence, Ricky making sure there was a good distance between them, but Wes never tried anything.

There was no sign of George Porter lurking in the trees, but if the old man didn't want you to know he was there, even Ricky wouldn't always sense it. He wouldn't admit it, but he didn't think he was top of his game now, anyway. Just as well.

He stumbled, as if to prove his own point.

Wes caught his arm.

He hadn't even noticed they were walking level with each other, or he had, but forgotten.

Wes held on to him a little longer than necessary.

Ricky's numbed skin tingled.

'Do you ever think about...?' Wes started to ask, soft and low, and Ricky shrugged him off.

'No.' It was an obvious lie. He shook his head. 'Sometimes.'

Wes nodded. 'Me too. Sometimes.'

Ricky nodded, head swimming unpleasantly. 'I'm going to have a lie down.'

The wire fence of Fairwood's back garden hove into view through the trees, tilted and slightly spinning, and the relief surged inside him, leaving him aching with tiredness.

'I'll sort Katherine out with the portal, we'll get her back there, we'll... we'll fix it. But I just need a – it ain't *easy*, comin' back after brain death and going straight into a full-body Change. Let me just say that.'

Wes nodded and let him go first.

'Safe and sound,' he announced to the house, and Ricky's cheeks burned.

Of *course* Wes had done this for *her*, gone after him for *her*, was worming his way into her good books, and bringing him home like a stray.

'I didn't need you to bring me back,' he snarled.

Wes kept out of punching range, light-footed in those flashy shoes despite the mud spoiling the leather. 'Want me to tuck you in, sweetheart?'

'Prick.' He couldn't hit him with the mistress watching. Buoyed by the light-headed fog settling inside his skull, Ricky marched back to the house, furious with Wes, his family, and himself.

Chapter 10: Heart of Darkness

15 January

Katy lay in bed hugging her favourite pillow, thinking about all the missing posters in college and running through her List in her head, along with all the things she hadn't done.

She hadn't had dinner the night before, or managed breakfast this morning. She hadn't been for a proper run in fuck knew how long. She hadn't done two of her assignments and the deadline for one of them had already gone.

She was a failure.

Gran had wanted her to be better than this.

Katy cuddled the pillow tighter, turning onto her side. She'd have to go back through the portal, and face the Throne, and Grandad Himself, maybe, and explain she couldn't do it.

What was it that she was most afraid of, and how do you just… turn it off? It was dawning on Katy that she had been afraid for most of her life. Her family had *made* her afraid, by design. When Gran wasn't around, they chipped away at her, controlling what she wore, who she spoke to, which events she went to, and when she…

Katy bit her lip.

When she'd complained to Gran, what had Gran said?

Of course they do. You're only a child.
Gran knew best. Gran knew everything.
Gran knew.
Katy swallowed hard. Gran had *always* known how the others treated her. And she'd let it happen.

Gran had let it happen, and then offered Katy the only place of safety left: Wundorwick. Where Gran could keep a closer eye on her, train her, make suggestions.

Who had said *You're getting more and more like your Aunty Janey every day...*? And Katy had dreamed of Aunty Janey.

Who had said *You'd better be careful of that temper, or you'll end up like Harry Shaw...*? And Katy had dreamed of Harry Shaw.

Katy shivered, the blankets too thin.

Had Ricky been right this whole time?

Who had warned her off him, anyway? Reminded her of how he'd ruined her birthdays whenever his name came up? Had never said a kind word about him until he turned up with various things she'd asked for, things you couldn't buy in a shop, and then she was all sweetness and approval?

Her chest hurt.

She tried sitting up, fighting to breathe, but an invisible dead weight crushed the air out of her.

Katy had never been afraid of *becoming* Ricky. They were poles apart, it just wasn't possible. And he had never been on the List. Had Gran wanted her to dream about him, too?

Wait – that's it.

She struggled to take proper breaths, shaking and forcing herself to count in her head as she inhaled and exhaled, but it was like something kept buffering in her head and she couldn't focus on the numbers. Her fingers tingled, the pillow barely registering beneath them.

What can I see what can I hear what can I feel I can't feel anything, shit shit shit...

Katy rocked, trying to get a grip on her world. Everything was slipping away and hanging on was like trying to catch shards of glass. Something inside her was dying, and she couldn't save it.

After ten minutes of hell, she wasn't dead, and the pain in her chest eased.

Someone knocked on the door. Her anxiety spiked again.

'Go away.'

'It's just me,' Wes said, his tone slipping in and out of her head. 'Don't you want any breakfast?'

Katy shook her head at the door, forgetting it was shut and he couldn't see through it.

'Katy? Just something small? Can we at least talk?'

She shuddered. 'I'm not... I don't want anything.'

There was silence. She strained to hear his footsteps walking away, but he wasn't going anywhere.

'Hey, so, do you remember that time I babysat for you, and you were sick, and I didn't know how to scramble eggs for you so I nicked Mum's cash out of the drawer for pizza and told her I'd spent it on weed?'

She snorted, despite herself.

'I was thinking about that, is all. You had those cute pyjamas. You wouldn't wear anything else to bed and I didn't know how to wash them properly and that was the first time you went to bed in a onesie instead.'

'You got me that onesie for Christmas,' Katy said, remembering.

He laughed through the wood. 'You remember?'

She hugged the pillow tighter, not answering.

'Why am I on the List, Kate?'

There was a slithering sound, as if he had slid down the door and was sat outside. She swallowed.

'Kate. Katy. You still in there?'

She cringed at the soft rap of knuckles on oak. He didn't touch the handle, though. Katy stared at it, unblinking. It didn't move.

'I just want to know.'

Katy found her voice. 'Do you really want me to die?'

Now it was his turn to be silent.

She tried to picture him the other side of the door, but could only focus on details of his favourite shirt, the creases on his designer jeans.

'I didn't *mean* to,' he said eventually. 'I just – yeah, all right, I voted against you, I'm sorry, I'm an arsehole, but I'm not – I haven't got a death wish. Not anymore. And I've felt bloody awful about it ever since, if that helps.'

'Not really, but thanks.'

He sighed. 'Can I come in, or…'

'No.'

She stared at the handle, but it didn't move. She pursed her lips.

'I want some time by myself.'

'Sure.' Still no sound of movement, no footsteps walking away. 'Sure, but… I just want to know. I mean, I figured I was going to be on there. I'm not anyone's definition of "strong", but… I was there for you, wasn't I? An' I been thinking… wasn't that strong? In a… different kind of a way?'

She couldn't answer him.

The silence was awful.

Katy didn't know what to say, but she thought he might be crying. She wasn't sure why she thought that.

Something in his voice, maybe, that she couldn't quite remember.

'It's not that,' she said, her pillow a barrier between herself and the door. 'It's nothing to – it's nothing to do with strength.'

'What then? What did I do that was so weak, or so... bad, or so... What did I do?'

Katy shook her head, pulling herself up against the wall. 'I don't *know*.' She rolled her eyes and talked to the ceiling. 'I... I just... It was all getting a bit much? Going out and stuff, we were going out every night, and...'

'Whoa, whoa, who's "we", what's this?' Wes flung her door open but stayed in the doorway. 'This is over the summer, right?'

'We all got fake IDs.' Katy had been dreading telling him about the Roar Shack and the Twilight, the two clubs that her friends had been getting into regularly. He could be such a hypocrite. 'Just a few mates, you know, we were just—'

'How many times, do as I say, not as I do.' Wes faced her, arms folded. 'You're a smart girl—'

'Fuck off.' Katy shook her head. 'We just go dancing, sometimes we take some stuff, it's not a big deal.'

'*Katy.*'

'You don't get to preach to me!' She wasn't taking a sermon from him, and the scorn poured off every syllable with more venom than she intended.

Although she forgot his expression, the twist of guilt it caused stayed with her. 'Oi! All right, bloody hell. I don't want you to be like me, do I? You can go to Uni and see the world and – fuck it, I'll pay for you to go, I said I would. Go travelling and that, do what you want. You're a clever kid. That's why...' He broke off. 'Shit.'

Katy nodded. 'Yeah, I think that's why I dreamed of you.' Every bone was made of lead. She slumped down, not looking at him, not feeling anything but heaviness, too tired for anything else. 'I thought I was turning into you. I don't want to end up just...' She sighed, suddenly numb. 'It's so fucking shallow. It's boring. I don't want to be your age and not have anything to show for it, and not have made my own *anything*, like what have you even done? Ricky gave you some winning lottery tickets and you just... like, what do you *do* every day?'

Wes was silent.

Katy hated the sound of her own voice, a flat monotone. 'I was just... I didn't want to think anymore, and then I was so scared, I was so scared I couldn't stop.' She rested her cheek on her pillow, stroking it and barely registering it against her skin. 'And I – I dreamed of you.'

'But not him.' She heard the crack in his voice and forgot it.

'No.' She shook her head. 'Not him. Not Dad. Not Mum. I can't imagine being like *them*.'

'But everyone else...'

Katy shivered. 'I can't remember what it was. What it was about them, I mean. Must've been something, something someone said, or something they did...' She frowned. 'Gran... Gran said to me, "What about Cousin so-and-so, wouldn't you like to be like them when you grow up?"' She swallowed sharply. 'Gran... Gran said stuff like that a lot.'

'Yeah.' Wes was watching her. 'She liked to pit us all against each other.'

Katy didn't want to hear this again, not now. 'Can you go away now, please? I know why you're on there, I can...

get over it, I guess, I don't know, just... I just need to be on my own.'

'You really want to know what I do every day?' Wes dug his shoulder into the door jamb. 'I do whatever the fuck I want. I have the life I want to live, yeah? I set it up so that I don't have to do a single day's work I don't want to do. I have two people who love me to death, fuck knows why, and I spend all my time trying to make them happy and be as supportive a partner as I know how to be, and Christ knows that's not very much but I try.' He ran out of breath and inhaled deeply. 'You don't need to worry about turning out like me, love. But I hope that you get to live the life you want, not the same one that I got, we're different people. I get that. I want you to live the life *you* want. I hope you can be like me in that way. That's all.' He nodded, voice cracking again. 'That's all I want for you.'

Before she could say anything back, he spun away and strode off, first out of sight, then out of earshot.

Katy didn't have any words for a long time.

They buzzed in her head too fast to catch.

Her lip quivered.

She instinctively went for her phone to call Rachel.

The battery, which had been at seventy per cent, was now at two.

'No! No, no...' Katy forced herself to get up and find her charger. 'No...'

'Let me.'

Katy screamed.

Carrie was in the room, as if she'd melted through a wall.

'Sorry.' Carrie didn't look human for a moment – there was something wrong with her skin. It rippled, going from woodgrain to a smoother plastered texture, and Katy closed her eyes. She was seeing things now as well.

Her heart juddered violently.

'Oh my God, don't *do* that!'

Carrie took the phone and cradled it in her hands. The screen lit up with the charging symbol.

Katy blinked. 'I... I need to call my friend.'

Carrie nodded. 'Not your mum?'

'What the fuck would *she* do?' Katy threw herself back onto the bed, wishing she was a kid again and Gran would come and take her away for a sleepover. The only peace she ever had was at Wundorwick. Aunty Ruby had taken Toffee the cat, although Katy had begged to keep him. Mum had said no.

Carrie sat on the bed and stroked her back. 'It'll be all right. No one can hurt you here.'

'Can I stay here?' Katy tried to sound mature, but it came out damp and high.

Oh, great, now she was crying. Perfect.

'As long as you like, but on one condition.'

Katy guessed what that was. 'I won't put Ricky on the List. I already promised that.'

'Just making sure.' Carrie gazed at her with windowpane eyes, and Katy thought she could see faces in them that walked the corridors of the strange woman's mind like ghosts. 'Want me to stay?'

Katy shrugged. Carrie was oddly calming. Like the house. She glanced at her phone in Carrie's hand and saw to her amazement that the battery had gone back up to thirty per cent already.

'How – how are you doing that?'

'Practice.' Carrie smiled at her. The smile was warm, and if not entirely human, was certainly humane. 'You coming for something to eat?'

'Not yet.' The panic attack had left her nauseous again, and she didn't want to spend today throwing up as well.

Carrie nodded. 'Understood.'

'Did you ever... get like this when you were, um, like, when you were... alive?' She wasn't sure if that was the right word, and a spike of worry jazzed through her in case she'd fucked it up.

Carrie grinned. 'I... didn't do well around people, sometimes. I'm not surprised you're anxious. I'm more surprised you didn't have a panic attack or something yesterday, to be honest, but... no, you've done really well.'

'I don't feel like I'm doing well,' Katy muttered at her lap. 'I can't do it. I'm not going to face my fear, I'm going to fuck this up and end up in the fucking Throne with the last Thirteenth and Gran and...' The panic was welling back up, the tightness in her chest increasing again.

Carrie's hand rubbed her back, firm and smooth, and Katy found herself leaning into the embrace of a safe, warm space where she could hide forever. She managed a deeper breath, and inhaled the scent of a garden like Gran's, mingled with old books and sun-warmed wood and leather.

'I really miss Gran,' she whispered, and started to cry. 'Is that, is that wrong, I don't... I don't even know anymore...'

Carrie held her as she dissolved into sobs, and even as she bawled her eyes out into the strange woman's cushion-soft chest, Katy felt safe for the first time since Gran's murder.

Wes sat in the passenger seat of his car again, toying with the idea of just going the fuck back to London and telling Katy he was sorry over the phone.

'That went well,' he told Charlie and Hugo's picture on his phone background. They were beaming at him from the patio of that villa in Thailand last year, Charlie in Hugo's lap with her arms around his neck, and three seconds after that photo had been taken, he'd picked her up like she weighed nothing and carried her off shrieking into the sea.

Wes had never wanted that holiday to end, but he never wanted any of the good times to end, ever. And they always did. Sooner or later, they went back to work, and he went back to... existing.

'I could get a job,' he suggested, as his partners smiled at him. 'No, I couldn't. I don't want to, anyway. And you know what I'm like. I was always crap at the basics, like showing up. Same with school, really.'

He missed them so much his chest ached.

He sent Charlie a video telling her he loved her, and sent Hugo a dick pic that remained unseen. He zipped his fly up, disgruntled at the lack of an immediate reaction, and sent the same one to a few of his other contacts just for a bit of validation. Someone whose surname he couldn't recall sent a heart-eyes emoji back, and he felt that was enough to buoy his ego for another half an hour, despite another reply telling him to fuck off. He put his phone away and considered his options.

There were a few pills left in the packet. It might be worth testing them out just once more, now he'd got the hang of it. Then he wouldn't need Ricky at all.

Nobody would.

Getting rid of him, though, that would be tricky, and he wasn't sure that's what he really wanted. There was a lot of history there, they didn't *always* needle each other, and besides, something Wes hated admitting was now an undeniable fact. Ricky was genuinely fucking scary. The Change in the kitchen, the way his coils bulged under the muscle, that genuinely rattled him. He'd seen what his cousin had become, and anything that could kill Gran and scare Uncle Marcus wasn't something Wes wanted to be in the same room with twice.

Maybe he'd made a big mistake.

'One way to find out,' he told the packet, rolling the glittering pills between his fingers inside the plastic.

—

This time, the first thought that greeted him outside his head was like a barrier, crackling darkly and stopping him from moving past it. Wes tried to push it out of the way, but it was hard and solid like a TV screen. He rapped on it with his knuckles, and a picture flared into life.

'*I don't believe in the future.*' Seventeen-year-old Wes scoffed at his cousin, shirtless and lying in the grass in Barrow Field. They usually went up there to drink and smoke weed, but it was magic mushrooms this time.

'*You don't believe in anything.*' Ricky was lying on his back waiting for the shrooms to kick in with the E. He had smacked Wes's hand away from his fly twice so far, and Wes wanted to try his luck a third time.

'Not this again, leave him alone.' Adult Wes watched his teenage self with growing unease, a gnawing guilt eating at him.

When teenage Wes was shoved off again and started bitching about how the farsight was fucking with Ricky's brain, adult Wes was mightily relieved.

God, he'd been an arsehole at that age.

'*The future isn't fixed until you look at it,*' teenage Wes was arguing, pissed off by his cousin's rejection. '*Why would you* want *to look at your own, anyway?*'

Oh, it was *this* argument.

Ricky had killed some girl from Wes's school the year before, just to read his own future. Wes was about to find this out, there was going to be a full-on fight about it, but by then Ricky would be high as fuck and they'd kissed and made up or some shit.

Wes didn't want to see all that again.

'Fuck this,' Wes said to the thought-barrier, and smashed through it, headfirst. The ground gave way and he pitched forwards through galaxies of bursting stars, landing face first on black sand.

Ricky was holding open a portal – adult Ricky, as he looked now, skin shredding off his monstrous eel-skin coils that swelled beneath his organs.

Wes saw himself, standing behind him.

How did Ricky get into the volcanic landscape he'd seen before? He didn't like it here. He was exposed, alone. A stone circle called to him, some way off, but he wasn't sure how far. Now there were monoliths dancing in rounds, shedding symbols into the air like sequins.

As he tried to focus on something else, orbs of memory popped up, the bad kind, fizzing and pulsing, bouncing towards him across the obsidian desert like that ball thing in *The Prisoner*. Wasn't that filmed in Wales somewhere? This didn't look like Wales. It looked like somewhere you went to die.

Wes knew with horrible certainty that if he got stuck there, he'd die there. He knew it, because he remembered it. Did that mean he was going to die, or just that he was going to be shit-scared?

Fuck...

Memories crowded him, bouncing against the dark sand.

One of them stood out among the rest, looming closer.

Charlie, on her knees with a utility knife in her hand, slicing off her own eyelids so she could stare hopelessly at a collage of his photographs until she starved to death. She'd soiled herself rather than leave the room, rather than leave the pictures of him.

'No, no, baby, no...' Wes whimpered, reaching for her, but he never wanted to touch that memory again. 'I thought if I left, you'd get better...'

The memory replayed from when he walked in the door. He spun around, looking for other memories, but there was only that one, replaying like a gif wherever he looked.

'No, no...' He closed his eyes, but it played on the back of his eyelids, and he couldn't switch it off.

Regret oozed out of his joints, slowing him down as he tried to run, and just as he collapsed in a heap of broken, numbed parts, everything twisted into a different shape and he was still strapped into the passenger seat of his car, his brain inside out, thoughts sucked back inside.

It took him a good ten minutes and another bottle of mineral water before he dared unbuckle the seat belt.

'Fuck, I've got to stop taking these.'

There was too much darkness in him, too much he never wanted to remember either backwards or forwards.

Wes shuddered. Regardless of what happened tonight, he promised himself, he would abide by the house rules and go back to London tomorrow. He needed a change of clothes anyway.

He stayed in the car with the radio on, listening to Classic FM to calm himself down until he felt stable enough to head back inside.

—

Katy came down for dinner and Wes let her go first. He wondered if leaving her alone had been the right thing to do, or if she would have appreciated him being there with her. Too late now.

'Hey! You all right?'

She nodded, not looking directly at him, but moved her wrists in the way she'd done as a little girl wanting a cuddle. He hadn't seen her do that in a long time.

Wes swept her into a tight hug.

Katy clung to him tighter than he expected, not letting go when he tried to pull away.

'Oh, okay. All right. Hey. Hey, you okay?'

She squeezed him and let him go. 'Yeah.'

'Promise?'

She nodded. 'Promise.'

He stroked her hair back from her temples, cupping her chin. 'Okay, then.'

She brushed him off. 'Are *you* okay?' There was a suspicious, pointed note in her voice. 'You look like shit.'

'That's all right. Blink, you'll forget all about it.'

Katy shook her head. 'That's not...' A vague expression crossed her face as she forgot what he looked like halfway through her sentence, and it died on her tongue. Wes chucked her under her chin, sadness squeezing his chest like one of her hugs.

'Right. Where's the god?'

Katy shrugged. 'Somewhere. Pretty sure he knows there's dinner in, like, two minutes.'

Wes wandered into the kitchen, nodded at Carrie who was setting the table, and took a seat. 'Alive and kicking, then.'

Katy winced. Ricky, on cue, swaggered out from the utility room, swinging the door shut behind him.

'Wotcher, Cuz.'

'All right?' Wes took him in. All trace of the brain death and ill-advised vodka was gone. 'You're looking much prettier.'

Ricky smirked. 'Ta.' He gave Carrie a pat on her back as he passed and took a seat at the table. 'Somethin' smells nice.'

'You're going to Change again, aren't you?' She went to the oven. 'You're getting the lion's share.'

Ricky winced. 'Fair enough.'

'Make him eat it.' Carrie dropped the baking-hot ceramic pot on the table without using oven gloves, a fact that Wes filed away for future reference. 'He needs it.'

Wes filed this away, too. 'Changes take it out of you, do they?'

Ricky didn't answer. He helped himself first, taking about two thirds of the casserole and leaving the rest for them.

Wes watched dinner disappearing onto his cousin's plate, and Carrie brought out warm crusty rolls.

Ricky refused them.

'Don't eat bread,' he said with his mouth full. 'You know that.'

'They're not *for* you.' Carrie clicked her tongue. 'We've got guests.'

'They ain't guests, they're fam'ly.'

Wes smirked. 'Speaking of which, how's your mum and dad?'

'Piss off.' Ricky scraped his chair back, tendrils disgorging out of reflex.

'You're so rude,' Katy muttered, not quite as shrunken in on herself as she usually was during family rows. Wes wondered if that was a good sign.

Wes shrugged. Trails of silver floated across his vision, as if he remembered this from before, as if this had all already happened, and he knew what was coming next. The images didn't come to mind, not exactly, but he had a feeling how it was all going to end, and somewhere up ahead was a pulsing red cocoon and Ricky lost in a landscape that wasn't the world they knew.

Wes's lip curled. 'Just asking after his old man, that's all.'

'Yeah?' Ricky talked around a mouthful of casserole. 'How's yours, still killing little girls for no reason?'

'All right, our dad's as much of an embarrassment as yours is,' Wes allowed. 'But at least he raised us lot in a decent house, not some shack in the woods without running water. Uncle George had all the same opportunities as our dad did, and he still *chose* to live like a fucking caveman.'

'Where's this coming from?' Katy demanded, but Wes had no clue.

'Uncle George barely bothers to hide what he does.'

Ricky swallowed. 'Why shouldn't he? Why should he hide what we are, we're top of the bloody food chain.'

Wes stabbed a carrot with his fork. 'Are you listening to yourself? Top of the food chain? What sort of fascist bollocks is that?'

'It's a *fact*.' Ricky sat back in his chair, glowering. 'We could be running the whole bleedin' world, and you're upset about Dad knocking off a few tourists.'

Wes scoffed. 'Who wants to rule the world? You know what that sounds like to me?'

'Hard work?'

'Admin.'

Ricky laughed in his face. 'I'm talking about destruction, death, bloody *power*. *Real* power. *This!*' He let his glory ripple and bulge, tearing the skin and splitting the stretchmarks along his ribs. The fabric of his hoodie strained as his glory fought to be free.

Carrie smacked Ricky on the shoulder. 'Oi, cut it out, calm down.'

Ricky rolled his eyes. Wes held his breath, but everything seemed to settle. 'Just sayin'.'

'He's leaving tomorrow, let's just have dinner.' Carrie shot Wes a warning look.

Wes nodded, unnerved by the speed at which his cousin could Change. He ignored their host, silver sparks crackling in his head.

'Go on then.' He jerked his chin at the back door, voice trembling. 'Point made. Off you go. Go rule the world.'

'I'd rather be left alone. Anyway. You'd have to be mad to want to rule the bloody world. What the fuck would you do with it?' Ricky visibly forced himself to relax, and Wes cursed himself and his mouth.

What was wrong with him?

Where do we start there, Wes, hey?

Something silvery tugged at his mind, and he found himself talking without registering his own words.

'I don't disagree with you. Maybe the three of us are the only sane ones in the whole family, the only ones who see that clear, do you know what I mean? Is this a coincidence, the three of us ending up together like this, or what?'

Ricky paused, staring at him. 'Are you high?'

Wes's lips twisted into something bitter, silver scudding away and leaving him woozy. 'Is that judgement I hear, Richard?'

'Just not my idea of fun.'

Wes seethed, nettled by the piety. *Oh, fuck off, you sanctimonious little shit.*

It didn't help that Ricky had taught him the word 'sanctimonious'.

He sneered. 'You want fun? Let's not forget who it was that actually got you off, shall we?'

There was a chilled, pregnant silence, a taut sheet of it that shrouded the kitchen and wrapped around his heart.

Ricky's face was burning.

Wes groaned, hating himself. 'Fuck. I'm – I'm so sorry. That was. It just slipped out, I didn't. I didn't mean…'

'I can open the portal well enough without you,' Ricky said finally, his voice tight. 'I don't need you here for that.'

'I know you don't.'

Ricky's eyes snapped up to meet his, fever-bright. He stood up and moved towards the fireplace behind Katy, who drew back in her chair and shot Wes a worried glower.

'Hell's bells and buckets of blood.' Ricky shook his head, staring at him and rolling up his sleeves. 'You think I *can't* do this without you? That what you think? You want to get your feet under the table here, make the mistress keep you on as part of some bloody triad, is that what you want? Want to see what *I* can do?' Two spots of ugly crimson bruised over his angular cheeks. His accent broadened. 'I c'n control gateways to worlds you ain't even *dreamed* of. It's part of her, don't you understand that? She needs me to do it, don't you, old girl? She needs *me*.'

Wes glanced awkwardly at Carrie, who was staring at Ricky in bafflement, one hand pressed over her heart.

His eyes were drawn back to the Pendle Stone, the hearthstone in the heart of the house, and a chill wandered up his arms.

He shivered, swallowing. 'I believe you.'

'*You* don't believe in *anything*.'

'That's not true. I believe in...' Wes hesitated, frustrated that Ricky wouldn't remember how sincere he was being. 'I believe in the people I love,' he mumbled at the table. 'Which don't include you, fair enough, but I *do* believe in some things.'

Ricky was vibrating like a tuning fork, cherry-red dots blazing in his pupils, and when he slammed his foot on the hearthstone under the old range Wes felt the shock reverberating through the stone tiles. There was ancient power in it, power that tugged at his skin, sucked at his forgettable face. He hadn't felt anything like that since...

His throat went dry.

Ricky was ready to rip the fabric of the world apart, and he was probably powerful enough to do it. He fought the rising panic in his chest, reasoning that he wouldn't, he wouldn't do anything like that, because he loved the house too much.

He'd never hurt Carrie.

It came to him then in a bolt of obvious clarity – somehow, Carrie *was* the house. He wondered how the hell he'd been so slow, and then how the hell that had happened. Never mind; now was decidedly not the time.

'Easy, mate, I...'

Ricky pared his full lips back in a sneer. 'You want to see? I'm a bloody god, I'm *your bloody god.*'

'Jesus, calm the fuck down!' Wes wanted to get between Ricky and Katy, who was cowering against the table and not knowing what to do with the power that was reverberating behind her. '*All right!* All right, you're scaring her, come on.'

'Hey!' Carrie's voice was soothing, the sound of a kettle on a rainy day. 'Ricky. He isn't thinking that. I know he's not.'

She's in his head, too, Wes realised. *Fuck, that can't be much fun. Rather you than me, love.*

'You haven't got *anything* to prove to him,' Carrie said, still in that calming tone. 'Look, you've made Katy cry.'

Ricky shot Katy a wild stare, an unhealthy pallor replacing the bruised blush. He swayed but kept his balance. Wes hadn't noticed Katy getting upset, and now he saw her fighting tears his heart twisted up.

Wes glanced at their stricken cousin, who didn't know what to say. 'Katy... love, I'm sorry. It was my fault, I pissed him off. I didn't mean to. All right, I took something, yeah. I'm a fuck-up, I'm sorry.' He leaned back in his seat, hoping to make himself appear less threatening and defuse things a bit. '*We're* sorry. His bark's worse than his bite, right?'

They both knew that wasn't exactly true, but Ricky shrugged and nodded. 'I wa'n't... I wouldn't hurt you, love. I let you kill me, remember? Bet that felt good.'

Katy sniffed. 'You're a pair of bastards.' She gave a watery smile, but it was brief. 'You know I could just kill both of you.'

'True.' Wes relaxed a little. 'But you *did* promise.'

'Yeah.' Katy rubbed her cheeks and swivelled on her seat to face Ricky, who had backed off. 'What's... No, you know what... Never mind.' She chewed the inside of her cheek and looked away. 'Can we just get this over with then? I just want... I don't know. I don't want... you two at each other's fucking throats all the time, it's like being at home.' She shot her brother a vicious glance that landed like a kick in the balls, and Wes swallowed.

'You want me to do it now?' Ricky asked Katy, who was dashing the tears off her cheeks.

Katy shrugged, miserable.

He nodded, looking at Wes. 'Yeah, all right, I'll do it now.'

'I don't want to see the Throne again,' Katy mumbled, voice thick. 'Not now, not... I don't want it, I don't want to be like this, I hate it...'

'Nah, come on, once you've figured the List out, it's up to you what you do.' Ricky gave her a weak smile. 'Let's get it over with, like I promised.'

Wes waited, recalling snatches of silver-edged hallucinogenic memory. It was tugging him into a groove, his direction carved out, irresistible. He wondered if Ricky could feel it, too.

'Can you come with me this time?' Katy whispered, big brown eyes wide and anxious.

'No,' Ricky mumbled, crouching down. 'We shouldn't. It's the Thirteenth's place. Not like where we go for our Changes...' He shrugged. ' 'Sides, we need to keep the portal open this side for you to come back.'

Wes tensed, pushing out the probing house and focusing.

Ricky didn't Change, not properly, but his skin split along his forearms as something pushed and bulged underneath. Bits of him ruptured under the strain, and the hearthstone began to ripple as if it were made of water.

Wes watched, fascinated. He really was going to do it by himself. It looked excruciating.

'Mate, stop it.' Carrie hung back, but her face was twisted in pain and Wes wondered if she could feel what Ricky did. He was using energy channelled literally *through her*, wasn't he? Did it hurt her as much as it hurt him? 'Ricky, I'm serious, let him help you.'

Fuck, he's going to do it, he's actually going to tear himself apart.

He needed Ricky alive, needed Katy to face whatever she had to. He couldn't let him do it alone. Not until she was done. Not until he was off the List.

Wes lost his nerve and started muttering under his breath, trying to take some of it into himself, connecting with it as words wove themselves into anchors and sank into the Pendle Stone.

Katy crept forwards, reluctantly dragging her feet.

He wasn't sure what to expect, but the swirl of vertigo when she connected with the rippling stone threw him off balance even though he was sitting down. He grabbed the table, which, for a split second, felt soft and malleable, like putty rather than wood.

His shoes sank through the tiles. In an effort to free himself he fell off the chair. Then the world swung back, his feet were freed, and he banged to the floor, jarring his knee.

He looked up.

Ricky was half-man, half coils, face splitting apart with nothing underneath it, a hollow thing of swirling darkness, shreds of himself hanging together by strings of skin. He'd seen this. He'd seen Ricky in the desolate landscape beyond the portal, he'd seen himself behind his cousin, exactly where he was now, he'd seen all this from the other side.

Maybe the future was fixed. It had to happen the way he remembered it happening.

How did Ricky go through the portal in his vision?

The sparks of silver coating his mind seemed to tug him into a solution. But he couldn't act, not yet.

Katy was still gone.

Chapter 11: Anywhere but Here

Outside

The black desert stretched out around her, but this time, on the horizon to her left, she thought she could see a pale white doorway in the sky, a perfect rectangle of white light where the thick curtain of navy hit the obsidian.

She couldn't see the Throne this time.

She wasn't even sure that this place was real. It felt like a limbo, a space between worlds, something tucked away and forgotten.

Was that all the afterlife was? Did you die, and your essence or soul or whatever it was, did that get sucked into the gaps between atoms, get lost in the cracks, forever stuck in the corners of time?

'Hello?'

She wasn't expecting an answer.

Hello, something echoed behind her. *Hello. Hello. Hello.*

It wasn't the voice of the Throne.

'I figured out the List,' Katy said, not turning around. She could feel it, heavy and hulking behind her, solid, real. More real than she was.

And you faced it, your fear?

'I... figured it out.'

Did you face your fear?

Katy itched to turn around, wanting to know what was behind her. 'I tried...'

Something sighed against the back of her head. She flinched, grabbing at empty air and her own hair, and spun around.

The black desert was empty, except for the Throne in the far distance, moving like a stalking predator, a great chair with many-jointed limbs carrying it forwards over the sand.

'Oh no...'

Her bead burned.

Katy wasted no time. She jumped back onto the Pendle Stone, a slab of rippling silicate, and tumbled back into the kitchen.

She didn't know if Ricky had noticed she was back, his ragged face was screwed up in effort. His coils were tumbling out of the ruins of his flesh, but he was controlling it well, keeping himself balanced between the two forms, a monster of eyes and mouths and torn skin.

'Did you do what you had to do?' Wes asked, catching her by the elbow and thrusting her out of range of the Pendle Stone.

She didn't know how to answer that. She tried positivity. 'Yeah?' She shrugged. 'I think... I mean, "facing my fear" is what I'm *meant* to do, whatever that means, but...' Before she could finish her sentence, Wes lunged forwards and pushed Ricky hard in the small of his back.

Caught off balance, coils thrashing, Ricky had time to swear in his own gruff voice before he tumbled into the portal.

Carrie lunged forwards too late.

Wes kicked at the coils writhing half in, half out of the dimension, as they grappled for something to lock onto and tried to attach to the hot range.

Katy blinked.

She stared at the spot where Ricky had been, at her brother, his wild-eyed exultation strobing in front of her as she saw, blinked, forgot, saw, then forgot again.

'What the fuck?'

'You don't understand,' Wes muttered, pale and shaking, flashing in and out of her memory. 'I had to. We don't need him anymore.'

Katy moistened her lips, not understanding. 'What the *fuck*?'

It was like a bad TV show. Her brother was a stranger to her. A cold, twisted stranger.

A coil flew out and looped around Wes's ankle as Ricky fought to extricate himself from the Thirteenth's dimension. Katy stared stupidly at it, not knowing whether to grab it and pull, or help her brother get it off him. Carrie shouldered her out of the way and lunged for the coil, forcing Katy into action.

Katy made a grab for Wes's hand at the same time as Carrie tried to grab the coil, but as Katy's fingers brushed her brother's, Wes was yanked backwards. He and the rest of Ricky were consumed by the shimmering haze rising from the limestone slab, and both of them disappeared.

Carrie stared at Katy, open-mouthed.

'I don't believe this.' Katy saw the Pendle Stone begin to stabilise, the portal closing.

She didn't have time to think it through.

She jumped.

(Fuck me, stupid bastard…)

Ricky fought to restore his human form, although he wasn't sure that was the best option. His coils bled out slick gelatinous skin, human shrink-wrap, and he oozed over the sharp anthracite. Wes was lying some distance away, where his coil had thrown him.

They needed the Thirteenth to get out of here, it was her place. The Pendle Stone, still open but barely, wouldn't let him back through.

'You sloppy tart,' he snarled at his cousin, trying to concentrate. 'What d'you go an' do that for?'

Wes stood slowly, unfolding himself from the black sand. 'You selfish prick, why did you pull me through as well?'

'*Me*, selfish?' Ricky balled up his fists, though a small rational part of his brain tugged at him to take stock of the situation first. '*Why?*'

'Because we don't need you!' Wes snapped, turning around. He strobed in front of Ricky's eyes, forcing him to raise a hand and look down at the black dust. 'I don't need you anymore! I was a single-birth too, farsight should've been *my* birthright. An' I *can* see. Uncle Barry unlocked it for me.'

'Uncle Barry?' Ricky dropped his hand, wincing as Wes flickered. 'Uncle bloody *Barry*, are you serious? Unlocked with what? Somethin' you snort?'

'It's a pill,' Wes said sullenly.

Ricky stared at him, for once almost lost for words.

He shook his head slowly, blinking.

'…You stupid bastard.'

'*Fuck* you.'

'What does it do to your liver?'

'Want to have a look?' Wes tugged his shirt up. 'Can't do more harm than that paint stripper you drink.'

Ricky flushed. 'I *don't* drink, all right, that was a… Look, I'm entitled if I want, I don't have to answer to you.'

Wes yanked his shirt back down. 'I want you to *see* me,' he said, his voice shaking. 'I want… I want you *all* to *fucking see me.*'

Ricky *could* see him.

The strobing had settled a little. There were two Wesleys here, one layered on top of the other. At the back, there was the one from after the Changes, fractured, almost invisible, the shards shifting into place and out again like tectonic plates. But there on top, like a flickering hologram, there was the Wesley his memory had been robbed of. Wesley as he'd once been.

That taboo pretty-boy with an obscene tongue, grown into his long looks and lanky frame, all moisturiser and eyeliner and mad fuck-me eyes, dressed up with a smile you could shave with.

Ricky had forgotten the edge of mania that had sometimes lurked in the corners of Wesley's eyes, in the slash of his smile. He'd forgotten he had learned how to smile like that from Wes.

'I *can* see you,' he said, but Wes didn't understand.

Katherine jumped through the Pendle Stone's dying light as Ricky finally lost his grip on it. For a moment they stood, a rough triangle, staring at each other.

'*What* the fuck just happened,' the Thirteenth said in between panting, then finally, plainly furious, words clipped, 'And *why did you do that?*'

Ricky clicked his tongue and jumped in before Wes made it somehow all Ricky's fault.

'Well, as far as I c'n gather, Katherine, your brother here had a really good idea when he was off his fucking face.' His limbs ached, joints leaden. 'You happy now, Wes? Now we're all here. Nice happy family.'

Wes stared at the sand, turning slowly on the spot, as if he didn't quite understand what had happened. 'If we're both here, we can just open the portal again from this side, right? It's the Thirteenth's place, Katy, can you, er…?'

Katherine stared at him. 'No?'

Ricky sighed, squatting to feel the spot where the Pendle Stone had been. 'You want the bad news, or the really bad news?'

The Thirteenth winced. 'We're stuck here, aren't we.'

'Yeah.'

'Is that the bad news or the really bad news?'

'Well, that's just… more of an overarching fact.' He gestured with a hand, making an arch in the air. 'The *bad* news is, I ain't got nothin' to open a portal with on this side. An' the *really* bad news is, I have no idea where to find something.' He straightened up, dusting off his hands. 'So, yeah, we're trapped. Basic'lly.'

'Okay…' She didn't panic, which boded well. 'What about that?'

Ricky followed the line of her finger to the odd, boxy horizon. There was a rectangle of bright light cutting into the navy wall like a door.

(Could be a trap.)

He eyed the light suspiciously, fighting the cold feeling he'd learned to identify as fear. Why was he afraid? They were alone here. But he couldn't shake an instinct, awakening in his gut, that sent prickles of warning through him.

Ricky hadn't felt like this before, except maybe that once as a kid, the first time his dad Changed in front of him and he realised he was a larva, a grub, naked, defenceless, and this shadowy, clawed, arachnid of a man was his insatiable, carnivorous god. He hadn't had words for it then, of course, only the feeling his four-year-old self couldn't express without soiling himself.

(Fuck that, abuseful old bastard. Now who shits 'emselves whenever I get a-nigh 'em?)

He rubbed the back of his neck.

'That what you think, is it?'

She shrugged. 'I think this is, like, a room.'

'A room?'

'A Throne Room,' she said, and Ricky's stomach plummeted.

His lips twitched involuntarily.

'The Throne, yeah. I bet it's a bit... I doubt it'll be happy to see me.'

Behind them, Wes found his voice. 'What's that?'

He had his back to them, staring off in another direction.

Lumbering around the edge of its confinement, Ricky thought he saw a malformed spider bearing something on its back. It had too many limbs, too many joints, and what were those things like snail-stalks growing out of it? What was that whisper, that greedy, slavering sound?

(That's bloody huge. Shit me, it's gigantic...)

His skin tingled, every hair rising, the last of the goo sliding off him as he shivered. His clothes were stained, ruined, but it didn't matter. The mistress would get him new ones. He needed to get back to her.

Instinct, primeval, told him to run.

Ricky Porter hadn't run from anything in years.

He backed off.

'It wants to hurt us,' Katherine said, her voice strained, and he didn't ask how she knew. He didn't doubt she was right.

Wes was staring at it in rapt horror.

(Of course – assimilation was your worst nightmare, wasn't it, Wesley? Allus stood out from the crowd.)

Not that he was any keener.

'Wes, shift your arse.' He couldn't tell distances in this place. How close was the doorway? Was it a doorway or a – a what? How far away was that thing, and how fast could it move?

Wesley didn't stir.

'Katherine, grab him.'

She was pale, frozen. 'You're stronger.'

'He's the one you jumped in to get,' Ricky snapped, the cold prey-feeling giving way to the other thing, the more familiar sensation of burning. 'Get him, then.'

She hesitated, so he left her there to make her mind up. Back off slowly. No sudden moves. Predators smell fear, prey stink of it. Sours the meat, better they don't notice until it's too late.

He kept up a measured pace, and by the time Katherine had sorted her head out and taken hold of her fuckwit brother, he was much further across the sands than he'd expected to be.

(Space is different. Like the way Dad does it.)

Bloody hellfire. So he could be halfway to the doorway (halfway out or halfway to his doom) or be nowhere near it, at the same time.

The anthracite powder shifted under his feet.

Was it coal?

He wished he was in the coal cellar of The Crows, soaking in her repressed, carbonised anger, gangrene-sweet, the darkness in her soul always keeping a welcome for him, no matter what else she thought or argued.

A few more steps, a quick check over his shoulder. The doorway was closer.

Katherine was dragging Wes and trying to close the gap between them, but the distance seemed to fluctuate as he tried to judge it. He didn't stop. Better one of them get out, better it was him.

(Not better for them…)

He frowned.

That was something the mistress would point out, dry and sarcastic. All right, he'd explain to her later, she'd understand.

You broke the curse.

Ricky stopped dead.

That wasn't his thought.

Not hers, either; he knew what she felt like in his head.

He didn't think it was the Throne.

Of course – if this was a Throne Room, where were they? Whose dimension were they in? Who spoke to him at night, whispered things, promised things?

'All right, Grandad?' he whispered, wondering where the old bastard was. He watched the Throne coming towards them, scuttling a few feet and then staying still, stalks waving, limbs tense. Its composite nature was clearer now that it was closer. 'That any way to treat your grandkids?'

They outlived their usefulness, so they have a new purpose now. But you, One and Only, you have proved yourself.

That sliced deep.

Ricky closed his eyes, fighting the urge to Change and rip the world apart.

'I ain't a fucking tool.'

You are the One and Only. Unique in your generation.

That was not the denial he wanted.

'But I'm *not* a fucking *tool*.'

'You're the biggest tool I've ever met,' Katherine snapped over her shoulder, dragging Wes backwards over the desert towards him. 'Keep going, dickhead.'

The Voice was gone.

Ricky licked his lips.

'Don't hate me.'

'What?'

He didn't know why he said that. He didn't know if it was even his idea, or if he was talking to her, or to Wes, or to Carrie, whom he'd probably never see again. Doubt, another unfamiliar foe, swept over him.

He didn't know what happened next.

He *always* knew.

What was this, this creeping sense of, of, of *desolation*? What was this, this emptiness, coming over him like a storm?

He shook his head and resumed his steady pace, but the door was further away now and he had a lot of ground to make up.

You have more to do.

The Voice was back as soon as he began to move. He didn't know if it could hear his thoughts like the mistress could when he wanted her to, but he pushed one up to the forefront of his mind anyway. About time someone gave the old man a piece of their mind.

(Look, Gaffer, if you wanted a champion you should've chosen one, not three girls who didn't give a rat's arse about anything except getting one up on each other and winning the bloody flower show.)

He gritted his teeth in a grimace, letting his anger overpower whatever else was going on inside him, this witch's brew of nameless sensation and hollowness.

(You chose the wrong fam'ly, an' that's on you.)

The light burned his back, and he paused, waiting for the other two to catch up.

He didn't fancy meeting his fate on his own after all.

The Throne stalked them inexorably across the wasteland of his nightmares.

Ricky snarled. 'Did you hear what I said?'

'You didn't say anything.' Katherine looked over her shoulder, nearly stepping on his foot. 'Shit! How'd you get so close?'

'Doant matter.' He took her arm and ran at the doorway of light.

-

The desert gave way to an island of black rock, the grey flat lid became a grey, clouded sky. A stench of rotting fish and seaweed, something vinegary, hit him in the face.

He'd read Grampa Nathan's memoirs, the human Porter who corrupted their particular line with his name and watered-down regular genes, and this looked familiar.

Grampa Nathan, between catatonic phases, had written out a lot of his dark experiments and was prone to flowery prose and over-use of words like 'stygian'.

If he was right, there should be some way of getting back home in a landscape like this.

The door behind them remained open, a flat rectangle of blinding light, clinical, harsh and out of place, but nothing else came through.

'At least this is *landscape*,' he said, and turned straight into Wes's fist.

Ricky stumbled back, nose a burning flare of pain. His tendrils disgorged, lashing in the fetid air, tasting the corrupt miasma and seeking Wes's spine.

He didn't even realise he'd thrown a punch back until a split second afterwards, when his guard was back up instinctively, and Wes was reeling from the uppercut he hadn't dodged.

Wes was bloody useless in a brawl, always had been.

Ricky forced his questing air-roots away, though they were itching for a taste of his cousin's spinal fluids.

Ricky licked a dribble of nose-blood away from his upper lip, sniffed it back and swallowed the iron. He grinned. 'About fucking time.'

He judged the distance between them and darted in close, feinted right and caught Wes with his left.

Wes blocked it this time and fought back, surprising him with a lucky blow, reminding him his nose wasn't healed.

Ricky swore, getting his guard up again to ward off a rain of hard, bony punches.

'*You* did this to me,' Wes said, heaving, landing hits on Ricky's protective forearms and a few in his tensed solar plexus. Some of them even hurt. 'This is *your fucking fault*! So – fucking – what – if I want you – *gone*, why couldn't you go *fucking quietly*?'

Ricky finally had enough. He got Wes good in the kidneys, landing his cousin on his arse without really trying, and leaving him doubled in agony on the rocks.

'Right, stay the fuck down.' Ricky circled him, tendrils twanging against his larynx on their way back up. He let them encircle his head like a cloud of retribution.

Wes actually tried to stand, and Ricky kicked his arms out from under him, landing him back on his face. 'I said stay the fuck down, I'm not joking.'

'This is – bullshit.' Wes rolled onto his back, spitting grit. He shielded his face as Ricky's tendrils swooped overhead, but Ricky was just making a point. This time. His nose really bloody hurt.

'Pushing us into the portal is bullshit, Wesley.'

'I pushed *you*. You were meant to be here. I saw it. I saw you.'

'Oh, well, ta very much.' Ricky shook his head. 'This your precious pills, is it? You saw me here, so you thought, oh, self-fulfilling prophecy?' He shook his head. 'If I'm meant to be here, I'd have got here without you pushing me fucking in, did you think about that?'

'More satisfying this way,' Wes mumbled against his torn sleeve.

Ricky seethed. 'Fuck you.'

(What if I can't get back?)

'*Boys!*'

The Thirteenth's voice rang out, drawing him up short. Wesley was panting, flushed, a pinkish glaze in his eyes that he hadn't noticed before – or had, but hadn't remembered.

Ricky remembered this time. There were still two of him, overlaid, the memorable image hazy but visible on top of the shifting fragments of the other.

He felt the bridge of his nose for breakage, wiping a smear of blood away.

His tendrils retreated.

'Absolute dickhead,' he muttered thickly into his cupped palm.

'You selfish bastard!' Wes took his chances and got back to his feet, wobbly and struggling to straighten up.

'Whatever those pills are, I don't think they agree with you,' Ricky said, deliberately averting his gaze. 'Your eyes look unhealthy.'

'Fuck you.'

Ricky grinned at the rocks, not looking back at Wes deliberately, yet still keeping an image of him in his mind. 'All pink, they are.'

Wes went quiet, realising that Ricky wasn't looking at him, couldn't possibly know or remember what his eyes were like. 'You made that up.'

'Do I sound like I'm lying? You need a shave.'

He chanced a sly glance at his cousin, slapping a hand to his cheek.

'Your eyes do look a bit pink,' Katherine said, uncertain. He waited for her to catch on, grinning at them both as his nose bled into his hand.

Katy got there first. 'Oh my *God*, I can see you! I mean, I know what you look like! Oh my *God*!'

'Where's a mirror?' Wes stood still as she threw herself on him with a squeal of delight, letting her hug him as she jumped up and down. 'Where's a – what's going on? Let me see, I need to see...'

Fuck, his nose *really* hurt. The pain was in his forehead now, he wished Katherine would stop squealing.

He let them get on with their celebration, slurping up the blood from his palm in case the rocks got bloodthirsty or in case something could sniff him out that way.

(Prey-thinking. I'm thinking like prey.)

(Yeah, well, I want to go home.)

Wes had dug his phone out, a useless block of plastic here, and was admiring himself in the black gloss of the dead screen like Narcissus.

Ricky rolled his eyes. 'When did you learn to punch?'

He cast about for any stray blood spots that might have fallen, but the odour of dead fish was still too overpowering to home in on a more subtle scent.

'Look at me!' Wes broke eye contact with himself and beamed, nearly weeping. 'I remember!' The adrenaline had obviously overcome the punches, and Ricky was almost jealous.

'Yeah, you're pretty. Come on.'

Below them, a few feet away, the rocks plunged into a grey sea. He didn't trust it. 'Let's get further inland. Who knows what's down there. S'giving me the creeps.'

'Scared?' the Thirteenth mocked, the most confident he'd seen her. Her delight for her brother had perked her right up. He vaguely remembered that, the selective invincibility of seventeen.

'As it happens, yeah.' It felt wrong, saying that out loud. 'So should you be, if you had the sense you were born with.'

He rubbed his nose gingerly, but the bleeding seemed to have stopped. He inspected the blood ingrained in his palm and scraped at it with his teeth.

'Mm. Right. What we're lookin' for then, like in the stories an' that, is a monolith.'

'A what?'

'*Monolith*. Dirty great big block of rock that looks like it shouldn't be here.'

Wes was still flushed, drunk with delight, but he caught up faster than his sister. 'Like in *Space Odyssey*. With the monkeys.'

Katherine wrinkled her nose. 'I fell asleep watching that.'

Ricky gave up on both of them. 'Come away from the edge, you don't know what's down there.'

'Where d'you think we are, though?' She started following him, throwing her arms out to keep her balance on the uneven ground. 'Is this, like, our world, their world, are we on another planet, is this the afterlife, what?'

Ricky hadn't ventured much further than Majorca, and that had been with Wes's parents when he was eight or nine. He hadn't seen much of it – it was one of those all-inclusive resorts. The sun was too hot, the people were too loud, and the other children cried all the time when he tried telling them about his hobbies. He'd spent the week hiding, being smacked for hiding, and having stones thrown at him by his younger cousins and human kids.

It had left him with the general impression that the rest of the world was boozy, sunburnt, vicious and exclusionary. He could get all that at home.

'Does it matter?'

'Don't you care? I know this is a bit of a shit situation but aren't you excited? Like not even a little bit excited?' Katherine danced over the stones, nearly slipping.

'I can *remember*,' Wes shouted after them, alight with glee. He realised they were moving off and hurried after them. 'I remember what I look like!'

'You're bloody welcome,' Ricky muttered.

Bloody typical. Try and do something out of spite (yeah, all right, be honest) and it turns into a golden gift. Maybe all those sacrifices he'd made over the years were also worthwhile in other ways, and he'd mercifully spared the world from yet more of the kind of people who took their kids to sodding Disneyland and claimed people who said 'fuck' had small vocabularies.

(Quotidian-aspiring cunts.)

Maybe he'd done the world a fair few favours he'd never be thanked for.

'Hey! What's wrong?' Katherine had caught up. 'You've got a face like a slapped arse. We can get out, right? There's loads of rocks around here.'

She wasn't wrong.

'Not just any old rock, love, I *told* you. Got to be something that'll make a connection, you know. Like the Pendle Stone. Has to have energy, that kind of thing, you'll know it when you see it.'

He scanned the landscape, wondering what exactly he could find, how many doorways of light they might stumble upon (that's bloody daft, for a start), and whether they'd come face-to-face-tentacle with some other apex predator who ate its own young but at least had the decency to do it literally and not figuratively, piece by piece, until they *wished* they were dead.

(I'm going mad, I've only been here five minutes.)

Wes gave a loud shout and nearly cannoned into him, forcing his sister to duck down.

Ricky turned.

Something was emerging from the sea, the water running off its hide as the waters boiled around it.

He scowled.

'Boiled'… he was starting to sound like Grampa Nathan. But that's what it looked like – the waters bubbling and foaming, churning up around the hulking shape as it rose in a hump of mottled seabed hues, bilge-brown, shark-grey, silt-black. A bulging eye, which he judged to be the width and length of his own torso, opened, two sets of eyelids blinking vertically and horizontally.

Ricky inhaled the amphibious stink.

'Cor. That's a bloody big frog.'

'*Cool.*' Katherine had found her courage, apparently, or was determined to enjoy their time here.

He shot her a frown, envying the elasticity of the youthful mind. Everything went downhill the wrong side of twenty-five, but he was far too young to die here.

Wes flickered in and out of his memory, layers of images shifting on top of one another as if the presence of the gargantuan creature was disrupting the signal, or whatever it was, which allowed him to be seen.

The head kept rising, water pouring off it in streams.

'Time to go.'

Wes was already pulling her away and didn't need telling twice.

'Oh my God, why doesn't my stupid phone work here?' She was actually trying to take a picture.

'Time to Change, don't you think?' Wes shouted at him, stumbling over the rocks, dragging the Thirteenth with him.

Ricky groaned. He hadn't eaten enough for that. If he Changed for any serious length of time now, or had to do anything dramatic, he'd pay for it when it came to Changing back. Muscles cramping into knots, organs dissolving themselves, bones crumbling, brittle as glass...

Better to wait, better to save it.

He heard the wet slap of a questing something-or-other on the rocks behind him and used his tendrils to keep his balance, mapping the world around him by taste and texture.

He was bent nearly double in the swift scramble, but their haste seemed unwarranted. After another rush of water behind them, the Thing from the depths sank back and sent a wall of dirty brine sloshing over the volcanic rock, catching his back in flecks of spray.

Wes paused some way ahead, Katherine in the lead. Ricky swivelled awkwardly on a jagged stone, scanning the sea around the odd finger of land, but it was empty. They waited, pushing their luck, but the waves settled back into their choppy splashing.

'Better keep going.' Wes sounded regretful, as if he'd expected more.

Ricky shared his disappointment, adrenaline fizzling out.

Katherine rotated nimbly, shading her eyes against the grey glare. 'It's pretty humid,' she remarked, and Ricky realised the clamminess against his back wasn't all new skin ooze and sea spray. He wiped his forehead, and his hand came away sweaty.

His little cousin was frowning. 'Not a lot of cover, except the clouds.'

'All right, look, there's something.' Wes pointed out a range of higher peaks in the middle distance, where the land widened out in a rocky sprawl of jagged coast. 'See? We can shelter there, at least.'

Ricky turned to look at the white door shining brightly at their backs, a neat shape snipped out of the landscape.

He didn't fancy their chances in the Throne Room, being stalked across a wasteland by the conglomeration of their dead kin.

'Sure.' His stomach growled. He couldn't be hungry again, not already?

His tendrils found the salty decay of a fish, rotting in the cleft of a rock, and cracked the tiny bones in a swift slurping gobble of spoiled flesh.

It left an aftertaste of salted slug, sour on the tastebuds of his human-passing tongue. He winced, his stomach churning. That was more the stress, he thought, they wanted him to sort everything out as per usual when none of them should even *be* here. It wasn't fair. He picked the rocks clean methodically as they trudged on, until his belly was tight and heavy, and he found himself out of breath.

How did that happen?

He looked up.

They had left the spur of land behind without him noticing and all around them now were the harsher, decidedly drier, outcrops of gleaming jet. It was difficult to get a good idea of the shape of the mainland, or if there was anything the other side of these taller spurs of rock at all.

His belly complained, a sharp stabbing pain slicing into his side from within. He held his side, releasing a pocket of sulphurous air, and belched it up with a grimace. The over-ripe seafood tasted worse the second time around, if only because this time he was paying attention.

'C'n we, can we slow down?'

Katherine was already scrambling half up the first large outcrop. 'I *knew* you'd be crap at cardio.'

He wasn't in the mood. 'It's the heat.'

Wes overtook her, a strobing blur when in motion, stabilising into the flickering layers of lanky fuckboi. He grinned: that was more the mistress's type of term. *She'd* at least see if he was all right, she wouldn't leave him behind.

He glanced at the empty space beside him where she wasn't, and slipped a hand in his pocket, hoping for a piece of her. There wasn't anything.

When he got home, he wouldn't leave the house without some part of her, not ever again.

'You carry on.' He waved them away irritably and slumped down. 'Good luck.'

Wes and Katherine made it to the top of the outcrop and stood balancing on it, scanning their surroundings.

'There's a big drop,' Katherine reported back. 'I think we can get around it? But it's just... rocks. Just a load of rocks.'

'Descriptive.' Ricky scuffed the pebbles, holding his angry stomach. 'Anything we can *use*?'

'Yeah, I see something.' Wes pointed off at an angle. 'Looks like a circle.'

Ricky rolled his eyes. 'A circle of *what*, Wes?'

The grin was audible. 'Rocks.'

Katherine giggled.

Ricky began to suspect they were doing this on purpose. 'Don't make me come up there, I swear to Grandad.'

'You know what you're looking for, lazy bastard,' Katherine called back. 'I don't know what to tell you. It's like...'

'Looks a bit like Stonehenge.'

Ricky gave Wes what he hoped was a withering glare. 'Are you takin' the piss?'

'No, there's a bunch of slabs in a circle, standing upright, over that way.' Wes shrugged. 'That what you wanted?'

'Stonehenge, fuck me. Everyone's a fucking druid.' Ricky raised his eyes skywards. 'What the bloody hell did I do to deserve this bollocks?'

'I dunno, maybe it was that time you killed Gran,' Katherine snapped, already scrambling down.

Ricky stretched out, which was a mistake. His belly groaned, full of long lines of pain cutting downwards. 'Bloody hellfire.'

'You been stuffing your face?' Wes dropped the last few feet before his sister and approached with a strobing swagger. 'See this? Remember this? This is my unimpressed face.'

Ricky rolled his eyes. 'Fuck me.'

'Not a chance.' Wes grinned, dropping into a light squat. 'Not even if you say please.'

Ricky fixed his eyes on a point beyond the distant door, jaw fluttering, thinking determinedly of things that wouldn't make him blush. He'd got better with that.

(The mistress likes to tease, but she never means naun by it.)

He swallowed, slipping a pebble into his pocket that he could rub with his thumb, pretend it was a piece of her.

Wes sniggered and jabbed him painfully in the stomach.

'Bugger off!'

'*Boys!*' The Thirteenth glared at them, bounding over with apparently limitless energy. She stared down at him. 'What's wrong with you?'

He rubbed the spot where Wes had jabbed him. 'I'll be all right in a minute, just... give me a break.'

'You can't have eaten anything, there's nothing here.' She scanned the spike of land they'd just clambered over. 'Except all the rotten...'

He burped, easing the internal pressure.

She scrunched her nose up in disgust.

'Oh, you're *kidding*. That's disgusting. That's worse than the eyeballs.'

'He can't help it.' Wes spoke over Ricky's giggle. 'He's always like this when he's under stress. Bloody liability.'

'Damn sight more disciplined than *you*,' Ricky murmured, waiting for his metabolism to catch up. 'It's not like I enjoy it.'

Wes shook his head and sat down. 'That's your problem. You never have any fun.'

'My *problem*,' Ricky said, keeping his eyes on the shiftless clouds, 'is the fact that I was at home, just now, and I did everything I was asked to do, even though I didn't have to bloody do it, and I get pushed into a bloody portal and now I'm *here*. With you.'

'You could've spared yourself that last part, in fairness,' Wes pointed out, fishing his phone out again to stare at his own reflection, 'but I guess you're a glutton for punishment, as well as rotten fish.'

'Got your face back, didn't you?'

'Die in a fire,' Wes said cheerfully.

Katherine covered her face with her hands. 'I hate you both.'

Ricky shrugged, a bulging coil rippling under his ribcage. He shifted position, skin splitting and sore.

'Hey, I'm sorry.' Wes tried to reach for her, but bottled it and sat back against the rock, too close to Ricky for his liking. Wes seemed unaware of this. 'I don't… It wasn't meant to happen like this.'

'D'you want to tell us what *was* meant to happen?' Ricky suggested, gritting his teeth. 'Or, tell *me* what was s'posed to happen, at the very fuckin' least?'

Wes grunted. 'Yeah, why not.'

Katherine was also waiting, arms crossed. All the excitement had faded from her face.

'I been Uncle Barry's guinea pig since September,' Wes said, not looking at either of them. 'Uncle Marcus handed me over to pay back the ket I stole, which was *for him*, by the way, slippery old bastard. Well, I mean, he got a cut. And he told me I could. Anyway.' He was silent for a moment and Ricky glanced at him.

He'd never been able to work Wes out, not even the summer they'd been inseparable, and he didn't like thinking about that. It all seemed so long ago now, so trivial, a blur of adolescent storms and things misremembered, but the shadow it cast almost reached him here, now, as if it was just over his shoulder.

Time was a strange beast.

Wes shrugged. 'He got these pills. I call 'em Silver Lining, but that's a stupid name, I'm not... anyway, I can sort of... it's more an aftereffect. It's like... it's not a... I remember stuff that hasn't happened.' He frowned, blinking. 'That's a better way to put it than "seeing the future", it's not like I'm... it's useful. I put a bet on, and I knew exactly what to bet, because... I remembered.'

Ricky rolled his eyes. 'Amateur.'

'That's so fucking dangerous!' Katherine was aghast, as if she'd never heard of such a thing, as if Uncle Barry hadn't been experimenting on everyone he could get his hands on for decades. 'So why did you push—?'

'What do you all need me for, if he can do my job?' Ricky winced, coils bunching and straining inside him. Pressure eased, discomfort waned. 'Does it work on everyone, or just single spawnings?'

'Lucy and Kirsty took some, said nothing happened.' Wes shrugged. 'You're s'posed to at least be able to see your own thoughts, like, externalise them, I can't explain very well...'

'Yeah, well, no offence, I don't think those two have ever had much in the way of actual thoughts,' Ricky pointed out.

'Fuck off.'

'You're an idiot,' Katherine snapped at her brother.

Ricky smirked.

She shook her head. 'I can't believe I'm stuck here because you had some stupid trip.'

'Did you not get the part where I remember stuff that hasn't happened yet?' Wes scrambled upright. 'Because that's pretty important.'

'Did *you* not get the part where we're stuck in another dimension? Because *that's* kind of more important, and *fucking unnecessary*!'

Ricky giggled. He couldn't help it. He fingered the stone in his pocket, sharing the joke with her as if she were there. He propelled himself upright, stomach gurgling but settled, energy restored.

'Yeah, well, Grandad doesn't want us to stay in here, does he? We're no use to him in here. *You* can't ascend as the Thirteenth, *I* can't be the One and Only, Wes...' He sucked air through his teeth. 'Whatever speciality you've got going on, I can't imagine you're exactly shining in a landscape full of rocks, so... let's have a crack at this henge, then.'

Wes took another long, lingering look at himself in the screen of his phone. 'It's like a 3D film without the glasses,' he whispered to himself, loud enough for Ricky to hear him.

'Sure. The henge is probably miles away.' Katherine had grown despondent while her brother was talking. She looked back over her shoulder. 'That thing's gone, is it?'

'I don't think it was after us. It just came up for air.' Ricky hoped he was telling the truth. That was an odd feeling, the not knowing. The hollowness he'd felt in the Throne Room hadn't gone away after all – he'd buried it in rotting fish-flesh, stabbed at it with tiny bones, gorged mindlessly and thought of nothing. That hadn't filled it.

He rubbed his chest, uneasy.

'Cor, it's, er. S'hard to breathe, innit? Diff'rent kind of air here.'

His cousins exchanged glances.

'It's a bit hot.' Katherine was uncertain, too. He heard it in her voice, but it didn't help.

He licked his lips. 'Yeah. Tha's what I mean. Bit hot.' He caressed the pebble in his pocket but it was an empty gesture. It couldn't help him.

'You said there was a chasm, other side of these rocks? How d'you want to go about crossing it?'

Wes pried his eyes away from his own reflection. 'I reckon if we follow it, it closes up along there somewhere, we could probably jump it.' He gestured off to the left.

'Great.'

(What happens if there's something in there, watching?)

(Prey-thinking, that's prey-thinking.)

Wes was calmer, no uncertainty there, posturing little shit. He went first, scrambling up the rocks as if he was mountaineering every bloody weekend.

'Scared?' he called back at them both, balancing on the top of the outcrop. 'No point me going first, is there?' He patted his pockets. 'Don't have the key.'

He treated them to a rakish grin, the kind Ricky had read about in books before he knew what it looked like, the kind Wes used to flash about all the time when he was still growing into that big mouth of his.

Katherine was hesitating this time. Scratching at her arms. Digging in her nails.

He cleared his throat, aiming for reassuring, the way the mistress would do it. 'Come on, Katy.'

She jumped, focusing on him.

Ricky cocked his head at the rocks. 'No reason he gets all the fun.'

Something was happening to her, but she wasn't sure how to tell them.

Ever since the Thing rose up from the sea she'd felt like there was something surging up inside her, too, something she needed to get the hell out of her.

Ricky was acting weirdly even for him, Wes was erratic and probably still on something, and they were stuck in another dimension.

She should have left them both to rot in here, be eaten by the Throne. Deal with the gap they left behind.

She swallowed as Ricky went ahead of her this time, as if to encourage her, cheer her up, and collected herself at the base of the outcrop. Apart from the fishy stink, which, if you kept breathing through your nose, you could get used to, there was something almost comforting about this place.

All these rocks are great hiding places, she thought, *so many places to be alone.*

The jagged shapes were dispassionate rather than sinister. They were what they were. Her bead was cool – nothing wished them harm, nothing was stalking them, nothing was wrong.

If it started to burn, would they see the predator before it was on top of them? Like the amphibious Thing that rose from the waves with its bugged eye and smooth curved head, were there others good at camouflage?

She'd feel better if Ricky Changed, or would she? What if he fed on them, sapping their auras and energy? What if he needed tribute, and took their eyes?

Katy joined them on the top of the outcrop, hands sore and scraped from not paying as much attention as the first time, and they set off in the direction Wes suggested, skirting the chasm below.

It looked like the mainland went on forever.

Almost all of it was the same, this strange volcanic landscape, jutting towers and slabs falling into crevices and rising, far away, into a mountain range of barren peaks and tabletop plateaus.

She wished her phone would turn on so that she could take a picture.

There was something glinting on the dark side of one of the mountains in the distance, but she couldn't make it out. Perhaps it was another door of light.

Wes was out in front, making the balancing act along the outcrop look easy. Katy made the mistake of looking down, at the sheer drop to a narrow ledge the other side, the slope below that littered with loose coal-black scree, the yawning fissure ending the incline abruptly with a sudden drop into nothing.

She wanted to be between the boys in case one of them pushed the other into the abyss, but she hoped Ricky had a little more dignity even if he had enough spite.

Every now and then, they'd look back to check she was following. It was getting hotter. Katy realised this when her mouth was dry and her top was plastered to her back, nape prickling with sweat. They had nothing to drink.

Carrie's kitchen felt so close, but there was no way to get there.

'If anything comes out of this hole I'm feeding you two to it first,' she muttered, sticky and irritable.

'Noted,' Ricky called over his shoulder, and she flushed, not knowing he could hear that well.

Every inch became leaden effort.

They left the outcrop to scramble onto a ridge that skirted the chasm, some parts flatter and easier going, others jagged with shards of sheer, razor-sharp spears of obsidian that slashed Katy's skin as she brushed by.

A red line opened on her nail-scratched forearm, and she didn't notice until it started to sting.

Ricky paused, emitting a tendril to lick up the blood and dribble numbing silver mucus on the wound. The stink of fish hit her again, but she let him. He gave her a look that was almost kind.

Wes waited, not looking at her, jaw tight as he studied their route. He flickered in and out of her memory, his layers stabilising as he stood still. As she got him back again, warmer-eyed than Kieran, good-looking like Liam, as tall as Ashley, skinny like Adam, she held on to the composite sketch of her older brothers and filled in the gaps that the shifting layers made it hard to see.

Ricky released her arm and she blinked, glancing back at him. He cocked an eyebrow, sour, as if to say 'you're welcome'.

'Thanks.'

He shrugged and turned away.

Wes led the slow, careful descent down the other side of the spur, where the chasm narrowed enough to jump across. The circle of stone slabs seemed a little nearer – still in the middle distance. The rocks seemed to be around another throne, or an altar with a vertical slab on one side. Katy hoped this one wasn't made up of their dead relatives.

'What's that?' she asked, shading her eyes against the grey glare.

'We'll find out soon.' Ricky shook his head and squatted down. 'Let's rest.'

'Don't you want to get home?' Wes asked, circling around him to help Katy down the last bit. She jumped, rubbing her arm. They had another slope to tackle now, a gentler one, but this was a good place to pause.

Ricky shrugged, pouting. 'Course. But it's hot. We're not even halfway. We got nothing to drink. She's hurt her arm. Let's rest a minute.'

'How fast does time move here?' Wes flickered, checking the sky. 'How can you even tell what time it is?'

'It's faster in here than out there, don't you panic.' Ricky settled against a rock, leaning back and breathing heavily. 'Grampa Nathan reckoned a few days here is barely a few hours at home.'

'A few *days*?' Wes paced, itching to cross the chasm.

Katy joined Ricky on the floor and shaded her eyes, her brother's constant flickering giving her a headache.

'Stay still, Wesley,' Ricky snapped at him eventually. 'You'll give your sister a seizure.'

'I'll give you a bloody seizure,' Wes muttered, but he gave up when he realised they really weren't going to be moving again any time soon.

Katy ground her molars. 'Can you both *shut up*?'

'Moody cow.' Wes's attempt at teasing her went down like a lead balloon. Katy glowered and his smile, weak as it was, faded.

He shook his head and came to sit the other side of Ricky, leaving Katy on her own.

They sat in mutual sulking quiet for a while, without any way to tell how much time was passing. Wes spent it staring at his reflection, or at least, that's what he was doing every time Katy glanced at him.

Ricky seemed to be meditating: his eyes were closed, his lips moving inaudibly, and he was playing with something in his pocket.

Katy, despite the situation, nearly fell asleep.

This was a familiar place, although she wasn't sure why. She was at home here, comfortable among the rocks, her wounded arm numb and not giving her any pain, and her bead remained cool against her chest. It had stayed cool when the amphibian rose up from the sea, too, so she wasn't as worried about the creatures that might live here as Ricky seemed to be.

He radiated anxiety, despite the relaxed attitude.

Her senses heightened, she breathed the reek of prey under his predatory mask.

She checked her arm, eyelids heavy. Was it scabbing over already? Or was that split revealing something under her skin? She poked the cut. Grey-blue flesh sat underneath, impervious to weapons, smooth and cold. That was good, wasn't it? She licked her lips. So thirsty. There was plenty to drink though, the two blood-sacks next to her would be enough for a few days. No need to worry.

One was still off limits, but she could change that. The other, she could start on now. Her maw gaped, sending three feelers from the back of her long throat to quest for his veins.

Ricky nudged her awake as she fell onto his shoulder. 'Oi.'

Katy started violently, scraping her back against the rock as she jumped.

Her brother, not blood-sack, *brother*, was fine, oblivious. She grabbed her throat, but it was the same length as it had always been, no feelers of any kind lurking in her tonsils.

Ricky eyed her warily. 'You, uh, feeling all right?'

She nodded, wide-eyed, hoping he wouldn't see her shivering. 'Thirsty.'

He grunted. 'Let's see what the night brings.'

'Night?'

He nodded at the sky. The uniform grey was darkening, patches of cloud breaking over the tops of the distant mountain peaks. Broken bands of cerise crowned them in bloody glory.

'This is my fault,' Wes said, unexpectedly.

Katy swivelled and stared at him.

Wes wasn't looking at himself anymore; slumped against the rocks, legs out, morose, his eyes were closed.

Ricky didn't say anything, but his expression told Katy he agreed.

'The only thing I regret is you being in here. You shouldn't be here.'

Ricky sniffed. 'I think he means you.'

'Course I mean her.' Wes shook his head. 'You – bloody hell. You did this to me. I'll never forgive you.'

'So much for "debt paid",' Ricky muttered, scuffing his foot on the loose scree. The light was shifting, dulling the landscape. It dulled his complexion, too, made him look shadier and more angular, highlighting the cherry-red dots in the centres of his eyes.

Katy frowned. 'Can you two just bang, or what?'

Wes and Ricky both burst out laughing.

'Shit me,' Ricky managed, after his giggling subsided.

Wes sniggered. 'You projecting there a bit, Sis?'

'What d'you mean?' Katy flushed, thinking of Rocket. Wes couldn't know about that.

'Aw, you got a crush? She got a crush.' Wes twisted around and his layers strobed. He twinkled at her, all dark mischief. 'No, it's nothin' like that. Can't you tell?'

'I don't know,' Katy snapped, folding her arms tightly across her chest, a barrier between her and further embarrassment. 'I don't know what this is about.'

'It's *about* his face.' Ricky answered for her brother this time, keeping a watchful eye over the chasm below them. 'He blames me for his face. He wouldn't do the sacrifices, thought it wasn't *cool*. So I did one on his behalf.' His grin was crooked, a twist of dark satisfaction misaligned with the angles of his skull.

Katy shook herself. Everything was twisted here, the light changing the way she saw things, the shapes of the rocks growing more sinister as the landscape darkened.

'He asked Grandad for something "special",' Wes said, his voice flat. 'He gave me something special, all right.'

Ricky sniggered to himself. 'Not like I was *specific*.'

'I could've forgiven you, that's the thing, I could've.' Wes sprang to his feet, unfolding his lanky joints and propelling himself upright. 'I nearly did, then after what this did to Charlie... I can't forgive that.'

Ricky stared at him, incredulous. 'You're blaming *me* for – give over, you spineless tart.'

'If it weren't for you, she'd be fine,' Wes snapped. 'Tentacles, ooze, weird bloodsucking growths, fine, she'd cope with that, she's a tough girl, she'd *love* that, all about the art, innit? But this...' He waved a hand in front of his face, making the layers crackle and break down for a moment, 'She's in love with something she can't even remember, I'm a, a, a black hole in her emotional universe.'

Katy licked her lips, a tingle of warning racing over her skin.

'You got given a gift, I didn't decide what it was. If you misused it, that's not on me.' Ricky's fists were balled tightly at his sides, his stance shifting slightly but perceptibly, shoulders squaring. 'You take some responsibility for yourself, Wesley.'

'What d'you *think* I've been doing?' Wes squared up too, towering over their cousin, and Katy became very aware of the drop below, narrow enough to jump over, wide enough to swallow one of them whole.

'Um,' she started, but her throat was dry and tight, and the sound came out as a tiny croak. Neither of them heard, or if they did, they took no notice.

Wes's nostrils flared, Porter-brown eyes feverish above those killer cheekbones she really hoped she'd remember when they got out of here. The Porters and the Wends had a decent set of human genes between them, and Wes seemed to have received the best bits of both.

Katy had seen Wes's expression in her own bathroom mirror a few times, alone with the door locked and the shower running, scalding herself on purpose under the hot tap. It welled up now in sympathetic kinship, borne from her belly in a boiling, impotent rage.

'I've shackled myself to her so she never has to go without seeing me again,' Wes snapped, voice deepened in his indignation. 'I made that commitment for her, for her health, for her wellbeing, don't tell me I'm not fucking responsible! I've never let Hugo or anyone else see me for more than a few minutes at a time, an hour max, unless they're strangers and it really doesn't matter! I've given up

Harvest Parties, eating meat, fucking *seafood* – I've thrown my patella collection in the sea... don't you fucking stand there and tell me I'm irresponsible, what the fuck would you know?'

'Shackled's an interesting choice of words,' Ricky said lightly.

Wes lunged at him and got him by the front of his hoodie. Ricky giggled in Wes's face, as Wes heaved him nearly off the floor.

'You little shit,' Wes hissed in his face, as Katy quivered with tense indecision, unsure where to stand or what to do, 'You never felt love in your whole life, you suck it up like a sponge and spit it back in our faces, where do you get off lecturin' me?'

'You never gave me anything wi'out you wanted something back,' Ricky countered. 'None of you. Not even you, and you can tell yourself diff'rent if it makes you feel better, but that's the truth. You allus wanted this.' He tapped his head. 'An' I made you rich, you can't deny that, and that was all you was after.'

Wes dropped him.

Ricky straightened his hoodie, taking his time. Katy couldn't see his face, but she read her brother's well enough.

Wes was wrestling with something, unblinking, jaw fluttering as he flushed, breathing hard.

'Ha, look at us, hey? No, maybe you're right, maybe you're always bloody right. You know what, you know what my consolation is?' Wes cocked his head. 'You and me, we're both special. All the others, they can hide what they are, change perception, but you an' me, the single-borns... people will always see us for exactly what we are, me a non-entity, fair enough, something of nothing...

but you? You'll always be a monster, and that makes me happier'n I can tell you.'

A jolt went through Katy as she realised what he was saying. If Ricky responded, she wasn't listening. No, he had to be wrong – others in the family had weird mutations that were on display, Nicole's spinal teeth, the triplets' seams. But when they chose, there was nothing there but some odd, light scarring, easily hidden with clothes and makeup. And the elders – Uncle George, even, not quite an 'elder' but certainly older – they could alter what you saw, mess with your perception. Cousin Ricky was the only one whose Change was outward and always visible. Wes's Change was unique.

What was the thing they shared, that made them special?

'But if you're both single-births...' she said, interrupting, 'and I am too, and neither of you can hide what your Changes are, then that means...' She looked down at herself, the tingling spreading under her skin. 'How am I supposed to go to Uni if I can't hide what I am?'

They fell silent, turning to stare at her.

'What d'you want to go to Uni for, anyway?' Wes asked after a long pause, attempting to sound casual. 'That's for regulars.'

'I want to learn stuff, I want to go out with my mates, I want to see new places, I want to go travelling,' Katy said, fighting down panic. 'No one said anything about *not being able to hide it*, I thought that happens randomly, what are you saying, that it... that single-births aren't...' she caught her breath. 'Are you saying I won't be able to hide my Changes *at all*?'

'No one's saying that,' Wes said, unconvincingly and too late.

Ricky shot him a look. 'Cor, they say I'm a shit liar.'

'*Not helping.*' Wes took a step towards her, and Katy shrank back into the rocks. 'Look, I – ignore me, I was just getting at him, I wasn't getting at you. It's just… false correlation, right, I didn't mean it.'

Katy shook her head. The tingling was getting worse, like something underneath her skin was fighting to get out. Her throat was constricting, not from emotion, but as if there was something stuck at the back of it. She couldn't cough.

'All right, deep breaths,' Ricky said, gruff but soothing. 'We can figure it out, course we can. We'll work on it. I already got an idea.'

Relief washed the tingling away.

'Moon's rising,' Ricky said, nodding at the sky, inching towards her, trying to smile. The light cast his face in fragmented patches of darkness. 'That's pretty.'

She darted a glance at it, but the white glare hurt her eyes. It peeked over the mountain range, a half-sucked lozenge, misty aura of silver around the visible edge.

'Look, ain't that nice? We'll get down to that circle soon, and we'll go home and fix it. You c'n have a proper drink of water. Something to eat. The mistress'll make us something. Yeah? You all right?' He reached her, holding out his hand.

Katy hesitated before she took it, her palm prickling at his clammy touch.

'Let's not fight,' Ricky said to Wes. 'She's gettin' stressed. We don't want that right now, do we?'

This seemed to jog Wes's memory about something, as understanding crossed his face, and his lips bowed in a warm smile while his forehead creased in worry. 'No need. Naun t' be stressed over.'

His accent mimicked their elders' and Ricky's when he lapsed, and made her smile.

'There we go,' Ricky said, pleased, helping her forwards and raising his eyebrows at Wes. 'There's a smile. Come on. Let's get this sorted.'

Katy nodded, relaxing. She let go of his hand.

'Thanks—' she started to say, but gagged. Something *was* at the back of her throat. She clutched it, coughing.

Ricky got between her and Wes, stopping Wes coming to her aid.

Spots burst in the gloom, pressure filling her head as she fought for breath. There *was* something inside her, and it was finally breaking free.

Chapter 12: The Metamorphosis

Outside

'I thought general wisdom was she'd be some sort of big, clawed, dog thing?' Wes said, not quite sure what he'd witnessed.

The sun, or whatever this place had for light, was gone, and the brilliant moon was higher, casting everything in stark black and white like a high-contrast graphic novel.

Wes had watched, powerless, as his little sister choked to death. Ricky hadn't let him near her, and if he was honest with himself, he hadn't fought very hard.

Eventually, purple-faced, she'd thrown up the sticky red mess splashed over the rocks, gleaming wetly in the sharp light. It had oozed over her as if it had a life of its own, eating through her clothes and skin, until she split open like a bloody, pulpy flower and petals of her flopped inside out.

What was left was a cocoon, a husk, about her height, pulsing gently with a slow, regular heartbeat. It was so quiet in the alien landscape around them that he could hear it, a gentle, muted boom that forced something within to circulate. He had a sense of déjà vu, as if he'd seen the cocoon before in a dream or lost memory, and he realised he'd seen it nearly every time he'd taken one of those pills.

Even Ricky looked slightly ill. 'Well, yeah. She will. But, um.' He swallowed. 'Shit me.'

That about covered it.

Wes wiped his mouth with the back of his hand, bile in his throat. 'She's only seventeen. I thought we had more time than this.'

'Yeah. Well. This place… and… it's, you know what, I shouldn't have been a dick. It's stress. You remember, mine came on a bit early, too.'

'You were eighteen, though.'

'Barely.'

Wes cast his mind back. One minute Ricky was screaming bloody murder at Granny Wend about something, the next he was on the floor clutching his head as if it would burst.

'I always thought that was something *she* did to you.'

Ricky scoffed. 'Nah. I did it to myself. Got all worked up, I'd felt it coming on before but I wasn't sure, you know how it is, how it feels.'

'Fuck, yeah.' Wes sucked in cool night air through his teeth. 'Yeah. Haven't thought about that in years, but… well, recently, I guess a few things have been coming back.'

'Yeah. I know what you mean.'

'Everyone says it hurts, but mine didn't.' Wes cocked his head, reflecting. 'Tingled a bit. Pins and needles. Yours looked like hell.'

'Worst pain I've ever had,' Ricky said, scratching his shaved head above the bald, puckered lips. 'Like an ice pick at first. Then more like a corkscrew. I could feel it coming out, you know, literally like a cork out of a bottle, except…' He gestured. 'It was out the back of my skull. Everything snapped, broke, my guts hurt…' He frowned. 'Or was that the second time? Full-body Changes fucking hurt, I can tell you. Split me open on the kitchen floor. All my organs, dissolving, eating themselves in there.' He pulled a face. 'It's not so bad after the fourth or fifth time, but that's not so much because it hurts less, more that you get used to it.'

Wes looked at the cocoon, where his sister was probably some sort of sentient soup by now. 'D'you think she's in pain?'

Ricky shrugged. 'Can't hear her screaming, can we? Even if she is, it shouldn't bother us.'

Wes curled his lip, a hot flush of anger — not all of it at his cousin — bubbling up. He shouldn't be here. What the hell had he been thinking?

Ricky sighed and gave him a pitying, hooded stare, as if preparing to dumb down a simple concept to humour someone being deliberately obtuse. 'Even if she is in pain, how can we help her? There's nothing we can do. An' if all you're going to do is mope about it like an old woman, we won't get anywhere near the circle over there and you'll drive yourself nuts. What use is that? So just as well, ain't it? Give us a hand with her.' Ricky jerked a thumb at the cocoon.

'You're kidding.' There was no way Wes was going to touch the wrong side of his sister's skin. It even *looked* meaty, veiny, structured with bone and rib.

Ricky stared at him. 'No?'

'You're *kidding*.'

'I'm not.'

Wes swallowed. 'What if we... left her here?'

'Can't.' Ricky spat on his hands and rubbed them together. 'We need her to get us back through. This is her place. We need her permission. Lock, meet key. That sort of thing.'

Wes shook his head. 'Nah, hang on. There wasn't a Thirteenth when Grampa Nathan tried it and he got back fine…'

'Hector was around then, he was Nana Deirdre's little brother, of course there was a Thirteenth.' Ricky motioned with his head for Wes to join him. 'Let's lever her off the ground, I'll take one end, you get the other.'

'There's no way we're getting her across the chasm,' Wes said, but rolled up his sleeves half-heartedly. 'I don't see…'

'We'll chuck her.'

'No.'

'Probably won't hurt her any more than being liquified is.'

'*No.*' Wes rubbed his face. 'I'm not *throwing* her. All right, let's see if we can get her across further up, it looks like it keeps narrowing.'

'You're proper conflicted, ain't you?' Ricky said, after a second's pause while he got into position behind the gently pulsing cocoon. '"Leave her here, no don't chuck her, hope she ain't in pain…" Bloody hell, make your mind up. She hasn't taken you off the List yet.'

Wes sighed, his heart sinking. 'I know. Don't go on about it.'

'I literally haven't said—'

'Just – just don't.' He got ready to lift from the bottom. 'Okay.'

The cocoon was slippery and rattled when they took hold of it, making a warning noise like dried peas in a percussive instrument.

'Nah, s'in-built, like a real caterpillar.' Ricky shrugged it off. 'C'mon, I'm ready.'

It was stuck firmly to the rock, glued down. Wes put his whole weight into it, or tried to, leg muscles protesting. It came free on the third attempt, surprising both of them with the dead weight of it. Ricky nearly buckled but adjusted his grip.

'Bl-*oody* hellfire, she's heavy.'

Wes strained at his end, but once it was more evenly distributed between them, the stickiness latched on to their clothes and hands, making it easier to grip and carry.

'This is *not* how I thought I'd be spending today, I got to be honest,' Wes grunted over his shoulder to lighten the mood.

Ricky grunted back. 'Watch your footing. If you go, we all go.'

That was an unpleasant thought. Wes didn't look down to the right, where the chasm was a dark rip in the rock. He focused on his feet, letting his eyes adjust. Every now and again the piercing moon glanced across his path as the clouds broke, dazzling him.

Ricky did a good job of his end of the cocoon, stopping it pushing him too fast, keeping pace. The slope down to the chasm had his heart pounding, but the stickiness of the cocoon's coating helped him keep his grip as his palms began to sweat.

A loose stone nearly sent him pitching forwards, and it was only Ricky digging his heels in that saved them from a nasty fall.

Wes could have kissed the flatter surface of the stony ground when they got there.

Since Katy's outer casing was now stuck to them in the way it had been attached to the rocks, tossing her over the gap was impossible, and Ricky seemed to dismiss the idea to Wes's relief. At least, he didn't bring it up again.

They trudged on, following the narrowing gap until the moon rose higher and Wes ached in every muscle fibre.

'They ain't eyes, are they?' Ricky asked casually, apropos of nothing.

Wes changed his mind about suggesting a rest. 'Where?'

'Nah don't look, let's just get her over.'

The spurt of adrenaline silenced his body's multiple complaints. 'Are you knackered yet?' Wes asked, knees about to give way. 'I am.'

'That's 'cos you're soft as shit. Come on. Get on with it.'

Wes eyed the crevice at his feet. There was nothing down there that he could see, certainly nothing that looked like eyes. He could hop over no problem, but this required them both moving at a measured pace.

'Don't stop the other side, that's all, keep going forwards.'

Wes took Ricky's advice, his heavy, agonised arms about to fall off at the elbows. It was his only shot at getting back to Charlie and Hugo, and the more time he had with them, the better. He'd never leave them for so much as a weekend away again.

God, Huey, I'll go with you to every conference, I'll never miss an exhibition, Charlie, fuck this, I'm so sorry... You're first from now on. Fuck the lot of them, I'm yours, not theirs.

By some miracle, he managed to force his fatigued legs into the short jump and keep moving forwards after the jolt of the landing, and he heard Ricky's cat-light thud behind him.

They pressed on, Wes focusing on finding the smoothest way forwards, trying not to slosh his sister around too much. Fuck, this was bizarre.

'Must be phosphorescence,' Ricky said finally.

'What?'

'Nothing, look where you're going.'

'Can you stop making comments like that, it's really disconcerting.'

'That's a big word for you.'

'Piss off.'

Ricky sniggered, and Wes smirked in spite of himself.

'We never did get on, did we?' he said after a few more moments, anything to take his mind off the pain in his arms and legs, the strain in his core, his lower back, the soupy, inside-out state of his baby sister stuck to his hands...

Oh, yeah, and the possibility of glowing eyes following them through the wilderness while they were stuck to a giant cocoon.

He clung to petty things to preserve what little sanity he had left.

Ricky didn't answer.

Wes pushed. 'Way *I* remember it, we were close for a bit. But I don't think that's true, I think I... I held on to the memories that made me look better. I don't think we ever even liked each other much, did we? You were a bit... I don't know, you wanted my attention all the time but whenever we got around to *doing* anything, you just... It was like you'd changed your mind. I've never been with anyone who *literally* lay back and thought of England.'

Ricky grunted. 'If it makes you feel better, I wasn't thinking about England.'

'We were never even friends.' Wes kept his voice down, but the monologue was helping. 'The more I think about it – we were always like this.'

'Speak for yourself,' Ricky muttered.

Wes sniggered. 'I must've *liked* you. At least a little bit.'

'The running away together thing?'

'What?' He hadn't thought about that for ages. 'Shit, yeah, I'd forgotten that. London, we said.'

'Brighton.'

'*Brighton?*' Wes pictured his teen-self, still figuring things out, struggling to fit in anywhere, thinking Brighton's Pride event was the best thing he'd ever been to. But to run away and live there? He reflected. Soho, Notting Hill, places he'd seen in films and on TV, heard about at Pride, *that* had always been his dream, and now he lived in a penthouse with access to a roof terrace and a swimming pool. 'You *sure* it was Brighton?'

'I dunno, you talked about it a lot.'

'*London*, that's where I always wanted to live.'

'Yeah, well, it was a long time ago. Maybe it was London.'

Wes heard the disinterest in his voice and scowled. 'You never wanted to go anywhere.'

'Not really.'

'Christ, you're boring.'

Ricky didn't reply.

Wes could barely see the circle anymore. He slowed to a stop and shook his head. 'No good. I can't tell where we're going. Put her down.'

They laid the cocoon on the ground, pulling themselves away from it with difficulty. Wes scrambled onto an outcrop to get their bearings. The circle was visible in the distance, jagged layers of rock in the way at varying heights, but he couldn't judge the distance properly or make out how many layers of rock there were between them and their target.

The moon found another break in the clouds and lit up the landscape in eerie silver, glancing off the strange shapes and hard edges, throwing off his perceptions with deeper contrasts and longer shadows.

He climbed down, throat dry, stomach growling and everything trembling and aching all at once. 'Over there. Can't be far, but I can't. I can't. Let's rest.'

Ricky didn't disagree. He put his back to a rock and closed his eyes, swaying a little.

'What were you looking at, earlier?' Wes wanted to know. 'The things you thought were eyes?'

'Nah, I don't know.' Ricky sucked absent-mindedly on his hand, pried from the cocoon's sticky outer membrane.

Wes leapt over and smacked it out of his mouth.

'*Don't* do that, bloody hell, you've no idea what that stuff even is!' He rolled his eyes. 'You know some species are toxic, right? To protect themselves from predators?'

Ricky giggled. 'Don't put me off.'

'That's...' Wes rubbed his own hands ineffectually on his jeans. 'Just don't. If you start seeing fucking bats everywhere, don't come crying to me.'

'I'm an ascetic, don't mean I don't know how to handle the odd trip.' Ricky paused and Wes watched the familiar expression of mild confusion slip over his face as his eyes unfocused briefly. 'Cor, actually. I do feel weird.'

Wes groaned. 'Oh, *perfect*.'

Ricky sat down heavily, frowning. 'On reflection,' he said, staring at his hand, 'that may have been a mistake.'

'Fucking hell.' Wes sat down beside him as Ricky began to shiver. 'You all right?'

'Is there an earthquake?' Ricky's teeth were chattering.

With a deeper sigh, Wes put an awkward arm around his cousin's shaking shoulders. 'No, mate. That's just you. Come here.'

Ricky made his flesh creep, but he pulled him firmly into a hug and let him curl up against his chest. Every muscle was fluttering, and he was starting to burn up.

Just as well, Wes thought selfishly, *it's getting colder out here now.*

He absorbed his cousin's feverish warmth, listening to the muffled grinding of his teeth.

'You all right? Ricky? Richard. *Richard*. Look at me.'

Ricky gave no indication he could hear him. Wes kept up a firm grip with one arm and tilted Ricky's head up so he could see his face. His eyes were open, but unblinking. It was hard to tell what was iris and what was pupil.

'That was daft.' He pressed Ricky's head back onto his chest, holding him more securely. 'All right. I got you.'

He held him in silence for a few minutes, until the vibrating in his body began to subside, and he felt the soothsayer relax. The back lips parted first with a dry smack, and a drunken tendril poked out to wave in the air uncertainly for a moment only to retreat back in.

Wes checked on Ricky's eyes, still dilated but not so sightless.

'Richard?'

'Don't call me Richard.'

Wes breathed out. 'You daft bastard.'

'Is that fucking real?' Ricky was staring at the cocoon.

Wes gave him a reassuring squeeze. 'Yeah. Well. Probably.'

'Oh, shit.' His eyes rolled upwards. 'What's up with the ceiling?'

Wes snorted. 'That's the sky.'

'What's that noise? That whispering?'

'Your conscience?' Wes wished he was quicker to think of things that might mess with him. Then again, that was unfair. 'Nah, joking. It's the wind. Promise.'

There was no wind.

'Right. Right.' Ricky nodded, evidently trying to get a grip on whatever was passing for reality at the moment. 'I'm fine.'

'Nah, you're not fine.' Wes let him curl up closer, wishing he was anywhere else. 'You're a bloody liability. An' in a minute, or an hour, or something, but knowin' my luck probably soon, she's going to hatch out and eat me, so get your comfort while you can.' He wrinkled his nose, turning his head away from his cousin. 'I'm not sure how this could get more ironic, honestly.'

'She's dreaming about you.'

'Great.' Wes felt him tense and heave, and pitched him over across his legs to throw up on the ground on his other side. 'All right. Get it out.'

The splatting puddle reeked of dead fish and Wes winced, nearly heaving himself.

Ricky coughed up a fish bone.

'Gorgeous.' Wes patted his back. 'More to come, or is that it?'

Ricky threw up again.

'Jesus.'

Ricky shuddered.

'Don't worry, I won't tell the missus,' Wes promised. 'What happens on tour stays on tour.'

This earned him a shy smile, but then Ricky shivered violently again and curled back into Wes's lap.

'She ain't my missus. She's...' He drifted off. 'I don't think you're going to die.'

'No?' Wes leaned back against the rock, ignoring the sharp jutting pieces that dug into his back. 'She dreaming good things?'

'She c'n hear us.'

'That's embarrassing for you.' Wes thought back over the past few... hours? Surely, it had been a few hours? Had he said anything bad? Anything that would upset her?

Maybe we could leave her here... shit.

'Are you... sort of connected?'

'Sort of.' Ricky's tendrils crawled out over Wes's chest and Wes batted them away until they slithered back into his head. 'Ow. She's... she's making her List.'

'Checking it twice?' Wes grinned. 'Finding out who's naughty or nice?'

'Don't be a twat.' Ricky shuffled into a more comfortable position for him and a less comfortable one for Wes, which earned him a poke in the ribs. 'Cut that out, I feel rough. What's that over there?'

'More rocks. And you'll feel a damn sight worse if you don't stop digging into me like that.'

Ricky grunted and moved.

Wes couldn't remember the last time they'd ever been this close for this long. Probably never. Well, never while sober. Nice that record wasn't broken.

Ricky was quiet, his breathing more regular, leaving Wes to accustom himself to the stink of the vomit puddle and occasional waft of breath.

So much for inter-dimensional travel. Hollywood made it look sexy, all those space suits and chrome and dramatic haircuts, being torn apart by alien lifeforms in an epic battle for survival, but this was more their family's style: *veni, vidi, vomiti.* I came, I saw, I threw up.

'Would you want to be seventeen again?' he asked, thinking of Katy and times gone by.

'Not a chance.' Ricky was still conscious, then. 'Don't remember half of it, an' the bits I do were shit.'

'Oh, thanks. Yeah. What an ego boost you are.'

'You got an awful high opinion of yourself as it is.'

Wes squirmed, hating him. 'Well, this is boring. Maybe I should give that stuff a lick.' He wasn't that desperate. Pushing the bile down, he decided to try and sleep. He hoped if anything came out to eat them, they'd go for Ricky first.

—

The Beast dreamed.

A creature of fear and nightmare, it chased down the things that made it afraid. It was as simple as that.

Hector, the only other one of its kind, had been leashed, chained, and did as he was told, until he tore himself apart, wrapped up in the web of his own fear.

Not this Beast. No such mesh encircled it.

It hunted.

Soft-breathed, light-clawed. Its long tail, prehensile, spiked, club-ended, whipped behind it and sliced through time. It ran through constellations in the vastness of space, through primordial waters, gliding, sliding, slipping tar-slick through the cosmos.

The Beast heard voices far away.

It paused.

Listened.

Remembered.

Before it crept a man the size of a mouse. The Beast sniffed at it, as the offering bent on one knee. Yes, there had been fear of this one, once. A blood-sack fit for the suckling, ripe flesh succulent and ready for claws. But he was... no longer to its taste.

The Beast was confused.

There should be fear in the kernel of its being, the fear of becoming like this man. It had been there, once. But he wasn't something to be afraid of. The Beast dismissed him and passed him by.

Further on, in the darkness of the swirling stars, a legion of the human-passing knelt to the Beast.

The Beast knew, deep in its core, that it was not like any of them, and yet they were part of it, they had shaped it. But now, what the Beast was, what it did, was not up to them.

Yes, some still glowed with the aura of fear, and those were the ones the Beast wanted to rip apart.

And yet...

The Beast wondered.

They did not control it. Wasn't it free?

The Beast craned its great neck to admire its gleaming, impervious flank, and thought, *Hang on. What's my name again?*

And it realised it was dreaming, dissolving, growing, Changing.

Its heart was beating in suspension.

It had no hands at all.

There was movement without motor control.

It wasn't human anymore, but the eyes were nearly done. Vision, that's what it needed.

Her name was Katy Porter.

She began to make sense of her fragmented senses.

And that was when she started screaming.

—

Wes was nearly asleep, despite the smell and the discomfort, when Ricky jerked awake, shocking him back into consciousness.

A low keening cry echoed around the craggy terrain.

'That a... what's that?'

It had the same guttural, barking scream as a vixen, the uncanny almost-human quality sending a shiver up his spine, accompanied by an underlying gargling sound.

Ricky grunted and shifted into a different position, away from Wes, pillowing his head on his arms.

'That'd be the sound of your sister realisin' she's primordial soup.'

Wes leapt up, avoiding the fishy vomit puddle, and came as close to the cocoon as he could. 'Oh, shit! Katy?'

The screaming continued, the cocoon pulsing faster than before. The outer casing seemed thinner, and as the moonlight fell on the swelling red mass, he thought he could see curved vertebrae sweeping around in a smooth arc, but it was difficult to make out anything else from that side.

He dared to touch it, the sticky red substance binding his hands to the shell.

'Katy, it's okay, I promise. I promise. It's going to be okay.'

The screaming died into a series of barking, gurgling sobs.

'Don't try and get her out,' Ricky warned, not bothering to turn over and look. 'Won't do her no favours. She has to break out by herself.'

'Is this normal?' Wes realised he currently had a tenuous grasp on normality at best. He shook himself. 'What the fuck am I saying? Why am I even listening to you, anyway? You're off your tits on caterpillar goo. What the hell is my life?'

Ricky was staring at something Wes couldn't see. 'It's what happened to Hector.'

Wes prised a hand off the cocoon, but left the other stuck to it, hoping Katy could feel he was still there.

'I'm not going anywhere,' he promised her. 'I'll be right here. So, um. If you break out… I don't want to die, all right? But.' He shook his head, giving up. 'Shit.' He slid his trapped hand down along the side of the swelling outer case, feeling the pulse of panic under his palm. 'I'm making this about me. Sorry. You're the one in the…'

There was another barking scream.

'Okay, okay, calm down. Calm down. Hector had a body, didn't he? You'll have one too. Don't panic. It's just the Changes, it's… it can't be very nice.' He winced at the platitude. 'God, I'm an idiot. I don't know what to say.'

'Shut up, then.' Ricky was evidently coming down, and he sounded irritable. 'Try and sleep.'

'You sleep. I'll sit up with her.' Wes slumped down by his sister, listening to the gurgling whimper from within.

'Shit me.' Ricky struggled upright, stumbled, and stood still, swaying. He came towards them unsteadily, slumping down on the other side of the cocoon. 'There, now we're both here.' He addressed the cocoon. 'You all right in there? Breathing, at least?'

Katy, or rather, the-Thing-that-was-Katy, Wes supposed, gave a burble that they interpreted as positive.

'Breathing's good,' Ricky said with an air of wisdom that Wes didn't think was warranted.

'You think there's anything else we need to worry about? What about that giant frog thing from earlier? Or those eyes you thought you saw?'

Ricky shrugged, accent broadening with fatigue. 'Dunno as they was eyes. Doant matter.'

'Er, I think it *might* matter, if we get ambushed and eaten.'

Ricky shrugged. 'We're with a, what's it called, an apex predator. I don't think anything's going to get within ten feet of us. This is *her place*. This is the Thirteenth's place. That's what Hector found out, or Grampa Nathan with him, or something. The Throne was meant to be his. Would've bin, 'til he destroyed himself.' He yawned. 'This place isn't going to have anything in it that's going to hurt the Thirteenth. And us by extension.'

'Why were you so worried earlier, then?'

He giggled. 'Wasn't high earlier.'

Wes sniggered. 'Fair.'

'You won't tell the missus about all this, will you?' Ricky added after a pause. 'Only, I sort of promised her a while back that… I wouldn't throw up on her floors, naun like that.' He laughed. 'Promised her that when I was fifteen, I think, but she still wouldn't let me in.'

'Cross my heart.' It took Wes a moment before he realised Carrie hadn't been around back then. She'd only moved in last year. He was talking about the house, as if he hadn't noticed it had absorbed a whole woman. He made a mental note to ask about that once they got out of here.

'And don't tell her I called her the missus, either.'

'Course not.'

There was a weird staccato sucking noise from inside the cocoon.

Wes frowned. 'You all right, Katy?'

Ricky chuckled. 'She's laughing.'

That was a relief. He grinned, pressing his hand against the outer membrane. 'Good.' He cricked his neck, stretching. 'Are *you* all right?'

'Me?'

'Yeah. You finished hallucinating?'

'Hard to tell.'

Wes sighed. 'This is going to be a long night.'

Chapter 13: The Sun Also Rises

Outside

Ricky let the Thirteenth's cocoon-dreams swamp him, submerged in images that came from her head. For a while he wasn't sure what was dream and what was waking, whether he was encased himself or not, or whether his limbs belonged to his own body. Perhaps he had borrowed them. Everything felt strange, disintegrated, disjointed.

It was worth it.

He saw what she saw, committing as much to memory as he could, hoping it wouldn't fade from him like a nightmare. But there was something else with them in the dreams – the eyes, the glowing eyes in the darkness, the watchers.

He took in the Thirteenth's form as it clawed and tore at their kinfolk, and wondered if his own form was a match for it, or if he'd ever need to find out. But he couldn't see that. She didn't dream of him.

Ricky watched her dreams unfold, filing the names and faces away, but something else repeatedly tugged at his attention. A glimmer of something in his peripheral vision, a flicker of light in the corner of his eye, distracted him. He turned to it, hoping to see the sun glaring on the mistress's windows, but with a stab of disappointment he saw it came from a dark, jagged mountainside, rising out of the barren landscape. The Beast and its dreams began to pull away from him, as the bright light pulsed and dazzled.

Ricky tried to return to the glimpses he had of Katherine's secret inner world, much preferring the knowledge he was soaking up from this temporary connection, but as he turned away, the light on the edge of his consciousness strobed and began to blind him.

The Beast and the faces of its victims fractured before he could adjust his concentration, and the strobing light filled his third eye with crystalline brilliance.

He didn't even have time to swear.

It swallowed him up, leaving him floating in a void of white. His feet found purchase on a hard floor. That certainly felt real, but he was pretty sure this was all still happening in his head. He turned and collided with something hard and nearly fell over.

He was now standing in a crystal cave, and a few dazed blinks brought everything more clearly into focus.

The cavemouth snarled out of the mountainside, and far below him was the circle of standing stones, and two tiny figures not far beyond that, sitting with a speck of red. The cocoon. Ricky rubbed his eyes. This couldn't be the future, then. Not if he could see himself. Nor the past, he'd never been here before.

The present, that was it. That's what it was.

He nodded and turned back around to find out what was so important about this place that demanded his attention. It felt familiar, like a place he had read about in a book, plucked from his mind. The geodes sparkled with no discernible light source, but he supposed that was an effect of his imagination. It was a globular space, reflecting and refracting energies his other form thirsted for beneath his writhing skin.

'All right,' he said aloud at last, when nothing seemed to happen. 'What am I doing here?'

He frowned, catching sight of himself in the facets, a hundred thousand fragments of himself. This place called for another language, an older one, and he repeated himself in Old English instead. For the first time he was self-conscious about it, knowing he was self-taught, worrying that he'd got it wrong, or wasn't pronouncing it properly.

As if in answer, a thread of energy caught his eye in its journey from one glittering crystal to another. Ricky blinked, following the darting path deeper into the cave. The thread sparkled, taunting him, and zipped off into a web at the cave's glowing heart.

His breath caught.

In the web he saw the Beast, saw her clearer than by walking through her stolen dreams, trapped in the centre like a giant fly. She could not hurt him. He saw the family, each one meshed in a miniature web of their own, though perhaps not all their own making. He saw the layers of decisions, the paths and their forks, their intersections, all laid out in the moving strands of light, and where they ended. Mostly, they ended with her.

Ricky knew better than to touch the web, although it seemed to invite him. His fingertips itched. This was the future, a three-dimensional model only partially woven, and if he wanted to, he could direct the warp and weft. It would burn. The energy sparked hot, crackled with prismatic colours, bounced from angle to angle.

It would burn, but it would work. He could manipulate the refractions if he wanted. And so what if it hurt? He could shed his skin, absorb the energy in his other form, drink it in, change back. Be good as new.

'Show me the cull,' he whispered in Old English, hoarse. Cold squirming trails of excitement coursed in his chest, clenching his heart. It hammered painfully in his throat, pulse racing. The energy sparked, obedient. The threads meshed and formed a cube, rotating until the corners smoothed in the air and it became a sphere.

Within the sphere, he saw the future he'd asked for, playing out in dancing pictures like a child's magic lantern. He'd always wanted one of those.

His heart hurt, it was beating so fast.

'Show me the next Head of the Family.'

The pictures swirled together, shrinking into pixels, and formed a face. Ricky tried to fix this in his mind, but it slithered away from him, resistant to memory.

'Shit me.' He licked his lips. 'Ain't we fucked.'

He winced, expecting someone to cuff the back of his head for the profanity, but nothing happened. No censure came. This was his place, after all.

He straightened up, swallowing.

'Show me the mistress.'

But all the pictures showed him was a house, out of focus, flat and inanimate. He shook his head, frowning. It was a postcard, poorly photographed, without the depth of Fairwood in reality.

'That's not what…' He broke off, clearing his throat. *'Show me the mistress.'*

The house flickered, coming into clearer focus. Yet there was something stopping him seeing it properly, something in the way of his vision. He squinted, wondering if this was because there was something wrong with his eyesight, but the excitement had turned to nausea.

He struggled with himself, now able to name the thing that was tugging at him, the idea that chased him through the wasteland. Maybe she didn't *want* him to come back. Maybe she wouldn't notice he was gone; she would wait a little, and then forget. All those years he'd spent outside, all for nothing.

How much of an imprint could he have made on her stones and bricks in a few months? Not even a year, barely a blink in all the time she'd been standing. Without him, she'd fill herself with light and life and people, erase him like dust.

The only thing worse than not getting back at all would be returning to her glower of disappointment.

(His mother's reaction when he returned after a three-month absence of sleeping rough, just before he turned seventeen, when all she gave him was one long, slow look of regret that dried his apologies on his dirty, dehydrated tongue…)

He hadn't thought about that for years, either. This place forced him backwards, into dark corners he tried to avoid.

It's not your sight, it's your conviction, whispered the Voice in his head. He'd been wondering when that would show up. *That's why you can't see her.*

Ricky swallowed down a lump of bile. He was looking at something that might not want to be seen. He gnawed his lip in unconscious imitation of his cousin, and when he realised, struggled to stop.

'What if she doant want me back?' he whispered to the cave, the Voice, the light before him.

The image in the sphere flickered and fritzed.

Ricky forced himself to look deeper, properly. His nostrils flared. 'I want to go home.'

You want power, the Voice corrected. *Here, you can control everything you see. Don't you want that? Their truth is whatever you say it is. You can break the curse of mediocrity, transform their dull ambitions. You can manipulate them, the way they always tried to manipulate you.*

'That the curse you want me to break, is it?' Ricky sniffed, cracking his neck to the side. He flexed his shoulders, still itching to touch the sphere, to feel Fairwood's aura burning through his skin with the energy that showed him its image. 'Ah. That'd benefit you, o' course.'

You are unique in your generation. The Voice turned silky, soothing, but Ricky mistrusted that particular tone. Gran had only deployed it when she wanted something, and he was willing to bet this slippery bastard was no different or he'd eat his own entrails.

'Yeah. Well. I can be unique at home, can't I?' His hands dropped to his sides, balling into fists. 'Wha's the point of this if I don't get what I want?'

You can have EVERYTHING you want, the Voice snapped, louder, echoing in his skull and around the cave.

'Yeah, the last time you said that she dropped dead and caught fucking fire,' Ricky pointed out, bitterly. 'So mebbe you doant know half of what I want, after all. I think she's better off wi'out that kind of bullshit, thanks. Prob'ly better off wi'out mine. But a promise is a promise, and you *promised me.*' Ricky glared at the geodes, flickering with power. 'This is nice an' all, but I'm having what was promised. It ain't even been a full year. I'm stayin' there, if she'll let me, an' I don't need your permission, *or* your bleedin' approval. I'm not doin' anything else until *I'm* ready, so you c'n stick your bleedin' cave.'

The Voice was silent. The cave began to melt away, dropping out of focus, out of sight. The power, the images, all the things he could have done, slipped from his grasp and he fell, stomach rising and flipping, into his body on the cold, hard ground.

—

It wasn't just the effects of the morning-after-the-night-before that brought Ricky gagging into the splintering light of dawn. There were the fragments of the Thirteenth's dreams still embedded in his skull like rusty nails, leaking into his own waking reality and distorting his perception. The crystal cave, its secrets and promise of power, danced out of reach.

His cocoon gamble had been worth it. He recalled with imperfect clarity the faces she'd dreamed of, the size and shape of things to come as they'd appeared in the web of light. Wes may suspect he'd done it on purpose, but Ricky thought he'd been pretty clever about it, even if the mistress would have seen through his cockiness in a blink. His chest warmed thinking of her, the only place he'd ever wanted to call home.

That was short-lived.

Wes was stretching, balancing on a rock and scanning the rocks. 'Morning, handsome.'

Ricky shook his head, shading his eyes from the stabbing of the dawn.

'You all right? All worn off?'

'More or less.'

'Ready for another go?' Wes spat on his palms and rubbed them together in imitation of him, rolling his shoulders back and flickering terribly as he moved.

Ricky couldn't look at him.

'Sure.'

'She ain't moving in there,' Wes said, bounding down and patting the cocoon. 'Can't hear her, either, maybe she's dreaming again.'

'Oh, she's dreaming.' Ricky saw the edges of a colour spectrum rippling over the obsidian, colours he couldn't recognise or name. Some of them looked alive, living colours, breathing colours, rippling and pulsing with their own strange life. 'You go first, I don't feel too clever.'

Wes nodded, eyes twinkling in mischief. 'Bet you don't.'

'She figured it out,' Ricky grunted, as they heaved the cocoon off the ground. 'I hope this bloody henge isn't far.'

They hauled the cocoon as carefully as they could between the outcrops and boulders, threading their way in a rough diagonal towards the stone circle. The cloud cover was dense once more, a blanket of blinding grey, but the heat grew oppressive.

They hadn't eaten or drunk anything for a full day, or at least Wes hadn't, and Ricky had thrown up. That made everything harder. Wes was bone-tired; he stumbled over loose stones, over his own ankles, over nothing, dragging his feet as sweat prickled through his pores and drained him of any moisture he had left. He couldn't go on much longer.

'The thing that's bothering me,' Ricky said eventually, in an ominous voice that made Wes groan, 'is...'

Wes waited.

Ricky didn't finish.

'Is what?'

'...What?'

Wes tried to swallow, dry-mouthed and irritable. 'The thing that's bothering you is... what?'

'Oh. Yeah. Priests. Haven't seen any.'

'Fuck me.' Wes thought his cousin was still hallucinating or something. 'Thought I saw some nuns over that way, we can have a chat to them if you want.'

'Don't be daft, you soppy tart, I mean Grandad's priests, don't I? The ones I could summon.'

Wes scowled. 'Since when can you do that?'

'What d'you think I had those tattoos for, afore I shed my skin? Decoration?'

'Well... yeah.' Wes hoped they could keep the bickering up; it distracted him from how rough he was feeling. He was certain the cocoon was getting heavier. 'That's what they're usually for.'

'I'm bloody wasted on you.'

Wes smirked. 'Nearly there.'

'Yeah, but it's like things are hanging back on purpose. Maybe it's not because we're with the Thirteenth, like I thought. What if it's Him?'

He could hear the capitalisation in his cousin's tone, but it wasn't entirely respectful. Wes empathised.

'I don't want to see Him.' He was starting to feel sick. False bravado pushed it down. 'He can bloody well give me my face back, if He does show up.'

'Three single-births together on this side,' Ricky mused, gruff and quiet. 'Why's that, then? I heard Grandad in the Throne Room, goin' round in my head like a bloody answer machine. What's he want with us?'

'I didn't hear anything.'

'Said something about me breaking another curse: opening up a portal for 'em is my guess.'

Wes went cold. 'Don't you bloody dare. I mean, we can't have an apocalypse *now*, Uncle Ray's just finished his barn conversion.'

'Would you listen to yourself?' Ricky's sneer was audible. 'Bloody barn conversion.'

Wes laughed it off, but worry niggled at him. 'You wouldn't, anyway. Like you said, who wants to rule the world? They'd only screw us over. First thing that came through'd lay waste to everything in its path and that includes your precious manor house.'

'Yeah, I did think of that.' Ricky grunted, tripping and causing Wes to stumble. 'If that's the offer, I'm not int'rested.'

Wes righted himself and they paused. 'Put her down a sec. We ain't far now.'

'If I put her down, that's it,' Ricky warned. 'She bloody stays where we set her. I can't. I can't go on much more.'

'All right, look, it's literally just over there, a few more yards, yeah? Then we'll put her down and hope she hatches out so we don't have to drag her.' Wes was desperate to wipe the sweat off his brow. It dripped into his eyes and ran down his nose, salty and stinging.

The henge loomed above them suddenly as they rounded another outcrop, overshadowing them with slabs of carved black stone, covered in columns of glowing green symbols carved into the smooth surfaces. The slabs were in threes, two uprights and one horizontal on top forming a blocky arch, laid out in this fashion in a large, perfect ring.

In the centre was a slab of gleaming obsidian, propped on top of smaller blocks. Another slab of rock was set flush against it, so that it reminded Wes of an armless sofa, or an avant-garde garden bench.

'Who d'you think did that?' he asked.

Ricky was wheezing.

Wes turned to check on him and frowned. 'Bloody hell, you okay?'

'Knackered.'

'Are you up to this?' Wes waved at the circle. 'This is what you wanted, right?'

Ricky didn't answer.

Wes dragged his weary, desiccated bones over to the nearest standing stone, and blinked at the symbols. 'These are glowing,' he said stupidly, tongue thick. 'Oi. Richard.' He sniggered, but winding Ricky up was pointless and only made him annoyed with himself. 'Ricky. Look. You seen this?'

'If that abuseful old bastard shows up,' Ricky muttered to himself, swaying on the spot, 'I'm going to lose my shit.'

Wes sniggered. 'You sound like me.' Something tugged at his attention through the haze fogging his thoughts.

I'm delirious, he thought. *Maybe it all seeped in through my skin. What even is this stuff? It's everywhere.*

The red ooze was splattered over his jeans and shirt and set like honey. Tiny crystals were forming on the edges where it had dried first, pinkish and hard as quartz.

There was a strange clicking sound that he hadn't been aware of before, but he couldn't pinpoint the source. He leaned against the stone, letting its cool surface seep into his flesh.

A line of green symbols danced before his eyes as he closed them.

Oh, shit, what now?

He couldn't pull away. His skin tingled underneath, like it had done the first time he'd Changed.

He became acutely aware of everyone his flesh had ever touched, everyone who had ever seen his image, heard his voice, and forgotten him. His sleeper soldiers, living, working, walking, sleeping, with him under their skin.

Call them, a Voice encouraged, buried at the back of his brain. *Call them, and they will come.*

Call them where? To do what?

If he woke up that thirst, they would become like Charlie, desperately seeking him at every party, every event, in every alleyway and crowded street, clinging to every photograph and cutting away their eyelids so they would never blink and forget again.

But they'd adore him.

Need him.

Do anything he wanted.

He had spent his whole adult life unknowingly sowing his seeds of madness in all who encountered him, like fungal spores embedded deep in hundreds, thousands, of random human brains, and now he had to wait for them to grow. People who'd glimpsed him in the street. In shops. In cafes, pubs, clubs, restaurants. People who'd seen the photographs Charlie tried to take, the countless hundreds on social media he wasn't even aware of, with him in the background. How many thousands of people had seen his forgettable face? And they would all, at one touch, one word, live to worship him. They'd claw their own children apart as sacrifices, offer him the world and everything in it just to see his face one more time.

Wes saw what he could become, the full glorious horror of it, and…

No.

He pushed himself away from the stone with a burst of energy, invigorated and charged.

'Fuck that! Fuck you!' Wes snapped at the sky. 'Fuck you with a chainsaw.'

The clicking was getting louder.

'Ah, wondered when they'd show up,' Ricky said conversationally, and fell over.

Wes ducked, as Grandad's priests burst down out of the clouds in a hail of locust wings.

One landed in front of him. Wes didn't take in too many details, but his brain registered the important ones. It was basically a chimera, a grasshopper with a horse-shaped head, except the face topping the segmented body was, firstly, fly-eyed, and secondly, had teeth that could slice through metal. The mouth set in that weird, long equine snout split all the way back to the base of the face, so it could cram as many of those teeth in as possible.

Wes didn't bother to count the legs or antenna.

He brained it with a rock.

It flailed about for a second, double-jointed limbs waggling like a half-dead cockroach, so he hit it again. Something blue squirted out, watery and pale, followed by some darker sludge. Some of it spurted onto his jeans.

'Great.'

Wes felt something slash across his back like a whip.

Two of them were on him, cutting through his shirt with the hooks on their feet. He thrashed against the rocks and rolled, feeling their bones break under him, and ripped his shirt off to get rid of everything they'd touched.

Ricky was in trouble.

They weren't getting too close, but his tendrils lashed about from the back of his head, oozing from nips and cuts as he tried to keep them off him.

Nothing was attacking the cocoon: probably because Katy hadn't pissed the old man off yet.

Wes used the rags of his shirt as part flag, part flail, whipping at the insectoids. He fought his way through the buzzing cloud and dragged his cousin over the rocks and into the stone circle by one arm.

The tendrils whipped around violently, covering their retreat, but as soon as he got them between the upright slabs, the priests swarmed around the outside, either unable or unwilling to enter.

'This is mine,' Wes said, hauling Ricky to his feet. 'The Throne Room's hers. But this place is *mine*.'

Ricky gave him a weary glance. 'I can see you better, at least. Here, don't leave her out there.'

He started forwards, out of the safety of the circle, and Wes grabbed him and yanked him back. Ricky lost his footing and sat down heavily on the ground.

'She's fine, they're not after her. It's us. We've *displeased* the old beggar.'

Ricky winced, putting his head between his legs. His back lips gaped mournfully, a few stray tendrils dribbling over the bottom lip as far as his shoulders.

'Everything *hurts*.'

'I'll give you a cuddle in a minute Princess,' Wes muttered, trying to keep Katy's cocoon in sight as the priest swarm buzzed around the outside of their shelter.

'Piss off.'

'Charming. You weren't complaining last night, were you?'

'Is that a sex joke?'

Wes blinked. 'No, mate. It was... what? No. Never mind.' The energy from the stones poured into him, refreshing his body and soul. It was not having the same effect on Ricky, who was much paler than before.

He wondered if the priests, all of whom had now had a good look at him, were susceptible to his seeds of insanity. Except, of course, he was memorable here. So much for that idea.

'What happens if I sit on that?' he wondered aloud, staring at the altar thing in the middle of the circle. 'Katy's got the Throne – what's this, my recliner? Chaise-longue?'

'Oh, of course you'd have something you can lie down on,' Ricky muttered.

'I'll have you know I do some of my best work on my back.' Wes paused. 'And fairly frequently on other people's.'

Ricky snorted.

Ignoring the angry swarming of the priests, Wes bounded over to his altar-throne and swung himself up onto it. It wasn't uncomfortable. Hard, but not uncomfortable. Quite warm, in fact. A few chenille throws, a cushion or two... He stretched out, hands behind his head.

'Well, this is nice. Could do a lot with this.'

Ricky stumbled up and joined him, casting a dispassionate glance from his head to his toes.

Wes grinned. 'See anything you like? Just say.'

The soothsayer rolled his eyes and dropped down near Wes's elbow, resting his back against the thick slab, where he could watch the arches.

'Where's your adoring court, then?' Ricky asked. 'This is what it was built for, ain't it? You lying in state, some poor sod feeding you grapes out of a golden bowl.'

'Peeled grapes,' Wes corrected.

'Yeah, of course.'

'Gave 'em the day off.' Wes cleared his throat, pretending he couldn't hear the priests, couldn't feel the stinging cuts on his back, wasn't covered in goo and weird alien blood and whatever else he'd picked up in this godsforsaken place. He was at home, Charlie was going to sashay through the door any second in a cloud of perfume and glitter and business cards, and Hugo was in the next room working on a presentation, stressed and dishevelled and sexy as all hell.

'We're going to die here.' Ricky's tone was so cold, so dull, so matter-of-fact, that a chill ran up Wes's spine.

He shook his head. 'We won't.'

'Look at that. We won't get through that. I can't open the portal. Not without her.'

Wes sat up. 'Give over.'

Ricky shook his head, shoulders slumped. 'Don't matter, anyway. I'll not be coming back through.'

'What the hell are you talking about? Don't be like that, what'll Carrie say if you don't come back? She'll blame me, you know. And, in fairness, it *is* my fault.'

Ricky gave a strange, bitter laugh. 'Yeah, well, shot myself in the foot there. Already set her up for life, haven't I? She don't need me, an' it's all my fault she's the way she is, she'll have other lodgers, I seen it. She wa'n't ever built for just the one person, it's not going to be the way I...' He stopped himself. 'I think it's better if I stay here. Do everyone a favour.'

Wes smacked him across the head. 'God, you sound like Granny Sylvia.'

Ricky twisted around with a snarl. '*I do not.*'

'"This will be my last Yule",' Wes mimicked in passable impression of their shared grandmother.

Sylvia Porter, daughter of Nathan and Deirdre Porter, mother of their respective mothers (and Ricky's father), had spent her life in a hard-done-by state of constant complaint, which made those family visits to her sitting-room a triennial chore. Wes couldn't remember seeing any other part of her house – he hesitated to call it a 'home' – except for that dingy sitting-room of faded blues and browns, stuffed with dated furniture, paisley patterns, and musty carpet. Finally, on one memorable November afternoon after one passive-aggressive remark too many, Uncle Nigel, the favourite son, had locked her in the big gas oven and turned it on. Yule hampers from Uncle Nigel and Aunty Mandy had been full of oddly rubbery meat cuts that year.

'Stop wallowing, then. Martyrdom don't suit you.' Wes sat up, watching the priests crawling outside their sanctuary, rubbing their back legs together with a strange keening chirp. 'Bloody hell, they're doing my head in.'

Ricky sighed.

Wes itched to shake him, but it wouldn't do any good. 'Where's yours, then? Must be near here.'

'My what?'

'Throne. Recliner. Whatever.'

He shrugged. 'What makes you think I got one?'

Wes gave him a proper nudge. 'You must do. You're the One and Only. Stand on here, let's have a look.'

'We can't get to it,' Ricky pointed out, but clambered upright half-heartedly. 'What's the point?'

Wes helped him up onto the slab so they could both scan the landscape behind the circle. The mountains rose behind them, one bald peak higher than the others, jagged and dark in the foreground.

'There we are.' Wes pointed at something gleaming about two thirds of the way up. 'That looks like something. Another door, maybe. Bet that's yours. Nice and inaccessible. Very Oracle of Delphi. Bet you got some nice pillars, bit of trippy vapour to inhale, bet it's really nice.'

Ricky smirked. Wes took this as a good sign.

'Prob'ly a bit of quartz in the sun.'

'What sun? Don't be daft.' Wes looked his cousin up and down, the niggling worry growing. Ricky wasn't himself. All the cockiness and swagger had leached out of him, leaving nothing behind except a gaunt, drawn tension and sulky self-pity. He was physically drained, too – filthy, stinking of days-old sweat now with the undertone of fishy vomit, hoodie and trackies completely wrecked by the red ooze, skin pale and pallid, eyes glassy and dry.

He wasn't up to opening a can of beans, let alone a portal to another dimension.

Maybe he was right. They were going to die here.

'Fuck it,' he muttered under his breath. 'Okay.' He turned Ricky bodily around to face him, hands on his cousin's shoulders. 'Hear me out. What if I drive people insane enough to start a cult and come looking for us?'

Ricky raised an eyebrow. 'Time is faster here than out there, so how long d'you think that's going to take them?'

'You don't seem surprised by the "driving people insane" part.' Wes wondered if the symbols meant anything to him.

Ricky grinned, a slice of his usual self reasserting itself. 'Nah, I've met you.'

'Fucker.' Wes pushed him away, grinning back. 'I *could* have a court, apparently. That's what He wants.' He pointed at the sky. 'That's why they're out there. All I have to do is... um. Activate this. Somehow.' He gestured at his body. No longer a strobing series of layers, here in the circle he was one consistent frame, one singular image, and he could remember the contours of his skinny ribs and bare, lanky arms, the paling post-Dubai tan.

Ricky was unimpressed. 'Right. An' how d'you reckon they're going to do that, if they're all mad? You met many occultists, have you? Physicists? Quantum mechanics?'

'I don't think that last one's even a job…'

'So, no, then.'

'All right, not a great plan.' Wes gave up. 'Plus, I mean, I don't think I could do it selectively. There's a lot of people I wouldn't want to mess up like that.'

Ricky gave him a twitchy smile and sighed. 'Well. At least we know how special you are.'

'Yeah.' Wes grinned. 'Fuck, should I get an Insta? I could break the internet. Literally.'

'If you break the internet, I'll break your face.' Katy, naked and dripping red ooze, picked her way between the priests and into the circle.

Wes's heart skipped.

She looked normal. That was a huge relief. Her hair wasn't the same: it had grown back in patches, some longer than others, most of her skull still bald. As she came closer, he saw that, underneath the ooze, her skin was mottled and raw. Some of it was peeling off with the red stuff, leaving slick shark-grey patches of rubbery flesh underneath.

'Katy! Oh, fuck, we missed the hatching. Oh babe, you look great.' He nudged Ricky, who was openly frowning. 'Don't she.'

'Beautiful, yeah.'

'You're such liars.' Katy was leaving a trail of sticky red slime behind her, and a few priests were stuck to it, drawn into the circle along the narrow red path she was creating.

Wes licked his lips. They didn't seem to be moving.

'Um, they... those things don't like us.' He gave his sister a wobbly smile. 'Are you all right? Shit, I'm so sorry. I'm so sorry about all this.'

Katy's face was strangely vacant. She shrugged it off and looked behind her. 'The Khly'k? They were singing to me. They woke me up.'

Wes and Ricky exchanged glances.

'Don't look at me,' Ricky said. 'S'prob'ly one of those weird names with an apostrophe in it.'

'If you're going to take the piss I won't tell you what they are.' Katy frowned at her brother. 'What happened to me? We were on the rocks, and then... I don't remember, I was coughing... and... where's your shirt?'

Wes kept a straight face. 'Working on my tan.'

She rolled her eyes. A glob of cocoon-ooze slid off her thigh, taking a few layers of skin with it. Wes caught a glimpse of red-raw flesh and sinew, human tissue, and switched focus to her face.

'You're not in pain or anything?' he asked, hoping she couldn't feel it.

Katy shook her head. 'I had some really weird dreams, nightmares, I thought I was, like, swimming but... I didn't have any limbs or organs or... I don't... I don't feel right. Some bits of me are a bit sore.'

Wes kept his voice light and gentle. 'Yeah, well, you're awake now, you don't have to think about it. Don't, maybe don't touch anything, or, or look, okay? Keep looking at me.'

Katy frowned and instinctively looked down at herself. Wes leapt off the slab and made her jump.

'Ha, no, no, there's no need to check, you're fine. You look fine. You look great.'

She backed away from him, trailing stickiness and bits of flesh. 'What? What is it?' She raised dripping hands to her face.

'Your *face* is fine.' Wes assured her, trying not to wince. She was becoming, as far as he could see, a torso of slow-cooked pork, meat pulling off the bone. There was something under there.

'Don't touch her, she's not done yet.' Ricky climbed down, stiff and slow. 'Katy, come here. Come here. It's all right. Am I glad to see you.'

He sounded genuine, which warmed Wes's heart. Wes stepped to the side, over the slime trail, to let Katy edge her way towards their cousin, more uncertain now as she tried to figure out what had happened.

'Am I really okay?' she asked, looking for the truth.

Ricky propped himself up against the slab. 'You're going to have to Change.'

Katy shuddered. Bits of her flopped to the ground. 'Ow...'

'Don't look,' Wes and Ricky chorused.

She closed her eyes, close to tears. 'What's happening to me?'

'You need to shed all that, that's all.' Ricky sounded confident, and Wes clung to the hope he knew what he was talking about. 'Hector did it. Came out of his cocoon looking like Swiss cheese, shed it all and there he was. Gran's beautiful butterfly.'

Katy caught her breath. 'Gran said that to me, she said I'd be a butterfly...'

'Well, it's more a big, kind of a, dog thing,' Ricky said with a wince, 'But, yeah, I mean, it's a nice metaphor.'

'But I can look like a *person*, right?' Katy swallowed. 'Like, I won't be... the Beast forever, right?'

'The Beast? Is that what you... okay. No, you can be a person.' Ricky nodded. 'Promise.'

'Really promise?'

'Absolutely. On my life. On the mistress.'

Katy took a deep breath. 'Okay.'

Wes closed his eyes and prayed to someone, anyone who was listening, that she'd really taken him off the List, that she had somehow figured it out, that he wasn't about to be turned into steak tartare. He also prayed, as a rather important addendum, that Ricky hadn't got it wrong.

There was a slick tearing sound, the sound of flesh being pulled apart. Katy was whimpering, but the whimper turned guttural, mutated and choked, then became a dog-like whine. Bones crunched and snapped. Something massive thudded down right in front of him, and the ground shook. He flinched, keeping his balance, cracking open one eye.

An enormous claw-tip was inches from his foot. He followed the claw back, expecting to see a paw. It looked more like a giant hoof, rounded like a horse's, with three more claws arching seamlessly out of it, irretractable. Hooves shouldn't have claws. He made the mistake of looking up. The forelimb went on forever.

His eyes watered as prickles of fear and adrenaline zipped through him.

He could barely breathe.

It was a giant hound, all right, but nothing like any hound he had ever seen.

'Ohh, *shh-hit*.'

'It's still her.' Ricky's voice was soft. He couldn't see him – the Beast was in the way.

The muzzle lowered, four petals of teeth parting like the trumpet of a flower to release a longer jaw from the back of the creature's throat. It sniffed Wes with this, its own scent oddly canine.

Wes was certain that, if he wasn't so dehydrated, he'd have wet himself by now.

'No sudden movements.'

No fear of that, Wes thought. He was clamped to the spot, terror in full, vice-like control of his extremities.

It didn't tear him apart.

The jaw retracted.

The petals furled up again. The Beast lifted its head.

Wes let himself breathe out, a long, slow jet of pure delirium. Spots danced in front of his eyes from holding it for so long. He filled his lungs with the unnatural scent of the Beast, and its long, prehensile tail curled around its body, nearly poking him with the tip.

Wes put out his hand, curiosity overcoming the numbing fear. The hide was rubbery, sleek, the way he imagined a seal would feel. He mentally added 'swim with seals' to his bucket list. Dolphins he'd already ticked off, with no regrets. It wasn't quite like a dolphin.

'How does she turn back?' he asked, wondering where all that flesh and bone could possibly go. Surely not back into the body of a seventeen-year-old girl.

In answer to this, the Beast began to shake itself.

Wes jumped aside, as, with a reptilian roar that ended in four coughing barks, the head split like a paper flower. It folded back on itself, regurgitating his sister's head and shoulders, collapsed like origami, the limbs folding up in a weird, twitching motion, the tail retracting, until the whole gargantuan mass of it was no more than his sister's height and width. She unfurled her arms, for a moment the toothy petals of its maw the only thing remaining, like dragonfly wings. Then they, too, folded up, leaking out human skin in the way Ricky's form did, binding up tight into Katy's naked body and leaving her almost exactly as she had been.

'Can I borrow your hoodie?' Katy asked Ricky, looking down at herself.

She turned, self-conscious, and Wes covered his mouth to hide a wince. She was indeed exactly the same, would pass for human well enough, and the only visible addition was a vestigial tail extending from the base of her spine. Well, that was all right, surely, she could wear skirts or something, that wasn't too bad. At least that was something she could explain to other people using normal human biology.

He hoped she'd see it that way.

Ricky tugged his stained hoodie off and handed it to her. 'You don't want that, it's... well.'

She took it anyway. It didn't cover everything.

Wes rubbed his forehead. 'Is it... are you going to be *that big* every time? Because... that's going to be problematic.' He looked to Ricky for answers. 'How the hell did Hector get away with that and not have them call the army in?'

The vestigial tail extended as Katy's eyes grew wide, darting from one to the other. It curled up on high alert, several metres long, spikes of bone pushing through it at intervals, a sharp point on the end.

Well, that was going to be a lot harder to explain.

Ricky shook his head. 'Nah, I'm sure she can manipulate the space she's in. An' don't forget, everythin's heightened because we're here. Like you. Look at you, pretty much a real person, now.'

Wes rolled his eyes, but that stung. 'Ha, ha.'

Ricky's eyes flicked to the bony extension. 'You got a tail, by the way.'

Katy twisted around on the spot to see it, resulting in a frantic, puppy-like chase that Wes tried not to find hilarious. He clamped a hand to his mouth, shoulders shaking.

'You bastard!' Katy was pink, pulling down the stained hoodie to hide her modesty, tail lashing in the air as she tried to get it under control. 'Stop laughing, I'll put you back on the List!'

This set Ricky off, sniggering as he caught Wes's eye.

'Seriously, I mean it!' She concentrated, the pink tinge to her cheeks deepening to bright red, and the tail slowly retracted beneath the hoodie's hem. 'Don't laugh at me! God, I hate you both.'

'Oi, we nearly broke our backs carrying you about. You weigh a bloody ton, Katherine.'

'Screw you!'

Wes swallowed his amusement. 'Aw, come on, you look great, and a tail is pretty cool, isn't it? At least it's not that mess he's got going on over there.'

Ricky shot him a look.

Wes shrugged. 'I think it's cute.'

'*I'm not cute.*' Katy was fighting a smile, he could tell. 'I'm the Thirteenth. And I want to go home. We've been here too long as it is. Who knows how much time has passed in our world, I've got exams and shit to do.'

That was music to Wes's ears. 'Oh, fuck yes. Yes please. Let's go home.'

'I'm starving,' his sister complained.

'You need to increase your calorie intake,' Ricky informed her, patting his bare midriff. 'Conserve more energy. And protein helps.'

Dehydration had done wonders for his abs. Wes, now able to remember that he was a skinny streak of nothing compared to his cousin, experienced a pang of envy at the aesthetic outcome of a lifestyle he'd do anything to avoid. The little prick could even be attractive if he tried, or at least modified his bloody diet. And had a personality transplant.

He was being petty again.

'Are you up to this?' he asked with a conscious effort to be supportive, as Ricky visibly steeled himself.

The priests had dulled their chirping to a low background drone, like cicadas on a balmy Mediterranean evening.

Ricky shrugged, studying the central slab for symbols.

'Can I help?' Katy approached as Wes hung back.

'Possibly, but it's his bloody chaise-longue.' Ricky curled his lip in Wes's direction, and Wes realised with a pang that Ricky, the family's new god, was jealous of him.

He joined them in the centre. 'What are we looking for?'

'I were hopin' it's like the Pendle Stone, or we could at least use it to connect with it.'

Wes nodded.

There were carved symbols all over it, and now that he was looking for them, he saw them plainly. They weren't like the ones Ricky had had tattooed on his arms, nor like the ones on the Pendle Stone, but they were similar to the glowing green things etched into the upright slabs surrounding them.

He cast a glance back at the arches in question, holding the priests at bay. The ones dragged in on Katy's trail of ooze were dissolving quietly, their legs twitching as they sank into deconstructionist oblivion.

'Yeah, I mean, there's all these symbols here,' he said, tracing the ones on the slab with his fingertips. 'Can't you see them?'

Ricky blinked. 'I thought... yes. I see them, but...' A vague expression came over his face. 'I... I must've forgotten they were there.'

A thrill chased up Wes's spine, but he feigned nonchalance.

'Ah, good. Makes me a bit less redundant. Hold on.'

This was *his* place.

Everything was calibrated to him, to his frequency, energy, heartbeat, brain chemistry, whatever. He didn't care how it worked; it felt as if it all belonged to him, had been made especially for him. When he traced the symbols in their natural order, they glowed at his touch.

He *could* awaken his seeds here, the little drops of forgotten image stored in the minds of others, be selective if he wanted. The symbols could show him how. He could have his own cult. Really be someone. Not have to harm anyone he cared about.

Was there a way of reversing it? Perhaps, if he explored this place thoroughly, learned all its secrets, took his time. He didn't need to go back yet, not if he controlled the portal this side.

The horizontal slab began to hum, vibrate, under his fingertips. His image began to break down as it did so, separating into layers again, some visible, others flickering in and out of existence and memory. He wasn't flesh at all – that was all illusion, there was nothing to him, only flat slices of persona, giving the impression of three dimensionality.

What was he?

He could only learn that here.

Yes, the Voice intoned in his head. *Stay here, Wesley. You will learn. Make us stronger, open the portal for us.*

Wes paused.

His layers wobbled.

Awaken your drones, spread your madness.

'Yeah, you know what,' Wes said aloud, feeling the tug of the Pendle Stone the other side, symbols connecting, 'Mr Wend, Shaw, Foreman, whatever he is, is a right piece of work.'

Ricky snorted. 'He in your head?'

'Oh, that creepy voice?' Katy folded her arms. 'The one that keeps telling me to "prune the tree" all the time?'

Wes winced. 'Oh, lovely. Yeah. I mean, probably the same.'

'Can we go home now?' Katy shuddered, glancing over her shoulder. 'Those things are creeping me out.'

Wes chanced a glance behind them. The priests had grown completely silent. Their equine snouts sniffed at the air, insect legs twitching, wings folded back.

'What did you say they call themselves?' he asked, thinking it had been onomatopoeic. 'The... Click?'

'Yeah, almost, Khly'k.'

'Click.'

'No, you're not listening...'

'...I *am* listening.'

'No, you have to scrape your throat but not *really* scrape it. Khly'k. Like that.'

'That's... that's what I said.'

'That's not...'

'Khly'k,' Ricky interrupted, getting it right first time. 'There's a glottal stop. Can you open the portal, please? Stop pissing about?'

Wes concentrated, the pointless bickering a welcome distraction from the madness-inducing powers he possessed, almost forgetting even the Voice in his head, and the slab shimmered as the connection was made.

'She taught you to say please, has she?' he asked, meaning Carrie. 'Cor, even Gran couldn't get you to say that.'

'I got manners,' Ricky said, affronted.

'Boys!' Katy tugged the hoodie as low as it would go. 'For God's sake, I'm fucking naked, can we *please* just get home?'

The ground shook, rocking Wes nearly off his feet.

Ricky's knees buckled, and he dropped to the ground, wincing.

Katy stumbled back. 'What *now*?'

It rose over the arches of the circle, although how they had been oblivious to its approach Wes couldn't fathom.

So this was Him, then.

He knew it instinctively — recognised the family resemblance. This was Mr Wend, or what Great-Aunty Olive's spawn called Mr Shaw, and what Great-Aunty Eileen's spawn called Mr Foreman.

How on earth could something that big sneak up on them? It must have slithered there, scaled body wet and gleaming, swelling bulbously as it dragged itself upright. Was this the form he always took? No, not always, surely; was this to keep them awed and cowed? He took it for a bigger version of Ricky's other form at first, all eyes and coils in its nether portions, but as it rose up over the arches its great forelimbs draped over the stones like a—

'What the fuck is *that* supposed to be? It's like a, like a *squid* fucked a *dragon*.' Katy was far from awed or cowed. Wes swelled with pride he had no right to feel. 'Tell me that's not... it's not. No way. How did... how did *Gran* spawn with... No.'

'All right Grandad?' Ricky got up, shaking. It wasn't fear – Wes saw pain scudding over his face, tight and drawn.

It is good that the Triad are here.

Wes glanced at the others to make sure they were hearing this, too.

Katy's eyes narrowed. 'The Triad as in, like, drug-deals and gangsters?' she asked, keeping her voice low.

Wes shook his head. 'No, er, I think he just means the three of us.'

My spawn should have populated the world by now, opened the portal fully, let us take more worlds than this.

'Well, like I said, if that's what you wanted, you should've picked someone who actually gave a shit.' Ricky was getting his swagger back, but the veneer was tracing-paper thin. 'Not three girls whose sole ambition in life was marryin' up and winning first prize at the local fete.'

We have waited a long time for this. Now the Triad will help us rise.

Wes rolled his eyes. 'Why in the ever-loving fuck would we do that?'

'Am I talking to my bleedin' self?' Ricky was breathing harder, scowling. 'I *told* you, no.'

Let me through.

'Hang on.' Katy took a step back. 'You... you can't do anything without us. Have I got that right?'

There was a great rumble from within the belly of their sire, which they took as audible assent.

'So... what... *good* are you?' Katy frowned. 'Like... you... managed to impregnate Granny Wend and her sisters, like, a hundred years ago or something, so you must've been able to... do *something*, once. And all you've done since then is... leave us to it.' She licked her lips. 'I have a *lot* of questions.'

Your spawn-bearers summoned me as they should, as they were prompted. But they did not fulfil their end of the bargain. I have been waiting, bestowing glory upon glory on my progeny, waiting for the Triad to rise. Unseal the door, let me through. Your world is my right.

'Bugger that,' Ricky muttered, loud enough for Wes to hear him. 'I want *my* bleedin' rights first, before you come marching in.'

Wes rolled his eyes.

Katy stepped forwards, staring up at the blinking eyes peppering the overlapping scales.

'*Excuse* me? Your *right*? Who the *hell* d'you think you are?' She squared her shoulders. 'I wanted to go to Uni, not kill my own relatives, but here we fucking are, I guess, so – so screw you! I want to go backpacking and *see* stuff, and I want my friends, and driving lessons, you don't get to just—'

'Uh, Katy...' Wes tried to catch her arm, but she shrugged him off.

'Get *off* me, I'm not a *child*.' She glared at their looming sire with a face full of hate. 'He's not doing anything, what's he going to do? If he was going to do anything, he'd have done it by now. But he *can't*.' She punched Wes in the arm. 'Come on. Let's go.'

The rage of their grandsire rolled over them like a tidal wave, forcing them to the ground beneath its booming power.

LET ME THROUGH!

Wes dropped to his knees clutching his head. But this was *his* place: made for him. He thought of Charlie and Hugo and the life they hadn't had time to live yet, and all the things they still wanted to do. He straightened up, pushing past the pain, gritting his teeth.

He regained concentration and the shimmering around the slab got stronger. He turned, and saw Ricky hanging back, that shifty, sulky look on his face.

Katy saw it too, gave an impatient huff, and marched over to grab him by the elbow.

'Don't even think about it. I need you to teach me stuff. And you're going to show me how to actually use those eyeballs properly.'

Ricky let her shove him at the slab but gave Grandad the middle finger before he went through.

She hung back. 'Wes, come on.'

Wes took one last look around the stone circle, the priests in their silent swarm, the power he could wield if he learned how.

The Voice was softer, probing his weaknesses, burrowing into his brain.

Stay. Take your place here.

Wes sighed. He would make a wonderful cult leader. Well, maybe one day. Today he was being a responsible adult.

He turned to Katy and took her hand.

'Let's go home.'

She beamed at him.

The ground shook with their progenitor's fury.

NO! Let me THROUGH!

Wes winced, and pushed his sister through the shimmering haze.

'Piss off, Grandad.'

He stepped through himself, and the world flipped upside down.

Epilogue: The Tempest

What's past is prologue.
—William Shakespeare, *The Tempest*

16 January

He peeled his eyes open, head fogged and pounding. Neither mouth was comfortable – the back was glued with dried mucus, while his tongue was thick and dry. Sunlight lanced into his skull like a scalpel.

'Morning.'

She smelled like warm boards and sun-baked brick, fresh dew on clinging ivy. He was home.

Ricky covered his face, trying to figure out where he was. The room was still unfocused. 'Fuck me.' He flung out an arm, disorientated, and hit the mattress. 'Oh, shit.' He struggled halfway into a sitting position, but his belly lurched, and he thought better of it. 'Why'd you let me? What did I do?' He'd forgotten she hadn't been there to stop him.

'Nothing.'

She was close, but he couldn't get a fix on her.

Ricky groaned into the pillow. 'I'll kill that bloody Wesley.'

'He might have pushed you in, but you did this to yourself.'

The mattress compressed as she sat down beside him and rubbed his back.

He belched up flavours he didn't remember consuming. 'What the fuck was I drinking?'

'You weren't.'

He lifted his head with difficulty, since it was apparently crammed full of lead weights. 'Is this... Bloody hell. I don't remember much.'

He was naked, the way he preferred to sleep, but back in his drinking days he'd invariably woken fully clothed. Relief smacked him in the gut.

He always slept naked, it wasn't unusual.

He was home, he was home. Everything was normal, and he was home.

'Thank fuck for that.' His memory was honeycombed with gaps. 'Where is he?'

Carrie lay down beside him and put her arm around him. The reassuring weight of her filled him with a deep sense of restfulness. That was disturbing. Worse, he didn't mind.

'Leave him be for now,' she advised, and he shifted sullenly against her, trying to unwind the thread of events. 'Anyway, he went back to London. He needed to see his partners.' She stroked his back. 'What happened in there?'

He blinked, wincing with another stab of daylight falling through the chinks in the curtains. Light burned his eyes like twinkling crystal...

'I can't think now, love. Tell you later.'

Another thought, or a half-formed realisation, flashed through his head in a razor-edged ribbon before he could fully grasp hold of it.

(Shit me, *Katherine*.)

He used Carrie to pull himself up. 'Where's she gone? Katherine?'

Carrie pushed him off her. 'Out, I think.'

'Yeah, out *where*? Did she say? Shit.'

He was remembering. Bits and pieces swam back into murky focus. Katherine, that scorpion tail extending over her head in a curved fan.

'Bloody hell, I can't think.'

The world spun, fragments of the Beast twisting through angles of time and into his brain.

Getting up took three tries, and when he was upright he wished he wasn't. He sat back on the bed, trying to force his thoughts to cooperate. 'Um. Is she... what did she say? It's starting, isn't it? She's... Has she gone? *Where's* she gone?' But he knew that. He leaned back against her. 'She's going to start it,' he said, remembering the dreams of the Beast, the pictures inside the crystalline web. 'She's starting the cull.'

'Well... isn't that the point?' Carrie was solid, warm. He rested his full weight against her, too tired to hold himself up. 'What are you going to do about it?'

He paused, frowning. He didn't know.

'I mean,' Carrie went on, pulling him back down and arranging his pillows, 'it isn't like *you're* on the List.'

She had a point.

Ricky grunted, swung his legs back onto the mattress and settled back down. 'It's just... you know. She's never done this before.'

'She killed you.'

'Oh, right, yeah. But not for good, you know, she's not... this is a big moment. Don't you think I should be there?'

Carrie stroked his close-shaved hair. Her touch soothed him with its intoxicating corruption. She had no right to do that, to make him feel like he belonged there, but he wanted to believe it so badly in that moment that he closed his eyes and let her.

'I think she snuck out this morning so that she could do this by herself.' She paused. 'You *do* belong here. The Pendle Stone is a part of me, and so are you, now. In a way. You know that, don't you?'

That hurt. He wasn't expecting that to hurt.

It wasn't the kind of pain he minded.

He grunted, swallowing hard and side-stepping the question the way she did, answering it with another one.

'Do you think she'll come back?'

Her hand on his head was gentle and rhythmic, lulling him into a groggy stupor. Her voice was soft and far away.

'Yes. She asked when dinner was, so.'

'When *is* dinner?' He didn't know what time it was now. He hugged the biggest pillow into his chest and his head sank into the softer pile of goose down forever. He was asleep before she replied.

—

Wes called in on Ricky's parents before he headed back to London. It was his mum's birthday, but he couldn't face her. He didn't want to be within ten feet of his father. He certainly couldn't explain to his siblings that he'd basically let Katy loose. That was all out of his hands now.

The question of whether or not he was fit to drive was moot, since he'd checked in with the Silver Lining and not seen any crashes in his future. Probably best if he didn't mention to Ricky he was still taking them. There was only one left now, anyway, and it seemed better than letting them go to waste.

He parked up in a lay-by and walked back through The Chase, cursing the undergrowth and mud.

Uncle George and Aunty Lettie lived in Bramble Cottage, a dilapidated shell in the woods with no electricity or running water. 'Lived' was a loose term. 'Existed' was more accurate.

The fly-tipped appliances in the garden and tangles of brambles were not the best for Italian leather, and Wes's silk scarf snagged on a twig.

'He ain't here,' Uncle George growled, answering the door in his string vest. He leaned back, fishing the dog-end out from behind his ear and taking a long drag. It burned all the way down to his tarry fingers.

Wes nodded. 'No, it was you I wanted.'

'That so?'

'Saw you in town the other day, week, whatever. You were hanging back.' Wes cocked his head. 'Didn't get too close when our lot were trying to grab Katy, did you? Don't blame you, really. I wondered if it was because you were scared of our Thirteenth, which would be sensible, but it's *him* you're afraid of, isn't it?'

Ricky's father snorted and flicked ash all over Wes's coat. Wes dusted off his brooch.

'But he's not keen on seeing you either, is he? I'm here to find out why.'

Uncle George sniffed, nostrils flaring. 'Better ask the old 'ooman.'

Wes nodded. 'Aunty Lettie's in, is she?'

Bramble Cottage reeked of death. When Ricky had lived there he'd kept it better than that, but Uncle George had apparently not bothered to clean for eight months.

'Coming in, are you?' His uncle stepped back from the door. 'You and your fancy shoes?'

Wes shook his head. 'I don't think so. I think you're going to take a good look at my face.' He unwound the scarf and Uncle George scoffed, used to his nephew's forgettable features. Wes's confidence was silver-edged, green symbols dancing in his head.

Uncle George's expression altered. There was a moment where his mouth grew slack, his eyes dulling with a vacant glaze.

Wes grinned, sharp and hard, in a way he hadn't grinned for quite some time. 'I'd make a brilliant cult leader.' He patted his uncle on the cheek. 'Hey, Uncle George. Go and get me whatever it is you've got squirrelled away in there for dealing with your boy, hey?'

He wasn't sure what the symbols *meant*, but he could go back to the circle and find out. He could learn a lot from the monoliths, maybe even a way to fix Charlie. Something told him Ricky wasn't going to like him opening the portal. He needed a bit of insurance.

Silver threads wove around his thoughts and turned them towards action.

He chanted something under his breath and didn't know what the words meant, only that he remembered what they sounded like. Remembered forwards, that is. He hadn't learned them yet. But he was going to.

Uncle George backed off, and Wes's face buzzed, vibrating around the chant. The words he didn't yet understand reverberated against his teeth.

His uncle moved like a marionette, losing conscious control of his form. His limbs grew, extended, many-jointed shadows tipped with solid claws. He scuttled like a stilted spider.

Wes covered his face back up.

Silver certainty flooded him, reassuring. It was good to feel certain of something. It made him stronger. He needed a purpose – no, a direction. He already had a purpose. Charlie and Hugo were enough. He told himself that over and over until it replaced the chant, and he could believe it.

'Here.' His uncle returned with a jar, hoarse voice dreamy and distant. 'Granny Wend made it for us. There's a little left. It weakens him, but he's a slippery bastard.'

'Yeah, I know.' Wes paused. 'You haven't given this to anyone else?'

Uncle George scoffed. 'Nah. Never know when we might need it...' His face clouded as he stared at the jar, as if he wasn't sure he was doing the right thing.

Wes took it from him before his influence could wear off. This trick didn't last as long as he wanted, but it lasted long enough, and if it worked once, he could do it again. Except... he couldn't remember the bloody words.

He backed away, the silver trails wearing off, symbols slipping out of reach. Why was his memory so shit on its own?

That'll probably be the drugs, you stupid bastard.

He turned, wasting no time, and jogged as fast as he could back to the car, wrecking his shoes and stumbling through the trees. He could get another pair.

He tossed the jar onto the passenger seat and sped off, fixing his scattered thoughts on his partners and the life he was going to build with them.

He would go back to the Outside one day soon, learn what he needed, and fix those symbols in his head without the need for pills. If Ricky didn't want him to go back or gave him shit for it... he could neutralise him for a while.

He picked up speed. Right now, he wanted to put as much distance between himself and Pagham-on-Sea as he could. He had seen what was going to happen, and it made him sick to his stomach.

—

Katy wondered what sort of transport would suit her best – maybe a motorbike. Probably not the bus, but that was what she had.

Her tail was uncomfortable to sit on, unless she sat just right and kept her posture. Gran would be proud. She sat upright all the way home.

Her old home.

She had a new one now.

The bus lurched through morning traffic, and Katy stared into the opaque, misted window, daydreaming about reinventing herself.

Everyone cut their hair short to be badass, didn't they, but she *liked* hers long. She could dye it. She twirled a strand around her finger, imagining herself with tight, lacquered curls, maybe purple and green, but that might look too cartoony.

The bus was taking forever. She definitely needed a bike.

Katy wondered about getting another job to afford one, and then remembered Ricky could just earn her the money in an afternoon at the betting shop. Or maybe Wes would lend her some.

Wes probably had a garage somewhere full of bikes and cars he wasn't even using.

She got off at her old stop and adjusted her skirt so the hem skimmed her knees. The cold pricked her legs an icy blue, but she didn't feel it. Her tail-stub tingled, the wicked point itching to be released. Petals of Other flesh rippled inside her, aching to open up and devour.

The Beast could smell its kin, and it was hungry.

The detached house was quieter now most of the kids had left home. It looked like all the others in the street, in need of paint and attention, a newer build on the edge of the industrial estate where Katy's dad had a storage unit.

That was his retreat from the family and the world, where his girls ended up after the soundproofed garage. His car was here, though, so he was probably at home.

Good.

She tugged the hem of her skirt automatically, and adjusted her jacket collar.

'What am I doing?' she asked herself out loud. It wasn't as if they were going to survive their disappointment. 'Right.'

She checked the street, but no one was around. It wouldn't matter if there was.

It was her mum's birthday. She'd be inside, grousing about no one turning up for it although she'd said all year she didn't want to do anything. Her dad would be in the living room, silent as a stone.

She fished in her pocket for her keys, but as she was unlocking the door it opened with a hard yank. Katy looked up at the looming figure of Ian Porter, lanky and grim, the outline of his second set of jaws bobbing in his throat like a deformed Adam's apple.

'Where the hell have you been?' he demanded, the most he'd said to her in months, if you didn't count kerb crawling and yelling her name.

Katy shrugged. 'Around.'

'Where's the soothsayer?' Her dad looked up and down the street. 'Come on your own, have you? Seen sense?'

Katy nodded. 'I hated it, I just wanted to come home but he wouldn't let me. I want to try Uncle Barry's thing, I'm sorry, I don't want to Change…' Rachel was better at the fake crying than she was, but she thought her performance was pretty good for a start. It got him to step back from the door.

He jerked his head down the hall. 'Your mother's in there.'

'Who is it?' Lottie Porter, breathy and shrill, appeared out of the dining room. When she saw her youngest child, she stopped and her face fell and twisted. 'Oh.'

'I'm back, Mum,' Katy said, trying not to let the tightening in her chest distract her.

Was this how Ricky felt *all the time*? She hadn't ever considered that. She'd always let herself be dragged around, never thought about how they'd treat her with Gran gone, never thought she would know what it was like to see nothing but disappointment and fear on her mother's face after time away.

Katy swallowed, digging her nails sharply into her palms, but that wasn't the release or relief she needed. The Beast inside her was poised to unfurl. The walls were bending a little around her, making room. Her dad must have felt it, because as she closed the door behind her, he backed off.

'Where've you been?' her mother asked. She had something in her hand, but Katy didn't get a good look before her dad obscured the view. There was a clumsy hand off behind his back, and she hesitated.

'Um. I just. You know, did what Ricky said.' She shrugged.

Her mother took her in. '*What* are you wearing?'

'Clothes, Mum.' Katy's tail flicked out and in again, readying.

Her dad's face clouded. Everything about him radiated tension. She wasn't quick enough when he lunged at her – she was never going to be quick enough, he'd practised this a thousand times on girls who looked like her – and when he stabbed her, the knife slid in cold between her ribs and the blood soaked through her top. She shouldn't have worn cream.

He ripped it out.

The wound didn't hurt. It just tingled. She pressed a faltering hand to it, unsure what to do.

A slow, sneering smile split her dad's face in two.

Fear spiked her stomach. She hadn't expected that.

Shit shit shit…

She stumbled back down the hall, staring at her dad's twisted, mirthless smile. She got a few paces back to the door and stopped. It should hurt. She couldn't feel anything.

The Beast stirred, unperturbed. Her tail released fully, squeezing out in the narrow hall with each armoured segment clicking as it telescoped into the killing point.

The changing expressions on her parents' faces gave her life.

Katy pulled herself together and gave her mum a thin smile. 'Nice try.'

She stabbed down, impaling Lottie Porter through the head.

Her mother split apart, silenced forever, spurting gore. A swing of the tail, and her mother's body crunched against the stairs. Katy's glutes ached, sinews stretching and twanging with the weight of her mother and the thrashing tail, but she wasn't sick. She didn't even feel nauseous. She didn't feel anything. She tugged her tail free, retracting it to curl above her head like an angry scorpion.

Katy glanced in the blood-flecked hall mirror and tried to wipe a splat off her nose but got it all over her face. The mess of blood and bone and viscera reminded her of Gran's cottage, that night a million lifetimes ago.

She regarded the broken, ruptured body with a rueful smile. 'No worries, Mum. I'll grab my clothes in a sec, once I've had a shower.'

Her dad had backed up into the living room and clearly thought he could defend himself better in there, where he could control the dimensions of the space.

What a fool, thought the Beast-that-was-Katy, and flesh flopped wetly into petals of invulnerable glory, bone crunched and lengthened, claws sprouted from great, unstoppable fused feet.

She hunted through the dimensions of space. She could stalk through the angles of time. She could give chase inexorably, forever, and there was nothing they could do to her in return. A living room wasn't much of a battleground.

Katy shook the scraps of humanity from her beautiful hide and let it splatter onto the carpet, dozens of feet below. The door became large enough to admit her, everything skewed and bending to her will. Her father couldn't fight back. None of them could. And if Katy Porter was the last person seen entering this house of death and nightmares, they would find Katy Porter's skin mingled with her mother's.

That might make college a bit tricky this term, but she'd figure something out.

The Beast-that-was-Katy sniffed out the desperate pheromones of Ian Porter, and saw him for what he was. It swiped him into the air with one bat of its thick tail, jaws open wide, and he burst between the petals of her fang-lined muzzle like a piece of rotten fruit.

Like a yoghurt bubble in one of those teas, the Beast-that-was-Katy thought, gulping down the fractured cartilage and bone, strips of flesh coming away like pulled pork as she raised her head and let him slide down her throat in pieces.

Who's next?

There was the tug of the List, but they could wait. This tug was towards her siblings – towards Wes, the oldest of them, and the Beast-that-was-Katy overrode this instinct with a shudder.

Not him.

The tug was not irresistible, and it eased off.

Who's next?

Katy pulled back into herself, folding up her great body like origami, a naked, slick butterfly with new human skin emerging from the ooze of the engorged flower.

The rooms went back to their normal sizes.

Blood and gore soaked into the furniture, splattered the TV, and was sprayed over the walls. She was a messy eater.

Her mother was lying in a bloody, shattered heap on the stairs, head and chest split in two down the middle, arms and legs at unnatural angles. Her own old skin and hair lay in a ruined heap with the rags of her clothes, slippery and grotesque. She should feel sick, but she didn't feel anything at all.

'Sorry for the mess,' she told her parents. 'I'll just get my stuff.'

She realised she was now naked and used the bannister to vault over her mother's corpse and run up to her old bedroom to towel herself off and get dressed. Her mum always kept spare cash for the window cleaner and food shopping in a tin in her bedroom. Katy peered in, but thought she'd better shower before she traipsed this mess all over her mum's clean carpet.

'I'll clean up, as well,' she called downstairs to the globs of flesh. 'You don't want all this hanging around. Oh, and if anyone touches my cousin, they're dead meat.'

She giggled into her wardrobe, picking out an outfit suitable for the bus ride home.

Downstairs, the front door opened.

Katy stiffened, listening.

'Mum! Happy birth— *Oh, fuck...*'

Her siblings' voices, raised in chorus, stopped abruptly. She heard Liam whistle through his teeth.

'Holy shit.'

The Beast growled in her belly, still hungry.

Katy bit her lip, dropped her clothes on her bed, and sauntered to the top of the stairs.

'Hi guys,' she said, as her siblings looked up at her in uncharacteristic silence. She drank in their paling faces, their collective and individual fear, and let it intoxicate her. She could do anything.

'Time's up.'

And the Beast unfurled.

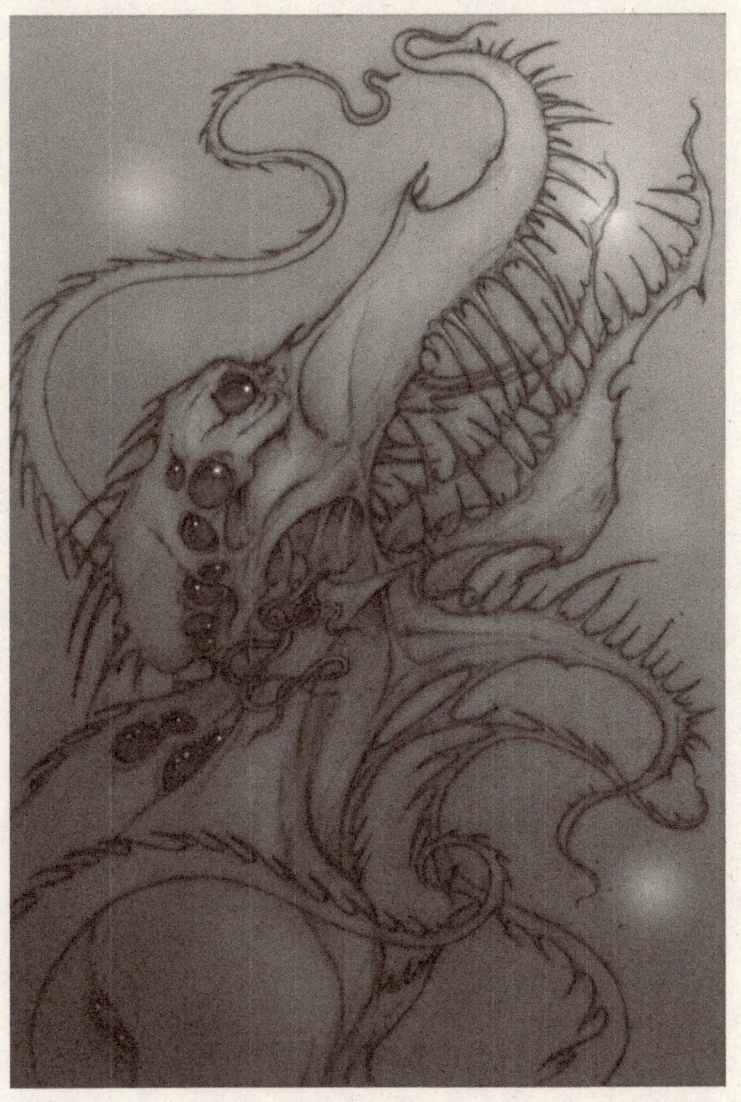